BETWEEN THE BIRCHES
BOOK ONE

AWAKENING

KP ROBERSON

Lunar Ridge Publishing

Author Note

This book contains sequences of graphic violence, gore, and disturbing imagery that may be unsuitable for readers under the age of sixteen; has adult language, involves cultists, attempted murder, character death, depression, animal death (NOT dogs or other domestic pets. Said animal is wild and its death is off-screen), mentions unsupportive parents, and contains non-explicit scenes of consensual sexual acts.

Lunar Ridge Publishing LLC

2800Scenic Drive Ste. #4 #144

Blue Ridge, GA 30513

www.lunarridgepublishing.com

A huge thank you goes to my family for putting up with my incessant obsession in extracting this story from my brain. Countless days and nights passed while writing this all-consuming story...as well as the second and third editions...and they still love me. All my love, always.

Prologue

SHE'D BEEN RUNNING FOR ages. Her skin was pulled too tight against her ribs as her lungs begged for air. Her second wind was long gone. In high school, she ran track and field for endurance, not survival.

But here she was, in the middle of an unfamiliar forest with no recollection as to how she got there. The sun had set an hour ago, but she'd seen no sign of civilization other than the trunk she woke up in.

Pine branches snagged on her hair and shirt, while briars tore at the skin of her bare ankles. No matter what, she couldn't stop moving. If she'd kicked her kidnapper in the jaw rather than the chest, he wouldn't be trailing her.

"Keep running, little rabbit!" The man's voice echoed through the trees. He was gaining on her. "I'll find you no matter where you go."

She hiccupped as a sob worked its way from her throat. It was difficult to discern which direction the voice came from. The man could be anywhere and everywhere for all she knew. Instinct was her only guide.

A gut feeling pulled the young woman to the left through the thicket. She couldn't tell why, but this direction *felt* like home. All she had to do was find the edge of the woods. There was bound to be a road...and with it, a way back to her family.

As if the universe heard her plea, a pair of lights flickered through the trees to her right. The road was so close. If she kept moving, she'd intercept the vehicle. Ignoring the full-body ache and how her legs felt like noodles, she pushed onward and finally broke through the tree line.

Instead of a road, she stumbled onto an open, grassy field. A large stone altar had been erected in the center. There were torches placed at the head and the foot, and two figures dressed in black waited nearby.

Her chin quivered and her feet became leaden, dragging until the weight of disparity pulled her to the ground on her hands and knees. Tears flowed in rivers down her cheeks. She dropped her head in defeat, unable to move. Her will to fight had vanished, taking with it what little bravery she had left in her reserves. Her dad would be disappointed with her giving up, but there was nothing in the tank. She was tapped out.

A pair of strong, calloused hands lifted her body. A wail of despair echoed through the trees as she was tossed across a set of broad shoulders like she weighed nothing. There was no strength in her limbs as he carried her toward the stones, swaying limply. Blood rushed to her face.

When her captor stopped, he gripped her by the hips. She was airborne long enough to gasp before being dropped unceremoniously onto the flat top. The back of her head bounced from the impact, creating multiple images of the man. He was also dressed in flowing black robes.

Darkness pressed around her periphery as more cloaked figures closed in, surrounding the stone. The pounding in her skull pulsed, forcing her eyes to half-close. Deep male voices chanted in unison, starting low and increasing in volume as her headache picked up. Whatever strange language they spoke wasn't anything she'd heard before. It turned her blood to ice.

The scratching of knife on bone had her screaming into the night. Something demanded passage into her skull. She grasped at the thoughts of her family to keep her grounded. Then, her head split open from the inside. All her memories drifted through the crack into oblivion. With each tear that fell, another part of her vanished until there was nothing left.

Chapter 1

BETH

"All packed and ready to go?" Tom asked as she zipped her backpack and placed it on the floor next to the bathroom door.

For Beth's twenty-fifth birthday, Tom invited her along on his annual hiking and camping weekend with the guys. They'd been going to this place since middle school, so it was her turn to see how beautiful the mountains and waterfalls were 'this year.'

"Yep. That's it, minus what we need in the morning." Beth turned and wrapped her arms around Tom's neck. His hands went to her hips, then slid around to her backside. He pulled her body flush against his. "What time is our reservation?"

"You sure you want to go out to eat?" He nuzzled Beth's neck, nipping just below her ear. "We're not going to have much alone time to celebrate your birthday once we're out on the trail."

Tom pressed feather-light kisses into the corners of Beth's mouth before brushing his lips over hers. The butterflies in her stomach became frenzied as her body ignited with need. Her free hand cradled Tom's cheek as he deepened the kiss.

Excitement built in Beth's lower abdomen. Tom knew his way around her body and often liked to remind her. Throughout high school, her parents had kept her too busy to date, but she'd always had her eye on him. They dated through college until four months ago when they married. So far, the honeymoon phase hadn't ended.

"Hmm." Beth broke for air, grasping at some sense of clarity. It was difficult to form sentences while Tom pushed all the right buttons. "Tempting, but we can't ditch our best friend."

"Grady will understand." Tom continued to convince her, kneading her backside while cupping her breast with his other hand. "He cancelled last minute anyway."

"What?" Beth pulled away from Tom. His head fell back with an annoyed groan. "That's two weekends in a row he's dropped us."

"His dad's welding shop has been slammed. Louis talked Grady into helping out, even though he has his own woodworking orders to fill." Tom's features softened when Beth's frown deepened. "He's probably exhausted and catching up on sleep for this weekend."

"I hope that's all." Beth laid her head on Tom's chest and hugged him tight.

Her friendship with Grady had a rocky start, but she had persisted because he was important to Tom. Eventually, Beth chipped away at his gruffness enough that he tolerated her. After Grady's mother passed away suddenly, the trio had become almost inseparable. Beth wouldn't admit it aloud, but she'd grown fond of Grady over the years. She tried not to take his absence as a personal slight.

"C'mon. We'll be late if we don't leave soon." Tom kissed the top of her head and pulled away.

"Wait." Beth wrapped her fingers around Tom's bicep, stopping him. She eased the bedroom door shut and put her back against the wood. "Cancel our reservation. We have other plans."

"Do we now?" Tom drawled in a low, teasing tone.

Beth's lips curled as she pulled her shirt overhead and dropped it to the ground. Tom's eyes dilated; his hungry gaze swept over her exposed skin with appreciation and tenderness.

"I love you," he whispered before crashing his lips into hers.

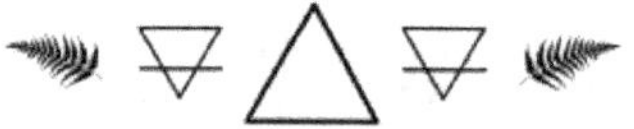

Beth dreamt she was lying on the forest floor, watching the trees sway as the wind wove through them. Ancient pines, white oaks, and red maples moved with quiet reverence. The softly rustling leaves spoke a language she didn't understand while the rest of the woods stood silent and still. She felt like she was imposing on some intimate moment.

She dug her fingertips into the cool topsoil and sighed in contentment. Her eyes fluttered shut as she inhaled the earthy aroma. So beautiful, so rich. While the area was unfamiliar, it warmed her to the core.

Opening her eyes, Beth was caught in one of those good stretches that left her feeling loose and relaxed. Sitting upright to study her surroundings. The forest floor was a sea of every shade of green. The sunlight bathed it in golden rays, creating a colorful kaleidoscope of the fallen leaves and moss. She stood and turned in a circle with her hands out at her sides and facing skyward. This forest didn't just warm her, it felt like *home*.

Beyond the tall trees, bundles of ferns, and a thicket of briars, Beth spotted a field of wildflowers. An invisible force tugged her body toward it, but there wasn't an opening.

The further she searched for a way inside, the thicker the shadows grew. Soon, the woods were starved of the sun's light. The hairs on the back of her neck rose. The pit of her stomach dropped with the thumping in her chest.

Beth scanned the dark patches of the woods closing in on her. When the shadows turned to wisps of smoke and an unnatural chill swept across her bare skin, she took off. Not once did she glance over her shoulder, for fear the watcher in the woods was following. Not even when her skin crawled. Instead, Beth picked up the pace. Her survival instincts ordered Beth to outrun the shadows.

Tree limbs became outstretched arms with sharp claws, like stinging whips across her cheeks. They tugged at her hair; she swatted them away. Fabric ripped, leaving her biceps exposed.

The forest didn't want her to leave.

Up ahead, Beth spotted a lighted archway shining like a beacon of hope. Finding her second wind, Beth pumped her legs until her muscles burned.

Just a little farther.

A sudden lashing burn across her back caused Beth's knees to buckle, but she didn't stop. Stopping would be giving up, and she wasn't a quitter.

The archway loomed, much closer. She could make out a hilltop beyond. Her heart leapt at the thought of her haven. She just had to make it before the darkness swallowed her. Her bare feet met the golden rays spilling from the archway. Beth clenched her teeth when a manic grin broke out. She was going to make it.

Beth yelped when something from behind yanked her hair. Without looking, she fisted her tresses and yanked back. The scent of rotten eggs followed a wave of heat at her back. Her fight or flight kicked in, pushing her legs to the point of done. A low growl came from too close behind.

The wildflower field beckoned her with a light breeze and the sweet smell of honeysuckles. The archway was so close she could taste them.

Beth launched herself through the entrance, tucking her arms and legs. The ground caught her rolling form until she was staring up at the sun.

She swallowed the lump in her throat and lifted her head to glance over her heaving chest. A blanket of darkness swirled on the other side of the archway as if stopped by an invisible force. Two oval-shaped dark embers glared back at her. Beth blinked away the sweat dripping into her eyes. The orbs were gone, taking the ill-natured murkiness with it.

Beth tilted her face to the cornflower sky, basking in its warmth and taking in a lungful of the delicate perfume of spring. When she turned to the wildflower field, a blanket of dark blue bachelor's buttons, white Shasta daisies, and gradients of pink and purple larkspur danced with the gentle breeze.

Despite the ache in her limbs, Beth pushed off the ground to stand. She squinted against the sunlight and made her way to the center. Her palms brushed over the tops of the soft, tall grass. The weather was the perfect balance of sunny and warm without blistering her skin. It reminded her of the Spring Break trips to Fort Polaski her parents took her on during her elementary years.

Wood-shingled rooftops came into view. As she crested the hill, they were attached to twin log cabins with bright white chink mudding.

She wanted to explore them, but her footsteps became like trudging through mud. The dream swirled to a gray mist, replaced by a familiar warmth and the scent of orange and sandalwood.

"Happy birthday, beautiful," Tom whispered as he swept a strand of Beth's dark honey-colored hair out of her face.

"Good morning to you, too," she groaned while managing a smile. "What time is it?"

"Time to wake up, sleepyhead," Tom replied as he traced her jawline to her chin and down the front of her neck.

Beth's arm shot out toward the nightstand. Her fingers grazed the cold rectangular device. She grasped it with a grunt, brought it to her face, and squinted. "Six-thirty."

Her finger hovered over the text messages. Nothing new. The splinter in her heart ached, but she was used to it after all these years. One thing she wasn't going to let them do was ruin her weekend.

Beth shot up out of bed with extra gusto. Tom grinned ear to ear when she kissed his cheek. Before she could make a break for it, Tom hugged her by the waist and dragged her back, giving her a toe-curling kiss.

Beth pulled away with a giggle and put her hand over her mouth. "Wait, I've got morning breath."

Tom's grey eyes were like an intense summer storm, ringed with the tiniest bits of blue. His face was rugged and masculine, with a chiseled chin that had a dimple she loved to kiss. He always threatened to grow a beard to hide his self-proclaimed 'butt-chin,' but Beth always protested and changed the subject by playing with his soft, dark blonde hair. It was a great tactic for getting kisses on demand, not that she needed to. Tom seemed to have some secret quota he met daily.

"I don't mind." Tom's not-too-full lips spread into a toothy grin. His eyes sparkled like they do when he's in a playful mood. "Besides, I love every part of you."

Each word came with another kiss. On the lips, her cheek, neck, and chest, ending with a raspberry on her stomach. Beth let out a raucous laugh. "Now," he said, with one last kiss on her forehead, "let's get out of bed before we spend the next hour getting into trouble."

Beth sped through her morning routine. It was her turn to go where the boys bonded every year, to see for herself the allure of this enchanted forest. There wasn't a moment she wanted to miss.

TOM

TOM LOCKED UP THE APARTMENT while Beth waited in the car. His stomach had these weird flutters all morning. He was about to take the love of his life to a potentially dangerous part of the woods. His best friend assured him it would be fine, that the threat had passed weeks ago, and their hike would be safe.

Grady's assurances had worn out.

He should have put his foot down and planned for a different part of the forest, far from the evil that tainted his most formative teenage years. Grady had an answer for moving locations, too.

"If we don't know the trails like the back of hands, Beth will catch on," Grady had argued, clapping Tom on the back. "I don't know about you, but I sure as hell don't want Beth pissed at me on her birthday. It's already a shitty time for her."

Tom gnawed on his cheek and eventually nodded. "Fine. But at the first sign of trouble we should leave."

"Do you have a backup plan if we need to hightail it outta there?" Grady's sharp blue-eyed gaze pricked his confidence.

"No. I don't." Tom ran his hand through his hair. "Fuck. I can't let her down, Grady. She's been looking forward to this for months."

"Then we adapt if shit hits the fan." Grady's face hardened as he squeezed Tom's shoulder. "Y'all are my tribe, my family. I swear on my life, if anything happens, I'll protect the two of you with my life."

"Just make sure Beth is safe." Tom sniffled as guilt gnawed at his gut. "No matter what, she gets home...promise?"

"Promise."

THE CAR HORN HONKED. Beth waved him over, an ear-to-ear grin plastered on her face. He could see her bouncing in her seat from here.

Flashing her his pearly whites, he bounced over to the open driver's side door. "Ready for a weekend outdoors, birthday girl?"

"Absolutely," she beamed, practically buzzing with excitement.

Turning over the engine, Tom wiggled his eyebrows, and then they were off. If Beth asked him to fly her to the moon, he would build a rocket ship and take her.

Tom's crush began in sixth grade when she beat him at dodgeball. His first loss, but not his last. Beth never noticed Tom until their first year in college. Both majored in education—Beth in early education, specializing in math, and Tom in middle-school history—so they had some classes together. Halfway through the first semester, he finally worked up the nerve to ask Beth on a date. One date turned into two and soon they were going out every Friday night and dated through college.

Beth was smart, witty, and had a great body. Her amazing eyes, green like spring ferns, darkened with her mood and held him captive. Their shared love of the outdoors was the final checkmark on Tom's list of 'perfect woman.' Even her stubbornness was endearing because her nose scrunched up real cute like, and when she crossed her arms it accentuated her chest. He made it official this past January, giving her his last name.

As they traveled toward the Tennessee-North Carolina border, he squeezed her hand lightly and glanced at her with a wide grin when she returned the affection.

"I'll be glad to be in the woods again," Beth spoke, bringing him back to the present. "I hope Grady is well-rested, because I'm ready to hit the trail."

"Me, too." Tom forced a half-smile. He had covered for Grady last night, but his best friend still hadn't explained what was so important that he had to go out of town at the last minute.

"Speaking of hiking, it's been years since you've mentioned Paul or Jeff. Are they coming?"

Tom's knuckles turned white as he gripped the steering wheel. Fighting the urge to grit his teeth, he let go of Beth's hand to cover a fake yawn. He needed to unhinge his jaw before it locked.

"Most likely not. We lost touch sometime after high school." Tom didn't want to rehash his falling out with Paul and Jeff before college. Not on his wife's birthday weekend.

Forcing those memories back into their box, Tom focused on the road and reached for Beth's hand again. He stroked his thumb over her knuckles in a soothing circle. Beth used her cell phone's Bluetooth to skip the song playing over the SUV's speakers.

"We're almost there," Tom relayed as they passed mile marker twenty-five.

Beth let out a sigh and wiped her palm on her canvas shorts. "I'm looking forward to it, but I'm nervous."

Tom brought Beth's hand to his lips. "I know it's been a while, but there's nothing to be nervous about, hon. We'll go your speed, okay?"

"That's not why I'm nervous," Beth replied before chewing on her bottom lip. "Last night I had a pretty intense nightmare about the woods. I guess I'm still on edge." She huffed out a chuckle, letting out a slow breath.

"Want to talk about it?" Tom asked, side-eyeing her with raised eyebrows. He watched for their turn, not wanting to miss the unmarked gravel road.

Beth nodded and cleared her throat, pulling her hand away to place both in her lap. "I was in a forest. And it was so beautiful, like what I would imagine my happy place to be. I didn't want to leave."

"Sounds like a real nice nightmare," Tom replied jokingly as he made the right turn.

"Heh, yeah. That was before everything went dark," Beth continued, visibly shuddering at whatever she remembered. "There was a creature chasing me. I barely made it to safety. Then you woke me up."

As Tom pulled into the parking area, his heart stuttered before dropping to his stomach. Jeff Putnam and Paul Larson stood on either side of Grady. The scowl on his best friend's face deepened when Tom made eye contact, flashing to dismay at seeing Beth.

The sinister smirk Paul wore confirmed his worst fears.

He almost turned the car around but couldn't condemn Grady. Summoning his best mask of calmness, Tom steadied his breath and parked the hatchback. If Jeff and Paul were here, that could only mean one thing: Grady was wrong...

...and Tom should have manned up and told Beth the truth.

Chapter 2

GRADY

"NOT ONE WORD, DO you hear me?" Paul growled. His face was screwed into grimace instead of a smile. The sandy-haired, lithe-framed man towered over Grady. Pain shot through his shoulder when Paul squeezed, promising to make good on his threat if Grady didn't agree.

"Of course...*brother*," Grady replied, barely able to contain the disgust in his voice. He would do well to play along for now.

Seeing Beth's bright face twisted Grady's stomach into a knot. He'd spent days here getting things ready for their arrival. His careful planning meant shit if these guys blew it and told Beth the truth... the real reason his dad and Tom's dad brought him and the guys out here every summer.

When Tom's hatchback crept into the parking spot, Grady jerked away from Paul's grasp. Grady glanced at Jeff, hoping he'd have an ally. He wouldn't meet Grady's gaze. Figured. Their red-haired friend had always lacked a spine.

With a heavy sigh, Grady readied his best and most charming grin. It was Beth's birthday. No need to alarm her until after he spoke to Tom. He'd have come up with a contingency plan since their talk.

Grady opened Beth's passenger door. He rested his arm on the roof and ducked his head. "Happy birthday, brat."

"Hey, you." Beth's luminous grin was like basking in the summer sun.

Grady backed up so she could get out. She slipped around the door and flung her arms around Grady's shoulders, squeezing him tight and rocking them. "We've missed you the past two weekends."

"I missed you guys, too," Grady answered, resisting the urge to toss her back into the car and scream for Tom to floor it. "I wouldn't miss your birthday hike for anything."

"Aww. You say the sweetest things." Beth ruffled his black curls and giggled.

Blushing lightly, Grady pushed the curls out of his face. He ignored Paul's intense stare boring into the back of his head.

"Ready to get this hike started?" He held out his elbow.

"Is the sky blue?"

Beth hooked her arm through his, resting her small, warm hand on his forearm. The unease in his stomach settled enough to flutter. He shook it loose because Beth wasn't his to have. Just because it felt right didn't mean it was.

Grady couldn't stand Beth when she started dating Tom. His best friend had pined for her through high school, but Beth never gave him the time of day. They'd only been dating a few months when Grady's mom passed away. Every day that summer, Tom and Beth took him fishing, camping, or whatever else they could think of to keep Grady's mind off losing a cornerstone of his life. Despite Grady's best efforts to keep his distance, they formed a bond.

And it continued to grow over the next three and a half years.

Tom was double-checking their backpacks when they rounded the vehicle. His jaw was hard set as he laser-focused on his task. Grady nodded hello, hoping Tom was ready to put on a show. Like a switch, Tom's Eagle Scout façade clicked in place.

"I'll leave you in the very capable hands of your husband," Grady said with a curt bow.

Grady jogged to his truck and grabbed his pack. He locked the doors and returned to stand next to Tom. His stoic expression promised pain as Paul welcomed Beth in a hug.

"Happy birthday, Beth. We're glad you could join us this year," Paul said as he rested his chin on her shoulder. The smirk spread over his face unsettled Grady to his bones. "Boy, do we have some surprises in store for you. They're gonna be killer."

Tom tensed beside Grady. He heard a grinding crack and hoped Tom didn't pop a filling. Grady frowned. Neither he nor Tom had told anyone else they were hiking this weekend, so how did Paul and Jeff catch wind of it? It wouldn't surprise Grady if his dad tasked them with keeping an eye on him.

"Y'all don't have to do anything special. *Being here* is the gift. I've wanted to come out here with y'all for years." Beth had a perpetual smile on her face.

Usually, Grady would be happy about it, but today it twisted his insides.

Jeff gave Beth a quick half hug while his gaze eyes darted around nervously.

"Come here. I'll show you the plan." Paul unfolded a worn map and spread it out on the hood of his SUV. He tugged Beth to his side with one hand. The other gripped the hilt of the hunting knife on his hip.

Point made, asshole.

"We are here," Paul said, pointing to the map at the head of the trail. Tracing a black line, he ended at a triangle on the other side of the map. "This is the trail we'll be taking to the campsite, here."

Beth studied the map closely and nodded. "Looks like that's about thirteen miles. Are we going the whole way today?"

"No. We have a few stops today before camping at the halfway point." Paul smirked over his shoulder at Tom, though his voice was tender. Focusing on Beth, he added, "Don't worry. We'll take it easy on you today."

Jeff let out a nervous giggle and hid his face. Beth chuckled and shook her head, unaware of the insidious turn this weekend had taken.

BETH

"LET'S GET GOING, OH fearless leader," Beth replied. Her cheeks already ached from smiling so much.

Despite Tom's excitement when they left home, he started grinding his teeth after they arrived, but seeing Grady melted her nervousness. Tom's tenseness must have been contagious, though, because their best friend's smile kept falling when he thought no one was looking. Whatever it was, she wasn't going to push the matter. She trusted her two favorite guys to let her know if something was wrong.

Paul led the way, followed by Jeff, then Grady. Tom took the rear close behind Beth. Their hike started off like a walk in the park in the cool of the morning. Dewdrops still hung to the lower foliage in the heavy shade. Their boots and ankles would be soaking wet before they made it to the first blaze where the hike really began.

Beth soaked in the nature surrounding them. She enjoyed the calming rustle of the trees, the birds singing, and the critters skittering away from the troupe of intruders.

Taking a deep breath of the dense mountain air, her heavy heart became lighter, freer. All worries about her nightmare were scattered among the fallen leaves and lost amid the sweet-smelling foliage. She'd missed this so much.

College graduation, planning a wedding, and moving into their apartment... Life had been full. This was the first time in months they'd been able to get out and do anything. Aside from their weekend movie nights with Grady, the newlyweds hardly saw anyone else.

The trail widened, and they came to a small clearing with two trees. One had a white diamond painted on it, the other had a blue diamond. Paul followed the white diamond blaze to the right. Tom sidled up to Beth and slid his hand into hers.

"The White Diamond blazes are part of the Appalachian Trail," Tom reminded her, pointing to the tree on the right.

When the path narrowed and steepened, Tom dropped behind Beth so they could walk single file. Despite the difficulty of the terrain and the slight burning in her lungs, Beth was more energized than she had in a long time.

The woods warmed quickly, but they made good time, getting to their first stop in a couple of hours.

Paul halted the group, turning to address them. "We're going to take this trail for our first stop." He motioned to the Blue Diamond on the tree to the left. "It'll be a quick sight-seeing detour, and we'll grab a bite to eat." Paul smiled, glanced at Tom, and started on the trail.

"Is this part of the normal hike?" Beth asked Tom, whose face was flushed red from either exertion or because he had something planned. He never was good at hiding secrets.

"It's not part of the normal hike. To be honest, I don't know what detours Paul has included this year," Tom answered. Beth detected a hint of annoyance in his voice. Before she could say anything, he added in a low voice, "Just stay close to Grady and me, okay? Don't go anywhere alone."

"Okay." Beth's grin fell a little. "Is there something I should be aware of?" Her eyes widened. "Does it have something to do with why you and Grady don't hang out with them anymore?"

Before Tom answered, Beth was startled by Paul's barking order, "C'mon, you two! We're burning daylight!"

Giving Tom an encouraging smile, Beth pulled him toward the others. He squeezed her hand, easing the tightness in her shoulders. Whatever was going on between these guys had nothing to do with her, unless Paul or Jeff was upset at having to postpone the hike. Beth never wanted to be an inconvenience. She'd find a way to thank them properly.

Tall pink and white Sweet Williams grew wildly in patches on either side of them. Further into the thicket, large ferns peppered the landscape.

"How beautiful," Beth remarked, letting her hand graze the taller flowers.

The trail gently inclined before opening ended at a small rocky outcropping. The farther they went, the louder the roaring became. Soon, they stood at the foot of a swimming hole fed by a beautiful waterfall.

"Wow," Beth whispered before turning to Tom, "This is amazing."

The mist from the falls felt cool on her skin. She wished they had time to go for a swim, but hike had barely begun.

"Hey, birthday girl! Come up this way!" Paul called out, breaking Beth from her quiet reflection.

Beth glanced at Tom, grabbing his hand before following Paul. As they passed Grady, he and Tom shared a look. She almost stopped to ask what their deal was, but Jeff stood behind Grady with a deep frown on his normally jovial face.

The well-worn trail took them to the top of the falls where more flowers grew among luscious ferns and ginormous mushrooms to their right. The sight reminded Beth the fairytale books her mother read to her as a child.

At the top of the path, Paul waited, his features indiscernible. When he stepped aside, Beth gasped.

Chapter 3

TOM

Tom's body flooded with adrenaline when Beth gasped at the top of the falls. He vaulted next to her, ready to defend against whatever trap Paul had set. His brows screwed together, and his lips parted. The fists at his side loosened.

Near the edge of the falls, a white cloth was spread over the top of the boulder. A large log had been rolled next to it for a makeshift bench. Strewn wildflowers surrounded the table.

"You shouldn't have," Beth choked, turning to Tom with watery eyes. "This is the sweetest birthday I've had in a long time. Thank you." Beth slid her arms around Tom's shoulders, pulling him down for a quick peck on the lips and a tight hug.

Over her shoulder, Tom glanced at Paul. The man stood there with a smug face. What kind of fucked up mind game Paul was playing? The pit in Tom's stomach was deep enough to swallow an elephant.

Erring on the side of truth, Tom replied, "This was all Paul's idea, honey. Honestly, this picnic is even a surprise to me."

Beth pulled back, a slight frown of disappointment on her face. "Really?"

"I thought you two would like to enjoy your last picnic in peace," Paul interjected.

Tom almost missed the irritation flashing across Paul's face. The man was schooled in hiding it.

"*Last* picnic?" Tom asked, raising an eyebrow. He'd almost missed it.

Paul wore an innocent smile. "Of course. No more picnics after this. We have thirteen miles to cover this weekend. Sorry, Beth, but we just don't have the time."

"Well, considering you didn't have to do this, I appreciate the grand gesture. Thank you," Beth replied earnestly. She gave him a pat on the shoulder and headed toward the makeshift picnic.

Tom went to follow, but Paul grabbed his arm. Speaking very low, he growled, "Not a fucking word or you get to watch them both die."

The gravity of the situation settled heavily on Tom so thick you could cut it with a butter knife. He fought the light-headedness and stumbled away from Paul. Beth was glowing with happiness by the time he joined her.

"This place is gorgeous. No wonder you guys come up here every year," she said, removing her backpack. She set it beside the log.

Tom forced a smile and followed suit, though his stomach turned like he'd eaten bad takeout. "Absolutely. And, with you here, this forest is even more enchanting."

Despite feeling like he was gonna hurl, Beth's enthusiasm doubled Tom's determination. He should've planned an exit strategy, but he'd trusted the man who never let him down. There was a first time for everything.

"We have apples, trail mix, and two kinds of jerky. Do you want pepper or teriyaki?" Beth pulled the bags out of her pack and placed them on the table.

"Pepper, please," Tom replied as he motioned to the seat. After Beth sat, he joined her. Holding both bags of jerky, he swiftly opened the bags in one swoop. "Here you are, my teriyaki baby."

Beth giggled and took the bag from his hands. When Tom looked out over the falls, Paul stood at the edge of the swimming hole, watching them with his arms crossed. The sinister smirk plastered on his face made Tom's skin crawl.

BETH

THE NAGGING FEELING that something was off wouldn't go away. Tom's mood soured the moment they pulled into the parking lot. Things had only gotten worse. She worried he was in danger of having another depressive episode. The last one was months before the wedding. High stress situation and all.

Maybe she could ask Grady for advice, but he wasn't acting normally, either. His brows were perpetually pinched, and he grunted replies more than he spoke.

Only Jeff, Paul, and herself seemed unaffected. Maybe talking about school would break Tom out of his funk.

"So, have you heard from the middle school about your schedule for the school year?" Beth asked before taking a bite of jerky.

Tom shook his head slowly, as if he barely heard her. "Uh, no. Not yet. I don't expect it will be much longer." He focused his gaze on her, giving her a half-smile. "Have you heard from the elementary school for yours?"

"Same," Beth replied, "but I've saved a ton of classroom themes on Pinterest. I think it'll be fun for the kids if I pull a semi-Ms. Frizzle act."

"I agree, but I doubt kindergarteners would get the reference." Tom chuckled, then stuck his chest out proudly. "No matter, you're going to be a great teacher."

Beth bumped shoulders with him and chuckled. "And you'll be the cute history teacher all the kids swoon over."

Tom's pride turned to adoration. "Oh, I'm sure there will be all kinds of little boys wanting to marry you when they grow up. I just hope I don't have any strong competition."

She started to laugh but was cut short when Tom leaned in for a slow, sweet kiss. Any worries Beth had about Tom's strange behavior were carried away. *This* was her Tom, her home, her place of comfort.

With a contented sigh, Beth nuzzled his forehead. "Nope. No competition, hon. You are my one and only."

Her heart fluttered like a hummingbird's wings when Tom placed a feather-light kiss on the tip of her nose.

"Good."

A loud whistle grabbed their attention. Paul waved his arm around his head once to signal it was time to wrap things up. Tom groaned. Beth glimpsed over at their half-eaten lunch.

"So much for our picnic," Tom grumbled before Beth popped a handful of trail mix in her mouth. "C'mon. Let's wrap the rest of this up."

So much for distracting his grumpy mood, Beth thought as she helped clean up. Tom helped her into the straps on her backpack before settling into his. She stood next to the waterfall, leaning over to peek at the pool below.

"How far down do you figure it is?" Beth pondered. "Looks to be a good twenty-five, thirty feet."

She turned to Tom for an answer as he stepped next to her to examine the ledge. Leaning over to gauge the distance, he grunted with a 'whoa.' Tom's arms shot out as he flailed to regain balance. Reflexively, Beth grabbed his backpack and pulled, grounding herself for leverage. Tom landed on top of her as the guys topped the hill, heading towards them. Grady was the first to bound into view.

"Are you two alright?" Grady asked, pulling Tom to his feet.

When Grady helped Beth up, he dusted off her back. Apparently, none of them had seen what happened.

"You scared me to death, Tom." she wheezed but it turned into a cough. Once she caught her breath, she asked, "Are you okay?"

His face was as white as a sheet.

TOM

TOM GULPED, GLANCING BACK at the falls. Goosebumps covered his arms. The hair on the back of his neck stood up seconds before *something* tried to push him over the edge.

"I'm okay, hon." He inspected his wet shoes and muddy knees. His wife had a brown stripe from neck to her backside. "You?"

"Mmhm." Beth's frowning face was scrunched up in confusion. "What happened? One moment you were peering over the edge and the next you were about to take a dive?"

Tom studied his wife before turning back to stare where he'd stood moments before. Rubbing the back of his head, he sighed. "I dunno what happened."

He glanced back at the cliff. The water running over the edge continued flowing as if it hadn't tried to send him over.

"I was looking down the falls when..." Tom's voice trailed off as he closed his eyes to run the scenario over in his mind. "I felt...*something* push my back." Avoiding Beth's gaze, Tom continued, "The next thing I know, I'm about to go over the falls, but Beth pulled me back. Then you guys came up."

Grady cleared his throat. "Thank goodness for Beth's quick thinking." Looking back and forth between the two nervously, he continued, slapping Tom on the shoulder, "But let's avoid any other dangerous waterfalls to be safe."

Jeff giggled like a hyena as he ruffled his wavy ginger hair. His soft crayon brown eyes belonged to a less muscular, less clumsy frame. His words came out too loud, too fast, "Parts of these woods are haunted, ya know."

Paul gave him a stern look, but Jeff seemed oblivious and rambled on. "There's a story I've heard since I was little 'bout a family of settlers that lived right here, in this very forest. They were cursed by a witch after she caught 'em stealing from her vegetable garden. Two weeks later, they all died of the plague."

When Jeff realized he had a captive audience, he lowered his voice and continued, "The garden they were supposedly stealing from looked like a regular patch of forest. Wanna know why everything in this garden grew so lush and green? The witch buried her victims there." His face stayed serious until he finally caught the death glare Paul was shooting at him.

"Enough," Paul said firmly through clenched teeth and hands. He readjusted his pack and barked, "We're losing daylight. Move out."

Jeff tried to play it off. "C'mon, Paul. It's just a story. Can't have a hiking trip without a scary story. It's tradition." He nervously cast glances at Beth and Tom before Paul shoved him toward the path.

As if in a daze, everyone grabbed their bags and headed back to the trail. Before turning to leave, Beth paused and turned her head to the side, then shook it. Looking confused, she strode toward the path after the others. Tom stopped, curious about what Beth had seen. Across the creek, he glanced over the area, spotting a stack of rocks that could have possibly been a chimney.

As Tom turned to leave, something caught his gaze. Icy tendrils crawled up his spine, chilling him to the bone. On the other side of the river, hidden in the shadows behind a tree, a wispy figure stared back at him with sunken, hollow eyes.

Tom froze to the spot. The figure lifted one long pointer finger to its shriveled lips, curling them into a sinister snarl. He tried to call out for Beth or Grady, but his tongue was heavy, and his jaw glued shut. Terror gripped his ribs with crushing force as it moved out from behind the tree and practically glided over the brush as it closed the distance. There had never been anything like this in these woods.

Not once breaking its gaze with Tom, the shadowy spectre floated across the water. Was this Paul's plan all along? Killing Tom and Grady so they wouldn't interfere? He couldn't leave Beth alone with Paul. Tom willed his body to yield to his command. Sweat broke out over his brow as the creature flew past the boulder with a sinister grin. If a round mouth filled with needle-like teeth could smile. Tom knew, without a doubt, he was going to die.

Frantic, Tom tried again to open his mouth, managing a tiny whimper as something warm trickled down his leg.

Chapter 4

TOM

Cursing silently, Tom resigned these moments as being his last. He wished he'd never brought Beth out here to the forest. He *should* have argued against Grady's promises that it was safe. But no. Tom wanted to share the experiences he used to have—before the rituals—with Beth. Now, because of that sentiment, he was going to die, leaving her unaware of the monsters she thought were friends.

And I should have told her the whole truth.

The creature advancing on Tom was close enough he could see the burning embers of hatred flickering in the depths of its soulless eyes. By the time the others realized his absence, it would be too late. Tears slipped down his face as his will gave up entirely.

Tom wanted to close his eyes, but the paralysis wouldn't allow it. He had no choice but to wait for his inevitable death. Imagining those jagged talons ripping flesh from bone, the searing pain that would accompany the brutal flaying was enough to make him sweat.

"Hon, are you coming?" Beth's sweet voice rang next to his ear.

Tom whimpered. It figured that was the one thing he *could* do. At least he and Beth would die together.

When he didn't react to her, Beth came around to his front. Her eyes widened as she gripped his shoulders. "Baby? What's wrong?"

Beth shook him, but he was stiff. Her warm hands cradled his chilled face. Despite trembling like a leaf, her voice was steady, "Please look at me, honey. Tell me what's wrong."

The icy air surrounding the wraith pressed in on them. Beth shivered. Its repulsive burnt mustard breath assaulted his nostrils when it stopped behind his wife. It raised a sharp-clawed hand, pausing when the shuffle of footsteps skidded to a halt next to them.

Jeff's arm flew up, straight as an arrow. He pointed directly at the creature, and stuttered for the first time in years, "W-w-w-witch!"

Beth whirled around, fists raised and poised to fight off Tom's attacker. When she unballed her fists, he knew she couldn't see the threat clear as day in front of them.

Eyes locked with Tom's, the creature hissed at Jeff's accusation. With a wild spin, the wraith disappeared into a mist that was carried away by a sudden breeze. The sickly sweet stench of composted animal flesh filled the area. By now, the rest of the group had caught up to them, made clear by the collective groan of disgust. The smell dissipated on the breeze like a thief leaving their calling card.

Tom took a deep, shuddering breath, startling Beth. She jumped and threw her arms around his shoulders. No longer paralyzed, Tom wrapped his arms around Beth, careful not to pull her against his soiled pants. As he rested his chin on her shoulder, Tom searched the woods for remnants of whatever the hell that thing was or if it had friends lurking in the shadows.

"Baby, look at me," Beth commanded with a slight shakiness in her voice.

Snapping his gaze to hers, the sudden rush of adrenaline crashed. Tom pulled Beth close, burying his head in the crook of her neck to hide the weakness leaking from his eyes.

"Shhh, shhh, shhh. I've got you," she whispered, fingers curling at the nape of his neck in a soothing rhythm.

Closing his eyes and breathing in the scent of Beth's warm lavender vanilla perfume couldn't shake the horrendous images from his memory nor replace the helplessness at being paralyzed. He held onto her, his body shaking until Grady finally spoke up.

"The faster we put distance between us and this place," Grady said as he surveyed the area, "the safer we'll feel." He came to Beth's side and placed a hand on Tom's back.

While Tom's gaze darted to search one last time for the creature, he met Paul's murderous stare. and his upper lip twitched. The message Tom received was loud and clear. He would keep two eyes on his old friend from here on out.

"Let's move!" Paul bellowed, breaking eye contact and slipping back into his more pleasant demeanor.

After putting a few miles between them and the falls, Tom called for a break to change. His piss-soaked clothes weren't the only reason he chafed in unmentionable places.

BETH

WHILE TOM CHANGED CLOTHES, Beth's adrenaline rush had worn off. The shaking started in her hands and spread to her toes. She hugged herself, working to smooth the goosebumps on her arms.

Tom was always so brave. She'd never seen him terrified enough to wet himself. She'd seen a fast-moving shadow but had dismissed it as a bird flying overhead. There was nothing else there.

An uncontrollable chill rolled down her body. She shivered, making her teeth chatter.

"Hey, hey, hey," Grady murmured before pulling Beth into a hug. He pet her hair with long, soothing strokes.

His familiar scent of cedar, wood stain, and freshly tilled earth eased her shaking muscles. Beth found calm in the blanket of Grady's safety. *He always gives the best hugs*, she thought, *like a big teddy bear.*

Grady pressed his lips against the side of her head and mumbled, "Don't overreact. Everything's gonna be okay."

Beth's anger flared. It was her parents' favorite response to anything Beth did that they disapproved of, which was a lot. Her parents often left her to 'deal with it.'

Nightmares? She was told to stop overreacting and got a pat on the head before being left alone in the dark again. Didn't make the cut for a school play? A tissue was thrust at her face with the consolation, "It's not Broadway, Elizabeth. Stop overreacting."

Her fears and shortcomings had always been reduced to an inconvenience. She'd learned by middle school to keep her mouth shut if it didn't make her family look good.

Beth pushed against Grady's chest, but the man was like a boulder. Unbudging. She leaned back with a scowl. Grady's gentle gaze edged on worry. Her face warmed. Why was he looking at her like that? And why did it make her chest flutter?

Ignoring the niggling at the back of her mind, she let her natural stubbornness take the lead.

"Don't give me that bullshit. *Something* scared the shit out of Tom, and no one is jumping to explain anything," she hissed.

Grady let her go and the corner of his lip tugged upward, studying Beth with a flash of satisfaction.

Was he riling her up on purpose? Funny thing was, it worked. She was thinking clearly again.

"What the hell is going on?" Beth narrowed her eyes at her best friend.

His penetrating blue eyes pierced the veil of his disheveled black curls. Running a hand through them, he flicked a furtive glance in Paul's direction.

"I'm not sure what to tell you, Beth." He rubbed his hand down his face. "Whatever that creature was, it's new to us. I've never seen Tom paralyzed in fear, and I don't care to see it again."

Her gut took a deep dive, making her stomach cramp.

"Am I the only one who *didn't* see this thing?" Beth knew the answer by the look of pity on Grady's face.

Tipping his chin up, Grady motioned behind Beth. Tom came out from behind the curtain, stuffing his soiled clothes into a bag. His eyes were glazed over, and he had a faraway look on his face. He'd stopped shivering uncontrollably, but his shoulders were hunched in defeat. Beth's eyes stung at the sight. There was no sign of the confident man she married.

"I'm going to go help Tom," Beth told Grady, not bothering to face him.

Before she could take a step, Paul walked up and put his arm around Tom's shoulders. Their heads were close as Paul spoke quietly. Tom nodded his head a few times, but his response was inaudible. Whatever was said seemed to satisfy Paul. Clapping Tom on the back, Paul cast a sidelong glance at Beth before heading back over to where a fidgety Jeff stood. When Beth turned back to Tom, he studied her. His face screwed into a pained grimace before he ducked behind the curtain again.

There was a deep ache in her chest. This was not how she saw her birthday weekend going.

Grady placed his hand on Beth's shoulder. "Go talk to him," he said, giving her shoulder a light squeeze. "We'll be heading out shortly. I'll stall Paul; give you two a moment."

"Thanks," Beth managed before Grady kissed the side of her head. She watched him walk over to where Paul was having an intense yet hushed conversation with Jeff before taking a deep breath. Grady was right, she and Tom needed to talk this out.

Gathering courage, Beth ducked behind the curtain. Tom was untying one of the knotted ropes holding up the curtain.

"Hey," Beth said softly, stopping behind her husband. She rubbed his back in soothing circles. "You okay?"

"No," Tom mumbled. With a sniffle and sigh, he turned, holding her gaze with tired, red-rimmed eyes. "You didn't see anything, did you?"

She shook her head. "I didn't, but that doesn't mean I don't believe *you* did. Whatever it was, Tom—whatever happened to you—scared the shit out of me." Beth took Tom's face in her hands and furrowed her brows. "But as long as you and I are together, we can weather any storm. Say the word and we'll turn back, go home. If we hurry, we can catch Benny's Pizza before they close, then spend the rest of the night cuddled on the couch with a movie."

Tom rubbed Beth's shoulders, smiling weakly. "It's your birthday weekend, but you'd do it, wouldn't you?"

"In a heartbeat."

He rested his forehead on hers. Before the moment could settle, Paul called for everyone to move out. Tom's sigh was deep, deflating.

"Trust in us," he murmured before placing a light kiss on her nose.

"Trust in us," Beth parroted, closing her eyes to gather strength.

Tom pulled away and straightened Beth's pack. She returned the favor before rejoining the group.

Grady dipped his chin to Tom. His gaze pinned Beth for a split second before it darted off and he turned toward the trail.

The group settled into a quiet march as they kept Paul's brutal pace over the rough terrain. At least one thing was clear; whatever was back at the waterfall *had* spooked Paul. For some reason, this tidbit of information didn't make Beth feel better.

Chapter 5

BETH

THE SUN WAS IN the late afternoon position as the group neared the ridge, the last leg before they made camp. Beth climbed the hill, struggling to catch her breath. Tom offered his hand. His jaw was set firmly, but he gave her a thin-lipped smile. Her chest tightened.

Tom's declining mood and the general disquietude of the group were her fault. If they hadn't gone off-trail, none of this would have happened.

"Thanks," Beth huffed, gripping Tom's hand to make the last step up to the ridge.

They were practically on top of the world. The rich valley below quieted Beth's troubles long enough for the breathtaking view to connect with her soul. Lush with dense pines and deciduous trees, it spread well beyond the hazy horizon. A few birds could be seen gliding effortlessly on the wind between the hills.

Her brief tranquility was abruptly interrupted by Paul's rough voice. "One more mile to go before we make camp."

There was just enough room to walk beside Tom. Beth quickened her pace despite her aching lungs and calves. Tom gently squeezed her hand before letting it go. She wiped her sweaty palm on her khaki shorts.

"Almost there, hon," Tom breathed. He took a napkin out of his pocket and wiped his face.

Beth took a swig from her water bottle and offered him a sip. Tom winked and took two heavy gulps before handing it back.

The last mile seemed to stretch, but at least it was uneventful. By the time they reached camp, the sun lingered three-fingers above the horizon. They had a good twenty minutes before it set, so the group got to work putting up their tents. Everyone worked quietly, speaking briefly to ask a question or give instructions. The tension hadn't dissipated much.

Beth imagined, had things gone differently, there would be lots of laughter and cutting up. They would have sat around the campfire eating dinner and regaling old stories. The quiet reality of the situation burned at her throat and chest.

I'm not going to cry and make this all about me, Beth thought, sucking up what little energy she had left to scorch that nerve.

Losing composure was how people got injured on hikes like these.

Instead of feeling sorry for herself, she busied her brain by helping Tom and Grady set up their tents. When the last stake was driven, Tom tossed the mallet to the ground and used the hem of his shirt to wipe the sweat from his face. The flash of his muscular stomach stirred her desires. Her husband could be a model on the cover of those men's fitness magazines. However, the grimace on Tom's face doused the fire.

"Beth and I are going to gather firewood and kindling," Tom announced. He kept his gaze firmly set on her as she stood and dusted off her knees.

Paul's lips pursed on his hardened face. He narrowed his eyes as Tom placed a hand on her lower back. It was like Paul wanted to argue but thought better of it. Jeff kept to himself, fussing with his tent and not looking at anyone. When they passed Grady on the way into the woods, he gave them both a warm smile.

Beth followed Tom, picking up fallen twigs while he gathered larger pieces of wood. When they were out of earshot, Tom stopped and glanced back toward the camp before setting his gaze on Beth.

"Did you mean what you said earlier? About going home?"

"Of course," Beth started, trying to gauge Tom's mood. He wasn't giving her much to go on. "But only if you guys are done. After all the stress, I wouldn't blame anyone if we called the rest of the hike off."

"Baby, I'm not asking because of anything you did. You were perfect," he whispered with a weak smile. Her stomach would have fluttered except for the fear flashing in his eyes. "I'm asking because we're in danger. Everything is packed and ready to go. We'll leave as soon as everyone is asleep. Head straight down the mountain, back the way we came. Stay off the trails so they can't track us."

"Wait. What?" Beth frowned, putting two and two together and whispering back, "Is this about what happened at the falls?"

Tom shook his head and stalked further away from camp. Beth hustled to keep up.

"Hon, you've got to explain. We can't just leave our friends," Beth tried talking him down. An unnaturally cool breeze made its way through the trees, making her shudder. "Help me understand. Please."

"It's *them* we have to worry about, Beth." Tom shivered as he looked her straight in the eyes and added, "I was stupid enough to think it was safe."

"Tom?" Her gut clenched as she clutched the sticks to her chest.

"Dammit. I should have told you everything before..." Tom stalked away, spit flying from his mouth on a curse. When he came back, his jaw ticked. "They're gonna sacrifice you tomorrow."

"You can't be serious." Beth stopped and let out a sharp chuckle. But one look at Tom's face told her that he was dead serious. She shook her head until wisps of hair fell from her ponytail. "No. I can't believe that. There's no way...*Human sacrifice?* Tom, I've known you guys our whole lives. We may not have always been close, but it's a small town. I think I would have heard something about a...cultist group."

"It's true, Beth."

"Grady wouldn't hurt a fly! He's one of those people that put spiders outside. How can your best friend..." Beth paused. Grady had skipped out on them the past two weekends. Could it be?

"No, not Grady," Tom said, smiling grimly. "Paul and Jeff. Every year, they come up here to perform a ritual. Grady said they—never mind. Please, Beth." He dropped the wood at their feet to grip her arms. "You gotta believe me. We need to leave while we can."

"You're scaring me." Beth jerked free of Tom's grasp and stepped back. The words 'ritual' and 'sacrifice' were on repeat inside her head, causing a chill to run down her spine. "If Paul and Jeff murder people in these woods every year, then why did you bring me?"

Her brain grasped for any rational explanation. They'd been together nearly four years. Tom never exhibited any strange behavior that would clue her in to cultish activities. Then again, they'd been under a mountain of stress before the incident earlier. Maybe this was new.

"I was stupid, okay? I wanted to bring you here, but my source was bad. I need to fix this. Please, Beth, trust me like you always have," Tom pleaded, his fear magnified by the welling tears. His Adam's apple bobbed. "I promise, as soon as we get somewhere safe, I'll explain everything. If we don't leave tonight, none of us will leave these woods alive."

Her wheels spun so fast there was smoke coming out of her ears. Beth gazed into his eyes, studied his body language. Tom was as scared as he was at the falls. Her shoulders dropped.

"We can't feel our way around in the dark, Tom. We'll get lost," Beth argued, trying to keep him talking while she figured out what to do. "And-and we can't leave your best friend if he's in danger, too."

Tom ran both hands through his hair in frustration and glanced back toward camp. "I'll loop him in when we get back. As soon as Jeff and Paul are asleep, we make a run for it. Grady will be ready."

She didn't want to believe him, that their friends meant to kill them. Why would he make up such an outlandish story unless it was an elaborate birthday prank?

Had Tom and his friends been murdering people for years?

One thing she knew for sure, the woods were not a safe place for her tonight. But she had nowhere else to go. The sun would be setting soon. Traveling in the woods at night was dangerous for advanced hikers, not for hobbyists like her.

"Come on, honey. You know I wouldn't lie to you." Tom's gray eyes were wet, and his hopeful grin fell with each passing second.

The sticks poked into her chest and breasts like dull pencils. The shadows darkened as the sun sank. Her heart nudged her toward believing him despite the little spark of doubt still niggling at the back of her mind.

What was she waiting for anyway? A sign? These woods were foreign to her, but the men knew them like their backyard. She didn't have a better alternative.

"Okay. We'll go back to camp...find Grady. We need to be gone before dawn." The tightness in her chest loosened. This was a good decision.

Relief painted Tom's features to match her husband's usual boyish youth. "I promise, we'll get you home in one piece." He gave her a tired grin and cupped her cheek.

The air around her thinned as another cool breeze surrounded them. The faintest whisper fell in their ears, soft but very clear.

"*Beth.*"

Whatever malevolent presence they had encountered back at the falls had followed them, and now it wanted her.

Chapter 6

TOM

Hearing Beth's name whispered on the wind made his heart stutter. He grabbed his wife's hand, scattering her kindling on the ground.

"Run."

Tom pulled her in a straight line through the forest, in the opposite direction of the voice. He didn't let go of her hand even when they went downhill. The further they descended, the darker the woods became. There was no stopping him...or his level of stupid leaving their packs behind.

"Dammit."

They would need their cellphones, flashlights, and compasses to find their way to the parking lot. It would take a miracle for them to make it out alive. To drive this point home, they found themselves in a blanket of black.

"Tom?" Beth's meek voice wavered.

He was an idiot. Had he forgotten his wife was afraid of the dark? This strike was added to the long list of tally marks he'd already racked up this weekend.

"I know, baby. Just squeeze my hand. Our eyes will adjust soon. We just need to keep moving."

"Okay," Beth whispered.

They slowed to a crawl. The only way Tom knew Beth was still with him was by the warmth of her hand in his. This whole weekend was fucked. He should have turned around when he saw Paul and Jeff.

Grady would have been fine. He'd have gotten out of sticky situations on his own before. Surely, he could give Paul the slip if they didn't make it back. But how would his best friend find them?

A twig snapped nearby. Tom's face flushed with pins and needles. He looped his other hand around Beth's waist and pulled her tightly against him, caging her against a tree. He couldn't hear much over his pounding heart. Whatever else was in the forest would either find them or move off. He prayed it was an animal.

Beth's fists tightened on his shirt. Her breaths were ragged and slow, barely there. Tom wanted to whisper words of comfort to console his frightened wife, but it would give away their position. Instead, Tom rested his forehead on hers, sharing every inhale and exhale.

By the time his heartbeat quieted, his eyes had adjusted to the dark. He leaned back and put his finger against his lips. Beth nodded, her eyes so wide the whites glowed. He gave Beth his back and scanned the woods for whatever was after them.

The moonlight provided scant light through the thick canopy of trees. Tom could make out the basic outline of white pines, bushes, and rocks. Nothing untoward.

When he was sure they were alone, he whispered next to Beth's ear, "Clear."

She nodded against his shoulder and sniffled. Taking her hand in his, he continued guiding them through the woods in the opposite direction of the snapped twig.

They would make it out eventually. There were no 'ifs' about it. They just couldn't stop moving.

BETH

NAVIGATING THE STILL DARKNESS was maddening. If what Tom said was true, there was little else they could do except keep going until they made it back to their vehicles.

Guilt filled some of the quiet. They'd left Grady behind. The thought of Paul or Jeff hurting her best friend because they ran away caused her chest to cave. More doubts used the opening to creep in.

Has Tom ever aided in these sacrifices? Or Grady?

The guys had been coming out here for almost ten years. How many of those had been for appeasing such a dark purpose?

Tom had to be mistaken. She'd have heard about all the missing persons, the murders. There couldn't be cultists in her little hometown.

Whatever was going on with the guys, Beth had no choice but to bide her time until they made it to the local police station. If the guys ended up being murderers, the officers would protect her.

Beth was lost in her own head when Tom whispered something. Her right foot caught on something hard and big, twisting her ankle sideways. Her chest hit the ground with a thud. Her 'oof!' echoed in the silent forest, breaking their spell of stealth.

She laid still, using her senses to assess the injuries. Her ankle was slightly warm, definitely sprained but nothing serious. Oxygen had vacated the premises except for the short, painful bursts. Her left hand stung, most likely scraped from trying to break her fall. She flexed it slowly just as Tom's hands found her shoulder. A relieved sigh was accompanied by strong hands moving up her body to her head. He gently swept the hair off her face.

"God, Beth. Are you okay?" he whispered so softly she barely made out his words. "Can you stand?"

"Maybe," Beth replied with a nod.

Tom wrapped her right arm around his shoulders and lifted. Once Beth was on her feet, he pressed his dry lips against her forehead. Tiny flutters danced in her stomach. Considering her mistrust, she didn't expect to be comforted by this small gesture. Tom was her doting husband, but she wasn't fully convinced he was telling the truth about the rituals. If he was sane and Paul was who Tom said, there was no way her husband would let them sacrifice her, was there?

The logical explanation was a birthday prank. They were all in on it, but now that she was injured, they'd let up.

"Where are you hurt?"

Tom's genuine concern eased the pinching in her chest and lungs. She relaxed into Tom's side.

"My ankle and hand are sore. It's nothing serious." Beth tried putting a small amount of pressure on her foot to prove her point.

A hot, stabbing sensation surrounded her ankle. She had to stifle the pained cry. *Dammit!* Prank or not, this sprain would ruin the hike anyway.

Tom adjusted his grip to wrap an arm around her waist. "I've got you," he whispered. "We'll try it again when you're ready."

Biting her bottom lip, Beth nodded. She was torn between wanting to cry in grief or scream in frustration. Instead, Beth swallowed her anxiety and tentatively took a step. With Tom's support, the sprain was minor enough that they could continue. "Take it slow," she said as Tom helped her forward.

"Yeah, we don't want anyone to get seriously injured tonight, do we?" A deep voice announced somewhere near them, freezing them in place.

A flashlight clicked on. Paul stood a few feet away. The light shining on his face cast a sinister glow before he lowered it to the ground. Chills ran down her back. For a prank, Paul sure was playing his part as sinister cult leader well.

Paul took a few steps toward her and Tom. Beth struggled to slow her breathing so her hammering heart wouldn't burst out of her chest. Her clammy hand was glued to Tom's despite the cool night. Bile threatened its way up her throat. She swallowed to keep it down.

"What are you two doing out here in the dark so far away from camp?" Paul asked, impatient as he took a few more steps toward them, not waiting for an answer. "Both of you know better than to hike at night without equipment so..." he said, leaving it open, no doubt to hear whatever lame excuse they came up with.

"The creature—fr-from the falls—found us while we were gathering firewood. I wasn't thinking; I grabbed Beth's hand, and we ran." Tom lightly squeezed Beth's hand and pulled her closer. "I know it was stupid, but I got spooked. We're okay. Thank God you found us."

Beth opened her mouth to call them out, but decided to go with it. "Yeah, I twisted my ankle after tripping over a rock. We're glad that's all that happened. Things could have been much worse."

She snuggled up to Tom, hoping to sell it. The niggling in the back of her mind was like a creep-radar. It went haywire with the way Paul watched them as if her was dissecting a science project. There was also a sliver of a chance what Tom said was true. In that case, how pissed would Paul be if he found out Tom had blabbed about the rituals? Best to play along for now. She could do scared to death and not fake it.

Paul smirked as he studied them. Seemingly satisfied at their answer, he whistled a signal. Once a reply came from far off, he knelt in front of Beth. "Which ankle is it?"

"Uh, the right one," Beth mumbled, watching the leader of their group turn her ankle over in his hand.

He gingerly prodded and turned it. Beth hissed when it smarted. When Paul whistled and tsked, she pursed her lips knowingly. The adrenaline pumping through her body must have been enough to dull some of the pain. Beth wondered how bad the gash in her hand really was.

"Alright." Paul stood and dusted his hands on his pants. "We'll carry you back to camp and get an ice pack on it. Jeff is already on his way back."

Silently, Paul and Tom slipped one hand each underneath Beth's thighs and locked their grip. They grasped the other's shoulder and lifted her into a two-handed seat. She put her arms around their necks for support. Her left hand throbbed from the pressure of being in a fist. She hoped it didn't need stitches.

They started back up the hill with the flashlight in Beth's lap to light the way. After walking a good twenty feet, another flashlight bobbed in the dark as it drew near. Beth recognized the black, curly mop of hair and fought the grin trying to break free. The concern on Grady's face was so believable that doubt stabbed at her heart again.

"Thank God you two are safe!" Grady exclaimed, looking at Tom before quickly settling his gaze on Beth. "Are you okay?" He examined her, focusing on the swelling in her ankle.

"Sprained ankle. Didn't seem too bad at first, but Paul said it needs ice. Guess I was wrong," Beth replied plainly. Trying to keep a cool countenance with the man who was her closest friend. "I'll be glad when we're back at camp."

This emotional roller coaster was getting the best of her. Beth closed her eyes, feigning pain or fatigue. However they wanted to see it. If she was wrong and this wasn't a prank, the last thing she wanted to do was put her husband and their best friend in more danger. Beth needed to figure out what was really going on. To do that, she'd have to wait until morning to suss out the liars. But if Tom was right, she wouldn't have tomorrow night.

Damn ankle.

She would sleep a few hours tonight, then leave before dawn, with or without her two guys. If things went off without a hitch, she'd have at least a four-hour head start.

A gentle breeze swirled around them much like the one before. This time, Beth's name wasn't whispered in the wind. It came into her mind as a thought. Peace washed over her with another message: *Trust.*

Chapter 7

GRADY

TOM AND BETH'S CARELESS ESCAPE plan made Grady's jaw hurt and gave him a headache, but it had worked in their favor. While Jeff and Paul searched for them, Grady used the opportunity to double back to camp. After he hid their backpacks in the hollow of a tree outside of camp, he used his pocketknife to cut a large but nondescript hole in the window of his tent and the Newman's. Zippered doors were too damned noisy.

Grady had barely rejoined the search when Paul's signal whistle cut through the forest, letting them know Tom and Beth had been found. Seconds later, Jeff whistled in answer. Grady thanked the goddess his blessings held out. A few seconds later, Jeff came rushing by, heading back to camp. Paul and Tom were close behind carrying Beth.

Grady had barely looked Beth over before she closed her eyes. His chest pinched uncomfortably, like when someone pulls at a single strand of hair, but this was more like a string to his heart. Everything had gone so wrong this weekend. He'd hoped to transition things a bit more smoo—

"Brother Grady, why don't you go ahead and help Brother Jeff with dinner? He should have the campfire going soon," he commanded with a gruff voice.

Grady's feet were rooted in place. Beth was injured; he didn't want to leave her. Tom's questioning frown cut him loose. He could use this time to rethink their escape.

"Sure," Grady grumbled, giving Paul a curt nod. He didn't dare turn back or else his resolve would weaken.

He headed back to town. It was clear that Tom didn't have a backup after all. If they were going to get out in one piece, it was up to him to figure it out. He'd have to let Tom in on it without alerting Paul or Jeff. Now that Paul was paranoid about losing his sacrifice, it would be next to impossible to get Tom alone. He'd have to resort to using some kind of code.

Soon, the scent of burning wood and white smoke came from the center of camp. Jeff had managed to make a fire after all. He whirled around with his eyebrows raised when Grady's boots crunched the ground.

"Oh...Hey, Grady. Where are the others?" The redhead wiped his brow and tossed another log onto the flames. The heat flared, sending cinders dancing through the air.

"They're coming. Paul sent me ahead to help with dinner." Grady squatted next to the food bag, searching through the Meals Ready to Eat they'd brought. A permanent marker rested at the bottom of the bag. He slipped it behind one of the meals. Finding the ones he wanted, Grady slid the bag over to Jeff. "Beth sprained her ankle. I've got to get an ice pack from Tom's tent."

"It's not bad, is it? I mean, Beth's ankle?" Jeff asked as he rifled through the brown packets.

Grady almost laughed at the mock concern in his so-called friend's voice. "Not serious. She'll be able to hike in the morning, don't you worry." He stood with the MREs in hand. "Be right back."

Without paper to write on, Grady had to keep the message short and sweet. He quietly ripped open a package and took out the bag of Skittles. He poured them out on Tom's sleeping bag and carefully opened the bag all the way. Using the Sharpie he wrote on the inside, "2 am. North window."

He signed the note with his typical symbol, a variation of his initials 'GC' within the symbol of the Triple Goddess. Same as the small blue tattoo on the meat of his left hand, below his pinkie finger. He placed the slip of paper underneath Tom's pillow and arranged the Skittles into an arrow pointing toward the note. With a quick prayer to the goddess, he exited Tom and Beth's tent.

"Any luck?" Jeff asked, steadying a pot of water over the fire.

"Nope." Grady shook his head and countered, "You wouldn't have an ice pack, would you?"

Jeff pulled a small squarish package from his backpack and tossed it to him. His face wore his signature goofy grin. "I got you."

Sure, you do, but not when it counts. Grady snorted internally.

The men worked quietly preparing the meal packets. They were almost done heating everything when a pair of heavy footsteps entered the camp. Tom and Paul both looked exhausted, having carried Beth the entire way.

Eager to get Beth away from Paul, Grady jumped to his feet to help. "Hey, you. Let's get you over to a chair."

"Thanks," Beth replied. She tried to smile, but it looked forced because her eyebrows were drawn together.

Once Beth was seated, Grady knelt in front of her and activated the ice pack, giving it a thorough shake. Before he had a chance to apply it, Tom knelt beside him.

"I've got this, Grady. Thanks." Tom took the pack from him and placed it on Beth's ankle. "How does that feel, hon?"

"Better." Beth studied Grady before answering Tom, "Really, I don't need to be babied. Y'all can carry on. I'll be fine."

Grady was used to her stubbornness, so he nodded. With a warm smile, he leaned over to the hot meals, plucked three, and stood. Handing one to Beth and the other to Tom, he sat on the log next to the fire.

"Eat up. Tomorrow is gonna be a long day. You'll need your strength." *Tonight is gonna be even longer*, Grady thought as he shoveled his food.

He hoped Beth could keep up.

Chapter 8

TOM

GRADY KEPT CODDLING BETH...AND it was pissing Tom off. He was used to the brotherly affection Grady gave her, but he couldn't shake the feeling that something had shifted in his best friend. There was a tenderness in Grady's interactions that went beyond what Tom was used to seeing.

He frowned. They were in a dangerous situation, and his imagination was making up shit that wasn't there. He needed to prioritize and focus on getting Beth out of harm's way.

Tom checked his watch. It was a quarter to two in the morning. He read Grady's note for a third time before tucking it into the front pocket of his pants. After dinner, he'd gone to get Beth a blanket from the tent and found it. At first, Tom thought the arrow made from Skittles was something his wife had set up before they had left for firewood. But he found the cryptic note underneath his pillow.

What does Grady mean by 'north window'?

"Hey, hon," Beth whispered as they lay in their sleeping bags. "You awake?"

Tom's bag ruffled as he turned toward her. "Yeah. You okay?"

She nodded but her face was pulled into a frown. "I can't sleep. Would you get my earphones from my bag? I need my music."

"Of course," Tom whispered before placing a kiss on her forehead.

With liquid movements as silent as a mouse, Tom slipped out of his sleeping bag in search of their packs. By the dim glow of electric candlelight, he searched the small two-person tent. Their backpacks should have been in the front corner, underneath the mesh bag the tent was stored in. He thought back to when he grabbed a blanket for Beth at dinner. They were missing then, he'd just been too preoccupied taking care of his wife for it to sink in. Panic rose in Tom's throat, burning as he swallowed back the bitter acid. Paul must have taken them.

The quiet ruffle of Beth's sleeping bag caught his attention. When he turned, she sat up. "Everything okay?"

"Yeah, it's, uh...Just one more minute," Tom whispered in reply. They couldn't leave camp without supplies...again. He fought the despair creeping into his subconscious. They couldn't afford having him fall into it, not with what was at stake.

Beth crawled out of her bag and shuffled over on hands and knees. She stopped to sit cross-legged next to him and held out her hand. "Hand me my bag. I know exactly where they are."

Tom's forehead lined with sweat. "I—"

"Psst!" A noise came from behind the tent

He and Beth froze. Her eyes were as wide as saucers.

Scanning the tent's windows, Tom narrowed his gaze until he came upon a face on the other side. He could barely make out anything but the sapphire blue eyes of his friend.

The NORTH window, you idiot.

"Grady?" Beth asked, crawling over to the window. "What're you doing?"

"Hey," Grady responded, a little too breathy for Tom's comfort. "Time to go."

Tom crawled over to draw Grady's attention. "Problem. Our bags are gone."

Beth put her hand on Tom's shoulder, forcing him to face her. She whisper-shouted, "What do you mean our bags are gone?!"

"Hey. I have 'em," Grady answered quickly before lifting their window. "C'mon."

Tom frowned when he saw the damage Grady had caused to his expensive tent. He turned away from the jagged edges to study Beth's reaction.

Her face was puckered in a scowl, but she slipped her shoes on and crawled out. Not wanting to waste more time, Tom followed suit. Once on the outside of their tent, he ignored the spurt of jealousy at seeing his wife in the arms of his best friend. Beth was only holding onto Grady's forearms while they waited on him. He was being irrational again.

As soon as Tom came to Beth's aid, Grady motioned for them to follow. They weren't far out of camp before the bushes rustled. A low rumble, almost like a growl, sounded from somewhere in front of them. The woods went silent, like someone had pressed the mute button.

Tom waited on Grady to wave them onward before following him to a hollowed-out tree. Inside, he counted three backpacks and was finally able to relax. Grady knelt in front of the opening and pulled a backpack out. Tom's tightened shoulders relaxed as Grady pulled out two more. Tom strapped on his pack, then slung Beth's over one shoulder.

When Grady stood, he pulled a map out of his pocket and opened it in front of them. He balanced a small flashlight between his chin and shoulder, illuminating the page.

"Here's where we're camping now," Grady pointed to the middle of the map. He moved his finger to a remote part Tom was unfamiliar with. "And this is where we need to go."

Tom narrowed his eyes. "I thought we were gonna go back home, not further into the woods."

"Trust me. This is the safest place we can go, safer than home. Paul won't be able to find us." Grady responded with such conviction that Tom found it difficult to argue.

He'd always trusted Grady, the man was like a brother to him. Tom's ride or die before Beth came along. But his brother had been acting strangely for the past two weeks. Tom decided it was best to keep him under a close, watchful eye.

"Look, I'm not sure what the hell is going on, but I'm not going anywhere until somebody explains," Beth interjected, concern hardening her soft features. Her stubbornness was magnified by the crossing of her arms.

Tom placed his hands below her shoulders in an attempt to soothe her. "Hon, I promise to tell you everything when we are safe. Please, give me—give *us*—a little longer. If Grady says he knows somewhere safe, I trust him."

He could practically see the wheels spinning behind Beth's eyes. When she nodded curtly, Tom held back his victory dance. Instead, he leaned in to kiss her, but she held up a hand to deflect him. The rejection stung almost as bad as her distrust.

"Let's not waste time," Beth huffed. She grabbed her pack from Tom, limped past Grady, and shrugged it on. Despite the protesting looks they both gave her, she made a flourish in the direction of the path Grady showed them. "After you."

Grady's wide-eyed gaze flickered to Tom before he shook his head and took the lead. Beth hobbled after him.

Tom's chest restricted, causing his breath to shudder. In the darkest depths of his psyche, the demon of doubt ate further at his resolve. His mental fortitude wavered, but he willed himself to remember that Beth needed him to be strong. She needed to be able to trust him again.

His gaze wandered past Beth to settle on Grady. Was he imagining the lingering glances his best friend cast at his wife? The man focused on getting them to this safe place *seemed* to be the same Grady he grew up with, but something was different. Even now, at the edge of his thoughts, a new fear formed. One he wouldn't dare put a name to.

Shoving the lurking darkness back into the strongbox in the corner of his mind, Tom tightened his backpack and followed his greatest treasure.

Chapter 9

GRADY

The weight over Grady's chest lifted when Beth finally nodded.

Behind her stubborn facade, Beth was scared and guarded. He'd seen the twinge on Tom's face when his wife rejected him. Grady had witnessed several minor arguments between those two, but she'd never been this distrustful afterward. Still, he remained cautiously optimistic. Once he got them to the Grove, they could fix whatever rift had formed between the trio.

You're only kidding yourself. Shit is gonna get worse, and you know it.

Grady crushed his intrusive thoughts with his proverbial fist. Tom and Beth were his family. His people. They'd understand after he explained.

"If we keep a steady pace, we should reach our destination in two hours," Grady said over his shoulder, a safe enough distance from the camp that he could raise his voice above a whisper.

Even with the miles they'd put between themselves and Paul, Grady still couldn't get comfortable. The silence between the trio was deafening, so he kept his attention focused on other things. Namely, the faint scent of a wild boar he'd caught shortly after leaving camp. The beast had been traveling away from their location, but the further they hiked into the woods, the more often he would catch it again.

Grady had made this same hike to the Grove over a hundred times. Usually, the ill-tempered porcine stayed far away from the main hiking trails. He'd never crossed paths with any. This past weekend, though, there was an unusual amount of boar activity near his route, but breeding season was still a few months away.

Nevertheless, he kept his wits about him. Something else was happening in his forest, something cloaked in malice. He was keen to keep Beth and Tom clear of it.

BETH

BETH MARCHED BEHIND Grady with Tom taking up the rear. They made as little noise as possible and the more distance they made, the more she felt like she'd made the right decision.

But that was two hours ago. Since then, Beth's thoughts filled with too many what if's. What if Tom was telling the truth? What if he and Grady were the murderers? What if they were taking her to be sacrificed right now? She could ask for a bathroom break and make a run for it, but what if she got hurt, or worse? Beth was a skilled hiker but surviving in the woods alone required a whole other skillset she did not have.

Chancing a look at Tom, he flashed one of his million-watt smiles before she turned away. Normally, it turned her insides to goo, but she only warmed at the gesture.

Beth focused on Grady, the way he moved with purpose, and surveyed ahead like he could see danger from miles away. As if he could feel her watching him, he glanced over his shoulder. Grady's features softened, making Beth's suspicions crumble. They didn't act like murderers. Despite the questions ticking away in her brain, it was difficult to feel anything but safe in their company.

"We need to rest. Beth is limping," Tom said, interrupting her thoughts.

Beth slowed, but she didn't stop. She hadn't noticed her slight limp. What else had she not noticed.

Grady turned and pursed his lips. "Where we're going is just past those bushes. Once we pass the boundary, we'll be safe. Can you walk a little farther?"

Considering it was nearly dawn and none of them had slept a wink, Beth was beyond tired. To add salt to the wound, now that she was paying attention to her ankle, it pulsed in pain. A safe place to sit would be a welcome reward for all her hard work. "I can make it."

By the time they got to the dot on the map, her foot felt like she was wearing a hundred socks. Looked about like it, too. Grady stopped next to a large, moss-covered rock with vines hanging down in front of it. He pulled the curtain of green aside to reveal a small passage through the rock. It was barely a person-sized crack. They'd have to go through sideways.

"Go on. I'll follow Tom." Grady's calm gaze penetrated her shields.

"Fine." Beth squeezed into the space, grabbing Tom's hand out of habit.

His hopeful grin made her cheeks warm.

Once Grady closed the vine curtain, a speck of light was visible on the other side. As she neared the end, Beth could make out a small clearing ahead. The wildflower field from her dream the night before flashed before her eyes. Her skin tingled like it did before a storm.

And then they arrived.

As soon as Beth stepped through and her feet touched the grass, the prickling across her skin sunk into her pores. It infused with her DNA.

Warm sunlight, soft wind carrying the scent of wildflowers. It was home but not. A child-like glee bubbled below the surface, the one she'd repressed when she longed to run free in the grass to chase butterflies and dragonflies. To stomp in mud puddles barefoot. To simply *be* without worrying about adult responsibilities and hiding away from the rest of the world.

"Just up this hill there's a sitting area." Grady pointed straight ahead. His face had lost the lines of grumpiness, leaving him more like the man she was used to.

Tom still held her hand. Beth was hard-pressed to let go of his when he looked at her with puppy dog eyes.

Beth tugged him onward. "C'mon before all the good seats are taken."

His grin finally won, making her heart happy.

She trudged up the hill, past the small clearing to a forested area, thick with white birch trees. Beyond was a much larger clearing opening up to rolling hills. Grady led them through the center and off to the left. A circle of stones had been placed around a fire pit. Three large cut logs were next to the pit as makeshift chairs. This place was more than secluded. The only way he could have known of its existence was having been here before.

"Beth can rest as long as she needs to. Nobody will bother us here," Grady explained as he sat and rifled through his pack for food and water. No other explanation.

Beth peeked at Tom, but her husband was just as puzzled. He shook his head and led Beth to the nearest log. Once she was seated, Tom dragged the last log closer to hers and opened his backpack. He rifled through it and handed her a protein bar.

"Thanks."

Beth elevated her ankle using her backpack, and opened the plastic covering. As she chewed, she scouted the area.

The field was full of orange coreopsis, purple asters, white Queen Anne's Lace, and tall wheatgrass. A gentle breeze caressed her skin, carrying with it a feeling of peace. This whole grove was one big bubble of serenity. Time seemed to move at a leisurely pace, and her worries diminished by the minute.

She was lost in the moment when something brushed against her ankle. Beth startled, but it was just Tom. His brows were furrowed in concentration as he moved it this way and that and prodded. Beth responded accordingly. He also checked her bandaged hand to make sure it was healing properly.

With a satisfied nod, Tom stood and planted a kiss on the top of her head. "I'll be right back. Have to take a leak."

Beth watched Tom as he walked away without a care in the world. It irked her, so she turned her attention to the firepit. The logs looked freshly used. Couldn't be more than a week old.

She bit into her protein bar and raised her gaze to the tree line. The morning sun's rays were nearing the horizon, painting the skies in a brilliance of pink, orange, and red hues. She stifled a yawn with no success.

"There are two cabins on the property," Grady said between bites. "As soon as Tom gets back, we'll go and rest up."

"Cool, but Tom promised an explanation." Beth countered, shaking her head. No matter how tired she was, there was no way she could sleep until her questions were answered.

"Alright." Grady sighed and rubbed his tired face before he studied her with a dejected frown. "Do you need to wait for Tom to get back or can I start?"

She felt guilty at seeing how low his shoulders slumped, but her curiosity was stronger. "What kind of cult are you guys in that requires human sacrifice?" The sting of her direct question visibly struck Grady. His face displayed an array of emotions going from surprise to serious. It was obvious he expected this discussion to take a different route.

"Um, right to the point." He started after clearing his throat, "First off...Tom and I are not part of any cult. Paul and Jeff are...as well as our dads."

"Whoa, whoa, whoa. My *dad* is part of this cult, too?!" Beth nearly screeched. The heat drained from her face as her jaw went slack. "No way. I would know."

"Would you, though? Small towns tend to have more secrets than residents." Grady's stoic frown spoke loud enough to make her confidence waver.

"Sorry. It's just difficult to wrap my head around. First Tom, then you, and now my dad." Truth be told, she didn't know her dad as well as she told herself. He came from the generation that left raising the children to the 'womenfolk.'

"Not your dad, just Jack, Louis, Elliott, and Curtis. At least, that's all I know of." Grady stood, gripped the edges of his log-chair, and effortlessly inched it closer to Beth's. "Let me start at the beginning."

GRADY

GRADY TOOK A DEEP breath and began, "The summer of our high school graduation, Paul, Jeff, Tom and I met up for our yearly hike. We'd been going on our own since Paul got his driver's license, so you can guess how surprised we were to find our dads waiting for us when we pulled into the parking lot.

"They told us we were ready to take over a sacred duty passed down for generations. The hike that year was to be our initiation. Paul and Jeff seemed excited by the cryptic way our dads were talking, but not Tom and me. It was downright unsettling, but we still followed. They were our dads."

Grady stopped long enough to take a drink of water. He allowed Beth time to ask questions before continuing. She took a sip of water by reflex, rolling her hand in a gesture for him to continue. He could hear Tom's legs cutting through the tall grass on his way back.

"So, we followed our dads into the woods. The first day was like usual. But on the second day of our hike, our dad's took us to a clearing in the middle of the woods. The closer we got, the bigger the stone in the center became. It was flat on the top, like a table, balanced on two smaller stones at the head and foot. That bad feeling I had earlier? It took a sharp, hard left when we saw that there was a woman tied to the surface. "

Grady rolled his neck. He'd never be able to look Beth in the eye again when she learned what a coward he was. He drew a deep breath.

"I'll never forget the look on her tear-stained face. The way her eyes begged for help as she shook her head and pulled at her bindings. They'd even stuffed a goddamn dirty cotton rag in her mouth."

Anger flashed in heat waves along his muscles the way they had back then. He'd wanted to do something, but there were six against two. Grady's fists were so tight his nails left crescent moons in his palms.

"She'd been there long enough there was dried blood on her wrists and the ropes were making fresh cuts. Our dads smiled and laughed like they were at some barbecue and not traumatizing some poor woman. And that's when I heard the words 'ritual sacrifice.' I thought I was gonna be sick."

He shuddered at the memory. The fear oozing from the poor woman was enough to constrict his chest. The blade in his father's hands. The quick slice and the squelching sound of blood. Grady had fallen to his knees, spilling his breakfast all over the ground nearby while the woman died. If he'd been stronger, if he'd known his true potential before that day, he could've saved her.

Tom squeezed his shoulder in support before sitting on the other side of Beth.

Grady continued, "They said the ritual was necessary, that an ancient witch demanded it in exchange for longevity and riches. Tom and I rejected joining them then and there, but they made us swear silence. If we told anyone, they threatened to make us watch as they killed our moms, and then they'd kill us. We've had to live with that guilt for seven years."

Hanging his head, Grady fought the urge to succumb to the shame. He couldn't bear to see Beth's reaction, knowing that he did nothing to stop his father and the others from cold-blooded murder. If he couldn't save the stranger years ago, how did he expect to save the woman he cared about deeply? Even with the magic he'd learned and practiced since then, would it be enough? Would *he* be enough?

The thought of Beth's disgust fueled his remorse until exhaustion crippled him. He couldn't raise his head if he wanted to.

But Fate was a fickle mistress.

He smelled Beth's soft lavender vanilla perfume as she knelt in front of him. Her presence was all-consuming, but he was drowning in trepidation. Her small hands cupped his face and raised his head. Grady's heart plummeted as soon as they made eye contact.

Her reaction was worse than he had imagined.

Chapter 10

BETH

As Beth listened in horror to Grady's recounting, she couldn't help but feel sympathetic. Grady and Tom had only been eighteen when their fathers threw them into a life of homicide. There was no way they could have changed the outcome against four grown men and their two friends. Paul's six-foot plus, spindly frame wasn't as weak as it appeared. And Jeff may be shy and a little soft around the middle, but he was no pushover when it came defending Paul. He'd use the few inches he had on Grady to Paul's advantage.

But there was still something Grady hadn't explained. Something she needed to know to feel safe if she wasn't going to bail on them while they slept.

Lifting Grady's face, Beth tried to keep a blank expression as she studied him. Yelling in anger would work against her. "If you and Tom aren't part of their cult, why did y'all bring me out here? Why not take me on a hike elsewhere?"

Tom grumbled something akin to, "I told him so."

Grady shot him a frown before bringing his attention back to her. Beth wasn't annoyed they communicated in their unspoken way, but the disconnect between them was concerning.

"We didn't know they'd be here, Beth. This was supposed to be a fun birthday weekend with just the three of us." Deep lines of regret were etched on his face. Grady took a shuddering breath. He glanced at Tom before adding, "As for hiking somewhere else, there are...other reasons we had to come out to these woods. Reasons I can explain, just...not yet."

"Not good enough," she breathed. At the same time Beth dropped her hands and stood up, Tom jumped to his feet.

"*What* other reasons, Grady?" he demanded.

Beth put her hands on her hips and twirled around at Tom's question. Either they were both messing with her or one of them was lying. Unfortunately, their reactions were pretty damn convincing. Tom leered at Grady with a reddened face, while Grady's body folded in defeat. Her eyes widened in realization. The possibility that Grady was lying chilled her to the bone. She almost believed his sob story.

"You brought us to a place where no one can find us," she whispered, running her fingernails across her scalp. "How could I have been so naive?"

Grady's head popped up. The terror of her unspoken accusation plastered across his face. "What? Gods, no, Beth. I would *never* do anything to hurt you...or Tom," he yelled, voice thick. His nostrils flared as he jumped to his feet. His face was as red as a beet.

Beth backed up several paces. Had she been wrong? Was *Tom* the one being untruthful? *Am I the one being delusional?*

"You two are the most important people in my life. Why would I want harm to come y'all?" Grady asked with a hoarse whisper. He held his limp hands out toward her and Tom, palms up, his deep blue eyes imploring her to see reason.

Not only did Beth's bones ache from tiredness, but her head pounded. No one was thinking clearly, and things had gotten way out of hand. They should table this discussion until they all have some sleep.

As if to drive her point home, the morning sunlight poured into the sky, bathing the area in a healthy golden glow.

"M-maybe we should get some rest. Clear our minds before we come to any other crazy conclusions," Beth replied, unable to make eye contact with either Grady or Tom.

Forget about sleeping in a cabin. Point her to the nearest cave, let her crawl inside, and roll a stone in front of the exit. Beth would be content to wait until her mortification dissolved before facing the guys again.

TOM

ONE MOMENT, TOM WAS livid with Grady for being untruthful about their reason for being here, and where he had gone the previous two weekends. How did his best friend somehow know a safe place in the middle of a federally funded forest anyway?

Then, Tom was surprised when Beth made the outlandish accusation that Grady was going to sacrifice them. Talk about whiplash. His emotional state had never dealt with such extremes in a matter of seconds.

Tom's jaw hung loose as he stared at Beth. Whatever occurred between Beth and Grady left *him* feeling like a third wheel. His wife was already distant, but now she wouldn't look at either of them.

Shit. He had to fix this.

"I think Beth is right," Tom replied. *That usually works.* "We're all exhausted. I don't any of us slept a wink last night. Some rest will do us good."

Grady's sad eyes met his. He gave Tom a slow nod and turned to pick up his bag. Beth didn't look his way but did the same. He was left there standing stupidly. Snatching his bag, Tom slipped it on and silently followed Grady up the inclining field.

When they crested the hill, twin cabins came into view. Beth stopped abruptly, staring at the buildings. Tom almost bumped into her, giving him an excuse to place a hand on her arm.

"What's wrong, hon?" Tom didn't see anything odd about them, other than they were well kept for being so secluded. And they were identical. "We don't have to go in there if you don't want to."

She turned as if noticing Tom for the first time. "It's nothing. C'mon. I'm about to fall over."

Tightening her hold on the shoulder straps of her bag, Beth continued after Grady. Tom knew something was still bothering her, but he refused to push the matter. He was skating on thin ice. What they needed was to sleep off the stress, if possible.

Grady stopped in front of the cabins and turned to face them. "Y'all can take the cabin on the right. I'll sleep in the other. Set your alarms to go off in six hours and we'll meet for dinner in my cabin."

"Understood," Tom said, placing his hand on Beth's lower back.

Not wasting any time, Grady left them alone. Beth rubbed her arms and shivered. Tom coaxed her toward the cabin, hoping a cuddle session would smooth things over. "C'mon, hon."

BETH

THESE WERE THE SAME twin cabins from her dream the night before last. She was sure of it. The central placement of the door with a single-pane window on either side, the white mud pressed between layers of hand-hewn, stacked wood logs, and the simple awning over a single step.

As they approached, Beth appreciated how immaculately maintained they were. Tom opened the door for her, offering a warm smile when she finally gathered the nerve to face him. They'd be sleeping in the same bed since their sleeping bags had been left at camp. The thought made her almost as nervous as the first night they were intimate.

To distract from the twisting in her gut, Beth scanned the one-room structure. When her gaze fell on the small twin-sized cot in one corner, one word came to mind: cozy. Unless the ladder led to a loft, they'd practically be sleeping on top of each other.

While Tom got to work fluffing the straw bed, Beth climbed up the ladder to peek over the ledge. As suspected, it was storage space for several baskets and tools. She swallowed her disappointment and climbed back down.

Beth's face flushed pink seeing Tom's shirtless back. The defined muscles flexed as he put on a clean shirt. Her breath stopped when he started to take his pants off, but she was stuck where she stood. Tom was a beautiful man, inside and out. Whatever doubts she still struggled with were pushed to the back burner when he flashed her a warm smile.

Coming over, he placed his hands on Beth's hips. "You know I love the way you watch me, but we need to sleep." Tom's voice was low and sensual.

He peered into her eyes as if trying to read her thoughts. She could lose herself in his stormy gray eyes. How could a man so full of love and devotion purposely bring her harm? He couldn't. Not on purpose.

Beth nodded, making his smile widen. Tom kissed her forehead as she pulled him into a hug. The comforting warmth was immediate. "I'm sorry." The words croaked out of her lips before she could think to stop them.

Tom took a shuddering breath and squeezed her; his face buried in the crook of her neck. "I'm sorry, too, hon."

When they released each other, Tom brushed away her tears with the pads of his thumbs. She smiled and whispered, "Let's go to bed."

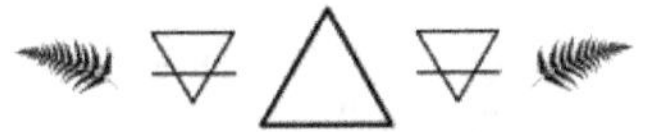

BETH'S DREAM WAS AS vivid as her memories. The second one in as many days. Both were connected to the same place—this beautiful grove surrounded by white birch trees.

She dreamt she was a healer who loved her work; curing people's ailments using what nature provided on her doorstep and, of course, *magic*. It was what she was born to do and gave her a sense of purpose.

Beth stood in the birch grove surrounded by lush grass with the warmth of the noonday sun on her face. A soul-deep warmth permeated her as the area hummed with joy. In her hands were a picnic blanket and a basket full of food. The gentle breeze nudged her onward. She smiled, knowing her lover would be meeting her soon.

In the center of the field, Beth spread the blanket across the grass, placing the picnic basket in one corner. Moments later, there came the sound of snapping branches. A tall, burly man with thick black curls came wandering into the clearing. He wore a beige long-sleeve shirt rolled to his elbows, brown wool pants, and a matching brown vest. He was ruggedly handsome and very tidy. An air of confidence surrounded him. There was also a familiarity Beth couldn't put a finger on. If only his face wasn't softly blurred.

"Good afternoon, Myrtle, my sweet," the man said in a voice as soft and rich as velvet. His sapphire eyes cleared the haze, gazing at her with such love that the air left her lungs. A small gasp escaped her lips.

"You're late, Barton Cooper," the woman said, voice full of confidence. Even though she was spectating, Beth's heart leapt with Myrtle's.

Barton raised her hand to his lips. "Fairest, please accept my deepest apologies. It could not be helped. Though my family has accepted our union, there are still obligations I must attend to. Being the eldest—and only—son, the responsibility of assisting my father in the family business falls to me. I promise, as soon as Solomon is old enough to learn the trade, he will take over."

"In due time, my love. For now, let us enjoy each other's company before you have to leave again," the voice breathed with exhilaration.

Taking her hand, Barton pulled Myrtle onto the blanket with him. He kissed her eagerly, holding her as close as he could while his fingers fumbled with the strings of her bodice. Beth tried to look away, but she couldn't. Whatever Myrtle saw, so did she. Soon, Beth was caught up in the fiery sensations of their romance.

The cool blanket beneath her warmed as Barton gently made love to Myrtle, kissing her neck and caressing her breasts. Beth felt guilty for enjoying the man in the dream, but that was just it. As vivid as the sensations or emotions seemed, it wasn't real.

Afterward, they laid on the blanket lazily feeding each other wild berries foraged from the forest, a bit of goat cheese, and some freshly baked bread. Myrtle watched Barton as he gazed at the sky, her heart filled to bursting with love. When he turned his blue-eyed gaze upon Myrtle, the rest of Barton's face came into full focus. Recognition came moments before the dream blurred and went dark.

Beth awoke before their alarms. The dream disappeared as if being sucked down a drainpipe too fast to hold on to, leaving only feelings. As quietly as possible, Beth turned her head to where Tom slept peacefully. Shame stabbed her chest.

Her dream only added more confusion and unanswered questions. The one that bothered her most: Why did the man in her dream look like Grady Cooper?

Chapter 11

TOM

Tom awoke with a heaviness in his chest, and it wasn't from whatever was going on between him and Beth. Something deep within his soul burned, like a seed that hadn't been buried deep enough and was being scorched by the sun.

He dreamt last night for the first time in forever. Shapeless forms surrounded him in flashes of purple, green, and red. Some seemed playful, teasing. Others exuded anger, lashing at him with windy blows that passed through him like ghosts.

Nothing about it made sense.

He lay there listening to the roof creak. There was no early evening birdsong, no crickets or tree frogs. Stillness like the center of a hurricane encased this place.

Careful not to wake Beth, he reached for his cell phone and lifted it enough to see the time. They were supposed to wake in a little over an hour, but he wasn't sleepy. Tired? Yes. But falling asleep after a weird semi-nightmare? Not happening.

He couldn't roll onto his back, and he couldn't get out of bed. Beth lay in the crook of his arm with her head resting on his shoulder and her arm draped across his chest. If he woke her, she might pull away from him again.

Instead, Tom rested his cheek on Beth's head and held her. Breathing in the lingering scent of warm vanilla and lavender from her shampoo seemed to ease some of his soul-deep ache.

Beth shifted in his arms with a quiet whimper. When her hips moved against his thigh, he stilled, waiting for her to wake. Her arm tightened against his chest, loosely fisting his shirt. Whatever nightmare she was having caused her breath to hitch. But, as her lips brushed against his chest, a soft moan escaped her lips.

Tom lowered his hand to cup her ass, ready to assist when Beth whispered, "Barton."

Who the fuck is Barton?

Anger surged, turning his vision red as the fires of rage swallowed him. He was about to shake her awake and demand to know who she was fantasizing about when Beth tensed. She jerked her arm back and stilled.

Forcing his breath to slow, Tom closed his eyes and pretended to be asleep, though his heart didn't get the memo. She slipped out of bed, leaving a cold draft in her place. He couldn't bring himself to open his eyes yet. He wasn't sure what to make of Beth's reaction when she woke up.

Her light footsteps didn't go far. A zipper opened painfully slow but only enough to get a hand through. When he heard clothes ruffle, he finally opened his eyes.

"Morning," Tom croaked. Beth went rigid and her ears turned dark pink.

She gave him her back and answered, "Morning."

Swinging his legs over the side of the cot, Tom stretched before he prodded. "How'd you sleep?"

"Fine," Beth responded without turning around. "You?"

Her hands shook as they fastened the clasps of her bra. She shimmied her arms out the bottom of her sleep tank before slipping the straps up to her shoulders. A classic Angry Beth move, hiding herself when she was annoyed at him.

"Fine," he countered, sneaking up behind her. His eyes traced the curve of her neck. He wouldn't touch her, not until she explained who Barton was and apologized.

Beth squeaked when she turned around. Her cheeks flushed red. She took a step back. "Wh-what are you..." she stammered.

Ignoring the vice grip squeezing his heart, Tom interrogated further, "Sounds like you had an interesting dream. Care to share?"

Tom was aware of the dangerous undertone of anger in his voice and the way Beth seemed wary of him. But, dammit, he couldn't help it. His wife had been dreaming of another man. That was almost as bad as cheating on him.

Confusion shrouded her pale features. She drew her eyebrows together in thought, backing away from him until her back hit the table. "I-I don't remember. It's..." She closed her eyes in concentration. "All the images are slipping through my mind like smoke. I'm—"

Beth quieted, opened her eyes, and stared at Tom. He didn't realize his hands were fisted at his sides until she closed the distance between them. She placed a hand on his chest. Some of his anger drained away. "Did I say something while I was asleep to piss you off?"

"Are you cheating on me with Barton?" The words were out of his mouth before Tom could stop them.

Beth's lips parted, her eyes narrowed, and she tilted her head to the side. "Who the fuck is Barton and why the hell would I cheat on you?"

The bite in her voice chewed at Tom. He wished he could take it all back—the anger, the pain, the accusation. He'd misread the situation again, but the thought of her being with another man threatened to destroy him. He buckled down instead.

"You tell me, Beth. You were the one calling out his name in your dream. Tell me, how long has it been going on?" Tom spat.

Beth withdrew her hand from his chest as if he had singed her skin. Balling her hands into fists, she ground out, "There is no one else, Tom. I don't *remember* my dream. And I sure as hell am not cheating on you with some Barton guy or any-fucking-body else!"

Her whole body shook. Fat tears rolled down her reddened face. She sucked in a breath but choked on a sob. "Fuck you," she huffed angrily before spinning on her heel and storming out.

Tom was glued to the spot as if she'd slapped him across the face. Hell, he wished she had. Then maybe she'd have knocked some sense into him.

I'm an asshole, he thought, *a stupid, jealous asshole.*

His admission freed his muscles. In three strides, he was out the door after her.

GRADY

"BETH," GRADY WHISPERED as his eyelids flew open.

He was drenched in sweat. The dream had been so vivid his heavy breaths and the ache between his thighs were difficult to dismiss. Until now, his wildest fantasies of Beth didn't hold a flame to the intensity of this dream.

He couldn't remember specifics. Only the green-eyed woman, Myrtle, who looked a lot like Beth, and the man named Barton, for whom Grady had a front-row ticket. He'd met Myrtle before in the dreamscape while meditating. It was there she taught him his heritage, his legacy. They'd never crossed into intimacy because, for one, Myrtle wasn't Beth. Myrtle also felt more like an aunt to him, despite having similar features to the woman who held his heart.

Rather than go along with his dream, he'd managed to change Myrtle's face to Beth's. It'd be less awkward the next time he met his teacher, but it left him with a bad case of stiffness.

Groaning, Grady forced himself to sit cross-legged on the cot. To repress his burning desire, he needed to meditate. Drawing in a deep breath, he exhaled slowly, letting his forbidden lust leave with it.

Grady repeated his exercise until his mind was clear and his libido calmed. When he opened his eyes, an almost imperceptible humming remained inside him. The feeling was like a harp string being plucked, and this single unseen thread was tethered to Beth. Even now, he could sense where she slept. Her essence was so strong, he could taste a hint of honeysuckle nectar that came with her scent.

Myrtle had warned Grady about the intensity of the bond that guardians share. He thought his adoration for Beth would be enough. He was wrong. Soon, Beth would be within touching distance, and it would take every ounce of his strength to keep Tom unaware.

Wiping his face vigorously, Grady focused on his work. His go-to method for shutting out the world was keeping his head down and tackling tasks. He'd handle this much stronger attraction the same way.

Wash up, get dressed, cook dinner, he repeated, stopping once when he felt Beth start moving around.

Heat flickered along their thread. Grady ticked his ear toward the other cabin. Muffled shouts. They were fighting again. His heart leapt, but Grady took a calming breath. It was best to play dumb, or else his questions would set Tom off again.

Too soon, a soft knock came at the door. Grady gulped. He wasn't sure he'd be able to hold it together.

"Come on in, y'all. Dinner is nearly ready."

When the door opened and Beth's scent wafted inside, he stood straight and stirred the stew with a little more gusto than necessary.

He was doomed.

"Coffee's on the counter next to the sink. There's only sugar and milk; no creamer," Grady said as he turned with the Dutch oven. Placing it on the center of the wooden table, his smile fell. "Where's Beth?"

Tom ran both hands through his hair and brought them down forcefully. He avoided Grady's gaze. "We, uh, had a fight. She ran out of the cabin and, well, I lost her. I dunno where she's gone."

Grady's gut churned. He knew she couldn't get far. There was only one exit, and she didn't know how to find it. Still, knowing how stubborn that woman was—with their luck—she'd stumble upon it.

...and then Paul would find her.

"How long ago did this happen?" he asked, coming to stand in front of Tom.

"Few minutes ago. We had words, then she told me to fuck off," Tom confessed, quickly adding, "I deserved it. I said some things I shouldn't have said—"

"Jesus, Tom." He interrupted, placing a hand on his friend's shoulder. "We need to find her, okay?"

When Tom nodded, Grady shot outside. He inhaled deeply, trying to pinpoint which direction Beth's scent was strongest. Even with the false trace where Tom stood, it was no use. She was everywhere.

Grady scanned the field and woods, trying to spot her outline. The setting sun hung on the treetops, hindering his line of sight with its blinding light. He wanted to yell at Tom but that wouldn't do anyone any good.

He was about to throw his hands up in the air and stalk off in a random direction when he remembered their connection. Focusing on the humming string that bound them, Grady felt the pull strongest in the direction of the entrance.

"This way." He sprinted off.

Tom's boots pounded the earth behind him. "How do you know for sure?"

Grady couldn't reveal how he knew without a shadow of a doubt where Beth was. He couldn't tell Tom the secret he'd kept for seven years. The secret that magic was real, and there were terrors too horrible to describe lurking beneath these hills. That the woman his best friend obsessed over for years was fated to be with someone else.

"She'd retrace her steps."

"Right," Tom agreed to Grady's relief.

He prayed they would find her before nightfall. There were a few more secrets Grady needed to keep until the right time. Beth and Tom being in the middle of an argument while being hunted by murderers was certainly not it. Grady needed things revealed tactfully and slowly.

If they could catch a break, the transition would go smoothly. Unfortunately, things had not gone his way lately.

Chapter 12

BETH

BETH BLINKED THE TEARS from her eyes for the hundredth time, pushing another low-hanging tree branch out of her way. It didn't work. Her tear ducts had sprung a leak, and they wouldn't stop dripping until the cracks in her heart were whole.

Leaving the Grove the same way they entered had seemed like the best idea at the time. Her rash decision to use the woods skirting the field as camouflage was a mistake. Now, Beth was lost. Adding insult to injury for her lapse in judgment, the sun was setting. The forest would be dark soon.

How can Tom be angry over a dream?

Their relationship wasn't perfect, but it had been great. In all their years together, Tom had never once accused her of infidelity. Apparently, the honeymoon phase lasts less than five months, if their fight was any indication.

What hurt most was something she had no control over was able to rock their marriage to ruin...and Tom hadn't come after her to apologize. What did that say about their relationship?

Tom was her first boyfriend, her first kiss, her first everything. If he wasn't going to fight for them, should she? Her chin wobbled.

Yes. I will fight for our marriage. I love Tom, and he loves me. The stress from yesterday turned him into an overbearing jerk.

Despite her resolve, the seeds of doubt had already been planted. She didn't feed the worry that Tom might not want to make things work.

Rather than wallow in self-pity, Beth got angry. The tears stopped flowing, and she shored up her situation. "Okay, Beth. Find the clearing, get your bearings."

Beth veered off her planned path in the direction she believed the field was in. It shouldn't take long, given she'd gone deep enough for cover but not so far that she couldn't see the sunlight. Except, now the sun had lowered beyond the treetops, limiting her little visibility.

And she was alone in the dark in strange woods.

The fact sent a wave of cold across her skin, leaving goosebumps in their wake.

"Well, Beth. You've gotten yourself proper lost. When you find your way back to the clearing, you are going to demand Tom take us to the hatchback so we can go home, and figure shit out." Talking to herself seemed to help. Her determination sharpened, allowing her to focus on wrangling anger.

"If I can't reason with Tom and he yells at me again, then I have no choice but to leave. I'll be damned if I'm gonna put up with this abuse." She stepped over a fallen log, sucking in a breath when her ankle seized. "Leaving means making it in one piece back to the car. Which should be easy enough. If I'm late checking in, the forestry service will send out a ranger...assuming Paul and Jeff don't off me first."

Beth's confidence fizzled. "If Tom doesn't come with me, I'll stay at my parents' place until he comes to his senses."

Her parents were on a cruise in the Bahamas with their friends. They weren't due home for another two weeks. Plenty of time and quiet to figure out what to do about Tom. She pictured the pain on his face again and took a shuddered breath. Her sweet, loyal, loving Tom...betrayed by a phantom dream she couldn't even remember. Given the current events, it didn't seem fair.

Sniffling, Beth stopped when she realized it was pitch black and the field was nowhere in sight. The loud growl coming from her midsection startled her. She closed her eyes and took several deep breaths to stop the scream welling up inside. She'd had a horrible nightmare, Tom had nearly died, they were supposedly in danger of being hunted by death cultists, and she'd been accused of being an adulterer. A bitter chuckle took the place of despair.

"I'm twenty-five for a day and it sucks already," she declared bitterly. Her shoulders drooped in defeat.

While her defenses were down, Beth felt a tug at her heart. Not like the one that was being yanked when Tom hurt her, but an almost physical one. Like a string being pulled taut. When she focused on it, the whisper of a new but familiar scent wafted past her nostrils. Closing her eyes, she inhaled. *Honeysuckles.*

The second before opening her eyes, Beth knew Grady stood in front of her. How she knew undeniably the scent was tied to him remained a mystery.

"Beth, thank God I found you," Grady breathed harshly as he rushed to her side, only to stop short like he'd hit an invisible wall.

The obvious distance summoned her frown. Tom told him about her dream? Was Grady disappointed in her, too? Beth's nostrils flared as she fought against the sting of new tears forming in the corners of her eyes.

She glanced over his shoulder. The blatant Tom-free space was a punch to her gut. Working things out didn't bode well if her husband was a no-show.

"I'm okay. Lost, but fine. Is everything else alright?" Beth hugged herself, digging her fingers into her biceps.

"Tom's...upset." Grady rubbed the back of his neck, eyes swirling with emotions while his face remained impassive. "Please, come back to the cabin so we can talk."

Beth shook her head. A lot of good *talking* did when no one else would listen. Besides, most of the fight left her sails the moment her husband didn't come for her. Their bubble of happiness had ruptured, and she wasn't the only one who realized it. She'd rather go home and forget this weekend ever happened.

"No more talking. I don't want to be here anymore." Beth used the ball of her palm to wipe her eyes. "Just tell me where the exit is. I'll grab my things and leave. Tell Tom—"

"Tell me what?" the man himself said with a cool, even tone as he appeared next to Grady.

A flash of hope flared behind her ribs. Tom's hands were jammed into the front pockets of his pants. Beth wished she could see his face, but his chin was glued to his chest.

Beth straightened her back. She wasn't backing down, not without seeming like she was waffling. "That I'm taking the hatchback and going home. You'll need to catch a ride with Grady when y'all are finished salvaging the rest of your weekend. I'll stay at my parents' place until then."

"No." Grady shook his head furiously, hands on his hips. "It's not safe."

"Wait, Beth." Tom was in front of her in a blink. He wrapped his arms around her, pinning her arms at her side. "Please don't leave."

Beth's eyes burned with new tears. Tom wasn't giving up.

He buried his face in her hair, and murmured, "I'm sorry I didn't listen to you before. Come back with us."

"Tom," Beth started, intent on telling him no. There was a bottle of wine in the pantry that had her name on it. But the look of distress etched into Grady's face, the glistening in his eyes, and the strain of his neck muscles as he held himself to the spot changed her mind. "Fine. I'll come back, but after we talk, I wanna go home."

"Thank you." Tom eased his embrace enough to search her face before giving her a cautious smile. "I promise I'll keep an open mind. If you still want to go home afterward, we'll find a way to get you there safely."

Beth nodded curtly, then stepped out of Tom's arms. "Let's go."

Glancing at Grady, he seemed to have chilled out, but his brows were slightly drawn as he led them out of the woods and back into the field.

Beth was done with the boys' emotional rollercoaster. What she needed was alone time with a hot bath and a glass of wine. Neither of which were here or happening tonight.

TOM

TOM THOUGHT BETH WOULD never let him touch her again. When she allowed him to hold her, even briefly, his chest fluttered and warmed. When she withdrew from him again, a bitter cold nipped at his heart. Surely this weekend wasn't the end. He hadn't fought against Paul and an evil spectre to lose Beth now. There *had* to be a way to work things out.

Grady's odd behavior perplexed him more. After finding Beth, the man bowed up and kept clear like their bad luck was contagious. After Grady's mom passed, he and Beth grew closer. It had always annoyed Tom how Grady never hesitated to give Beth a hug, but he'd never been jealous. Had he?

When they arrived at Grady's cabin, his friend stood behind the door, holding it open as if it were a shield. Once they were seated, Grady took the chair farthest away from Beth.

"So, y'all wanna tell me why Beth felt the need to leave tonight?" Grady pegged them with his discerning gaze.

Beth stared intently at her clasped hands resting in her lap. He'd step up, own his mistake. Maybe it'd be enough to get out of the doghouse.

"I accused Beth of cheating on me because of a dream." The words spilled from Tom's mouth, leaving a bad taste. His mouth went dry when Grady winced.

"A dream I don't remember having," Beth added, picking at a grain of wood on the table. "About someone named Barton. Until today, I'd never heard the name."

"Wait," Grady said, voice tight. "So, Beth has an intimate dream about someone she's never met and doesn't remember, and you get upset because she *should* remember? I'm confused."

"When you put it like that it sounds stupid," Tom admitted, cheeks hot as he placed his palms flat on the table. "But yeah."

"Well, if she doesn't remember the dream, you have either two choices. Forget it or ask her if she's been unfaithful." Grady wore his poker face; eyes slightly wide, chin tucked, lips pursed but downturned at the edges. His best friend was hiding something.

"That won't be necessary," Tom said, his chest fluttering when Beth covered his hand with hers. He eyeballed his best friend. "I don't need to ask Beth if she's been unfaithful because I know she hasn't. I overreacted."

Beth's stomach rumbled. Tom got up and came back with an apple. He shined it on a napkin and handed it to her.

"Thanks." Beth's tired grin made his stomach somersault.

Tom placed his hands on her shoulders and kissed the top of her head. When her soft hand slipped over the top of his, the weight of the world took a hike.

Grady's gaze hardened. "I'll reheat dinner."

He stood, taking the Dutch oven to the woodburning stove. He dropped it on top with a loud clang. "It'll be hot in twenty."

Tom took it for the dismissal it was. "Come on, Beth. Let's wait outside."

As Beth stood, Tom caught Grady's furrowed stare pinned on Beth. Another spurt of jealousy speared Tom's ribcage. For longer than he could remember, Tom trusted this man with his life. He wasn't sure that was the case anymore.

Chapter 13

GRADY

GRADY STUDIED THE GROOVES in the table after dinner. *This isn't how things were supposed to happen.* Raising his gaze to Beth's, he prayed for the goddess to guide them. The fate of the world depended on Beth's acceptance of magic and their roles as guardians.

"So, you don't remember anything from your dream?" He had to know if she retained even a sliver of *something*. It was important for her awakening.

A loose strand of hair had worked free of her ponytail. Beth tucked it behind her ear. "Nothing specific, just blurred lines. The images faded and disappeared as soon as I woke up. The sensations lasted longer but they, too, were gone before I could hold onto anything."

She cast a furtive glance at Tom. His back was turned while he washed dishes. He made no move to add his two cents.

Grady nodded absentmindedly. The negative energy from her argument with Tom probably blocked anything from taking root. He scrubbed his hand down his face. One touch is all it would take. He could simply brush his foot against hers, and she would remember.

He resisted. Taking the slow route would risk pissing his best friend off less. At least, that's what he kept telling himself.

"It's okay, Beth. This place has a way of...showing you things. It's special. Magical, even."

"What do you mean by *magical*?" Beth asked, her face narrowing in suspicion. Grady didn't expect her to be so skeptical after the past few days.

The sound of cleaning stopped abruptly. A moment later, Tom dropped into the chair next to Beth, his arm going around her shoulders. "What's this I hear about magic?"

Grady shifted in his seat, unable to hide the smile tugging at the corners of his mouth and nodded. "That's why I've been coming out here for the past seven years. To learn and practice."

"You're joking, right?" Tom scoffed, sitting back in his chair. "If you've been practicing *'magic'* for seven years, then why didn't you tell me?" He emphasized the word 'magic' with air quotes. Grady didn't miss the clenched jaw.

"Well," Grady began, "it happened a couple of days after our 'initiation' ritual. I wasn't feeling up to sharing after that nightmare." Tom's face went ashen. He then pursed his lips and dropped the issue. Grady continued, "It's also why I missed our last two Saturdays. I was getting everything ready for this weekend, stocking food and stuff."

"That's how you knew this place was safe, because it's protected?" Beth surmised as she turned to stare out the window. He wished he knew what she was thinking.

"Exactly. Only those with the genetic predisposition to the metaphysical can enter." Grady paused to give his best friend an apologetic grin. "Someone like Tom can only enter if allowed passage by one who does." He left that information hanging to sink in.

"Wait. If you have to have magic to enter the Grove." Tom frowned in thought. He stood, muscles tense as he came behind Beth's chair, gripping the back. "Then Paul can get to us."

"No." Grady shook his head. "Paul doesn't have the right kind of magic or the blood ties to this place that we do." He motioned between himself and Beth. "Whatever dark entity Paul serves *gifted* him with some kind of perverted power. By design, none of it can pass the gate."

Beth leaned on the tabletop, her arms crossed in front of her. "How can I have magic in my blood? Y'all met my parents. They're the most boring, ordinary people I know. And I've never done anything extraordinary in my life that wasn't hard-earned."

"Not your parents, Beth, but Myrtle." Grady sat on the edge of his seat for her reaction.

"Myrtle?" she asked, tilting her head to the side as her brows drew together. "Doesn't ring a bell."

Grady's hope withered. "She's your predecessor and ancestor. Myrtle died over three hundred years ago, but her magic was passed down to you. This weekend was supposed to be your awakening, but Paul crashed the party."

"So, *that's* what's different between you two." Tom sat down, rubbing his chin in thought. "I mean, I sensed *something* but couldn't quite put my finger on it." His brows were drawn together tight when his jaw flexed.

Trying to keep his cool, Grady cleared his throat, ignoring Tom's comment. He was too close to hitting the nail on the head. Tom didn't need to know *how* much had changed, but he would in time. Once Grady figured out how best to tell them. "Yes. And, now that we're here, Beth can begin her training."

"Whoa. Hold your horses, Grady. How can I begin training when I don't even believe in this hocus-pocus stuff?" Beth was back to her usual sarcastic self. "And, in case you two have forgotten, we still have the Paul and Jeff situation to sort out."

"Don't worry about Paul and Jeff. Grady said they can't enter the Grove, and they can't stay in the woods indefinitely," Tom answered matter of fact.

"What about our vehicles? If they come looking for us, they'll assume we went for our vehicles. What's to stop them from slashing our tires once they find out we're still here?" Beth asked. Her concerns were valid, but Grady kept his cheeks in check.

"Time moves like molasses outside of the Grove. We left before two a.m., right?" Grady placed his phone on the tabletop and pressed the home key. The time read 4:13 a.m.

"Paul and Jeff are still asleep in their tents." He smirked when Beth's and Tom's jaws dropped.

"How's that possible?" Beth whispered as she scrambled to bring out her phone. "Wait. The sun *just* set. How can we be sure?"

"You just have to trust me," Grady challenged, pinning Beth with his gaze.

Their connection pulled like magnets to North. His fingers stretched toward hers. He blinked and hers were reaching for him, too.

"Grady," she admonished weakly, though her fern eyes held a sparkle.

"It's magic," Tom supplied, breaking the spell.

Grady pulled his hand away and crossed his arms. His heart thudded against his chest.

"Beth, I think you should take Grady up on his offer. He can teach you magic, and y'all can practice until we run out of food." Tom's leg bounced so high Grady could see his knee over the table.

"I dunno. Don't you have to believe in magic to *do* magic?" Beth put her hand on Tom's knee, giving him her 'teacher brow.' He stopped with a goofy grin.

"Belief isn't necessary, but it makes things easier." Grady stood and put more space between himself and Beth, leaning against the counter.

"I still don't know what to believe," Beth mumbled, tearing her paper napkin into strips. After a long silence and lots of frowning, she sighed. "Tell me again how the time difference works."

Grady bit his bottom lip to keep from smiling. "For every full twenty-four hour day spent here, only an hour passes outside."

"That's..." Beth trailed. Her eyebrows were drawn so deeply they nearly touched.

"Amazing," Tom finished, his eyes sparkling.

"I was going to say impossible," she corrected, shifting her hardened gaze to Grady. "Please, tell me this is all a joke. That this whole weekend is some kind of prank y'all pull each year and I'm the dummy."

Grady wiped his face and sighed. "I wish I could tell you that, but Beth, know one thing"—he licked his lips when his mouth suddenly went dry—"I will never lie to you."

BETH

THE CONVICTION IN Grady's words made Beth's heart clench in her chest. She wanted to believe this weekend was a hoax and that magic didn't exist, but there was an unexplainable trust she felt with Grady that ran further than bone deep. It was seated in Beth's very soul. Since when did he have her complete confidence, even more than her husband?

Beth studied Grady's face for any shred of deceit but there was none. An image of a man with Grady's features smiling at her with such tenderness flashed in her mind. She gasped lightly, ignoring Tom's inquisitive gaze. This was all too confusing. She needed clarity—and fast.

"Okay," Beth finally said, averting her eyes and sitting back in her chair.

Grady's scrunched shoulders relaxed at her reply. "Okay."

"No," Beth answered firmly. She crossed her arms and raised an eyebrow in challenge. "If magic is real, and this whole weekend isn't a prank, then *prove* it."

"Fine. I can do that." Grady cleared his throat and stood, wiping his hands down the legs of his pants. He leveled his gaze with Beth's. "You promise to stay after I show you?"

Beth leaned back in her chair, balancing on the back two legs and nodded. "I promise." *This should be good.*

Closing his eyes, Grady lifted his hands to his sides, palms up. He took a few calming breaths, but nothing happened for several seconds. Beth was about to stand and leave when a stream of sparkling, green light entered through the open window behind Grady. It swirled around his body, snaked around his arms, then landed in the center of his hands.

Beth gasped, her mouth opened in astonishment. The cabin filled with the scent of fresh-cut grass. When Beth raised her gaze to Grady's, he wore an 'I-told-you-so' smirk.

She snapped her mouth shut, lips twitching to curl upward. The fluttering in her chest was reminiscent of the childhood wonder her parents snuffed out before she could enjoy it. She wasn't going to let this opportunity pass.

"Cool. You can command glitter," she challenged. "What else you got?"

"Oh, there's plenty more where that came from." Grady winked, combined the two green orbs, then tossed it over his shoulder without looking.

It landed outside the window onto the grass with a pulse.

"Dude," Tom whispered, rushing to the window. He craned his neck to see better. "That's incredible. Beth, come see this."

Beth joined Tom and, sure enough, whatever Grady's green fairy dust touched was like a fast-forwarded time lapse. Dandelion buds bloomed, wheat went to seed, and the color of the grass was more vibrant. She cocked her head to the side and pushed her lips out in thought. The prospect of learning magic made her giddy, but the way her heart thumped in her chest at Grady's show was concerning. She would have to keep her walls up.

"A promise is a promise," she finally said.

The triumphant glee on Grady's face was charming. She focused her attention on her husband.

"Does this mean we'll stay, and you'll learn magic?" Tom asked as he wrapped his arm around Beth's waist.

"It does." Beth nodded.

Tapping the countertop with his palm, Grady's grin was ear to ear. "Fantastic. Let's turn in for the night. Tomorrow's gonna be a long day."

Beth sighed. She was still nervous knowing Paul and Jeff lingered outside the Grove, despite Grady's assurance that the magic here would prevent them from entering. She doubted she could sleep with her brain so occupied. "Well, goodnight, then."

Beth went to hug Grady, but he moved away and busied himself with his backpack. His soft rejection caused her chest to tighten uncomfortably.

Grady must still be upset at me. Which didn't make her feel any better.

Tom pulled her against his chest and murmured, "C'mon, hon."

"Okay," she mumbled softly, letting Tom lead her.

"Sleep well," Grady called out as they went through the door.

Beth's wheels were turning. Grady sat as far as he could from her and wouldn't give her a hug, going out of his way to make sure they didn't make any physical contact.

She'd never shied away from spending time with Grady, but how would he teach her magic if he actively avoided her?

The thought of being alone with her friend caused her pulse to quicken. Something in her memories nagged, something important. When Beth reached for it, it faded.

Maybe staying was a bad idea.

Chapter 14

TOM

Beth was unusually quiet as they trekked the short distance to their cabin. Once inside, Beth went straight to the cot. Tom stopped by his backpack to find a sleep shirt. When he turned around, she held an armful of blankets.

"What are you doing?" Tom asked with a nervous chuckle. He thought things were on the right side of getting better. Clearly, he had missed something.

Beth smoothed the top of the fabric, avoiding eye contact, and sniffled. "I thought... What if I have another dream like last time and we can't come back from it? I can't go through that kind of hurt again, Tom. I don't want to lose you."

"So, what? You're gonna sleep outside?" Tom asked, his face flushed as hot as an iron. He shook his head. "Don't be ridiculous, Beth."

"But—"

"Not up for discussion," Tom cut her off. Gently taking the blankets from her arms, he trailed a finger down her jaw. "You take the cot, and I'll see you in the morning."

He pressed a chaste kiss on her lips, but her admission was a vice squeezing his heart. Tom didn't want her to see the suffering pinching his brows, so he turned away. He did this. He should've listened to her side of the story, trusted her when she said she would never be untrue. Tom damned his stubborn pride.

He took two steps toward the firepit before stopping at the sound of her small voice. "Tom."

When he turned around, his anguish was reflected on her face. Beth stood where he'd left her, shivering as she hugged herself. He took a step forward, hoping she'd changed her mind. All he wanted was to fall asleep with his wife in his arms

Sucking in her bottom lip, Beth released it only to whisper, "Thank you." She turned to go inside.

Tom couldn't leave it at that. "Beth."

She stopped but didn't turn around. Her shoulders shook, as if she were crying. It took every ounce of his strength to keep rooted to the spot. So, he did the only thing he could. "I love you."

Time froze. Beth's shivering stopped. Tom held his breath as she turned enough to make brief eye contact.

"I love you, too," she whispered over her shoulder. She darted inside, and the door closed with a soft click.

An hour later, the weight on Tom's chest was so heavy it was difficult to breathe. Defeat threatened to send him spiraling into the depths of his depression, but he remained afloat, clinging to a glimmer of hope: Beth had kissed him back. She'd told him she loved him back.

Tom pressed his eyes shut, willing sleep to come, but the fickle duster of dreams denied to visit. Sleeping on the ground wasn't new to him, but sharing the bed with Beth these past five months had him spoiled. No matter which way he turned, he found a rock or a lump. He was cold and worn out and hated himself for putting a wedge between them.

Turning on his side, Tom balled up the blanket that smelled the most like Beth and hugged it. It wasn't enough. He needed to take the initiative; to show her he wasn't intimidated by a dream.

BETH

BETH SIGHED RAGGEDLY, draping her arm over her eyes. For the past hour she'd stared at the ceiling, replaying the events of the evening. She'd wanted to throw the door open and drag Tom back into the cabin, but what if she had 'the dream' and he flipped out again?

Her life had fallen to pieces, capsized like a boat and left her helplessly floating without a way to ground herself. Were it not for the invisible string connecting her to Grady, she would have drifted away.

Fighting the sobs choking her, Beth bit her bottom lip and beat her chest with her fist. Her heart ached, torn between wants familiar and new. Her mind scolded her heart, reminding her who had first dibs. Familiar won in the end as she whispered his name, "Tom."

She shivered and curled into the fetal position. No matter how many blankets she piled on, they couldn't warm the coldness boring into her core. She pulled the sheet up to her nose and breathed in what she could of Tom's scent. It wasn't enough.

Beth closed her eyes, but it was no use. Her mind raced, keeping ahead of sleep. She was afraid the people she'd known her whole life were cultists, afraid of strange dreams about a place of magic. Most of all, she was afraid of what this new connection to Grady meant and how it fit with the dream that made Tom accuse her of infidelity.

There was a soft knock at the door. Moonlight flooded the cabin walls. Beth rolled over to find a Tom-shaped silhouette in the doorway. He stepped inside, shoulders pulled back and jaw set. The look in his eyes was full of regret and longing.

Tom closed the door and dropped the blankets on the table without breaking eye contact. In three strides, he knelt beside the bed. "Beth, baby, I'm not afraid." His whisper was light but held the weight of a thousand promises.

He cupped her face with both hands and placed a kiss on her forehead. "I can't sleep knowing I did this to you—to us. I need my arms around you like the sun needs the pull of the moon to rise."

"But what if I have another—" Beth asked, but Tom captured her lips with his in a melting kiss.

"I've loved you as long as I've known how to breathe," Tom declared, running his thumb along her bottom lip. "I'm not letting a dream come between us."

The torn pieces of Beth's heart slowly knitted together. As she wrapped her arms around him, he slid into the cot and pulled her against his chest. Beth tucked her head in the crook of Tom's neck. This was where they were supposed to be. Together forever just as they promised on their wedding day.

"We're okay?" Beth whispered, nuzzling his jaw. His faint cologne pushed away her fears.

"Yes, hon. Better than." Tom heaved a sigh and tightened his embrace. She felt loved. "When we get home, I'm gonna pamper you with a bubble bath and a bottle of red Moscato. I'll rub lotion on your feet while you relax with a face mask."

Kissing the side of Beth's head, he continued, "I'll take care of you all night. In the morning, we'll pack up and head to the beach for a real vacation. Just you, me, and the sunshine."

Beth's breath hitched as Tom's hand slipped past the band of her sleep shorts and kneaded her backside.

"We'll make love at sunrise every day," Tom continued as he kissed down her jaw to her neck. He climbed on top of her, grinding his hips into her core as he whispered against her lips, "and stay in bed until you're fully convinced that I will never leave you."

Beth was left breathless, caught in the moment. She tangled her fingers in his hair as Tom lifted her thigh, tucking it around his waist. Dominant Tom was very sexy. She let go, falling into the abyss of their passion.

When he gave her a second to breathe, Beth whispered, "Make love to me, Tom. Please."

"As you wish," Tom replied before doing just that.

Chapter 15

GRADY

"Take your time and practice breathing. This isn't a race." Grady sat in front of Beth, both cross-legged in the patch of grass near his cabin.

The rhythmic thumping of Tom's axe splitting wood was not only soothing but a reminder of how careful he had to be. The world hung on a delicate balance between duty and loyalty, and it all rested on his shoulders.

Beth's eyes were closed, giving Grady a chance to watch her without seeming like a creeper. Her eyelashes brushed the tops of her cheeks, and every exhale made her full lips puff and pucker. He wondered if they were as soft as in his dreams. He knew her hair was like honey-dyed silk. Would she lean into his touch if he swept away the loose strands in her face? Grady's insides swarmed with butterflies.

No. He banished his daydream with a mental flick. *Focus.*

He maintained a healthy distance, especially after last night. Grady knew everything that went on in the other cabin. Their metaphysical bond was growing rapidly. Whenever Beth's emotions were heightened or intense, it affected him. Last night had him sweat-soaked and grabbing a shirt before he made a mess. The shame and loneliness were anchors on his soul. The only reprieve he found was on a run, looping the Grove until his body was exhausted to the point of numbness.

If the couple engaged in those kinds of activities nightly, Grady wasn't going to survive being here for days. It was one thing to have feelings for your best friend's wife, even if it was mostly because of their magic. But to act on that attraction? Tom was the brother he never had and more like family than his own father. He'd never betray his best friend, no matter the cost of his own happiness.

"Good," Grady murmured. "Now that you're relaxed, let's practice connecting to the earth element. There are three main attributes: deep-rooted, stable, and stubborn. You should understand the last one well." He smirked when she opened her eyes and pursed her lips to hide the upward curve trying to form.

"I am a master of the art of stubbornness," Beth jested, biting the inside of her cheek.

Grady's face warmed. Even her everyday banter even seemed flirty.

Goddess, give me strength. Grady silently prayed and continued their lesson.

"Take off your shoes and socks. The best way to connect with the earth is by physical touch. Practice doing this with bare feet so your hands are free for other tasks."

Beth took off her socks and shoes, placed them next to his, and returned to the cross-legged position. "Now what?"

Grady sat with his back straight and drew his knees to his chest. His feet were flat in front of him. "Sit like this. You'll use your hands to direct the energy you draw, but for now, put your hands on the ground."

"How do we draw energy? Doesn't that hurt the earth and plants or whatever?" Beth asked as she mimicked Grady's pose.

"Not the way I was taught." He shook his head and grinned. "Think of it this way. Drawing magic is like drinking water. When you're thirsty, you drink what you need. Drink too much, and it can be harmful."

Grady closed his eyes and focused on his breathing. Every inhale, the loose dirt around him swirled like tiny dust devils that tickled his feet. Exhaling, his body sunk slightly into the earthen floor, taking root where he sat. The air around him crackled with energy.

He opened his eyes and focused on an unopened wild violet bud next to Beth. Flicking his hand in a lazy wave, he sent a small burst of energy into it, making the flower bloom.

Beth gasped and a smile lit her face like the sun. "That was amazing, Grady. How did you do that?"

The wondrous sparkle in her eyes was enough to take Grady's breath away. He managed to answer despite having his heart in his throat, "I borrowed a drop of the earth's energy and gave it to the wildflower. I'll give the rest to you."

He waved in Beth's direction with the same flourish. The rush of transferring the power caused his skin to prickle. Beth shivered as it passed through her and back into the ground. When she opened her eyes, her irises were bright and colorful like ferns after a good, soaking rain.

"It's warm. Reminds me of something." Beth clicked her tongue against the roof of her mouth and tilted her face toward the sun. "There was this plum tree at my grandparents' house with the softest patch of grass. Every summer I would lay there to cloud-gaze. That's what it feels like to me."

"Yeah," Grady breathed, unable to speak much else. Beth's description of how earth energy felt was exactly how it was for him. Now that he had someone to share the gift of magic with, he was eager to explore more with her. "Sounds perfect."

"It was," Beth replied with a hum.

She studied Grady with curiosity, making his stomach flutter and his heart melt. The urge to cup her face, to give her the world and all its wonders was disintegrated by the thunk of an ax and Tom's grunt.

"So." Grady cleared his throat and tried to sound like he wasn't dying inside. "It's your turn."

BETH

GRADY'S SOFT TENNESSEE TWANG was made for radio. She'd always thought so anyway. His soothing voice stirred some unknown need deep in her being as he instructed her to 'be the seed.'

Beth locked it down and erected a twelve-foot tall wall around whatever feelings were trying to take root.

"Burrow into the ground, let yourself sink until you feel like you're covered under a large, heavy blanket," Grady explained.

Beth imagined herself making a hole in the dirt and burying her seed in it. "Done."

"Now, imagine yourself basking in the sunlight like when you were a kid. Let the warmth permeate your skin, soak into every pore. Then I want you to raise your arms as high as you can and reach for the sky."

Beth closed her eyes and dug her toes into the dirt. Letting the memory of the summers she spent beneath the plum tree fill her mind. The sunlight kissed her skin, warming every exposed inch. She stretched her arms as high as her seated position would allow. She waited for the crackling air to come as it had with Grady. And waited...

She opened an eye. Nothing. Not even the green glow.

"It didn't work." Beth pinched her lips together as her stomach knotted.

Grady made it look so easy. What if he was wrong, and she didn't have magic?

"Don't lose hope, Beth. It was your first time. Try again," Grady commanded softly. The determination in his eyes gave her a boost of confidence.

"Right. If I got it on the first try, that would have been crazy amazing," Beth chuckled, trying her damnedest to hide the uncertainty circling her convictions like hungry buzzards.

Taking a deep breath, Beth straightened. She adjusted her feet, making sure they were level on the ground and tried again. The warmth surrounded her again. She took even breaths and saw herself as the seed this time. The dirt covered her like a safety blanket, sustaining her with nutrients from the earth. She exhaled and a crack formed in her shell. On the next one, a sprout unfurled. Reaching up to the sky, she visualized the sprout breaking through the dirt, seeking the life-giving sunlight, but it wouldn't grow further.

She sat like this for long minutes, breathing in and out, stretching toward the sun. Each time her sprout wiggled, but it didn't breach the layer of dirt above.

Eventually, she banished the image with a huff. "What did I do wrong?"

Her confidence had been smothered by failure. Tears stung at the corner of her eyes as she blinked, trying with futility to rein in the overwhelming sadness that gripped her.

Grady sat there, quietly staring at her with his brows drawn together.

Beth waited for him to confirm what she already knew. He was wrong.

There was nothing special about her. Every single one of her accomplishments were earned because *she'd* made it happen. Not because she was talented or because it was genetic. Beth had busted her ass at the gym, put in hours on the ground to earn her track team the gold. She'd endured worm guts and infections from hook scratches because her dad didn't think fishing was a woman's sport and refused to let her tag along. And when her parents cut her off financially after her first year in college, she'd worked part-time, waitressing at the corner diner down the road from her dorm to keep afloat.

"I don't understand." Grady mumbled, rubbing his chin.

"It's simple math, Grady. Myrtle was wrong, and I don't have magic." Beth couldn't keep her voice from cracking, but she'd be damned if this was gonna make her cry.

"Oh, I have no doubt that you do," Grady countered, shaking his head. He stared over her shoulder, at the trees behind them. "We're just missing something...a key, or block."

"I dunno, Grady. I can't even channel energy, and that's basic stuff," Beth mumbled, then plucked a blade of grass. She played with it, ignoring how her ribcage shrank and her nose prickled.

Grady shifted to sit on his knees. "Please don't give up, Beth. It's your first day. You can't expect to master the basics after two tries. Don't give up on—just...don't give up yet."

Face flushing pink, Grady dropped his gaze. There was something oddly endearing about seeing him blush. Their friendship was strong, so Beth continued to ignore the niggling in the back of her mind telling her things were changing. But it was hard not to when Grady hadn't hugged her since her birthday or when the inches he kept between them felt like miles.

Beth missed his hugs, especially when she felt so damn vulnerable.

Tom's panting echoed in the break. He was shirtless in all his golden boy glory. Sweat gleamed off his tan skin as the sunlight yellowed his sandy blonde hair. The muscles in his arms and back flexed as he took another swing, splitting the log in half. If it weren't for the working man stink, she'd go to him for a hug.

Beth dropped the blade of grass she was twirling and returned her attention to Grady. He quickly averted his gaze, hiding behind a soft curly black lock of hair.

"What about Myrtle? Maybe she could watch and tell us what I'm doing wrong."

Grady stamped out her hope with two words. "She can't."

"But why wouldn't she—" Beth asked, but he kept talking.

"Myrtle doesn't exist in our world, but in a dream state. Well, more like her spirit and memories...I think. She only ever appears when I'm sleeping or meditating," Grady explained. "Myrtle first came to me in my dreams a few nights after our dads tried to initiate us into their cult. That's when she told me of our ancestry."

Beth was glad to be sitting. The sudden swirl of questions spiraling through her brain would've floored her. If she hadn't watched him perform magic, she'd have thought he'd lost his marbles. Perhaps *she* had gone crazy. Was this all a dream? She pinched her arm and yelped.

"Why'd you do that?" Grady eyed her cautiously. It was like he could sense her disbelief.

"To see if I was dreaming or if I'm just crazy," Beth sighed deeply, reaching for his arm.

Grady rocked back and rolled to his feet before she could touch him. He avoided eye contact, shrugging one shoulder. Hot and cold. This was her best friend's new game.

"Okay," he said, swiping his shoes off the ground. "We'll break and try again after lunch."

Beth's gut dropped like a cement block in a lake. She'd hurt his feelings. "Grady, please don't be like this."

"Like what, Beth? I've not given you any reason not to trust me." Grady's shoulders fell in defeat, adding quietly, "but you still don't believe me."

"You gotta understand how insane this all sounds to me. This whole weekend has been a lot. My emotional battery is drained. While I was excited about the possibility of having a superpower, the reality isn't as pretty. What I want now is to go home. I need some semblance of normalcy." Beth shielded her eyes from the sun. Looking up at Grady from this angle made him look like a Greek god carved from marble.

"Fine." Grady's jaw tightened and flexed. He rolled his shoulders back and held out his hand. "We leave first thing in the morning."

"Thank you." She stared at Grady's outstretched hand, a peace offering. Beth's stomach cartwheeled as she reached for him. "I think I can manage one more day here."

Soft static electricity arced between their fingers, but she didn't snatch her hand back. It didn't sting. It was like curling up on the couch with a book and a hot cup of coffee on a winter's day. Grady's eyes widened slightly, and his lips parted.

Tom swept Beth's hand into his, pulling her to stand. "Done already?"

The world was engulfed in a glumness filter. She cleared her throat and tucked her hair behind her ear. "We're taking a break."

Tom put an arm around her waist and rubbed her lower back. His comforting scent of orange and sandalwood was soured by the musk of sweat. "How did it go? I bet you aced it like you did all through high school and college."

His smile was sweet and would usually send her heart pattering, but everything was off kilter. Nothing was going right and failure was not something Beth was accustomed to. She knew better than to snap at him. Her inability to do magic was not his fault.

"Next time, perhaps." Beth pulled away from Tom, forcing herself not to shove him away. "I'm gonna go lie down for a bit."

Kissing Tom's cheek, Beth hurried back to the cabin without a glance back. She knew Tom was watching her go, but it was Grady's gaze that made her squirm. He saw clear through her bullshit straight to her soul. That fact tested the walls she'd built.

Chapter 16

PAUL

"Wake up, you worthless sack of shit!" Paul yelled, kicking Jeff's thigh.

"Ow, Paul. What did I do?" Jeff scrambled to his knees, rubbing his leg.

"You let them get away." Paul's eye twitched.

"Sorry. Didn't mean to fall asleep, Brother." Jeff scrubbed his face with his hands before rolling up his sleeping bag. "Why'd they leave with Beth's ankle as bad as it is?"

Fuck if I know. But he couldn't admit it to Jeff.

"Because they think a head start is gonna help them out-run us."

Somehow, Tom and Grady managed to talk Beth into leaving with them. Dawn hadn't broken yet. They couldn't have gone far, not with her seriously sprained ankle. Thank fuck Paul needed to take a leak after dozing off, or else the trio would have made it back to their cars and Mayes Hill before the dew set.

Jeff grabbed his pack, and a sketchpad fell out. It opened to a page with a detailed pencil drawing of Beth and Tom sitting by the campfire last night.

"Shit!" Jeff swore, diving at Paul's feet for it.

Paul was quicker. "What do we have here?"

"P-please, Paul! G-give it b-back!" his friend cried out, scrambling out the tent and across the ground on his hands and knees.

Paul flipped through the pages. Pencil and ink sketches of people, mythical creatures, and colored pencil landscape art littered the sheets with masterful strokes. He couldn't have guessed Jeff was so talented.

"Looks like a ten-year old drew these." Paul cackled before slamming it shut.

Jeff cowered on the ground, watching Paul with terrified eyes. "I-I know they're not g-good."

Paul didn't care. Jeff and his hobby were slowing him down.

Rolling his eyes, Paul threw the sketchbook. Jeff covered his head with his arms, and the book bounced off his back. He scrambled to pick it up.

"Right. Leave the rest of our shit. We'll be back after we find our lost lambs." Paul rolled his neck and shoulders. He had his map, knife, and all four of his 'contingency plans' ready to go.

"W-what if some'un comes along?" Jeff stuffed more things in his backpack, putting the sketchbook in last. "Pop'll tear me a new one if I don't bring his new tent back."

"Don't worry. If Louis Cooper did his job, there won't be anybody else in these woods but us. We have all weekend to look for our little sacrifices."

"Oh, good."

Paul didn't tell his dimwitted friend about the very real time limit hanging over his head. Ja'azul promised immortality and absolute rule over this world to the one who brought the final soul that freed him. Over the past seven years, Paul had delivered over a hundred sacrifices, but that number meant shit if he didn't deliver the final one. Paul would, though; his mother predicted it.

She'd always told him he was destined for greatness. Ruling the planet is about as great as you can get.

Paul checked the time. 3:30 A.M. He pulled the straps of his pack tight and took off toward the path they'd come in on. Jeff followed, his backpack ruffling and clanking like a broken alarm clock.

He whirled on the half-wit and growled, "Can't you be quiet?"

"Sorry, Brother. I'm carrying all the cookware and food stuffs." Jeff frowned with a sniffle.

"Drop it," Paul demanded. "You can keep a few bars for later, but nothing else."

"O-okay. Gimme a second."

Paul huffed as Jeff knelt next to Grady's tent to unload the dead weight. Rather than stand around, he decided to do a perimeter walk. He'd barely started the circuit when he found a hollowed-out tree trunk. Brown and black tree dirt was scattered around the base, some tossed out into the surrounding brush. The meat had been scooped out. There was enough room for three adult-sized backpacks to fit inside.

A wave of excitement coursed through his veins, electrifying his muscles. Paul knelt and shone his flashlight over the landscape. A large clump of tree matter had the impression of a small sneaker. He followed the bent leaves and broken branches to a bush. The dirt had been freshly scratched, exposing some of the roots. Small clumps of black scat were nearby.

Boars.

"I'm ready, Paul," Jeff panted, stooping to study the bush. "Isn't it early for wild pigs to be rootin' 'round here?"

"A bit." Paul stood and dusted his hands on his pants. "Tom and Grady are taking Beth further into the forest."

"Why'd they do that?" Jeff asked, scratching his forehead. "Don't make no sense."

"No, it does not."

Paul knew Grady was up to something, he just didn't know what. Louis Cooper told his dad, Elliott, that Grady had been seen in the area the past two weekends. Whatever he was up to, Paul wasn't letting Grady get away, not this time. He and Tom had gotten off easy at their initiation. If the dads had listened to Paul, Ja'azul would've had two more souls that weekend. Weak old men; all of them.

"Run, run, run, little rabbits." Paul murmured. He was as cool as a cucumber on the outside, but his blood was running hot for the hunt.

JEFF

JEFF WASN'T INTERESTED IN RULING the world like Paul. His needs were simple: Protect Audrey Pebblebrook, his high school art teacher and the object of his affections.

She was the only person in this town who understood him, made him feel important. And it wasn't because she was six years his senior, either. Audrey said he had a gift. That he saw the world the way it was meant to be seen. His paintings covered her parlor walls, which was why he was doing what needed to be done.

The only way to ensure her safety was to barter with the devil, so that's what he did. Even when it meant he endured every slap upside the back of his head, every punch to the gut or ribs, every single goddamn degrading name Paul could think to hurl. Some of them were worse than the ones his dad, Curtis, called him. Then again, the only peace Jeff found with his old man was under a hood. Jeff was handy with a wrench and knew his way around an engine. Was the sole reason his Pop hadn't kicked him out of the house yet with him being twenty-seven. That, and he was cheap labor.

After this weekend, he was gonna finally put a deposit on the apartment across town. Once he was settled, he'd ask Ms. Pebblebrook to make things official.

"Dammit, Putnam! Stop dragging your feet!" Paul barked. "We should have found them by now."

Jeff adjusted his pack and picked up the pace. They'd been walking for a while with the sun playing peekaboo above the trees' roots now.

A low growl came from a nearby rustling bush. Jeff slowed to scout the area. If it wasn't something solid, he wasn't to bother Paul.

The treetops swayed side to side in a lazy dance. Something sweet hung on the wind, something akin to vanilla with a sour note. A dark figure, low to the ground, darted out of the bush and weaved between the trees in the opposite direction.

"Probably a boar," Jeff whispered to himself.

The thought of an angry wild pig coming after him with those pointed tusks and without rhyme or reason made Jeff shudder. He hurried to catch up with Paul.

Their quiet march lasted until the sun reached the underside of the canopy. A deep rumble and the sound of raining dirt came from behind. Jeff's chest tightened. His body broke out into sweats.

"Run," Jeff panted, jogging to keep up with his friend.

An unearthly roar kicked his gears into a full run.

"Shit," Paul swore when he glanced back at Jeff.

Paul grabbed Jeff's sleeve, pulling him along with his longer legs. Jeff's lungs were swollen from the effort, and his legs burned. The game trail there were on was not forgiving. He had to negotiate twice as many rocks and stumps to stay ahead.

Jeff chanced a peek over his shoulder. The boar was as big as a full-grown hog, but this one's eyes were glowing red, and it was spitting a trail of yellowish-white foam. The beast squealed a roar filled with the fury of a runaway freight train on a track to hell.

And it was gaining on them.

I'm not going to make it. Jeff could practically feel the heat and spittle of the wild beast on his heels.

He didn't want to have his throat slit to bleed out like the others, choking and gurgling on the sanguine liquid as their life slipped away. If Jeff was going to die this weekend, he wanted to go on his own terms. Paul was the only one who could bring him back, so he'd be the distraction.

Before he could change his mind, Jeff pictured his first love and faced his demon. Drawing his pocket knife, he exhaled her name, "Audrey."

Jeff screamed as white-hot fire spread from his abdomen as its tools of destruction lay waste to his thigh. He sunk the knife into the beasts flesh, but the damned thing squealed in anger and shook him like a rag doll. The sickening rip of flesh was followed by the crunch of bone. His stomach pitched, head rolling loose as his sight faded.

The bloodthirsty beast suddenly dropped him and squealed. Seconds later, Paul's unfocused face hovered over him. It sounded like he was shuffling around in his pack.

Jeff's breaths were short and sharp. Everything was cold. He was pretty sure he'd lost more than just a chunk of his leg.

"Hey," Paul murmured, grabbing his hand and squeezing it. "That wild boar got you good, there, Brother."

No shit. Jeff wanted to say, but he wheezed instead. The taste of copper coated his tongue.

"You know what needs to be done."

Jeff nodded weakly, and Paul let go of his hand. His body was going numb. That was good. At least he wouldn't feel any more pain.

Paul raised his ceremonial knife in one hand, the other held the Babe Ruth signed baseball Jeff's grandfather had given him. Jeff blinked the sweat clouding his sight, but the dark edges closed in.

Paul plunged the knife into his heart. Jeff grunted and his chest rocked from the force. He grimaced as the tip nicked a rib bone.

"By the power of the Dark One Ja'azul, god of chaos and death, I bind the Eternal Soul of Jeff Putnam to this item of great importance."

A spark of glittering light the size of a marble rose from his chest. Paul pulled his blade free. It made wet suctioning sound. His soul followed the bloody knife as Paul touched the blade to the baseball. It glowed with a soft, yellow light when his essence settled.

"You did good, Brother," Paul cleaned his blade and placed his baseball on the ground at his side.

As the world became silent, Jeff's head rolled to the side as he exhaled for the last time. Before the lights went out completely, he saw three more bundles in Paul's backpack and understood.

None of them were meant to leave the woods this weekend. None except Paul.

Jeff's heart ached in a way no slice from a blade could. *I should'a kissed Audrey at the art gallery.*

Chapter 17

TOM

AFTER RECONCILING WITH BETH last night, the heaviness weighing on Tom's chest had eased. Splitting logs while she learned magic had given his brain something else to think about.

Grunt, swish, crack, thump, thump. Repeat for hours.

The rhythm had mellowed his cloudy mood quite a bit.

But his chill took a nosedive when Grady offered his hand to help Beth stand. His best friend practically had googly-heart-eyes.

Tom knew it was a jerk move, swooping in like that, but he didn't want Beth to be more friendly with Grady than she was already.

He'd stepped in it again with his overly energetic optimism. Tom had been so worked up about Beth's abilities, he hadn't noticed the red rims around her eyes or how her shoulders drooped. Beth was great at everything she did. How was he to know she wouldn't ace this stuff, too?

"Now I feel shitty."

He didn't mean to say that aloud.

"Naw, man. She's had a rough morning is all." Grady toed the grass with his bare foot. "She was so close to getting it, Tom. Until today, I don't remember a single time Beth put her mind to something and it not work out. She's always been tenacious."

Tom's gut twisted uncomfortably at Grady's words. His tone held the same awe and wonder for Beth as Tom had every day. He forced a chuckle. "Yeah, and my girl can still out-fish the both of us with one hand tied behind her back."

Grady winced and nodded. "That she can."

Silence followed for a long beat or two. Tom didn't usually mind, but if he didn't do something soon, his brain was gonna put him through the paces again.

Grady cleared his throat. "Wanna help me with dinner? Bet you're hungry after mutilating trees all morning."

"I could eat." Tom's stomach growled, getting a snort-laugh from his best friend.

"Good." Grady started toward his cabin, casting a quick glance next door. "Magic has a cost. Beth'll be hungry when she wakes."

A MEATY STEW SIMMERED on the wood stove top, filling the single room with the scent of rabbit, thyme, tomato, and root vegetables. When Tom asked where the meat came from, Grady said he couldn't sleep last night, so he'd gone hunting.

The door to Grady's cabin swung open.

Beth stood in the doorway with her backpack in one hand and her chin jutted. The setting sun cast her in a golden halo.

"I'm ready to go home."

Tom was on his feet next to her in no time. "Grady and I made rabbit cacciatore. Come and eat first, then we'll go."

Beth had bags under her bloodshot eyes. Though she raised her chin, there was a slight shakiness to her backpack arm. She stared at him, eventually giving him a slow nod. Tom relieved her of her pack, placing it next to the door.

"Smells good," Beth remarked as she plopped down into the nearest chair.

Grady placed three wooden bowls filled almost to the brim with the steaming stew on the table. Tom readied some coffee, making Beth's with sugar and powdered creamer since there wasn't anymore milk.

By the time he and Grady were settled next to Beth, her bowl was half empty. Tom's face split into a smile. Beth liked food, it was one of the things he liked about her, but she was usually prim and proper, wearing a napkin on her lap and such. She spooned more into her mouth as quickly as possible, slurping with each bite. Thank goodness her mother wasn't here to see it.

"This is so good. Is there more?"

"There's plenty," Grady said with his own ear-splitting grin. He slid his bowl across the table. "Here, I'll get another."

"Thanks," Beth mumbled around a mouthful.

She tipped her bowl, scraping the last bits into her mouth. Reaching for the bowl Grady gave her, Beth paused. Her cheeks were dusted rose.

"What?"

"Nothing, hon." Tom didn't realize he'd been staring, so he cracked a warm grin. "Need another bowl?"

He was glad to see the shaking in her hands had stopped and her face had her usual healthy glow.

"Thanks." Beth remembered herself and dotted her mouth with a napkin. "But I think two is my limit."

Grady placed the Dutch oven on a potholder in the middle of the table and winked. "Just in case."

He used Beth's empty bowl for his own, making Tom's eye twitch.

Is there a bowl shortage or something?

"How much time has passed since we left?" Beth asked, lazily lifting another bite.

Grady checked his cell phone. "Little over two hours."

"What do we do if Paul and Jeff are waiting for us when we step through?" Beth asked, pulling her hair back into a ponytail.

Tom eyed Grady before chiming in. *He isn't the only person with answers.* "We'll protect you, Beth. If things go south, Grady will give you the map. Run back to the Grove entrance. We'll meet you once they're dealt with."

The thought of having to possibly kill their lifelong friends made his stomach lurch and bubble. If it weren't for Paul threatening Beth's death, Tom wouldn't be up to the task.

Grady nodded. "If—by some chance—they woke early, they're probably finding out we didn't go back to our vehicles. I'm betting we can beat them to Jeff's car."

"What good is Jeff's car if we don't have the keys?" Tom asked, hands on his hips.

Grady reached into his jeans pocket and pulled out a sandwich bag. He dangled it and asked, "Who said we don't?"

A huge smile lit Tom's face. He peeked at Beth to see her smirking and his heart leapt. "Good thinking."

"One other thing before we go." Grady pocketed the bag and handed Beth his map. "There's been an awful lot of unusual boar activity. Something doesn't feel right about it, so keep your eyes and ears open."

After dinner, Beth washed dishes while he and Grady packed. The thought of leaving Beth alone with Grady gave Tom indigestion. He wanted to argue, but it'd only serve to push Beth farther away. Tom had never packed so fast. When he exited their cabin, Beth stood outside putting her pack on.

"Almost set."

"Turn around for me." Tom adjusted her neat backpack so the weight was distributed more evenly.

The cabin door opened. As Grady stepped out, his gaze went straight to Beth before flickering to Tom. "Y'all ready?"

"Yes." Beth's short reply came out soft, unsure. The set of her jaw and the way her shoulders were pulled back showed differently.

Grady grabbed his shoulder straps and wordlessly led them down a worn trail beside his cabin. After about a mile, it ended at a six-foot wide archway between two paper birch trees. Looking past the trees, the forest appeared normal.

"All you do is step through. You'll come out about six or seven miles past where the entrance to the Grove is," Grady assured.

Tom was eager to spend time with his wife with ample space away from his best friend. He'd been thinking of the different ways to make this weekend up to her. For months, Beth had been dying to try breakfast at the fancy corner restaurant.

He glanced her way. She white-knuckled her shoulder straps as she looked back down the trail toward the cabins. Her eyes watered, like the thought of never returning was painful.

"Another thing. The passage is one-way. Once we go through, we are outside the Grove. The only way back is through the entrance. I've circled it on the map." Grady made eye contact with Beth. She nodded. He studied Tom, who gave him a thumbs up. "Good. I'll go first."

Before Tom could ask how long to give him, Grady was gone, somewhere between the birches.

"Ready?" Beth asked

"Wait." Tom turned Beth to face him and cupped her face. "Before we go, I want to say I'm so, so sorry, Beth."

"I know you are, Tom," she said, placing her hand on his. "Can we just forget this weekend ever happened?"

"I would love that." Tom placed a chaste kiss on her lips. "Elizabeth Marie Harper-Newman, I have always loved you and will forever. I promise to make everything up to you."

"I'm looking forward to it." Beth's eyes glistened and her pouty lips formed a smile. "I love you, too, Tom."

His heart leapt in his chest. The danger hadn't passed, but their chances of survival skyrocketed. They always said, together they can conquer anything. In that moment, he believed it to his core.

The only problem concerning him was the man waiting on the other side.

Chapter 18

BETH

THE WOODS OUTSIDE of the Grove were so dark, Beth's chest caved. Tom gripped her hand tightly, causing her wedding ring to pinch her skin. She was too busy worrying about how much time had passed to bother with the discomfort. Was it possible Grady was wrong about the time difference? Speaking of Grady, where was he? She and Tom hadn't taken *that* long to step through after him.

A pained groan came from several feet away, in the southwestern direction they had planned to head. Tom stepped in front of her just as Paul stood with his knife in hand. It dripped with blood.

In the back of Beth's mind, she knew whose blood was on the blade but there was so much. He couldn't be dead. She could still feel the thread between them, though it wavered.

"Where's Grady?" Beth asked but the words came out in a whisper.

A cruel, maniacal grin spread on Paul's face, like he could sense her fear and got off on it. In answer, Paul lifted the knife to his lips and made a show of licking the blade. Turning his head, he spat on the ground. "Traitor blood...never tastes as sweet as the blood of the innocent."

"No," Tom whispered at her side before dropping her hand.

He took a few stumbling steps toward Paul before he steadied. Some unseen force had to be holding Tom up. Beth knew she'd crumble if she tried to move.

"You're dead!" Tom screamed as he rushed at Paul.

Paul raised the knife over his shoulder, curling his lips into a victorious smirk. The second Beth realized his intent, the wind around her shifted, lifting her hair lightly as an invisible force pushed from her chest at the same time Paul hurled the knife with a growl.

It whizzed through the air with the pointy end aimed at Tom's heart.

Beth's burst passed over Tom and redirected the knife's trajectory by a few inches. Tom's face reflected in the silver blade as it passed him and headed for her.

She jumped sideways, but the sharp edge of the knife caught the outside of her right bicep before disappearing in the tall grass. She landed on her left shoulder hard enough to jar her but not to dislocate it. Luckily, she missed any rocks.

"Impossible," Paul whispered. A loud crack echoed through the trees.

Scrambling to her feet, Beth covered the gash on her arm with her hand, hissing at the sting. Paul was doubled over as Tom brought his knee up to his jaw. The man fell to his side, while her husband towered above. He gave Paul two swift kicks to ensure he stayed down.

"Tom," Beth breathed, rushing to his side. Her eyes were wide, and the air was too thin. "We need to find Grady."

Tom placed his foot on Paul's head, pinning him to the ground. He scanned the area and pointed at an indent in the tall grass. "There. Go, I've got Paul."

Beth nodded and took off to where Tom pointed. "Found him!"

Grady lay on his back, still wearing his backpack. One shoulder was soaked dark red, and he blinked rapidly. Quiet grunts came from his throat as he mumbled incoherently. There was so much blood. Her heart fell into the pit in her stomach.

Beth knelt at his side. The straps were too tight, cutting off circulation. If only she'd thought about grabbing Paul's knife.

"Hold on, Grady. We've got you."

Her hands trembled, taking twice as long because the nylon wouldn't cooperate, but she managed to open his shoulder straps as wide as they'd go. Grady whimpered and ground out a groan.

Where's Tom?

She cast a quick glance behind her. Tom's back was to her. His stance was low, fists balled. Tom swung and Paul grunted. She needed to hurry.

Beth reached for Grady's injured arm, but he wheezed and shook his head.

"Hey, I'm trying to help. You need to lie flat on the ground."

When her fingers made contact with his elbow, images flashed in her head like a sped-up home video from the 90's. She grabbed her head, catching glimpses of a picnic for two, a lover's embrace. At the end, a set of hauntingly beautiful and familiar sapphire eyes pierced her soul.

Like a surging ocean crashing along a cliffside, wave after wave of emotions pummeled her. Friendship, adoration, love, want, desire, and *passion*. She was no stranger to these feelings, but they were directed at someone other than Tom. They whorled inside her like a maelstrom, plucking at the string connecting her to Grady. The tune was low, steady, and constant; reminding her of the 'oms' monks chant while they meditate.

Beth focused on the hum. The storm inside her calmed and she could breathe. When she opened her eyes, Grady studied her. His poker face was on point for once.

The sound of grunting and scuffling broke the spell. Beth shot a wide-eyed glance over her shoulder to where Tom recoiled from Paul's jab. Tom turned his face to spit blood. She could make out the beginnings of a black eye. She opened her mouth to call out, but he gave Paul a shiner to match.

Something warm and smooth was shoved into the palm of Beth's hand. Startled, her head whipped around. Grady's eyebrows scrunched together, and his fingers wrapped around hers. The corner of a plastic bag peeked out between them.

"Beth...run," he whispered with a grimace. "Please."

She didn't want to leave, but now was her chance. Tom and Grady had done all they could to protect her. If Paul wanted a sacrifice, he was going to have to catch her first.

Placing her hand on his cheek, Grady's eyes fluttered shut and he sighed. "I'll come back with help," she promised.

Jumping to her feet, Beth gripped the plastic bag tightly and sprinted through the woods toward what she hoped was the right path.

The sharp tug in her chest, the one urging her to turn and fight, disagreed. Leaving the men she loved behind was almost impossible. The only thing that kept her moving was cowardice. How could she possibly face Grady again after what she saw?

She'd cross that bridge when she got there.

Sweat ran down her back and arms, dripping off her elbows. It had been months since she'd had to run like this. Beth wasn't sure how far she'd gone. She put one foot in front of the other and didn't plan on stopping until she was at the parking lot. The trouble was, she couldn't remember which marker to look for to get her there. What good was having a car key when you didn't know where it was parked?

Grady's map poked her in the side. If she stopped to figure out where to go, Paul would catch her. It was best to *just keep running*.

The words played on loop, keeping her focused on putting as much distance between herself and Paul.

Every cell in her body screamed to turn back around. To run back to Grady. For once in her life, her heart was at war with her body.

Whatever was going on between her and her best friend took a backseat. None of them were out of danger yet. There would be plenty of time to unpack all of this later, if they made it home in one piece.

Something in the wind shifted. Beth's senses picked up the scent of a wild animal. She remembered what Grady told them. *Keep your eyes and ears open.*

An angry squeal came from behind her, along with the sound of hooves tearing through grass and roots. Her face felt like she had stuck her head in a bed of needles. She'd probably wandered too close to the wild pig's nesting grounds. Whatever the reason, Beth wasn't slowing down. She silently prayed the boar would lose interest.

Beth growled as she pushed herself past the limits, igniting her lungs. The fire in her legs grew stronger. She wasn't going to make it. Tears stung her eyes and then pain rippled through her calf when something sharp nipped at her leg.

"Stop!" Beth cried out, refusing to let the beast keep her from getting help.

She sucked in a painful breath and nearly sobbed when another animal came barreling toward her—a golden mountain lion. Whatever good fortune Beth thought she had was spent, but she wouldn't go down easily.

The mountain lion leapt through the air and Beth dove to the side, tucking and rolling to her feet. She expected the boar and the panther to follow, but they didn't. The large cat's jaws were locked around the larger beast's neck. A deep, otherworldly and unnatural squeal came from the wild pig, freezing Beth to the spot.

The beast shook it loose and swung its tusks, grazing the cougar's neck. It roared and turned with lightning speed, sinking its teeth into the wild pig's jugular. The pungent scent of copper was thick in the air. Jerking its head, a sickening crack echoed around them, and the mountain lion dropped the boar.

Beth's movement returned, but she didn't run. Big cats liked it when their prey ran. The panther's golden eyes stared at Beth with curiosity. Oddly, the longer they held eye contact, the less erratic Beth's heartbeat became.

"Thanks for the assist, but this weekend has been really, *really* crappy. I ain't ready to die yet," she whispered. The absurdity of talking to a wild cat was not lost on her until it tilted its head in reply. "So, unless you can take me to the parking lot, how about we part ways and leave each other be?"

Inching her way toward the path without taking her eyes off the panther, Beth kept her hands out in a non-threatening manner. What was she thinking? Did she really believe negotiating her freedom with a wild animal would work? Crazier things had happened this weekend, and it was far from over.

When the large cat made no move toward her, Beth kept moving away. One misstep on her injured calf caused her to cry out as it spasmed. Sweat formed on her brow, but she persisted. "That's it. I'm gonna hobble away before Paul catches up to me so I can get help. Oh, I have two friends out there...Please don't eat them."

The mountain lion tilted its head in the other direction as its tongue lolled out. Beth swore the cat was smiling. It cantered past her, down the path Beth was taking, and stopped to glance back.

"You want me to follow?" Beth was surprised when the panther gave a curt nod and continued. "Interesting, but I'll take it."

They traveled quietly at a snail's pace thanks to the throbbing gash in Beth's leg. Finally, she had to rest. "Sorry. Gotta take care of something real quick."

Finding a log, she sat to assess the damage. The panther eased next to her, sniffing the cut before licking it. "Hey!"

Beth pulled her leg away, but the cat nudged her, trying to finish cleaning the wound. The thought made her cringe, but she let the animal work. When it was finished, Beth ripped a strip off the bottom of her shirt.

"Thank you," she murmured as the large cat waited on her haunches.

Beth tied the cloth firmly around her calf, effectively stopping the bleeding. When the mountain lion hissed and stood, her hackles raised, Beth startled.

The large feline sniffed the air and posited itself behind Beth. Her senses flared just like when the boar came, but she didn't detect the scent of a wild pig. A thick, coppery tang wafted around them, along with the stench of death.

Beth whirled when the panther snarled. Paul stood behind them. The whites of his eyes were in stark contrast to the sticky blood and dried mud covering his face.

"Well, well, well. It appears the little rabbit has made a new friend," he sneered, before cracking his bloodied knuckles and advancing.

The forest grew silent as Beth quickly assessed the situation. Even if she could call on her magic again, she was no match for Paul. The only reason it activated earlier was because she'd needed to protect Tom.

She tried to focus on the raw emotion evoked with that need. Placing her hands out in front of her, palms out, she pushed. Nothing happened. Huffing in exasperation, time sped up back to normal.

The panther was poised to lunge. It screeched before launching at Paul, teeth and claws glinting in the sunlight.

Beth turned on her heel and ran. Her leg cramp turned into a full-on spasm before she could get too far. She fell to her hands and knees, crawling away searching for a place to hide.

Behind her, the snarls of the panther were cut short, ending in a sharp and painful whine. Beth picked up her pace, ignoring the stings of fresh cuts on her hands and knees. It was just like her dream. The woods here didn't want her to leave.

She spotted a freshly fallen pine tree with enough limbs and green needles for camouflage. Changing direction, Beth scrambled through the brush toward her temporary salvation. Her breaths came in heavy pants, muffling any other sounds.

There was a hard blow to the back of her head, robbing her of any adrenaline she had left. Her head throbbed and dark blots swam in her vision as her hand grazed the greenery. Maybe she'd wake up and this would all be part of her nightmare.

Chapter 19

TOM

HIS LEFT EYE SNAPPED open. The disorientation cleared, and Tom scrambled to his feet. The sudden movement sent a sharp stabbing pain through his sides. He cried out, sheltering his rib cage while fighting the urge to lay back down.

If he didn't remember being beaten within two inches of his life, Tom would think he'd walked in front of a speeding train. There wasn't a single muscle, bone, or inch of skin that didn't hurt.

"Beth?!" he called out in a hoarse voice, searching wildly for any sign of her but he was alone.

A low groan came from the ground a few feet away followed by a pained whisper, "Tom."

He hugged his ribs and shuffled to Grady's side. "I'm here, Brother!"

Grady's pale skin was coated in sweat and dried blood. His hands hovered above his stomach, shaking uncontrollably as he took shallow, quick breaths. Tom took one of Grady's hands in his and his friend's eyes snapped open.

His free hand grasped Tom's arm. "F-find, Beth. She's the...key," Grady breathed, barely getting out the last word before he stilled into a death-like sleep.

"No," Tom whispered, a sob stuck in his throat. "Grady?" He felt his neck for a pulse and choked when he felt a faint heartbeat. "I'll be back for you, I promise."

It about killed Tom to leave his dying best friend, but if there was a possibility Beth was still alive, he needed to find her. He closed his eyes, trying to remember which direction she ran and remembered Jeff's key. Careful not to jostle Grady too much, he searched for the sandwich bag but came up empty.

"Does Beth have the key?" he asked himself, almost facepalming when he realized what

Grady said. "Beth isn't *the* key; she *has* the key."

Tom jumped to his feet and took off after her, toward the trail to the parking lot. The restricted airflow left him huffing, squeezing his lungs with every intake of breath. Paul had done a number on him. His body screamed to rest and heal, but Tom was too jacked up on adrenaline to care. Broken or bruised, he'd find his wife.

An image of Beth lying on the stone table with her throat sliced open, of her blood spilling onto the softness of her neck to stain her sun-kissed skin taunted him. Tom's scream echoed around him, shattering the image. With a grunt, he pushed himself beyond human limits.

Determination wasn't the only thing keeping him going. Tom had to believe Beth was still alive because the world wasn't on fire yet.

Glancing at the position of the sun, he guessed he had been asleep for a good half hour. She had at least a fifteen-minute head start before Paul knocked him out. Beth was a fast runner, but she hadn't participated in any 5k races since they got married. *She'll make it, she has to.*

The scent of burnt copper and spoiled sweet meat clung to the humid air like a wet cloth, thick and moist. Tom's heart hammered in his chest as though it was trying to tear free. He tasted bile at the back of his throat.

"Please, God. Don't be Beth, don't be—" he stopped dead in his tracks at seeing the body...then another nearby.

A wild boar lay with its jugular torn open. The beast's eyes were white, mouth wide, tongue rolled out, and bloodied. Tom prayed the blood was not Beth's. Putting his arm over his nose, he pressed onward to the next body. The golden fur of a mountain lion was matted with blood. Its head was twisted in an unnatural way. Blood still seeped out of the cat's mouth, meaning it hadn't been dead for long. Had Beth killed both of these animals or had this been Paul's doing? He shuddered. His wife loved animals, but she had magic she didn't understand yet. He shoved the thought away.

"Beth!" Tom called out, scanning the surrounding shrubbery frantically. She couldn't have gone far.

He was about to move on when he spotted something light blue near a downed pine tree. He hurried over and leaned down to pick up the strip of cotton fabric. It was mostly soaked in blood, but Tom was sure it was part of Beth's shirt.

He clutched the cloth in his fist. His whole body vibrated with a terrible rage he didn't know existed.

Tears stung his eyes as Tom pushed himself to stand. Beth was injured and alone in the woods with a madman. He prayed his wife was still alive, and he would make it in time.

Wiping his face using the back of his hand, Tom swallowed the dread of returning to the place of his nightmares. He swore to never step foot in that field again after the day his reality shattered. Taking several deep breaths to settle his nerves, he made his way to where Paul had taken Beth: the sacrificial altar.

GRADY

"GET UP! YOU CANNOT give in when your beloved needs you!"

Grady gasped for air. He'd been too close to the brink of darkness when Myrtle urged him to wake up.

She wasn't just his mentor and instructor in all things magic. Over the past seven years, she'd become his confidant. Myrtle taught him his family history and all she knew of magic while Grady slept or meditated.

The Friday before last, Myrtle dropped the bomb that Beth was his destined one. She also said their bond would be the most powerful among all guardians. At first, he was pissed, taking his aggression out on sanding and staining the California king bedframe one of his customers had custom ordered. Why would fate or destiny set him up with his best friend's wife? Grady knew he wasn't perfect, but he wasn't a bastard like his dad.

Once the anger passed, Grady threw a pity party at his dad's welding shop as punishment. His old man is in the business of charging new metal prices for rusted parts he finds at the junk yard. Working with Louis Cooper only served to ruffle Grady's feathers, but he'd come to an understanding: Beth was his best friend before his 'anything else.' He'd had years of practice pretending his relationship with Beth was strictly platonic. Until this weekend, Grady had pulled it off well.

He groaned, forcing himself to sit to assess his injuries. His shoulder still throbbed, and, though the blood had slowed, he wasn't able to move the arm. It just flopped at his side. Paul must've hit a tendon. Grady thanked the goddess it didn't nick an artery or else he wouldn't have woken at all.

Using his good arm, Grady rolled to his knees and caught his breath. He reached for the thread connecting him to Beth. It was still there, warm and steady. He grinned.

She was too stubborn to die so easily.

Grady was more worried about Tom. His face was puffy; right eye swollen shut, left eye bloodshot. Paul had the heart of a killer and gave Tom a hell of a beating. If he and Tom were still breathing, it was because Paul wanted them alive. Grady had a few guesses why, none included them going back home. Too bad for Paul, but Grady wasn't planning to be here when he returned.

Time hadn't made it a habit to be on his side, so Grady did the only thing he knew to do. He forced himself to stand and stumbled toward the field, toward the sacrificial stone altar.

Once he was steady on his feet, he picked up speed until he was sprinting. A deep growl echoed in the woods. Black fur burst free, taking the place of his skin as his bones cracked to accommodate the change.

Grady landed on all fours, tearing up the landscape on a one-way mission to rescue his...best friend's wife.

Chapter 20

BETH

THE BLAZING SUN WAS high in the late afternoon sky when she finally awoke. At least an hour had passed since knocked unconscious. Beth needed to figure out where she was and how to get away from Paul. Her men's lives depended on her escape.

As her sight adjusted, Beth found herself in the middle of a field, surrounded by dark woods. The last thing she remembered was trying to find a place to hide while Paul wrestled the mountain lion. Then, everything went black, and she was falling like a feather.

She turned to get a better look at the situation and winced. The surface beneath her was rough and uneven. The back of her head throbbed. She raised her hand to feel how big the bump was, but her arms wouldn't move.

Pulling again, Beth panicked. The heaviness keeping her limbs from moving were ropes. Paul had tied her down. To the ritual altar. Sweat formed on her brow. Her heart pounded a frantic SOS that only she could hear as a scream caught in her throat.

She swallowed it down. Paul wouldn't have gone far. Keeping a clear head was key to survival.

Giving another tug, Beth tried not to cry out with the exertion. Every time she fought against her restraints, her head pounded. It was no use because the ropes weren't budging. If anything, they seemed to tighten.

Defeated, Beth lowered her head on the rock. Someone had let loose a dozen jackhammers inside her skull. A small whimper left her lips as a warm tear rolled down her temple, falling inside her ear. *This can't be the end. Tom and Grady will come. They promised.*

The sound of heavy footsteps came from her left. Without turning her head, she strained her eyes to get a better view. The sight made Beth's stomach sick. Whatever clear-headedness she thought she could muster was out the window.

"Paul," Beth squeaked, barely able to find her voice. "You don't have to do this. We aren't your enemies. We're your friends!"

A hooded, black-robed figure headed toward the stone altar with a knife in one hand and a baseball nestled on a piece of fabric in the other. The hood shifted, and Paul looked down at her. His usual blue eyes were black and empty, as vast as a thousand galaxies and very cold, completely devoid of humanity and compassion. Fear coiled around her neck like a noose. A blood-curdling scream fell from her lips, raw and jagged at the edges.

He smirked and chanted in a guttural language that sounded as old and ancient as time itself. The un-words crawled underneath her skin, spreading a terrible emptiness.

"Let me go!" She yanked at the restraints in futility. The light glinted off the blade in Paul's hand, breaking any composure she had remaining. If she were to die today, it wouldn't be without a fight. "Listen here, you piece of shit! You won't get away with this. If Grady doesn't magic your ass to hell, you can bet Tom will finish what he started by beating the ever-living *shit* out of you!"

The smirk on Paul's face grew as he continued, ignoring her threats. Beth's brain was fuzzy as a pencil-sized shard of ice formed in the recesses of her consciousness. It melted and seeped through the crevices, weaving its way through her mind like cracking glass.

Alarm bells sounded. What if the guys didn't get here in time?

"Tom!" She screamed as loud as possible. Her throat stung from usage, transforming her pleas into broken screeches. "Grady! I'm here! He's—"

The fractures in her mind shattered into a million glass shards. Like stepping inside a blast freezer with the top of her skull missing, her subconscious was left wide open as she floated among an infinite body of stars.

Her whole life passed before her eyes: the sporting events, the fishing trips, romantic nights spent with Tom underneath the stars or in candle-lit bedrooms, the promise of children and of growing old together. All her cherished memories and those she had yet to make. They slipped away into the void like the pages of a book with poor binding, falling out one by one until nothing would remain but an empty shell.

TOM

NOT MUCH HAD CHANGED in the near decade since his dad and the others performed their dark ritual.

The trees were still as thin, sickly. Like they'd been caught between a black and white movie being restored to color, but the technicians ran out of ink. Wispy leaves and brittle pine needles clung to drooping limbs, afraid the next gust of wind would render them to forest mulch.

For a clearing on top of a mountain, it sure seemed dark with its perpetual dusk. Even when you stared at something straight on, it wasn't fully in focus. Everything here had an imprint of itself, just off to the side. The whole place made his skin crawl enough that the animal part of his brain shouted 'run.'

The sun touched the treetops when the stone altar came into view. Tom's knees gave out when he saw the hulking, black-robed figure standing next to the ritual stone with his arms held high. The glint of the knife was clean, but Beth's body lay limp, and her arms had been secured with ropes. Panic ripped Tom's heart in twain and twisted his gut in knots. He wouldn't make it in time.

Tom's nostrils flared, his blood pumped fire through his veins. He grabbed the first rock he could find and hefted it above his head, charging the rest of the way with a roar.

Paul stopped chanting and spun. The rock in Tom's hand itched to be embedded in the bastard's head. Paul snatched his wrist with a vice grip, pulling Tom close.

"You're no match for me, *Brother*." Paul's voice was distorted, scratchy and deep, as if he was speaking through a voice-changer.

A chill went down Tom's back, same as the day at the waterfall. Paul jerked and twisted, dousing Tom's wrist in liquid fire. The noise coming from his mouth reminded him of the one iconic movie scream but more drawn out.

The rock tumbled to the ground. The force against his chest sent him sailing through the air. Tom landed with a thud several feet away, cradling his broken wrist against his ribs. Stabbing pain shot through his chest. He took short quick breaths and blinked away the sweat dripping into his eyes. No doubt, his ribs were broken. Without the adrenaline rush, he could feel each fracture.

Paul continued chanting. Tom couldn't remember the words from when their fathers had tried to initiate them. He'd been too busy looking anywhere other than the poor woman on the altar. Whatever noises coming from Paul's mouth weren't words. They sounded like breaking glass and gurgling pops chanted in a rhythmic tone that caused the sky to dim underneath a smoky lens. The air thickened with sulfur.

Tom certainly didn't remember this either.

He had to do something. Tom tucked his legs and rolled to his knees. His entire body pulsed with one heartbeat. His vision blurred and he swayed. Bile stung his throat.

"Is that all you got, *Brother*?" Tom's words were slurred, but there was nothing left in the tank. There was no way he could get to his feet.

A black blur whipped past him, heading straight for Paul.

It jumped on the hooded man with silver claws and white fangs flashing in the waning sunlight. There was a sickening crunch followed by an inhuman howl of pain. Tom wiped his eyes and hissed. It was a large black panther. Its jaw latched onto Paul's right arm, tossing its head like it was shaking a rag doll. Tom realized Paul wasn't holding his knife. It must have fallen somewhere on the ground nearby.

He couldn't waste this distraction. He swallowed the sick rising in his stomach; let the hurt roll over him. Embraced it. Tom stumbled to his feet and rushed to Beth's side.

He fumbled to get the knot holding her hands loose, but it was too tight to loosen with his fingers. He needed leverage. A stick or something. A knife. He found his rock instead. Tom knew the effort needed to smash the knot loose was costly. He'd have the piper add it to his bill.

Tom unfastened the rope, and Beth's free hand dangled off the edge. When her head rolled to the side, he glimpsed something red and sticky on the back of her head.

Fucking Paul. Tom's face was hot enough to fry an egg. He couldn't let the bastard complete the ritual. He needed to find the knife and end it.

Tom ducked underneath the table. Paul's feet shuffled around, kicking loose dirt and the blade toward him. Stifling a cough pinched his ribs, starting a chain reaction to his stomach. Nausea stirred in his gut like rancid milk. The panther hissed and there was a grunt. Tom pushed past it all and bent as far as he could, his good arm stretching. Every inch was a mini-victory. Dirt crowded underneath his fingernails as he clawed closer. His middle finger touched something smooth and sharp.

Just a little farther.

There was a thump and a whine a ways off. Paul's bloody hand slammed down on the hilt of the knife, and it disappeared. He may as well have punched Tom in the gut, because he was out of ideas. He couldn't fight Paul directly when he could barely stand, but he couldn't lay here and do *nothing*.

The chanting restarted. Paul's strong voice was strained and broken. Tom wiped his good hand on his damp shorts and pulled himself to stand across from Paul. The man he'd grown up with looked through Tom like he was mist, giving him time to look for a weakness.

His former friend's face had four, even claw marks over the center of his nose. One eye was split so badly that the blood running from it was black, and his bottom lip was sliced. Despite the damage, Paul's hands and body radiated strength as if he hadn't been lingering at the edge of life and death.

Fuck.

Tom took several quick breaths, then hoisted himself onto the stone next to Beth. Paul raised his face to acknowledge Tom but made no move to stop him.

His injuries were serious. The likelihood of his getting out of here alive were next to none. With luck, Paul would return to normal and Beth could finish him off. She would be free to find Grady, and they could come back for his body.

Leaving Beth after they'd had their first real fight and reconciled shattered Tom's soul, but he wouldn't trade his time with Beth for anything.

"I'm so sorry, Beth. I love you, forever and always," Tom whispered before he kissed his princess like the prince in the storybooks.

It was now or never and stupid, but it was the best he could come up with. Tom laid his torso over Beth's. If Paul wanted a sacrifice, Tom would take her place.

Chapter 21

UNKNOWN

HE WATCHED FROM THE shadows of the forest line with bated breath. The woman's magic had called to him across time. By the time he had answered her siren call, she had summoned two other men. Pity, he was not in a state to take them on for her favor. He would simply wait it out. Whomever was left would be damaged enough to ensure an easy victory.

He lurked through the tall grass for a closer look, stopping when the woman levitated in the air. He had not seen such unlimited power in many moons. Whomever this new guardian was, she was magnificent.

She would be his greatest conquest.

He kept low to the ground, not wanting to miss a single detail of the spectacle. Fascination and curiosity were his constant bedfellows, often getting him into awkward situations given his acuity to learn everything about the world. This event was most enthralling, piquing his interest far more than any modern marvel or scientific discovery had in quite some time.

The brunette's eyes flew open, glowing bright white. The raw power emanating from her made his skin prickle with excitement. The hooded fellow paused to look around as the wind picked up, swirling his robes so the entangled his legs. Remarkably, her hair flowed gently around her face, unbothered by the whipping winds.

The hooded man continued chanting, his voice growing louder, more frantic, as he struggled to complete the ritual. The woman frowned in concentration, chanting a counterspell he was very familiar with, having written it long ago.

When she finished, blue flames consumed her entire body. They danced across her skin in waves, leaving her unharmed. She tossed her head back, and the flames burst from her in a ring. Her adversary stumbled back, dropping his knife. He swatted and punched the air like a drunken sailor, sending something round to the ground that rolled underneath the stone.

Pulse after pulse of fire pummeled the hooded man. His movements slowed as he disintegrated bit by bit into dust in the wind. He was, as the newer generations called it, 'on the edge of his seat.'

Large pieces of ash floated past his hiding spot. Had he not been keen on staying out of sight, he would have reached out to catch it, to learn more of the hooded figure, but alas. Though waiting was not his favorite game, he was well-practiced in the art of patience.

The woman drifted down until she was lying once again upon the stone table. The yellow-haired man from earlier ran to her side. Not far from them, a black panther rose to its feet. Neither had been destroyed by her attack; both seemingly in perfect health.

Pity. He was so looking forward to a good scrap.

The feline watched the others and moved more like a human than a cat. Its head swiveled in his direction. When the panther's gaze found him, he went still as the dead. The cat stared for several moments before cantering out of the field, away from the prey. *Very curious.*

Even more inexplicable was this mysterious woman. He had to know more, had to learn everything about her and the unique power she possessed. There had not been a female guardian in over three hundred years, yet he was fortunate enough to witness the birth of the most powerful one to have ever existed.

TOM

TOM AWOKE ON THE GROUND, curled into a ball. It was not one of his proudest moments, but that hardly mattered now. The darkness shrouding the area had lifted and birdsongs returned. It was finally over.

He stood, expecting a full-body ache from his injuries and dusted himself off. Not a single twinge or sharp stabbing pain. He felt great...more than great. *Energetic.* He rolled his broken wrist with no issue and prodded his face. It was smooth and bruise-free, no puffy eyes or cheeks. Beth must have healed him when she went all glow-y and shot out those rings of fire.

The patch of grass a few feet away rustled. The panther rose and stretched. It studied Tom for a long heartbeat before staring at something in the distance. Finally, it nodded and took off. Tom forgot the panther and scrambled to Beth's side.

Her eyes were resting shut, mouth slightly parted. She looked like a sleeping angel, but Tom needed proof or else he was going to have a coronary.

"Beth, baby. Please be okay," he murmured, brushing the hair off her face and neck.

When she didn't respond, his chest caved, and his legs wanted to give up. Instead, he forced his weakness down and checked Beth for a pulse. It was strong and steady. Tom internally whooped in celebration as he scooped her into his arms and surveyed her sleeping face. His wife was alive...it was a miracle.

As soon a he'd given Beth her fairytale princess kiss, her eyes opened. The brilliant white had his body clenching in fear, but the levitating, the silent screaming, and rings of blue fire had him huddling on the ground stuck between being small and wanting to cheer her on. Once the healing flames rushed over him, so did Beth's lavender vanilla perfume and a feeling of connectedness. He'd never seen magic like that before, not in real life.

He should be terrified after watching Paul disintegrate, but Tom couldn't help it when his chest puffed out. He sure as hell didn't want to lose her now, not when they'd been given another chance.

Tom pressed a kiss to Beth's forehead and carried her out of the field. They needed to find food and shelter before the sunset stole the day's light. Tom cursed silently and headed into the woods, away from the field of terrors.

The woods were darkening the longer he walked. He still hadn't found a safe place to rest, nor had he seen any blazes to give him a clue to where he was. All he knew was that they were on a game trail, probably made by deer. Beth was still asleep, but at least he wasn't tired. He could probably climb Mount Everest if he wanted to.

Tom rounded a boulder and spotted the black panther sitting in the middle of the path. He stopped, ready to backtrack and go another way, but the cat stood and cantered toward him. Its sapphire gaze was strangely familiar, peering inside Tom's soul as though it wanted to plant understanding. It cast a glance over its shoulder, then looked at Tom again and cocked its head.

"You want me to follow you?" Tom asked the large cat. It nodded.

He huffed a laugh. Tom's brain told him this was ridiculous, but his heart urged him to follow.

"I hope you know what you're doing," he mumbled under his breath. Piercing the beast with sleek black fur with his most intimidating gaze, he said louder, "Lead the way."

The feline's tongue lolled out the side of its mouth and it dipped his head in agreement. Tom adjusted his hold on Beth and kept his distance. The panther led them to a small cave not too far away that'd been made into a lean-to shelter. There was space for a campfire outside and two cots on the inside. Stalks of sugar cane were lashed together into a makeshift door that was propped up next to the opening.

"Huh." Tom said aloud as he made his way closer. The cat circled a spot next to the 'door' and curled up with a wide yawn. Its large teeth made his gut clench.

"Don't eat us while we nap, okay?"

It rolled its eyes and rested his head on its large paws.

Tom passed the sleeping panther to one of the cots inside. He gingerly laid Beth down and straightened her head, doing what he could to make her comfortable. She sighed and relaxed into the drooping canvas.

"Sleep, baby. I'm not leaving your side." Tom petted her head before pressing a tender kiss on her cheek.

Looking over his shoulder, the panther had one eye open, peeking at them. "Thank you."

The feline closed its eye and settled into sleep.

Tom propped up the 'door' and gave it a good shake. It wasn't going anywhere unless another person or a bear wandering by got curious.

He cupped Beth's cheek and placed a chaste kiss on her lips. "Goodnight, my love."

When she didn't stir, Tom took that as a sign to rest. His brain still buzzed, but he laid down and closed his eyes anyway.

Chapter 22

BETH

Beth was aware something was happening, but her muddled mind couldn't comprehend where she was or what had happened before this place. Only that she and the movie screen were the sole inhabitants, and the images—while familiar—played in reverse.

A young woman wearing a tank top and shorts lowered her raised arms as she stumbled away from a self-repairing ribbon. Her ponytail swung like a pendulum, and Beth fell into a trance. A spark of light illuminated the girl's chest. It grew larger, causing the images to flicker.

Beth tried to get up, but she was suspended in the air, unable to move anything but her arm. The ball of light drowned out the darkness as it floated toward her. She must've been watching the movie for a while because her eyes were heavy, and her body was ready to rest.

Warmth covered her torso as the essence sunk into her chest. It blanketed every atom until an explosive force cracked the chains binding her. Rage unlike anything she'd ever felt made her blood boil. Something had been taken from her. Something important.

Behind the movie screen, Beth noticed two burning balls floating side-by-side. Meteors the size of cars. They flared, sending cinders around the edges. The fog surrounding her brain closed in and became dense. Her limbs weakened. It was killing her.

Beth's chest tightened and sweat surfaced through her pores all at once. He needed her. No, not he. They. Ghostly shadows, imprints of forgotten memories, floated on the other side of the cloudy vale. No matter how hard she focused on finding details, their gray silhouettes remained hidden.

The evil entity belonging to those hateful eyes was slowly draining her life force. She screamed into the emptiness, directing all her anger and vengeance. It flinched. She fell.

Beth's gut clenched as she plummeted into the unknown. She looked down past her legs. A boundless lake stretched beyond sigh, and she was headed straight for it. She had a split second to grab a gulp of oxygen before plunging into their depths. Had the water been cold, she'd have lost it. The lukewarm water swallowed her without a splash, and as she sank, the surface ignited with blue flames. The way out became a hazard.

Her skull itched. She shook her head, breaking through the fogbanks like a lighthouse on the cliffside. A deluge of memories forced their way back inside her mind. Her days in high school, crushing on the boy with the stormy gray eyes whom her parents told her she didn't have time for. Her first days in college, and the way she giddily danced in her dorm room after Tom asked her out. Their first date and first kiss. The first time they made love. Their wedding day.

Grady's sapphire eyes and boyish grin as he taught her how to harness the magic from which she was born. His hugs that felt like comfort incarnate. The emotion she dared not put a name to every time he looked at her this weekend.

Happiness burst behind her ribs. Every precious memory Beth recovered fueled her fighting spirit. On the other side of the lake of azure fire, those cursed eyes watched, seething with an inhuman rage. Beth glared back. It was time to end it, but she wasn't sure how to fight it.

She looked around. Which way was up? Beth gritted her teeth against the imminent collapse of her airways. Her heart raced, stealing the blood from her fingertips. Panic clawed her chest, proving that her brain didn't get the memo that this was a dream. Gods, she was screwed. There was no coming back from this. Paul had seen to that.

A stream of bubbles left through her nostrils and clenched teeth, bleeding her lungs dry. When she kicked her feet to swim to the surface, an unseen force kept her suspended in water. Her lungs squeezed as the last of her air vacated.

An unbidden thought wormed its way inside. Would the world even miss her insignificant existence if she was gone?

The domino effect of this question led her to a heart-crushing truth. She'd left Tom and Grady when they needed her. They weren't going to survive the extent of their injuries, and she'd left them to die. Alone, scared, and unloved.

Beth's tears mixed with her ocean tomb. She wasn't even worth the earthly resources she so greedily consumed. Her parents had been right all along. Beth was a waste of space.

Her life had been a series of other peoples' expectations, namely her parents. The only time Beth asked for something she wanted and got it was to marry Tom. And in his time of need, she let him down.

Her body jerked.

Dreams, magic, fated lovers. She hadn't asked for a reality shift on her birthday. Was it so wrong to want a simple life? Teaching kids, being Mrs. Tom Newman, raising children.

Beth's eyes bulged as her body jerked again; her body fighting against the lack of air. The edges of her sight dimmed.

Closing her eyes, the flash of sapphire orbs chased back her fear. Even faced with death, her thoughts went to Grady before her husband. She reached for the thread connecting them, expecting dead space, but her metaphysical fingers plucked it. The thrum was like a second wind.

Grady was alive. Tom could be, too.

Her lungs were given what they needed, and her eyes shot open.

The blue flames dove through the water to encircle her, unbothered by the source of its demise. On its tails, an endless ocean of stars crashed against Beth's weakened will with enough force to give her whiplash. This cosmic being tried to forcefully steal her most cherished memories and made her question her self-worth. Beth was done with being bullied.

She pushed back, sending wave after wave of her goddess-blessed flames against the darkness. This was the magic she held, her retributive power against the denizens of annihilation. The star-swarm continued to charge, each time knocking her back. Her fiery blasts kept chipping away, but it regenerated. They were at a stalemate.

Beth's lungs were on the verge of needing another refill, but the only way was down. She sank until her feet touched the bottom. Like a flat tire being filled by an air compressor, pressure built in her stomach. Once full, it had nowhere to go except to press against her skin. The feeling came back to her fingers, but her nails felt like they'd pop off.

Her arms were flung to the sides, mouth open wide on a soundless scream. It was like pulling the plug on her tub drain.

Water rushed inside down her throat. She tried to snap her lips shut, but there was too much, too fast. Before Beth could worry about exploding from taking on an entire lake, she fell to her hands and knees. Mud squished between her bare toes and fingers. Her stomach muscles twinged. Something deep inside Beth's being pulled her nerves into a bundle and tied them in knots. She heaved, pulling in oxygen as quickly as she exhaled.

The water inside her was changing. She didn't know how or why, just that it *was*. Whispered words she couldn't make out flew from her lips, ending with a clear, "So mote it be."

Her burp was like a popping cork. The lake worked its way free, stretching her throat and turning into a tidal wave that towered over the darkness devouring the edge of her sanity. Ice crystals formed around the exterior, but the surging water broke it off in chunks, dissolving the murkiness.

The waves enveloped two other energies in its path. It recognized them, repairing their wounds and leaving them otherwise safe.

At last, Beth was empty, and her energy was spent. She collapsed to the now dry land and closed her eyes. Her heartbeat steadied and calmed as an unfamiliar weight rooted itself in her core. It wasn't uncomfortable. It was new and warm like the sunshine in spring and had cunning roots that ran deep. Beth could feel every living thing connected to the earth, which promised the wisdom of generations. She was almost whole.

Someone beyond the foggy veil beckoned with a whisper, "Guardian."

She managed to pull herself to her feet and slowly spun around. Beth had come full circle when a path appeared. She followed it to a small cottage in the forest surrounded by white birch trees. To the left of it was a beautiful garden lush with vegetation.

She entered the cozy cottage, and her eyes widened. Giddiness tickled her chest. Wreaths made from twigs and branches found in the forest hung on the door, above the fireplace, and in the kitchen window. Bundles of dried herbs and flowers hung from the ceiling with cotton twine tied to the rafters. More were stored in bottles on shelves.

"Grady would love this place."

On the mantelpiece were little knick-knacks and a small statue of a woman holding a bowl overflowing with water. Carved at the base of the statue's feet were various woodland creatures bringing her flowers. The peaceful smile on the woman's face warmed Beth, blanketing her in calm.

She continued wandering around the tiny space until she was met at the doorway by a familiar face. "I know you."

"Hello, Beth." Myrtle smiled. "I have long awaited our meeting."

Myrtle's aura brightened the whole room. She stepped inside and embraced Beth like a daughter. The same overwhelming power from the magical lake surrounded them in a soft blue aura.

"What is this place?" Beth blurted the first of a hundred questions.

"Come and sit. We have little time, and there is much you need to know," Myrtle said, guiding her to the two stools under the island in the center of the kitchen space. "You and I are the same. And so is your destined one, Grady."

"My destined one?" Beth asked, her face scrunched in confusion.

The corners of Myrtle's lips curled up. "Of course he is, my dear. Grady is your beloved. Your perfect match and guardian counterpart."

Beth's eye twitched. "You keep calling Grady my beloved and my destined one. He's my *best friend*. I'm happily married to Tom. I don't feel that way—"

"You will in time, my dear." Myrtle held up her hand and cut her off. "I am sure Tom is a good man, but he is not the one fate ordained for you. You have magic and he does not."

Beth's neck was tight, and her face flushed hot. "What does magic have to do with who I'm destined to be with or not? I love Tom. *He's* my soulmate." She put her hands on her hips, challenging her to argue.

Scoffing with a wry smile, Myrtle crossed her arms. "Magic has everything to do with your destiny."

Beth narrowed her gaze while Myrtle explained, "Without you and Grady and your magic, evil will prevail. Ja'azul, the god of chaos and death, will destroy everything that is and ever will be if he is set free. You and Grady are light-bringer guardians, responsible for keeping Ja'azul imprisoned until he can either be destroyed or banished to his dimension."

"Okay, put a pin in the whole 'evil asshole and the end of the world' stuff. If I have magic, it's broken. Grady tried to teach me, but I couldn't do anything until someone I loved was threatened." Beth crossed her arms and sniffled. "Y'all have the wrong person."

Admitting she wasn't some magical savior destined to be with Grady made her nose and eyes sting. She shouldn't feel this way about the man who'd been like a brother to her for the past three years. Nothing made sense anymore.

"My brave girl," Myrtle placed her hands on Beth's shoulders and raised her eyebrows in sympathy. "You opened yourself, accepted part of your destiny, thus beginning your magical journey. Now, you can access your full potential and protect the world as you were chosen to do."

"I don't understand." Beth frowned. She didn't do anything other than scream and fight against well-knotted ropes. "Passing out and having trippy dreams isn't exactly 'saving the world' type of behavior." She rolled her eyes and shifted her weight to the other foot.

Myrtle grinned ear to ear. "Oh, you did much more than you realize. You fought back the darkness to save everything you hold dear, and in doing so, you vanquished the enemy's vessel, Paul."

Beth dropped her arms at her side, the weight of Myrtle's hand on her shoulders settled as heavily as her words. She thought back to the beginning of her vision. "Are you saying everything in my dream really happened?"

Her chest shrunk in on itself. She'd nearly lost herself, *forgotten* everything.

Cupping Beth's face, Myrtle gave it a wiggle. "Yes! You embraced your destiny, letting your magic flow naturally, and released your power. Fighting against your magic is the same as fighting against the color of your eyes. You cannot change it or make it go away. It simply *is*, and you need it to function."

Ha! I can change my eye color if I want. Beth thought smugly, but Myrtle's words stuck with her. The awareness at her core palpitated with warmth at her declaration. It wanted her to heed the edict of her ancestor. Some parts of her wanted to, but not at the cost of letting Tom go. Whatever destiny she shared with Grady would have to wait.

"Right. So, what happens now? Am I going to wake up in the morning and just *know* how to keep this darkness at bay? There's so much I don't understand. What if it comes back while I'm awake?"

Using magic unconsciously was simple. Her rational *awake* mind wasn't going to be so easily assuaged.

"I have been teaching Grady the craft for several years now. He and I will help you so that the prophecy is fulfilled," Myrtle said, turning to the window. The ball of light keeping the place lit dimmed like the setting sun. She spun back to Beth and continued, "Mark my words, Ja'azul *will* be released. The prophecy speaks of a child, a daughter born of magic in a time when magic was believed to be dead. She will defeat the darkness for all time. I believe *you* to be this child of prophecy, Beth, but you must embrace your destiny and complete the bond with your beloved."

Magic, destiny, prophecies...her head hurt from spinning so fast.

"I don't understand."

"You and Grady must come together as one or else the end of everything you know and love will perish when Ja'azul is free." Myrtle brought her hands together in front of her stomach. Her patience annoyed Beth.

"I can't cheat on my husband with our best friend." Beth couldn't calm the anxiety welling up inside her. Having sex with Grady was a large leap from her newfound attraction to him. It was all too much.

"In the end, you will see there is no other choice." Myrtle's voice was firm but not uncaring. "There is more."

"Of course there is," Beth scoffed. If her chest contracted much more, her heart would implode. She wanted to wake up, not hear more bad news.

Myrtle glanced at the window and swallowed. "Now that your power has awakened, any non-magical man you lie with will have a shortened life. Think of it as a type of magical radiation. Only those with magic have the power to survive a coupling."

"So, you're saying the only choice I *do* have is whether I slowly poison my husband or not." Beth's gut was a ball of thorns in a vat of acid. "Jesus, lady. You know how to sell this whole 'saving the world' thing."

"It is not the end. While your time with Tom will be short, the love and happiness Grady can offer will last centuries, just as my Barton loved me. Of this, I promise."

"How can you stand there and tell me that I can't have sex with my husband, or he'll die?" Beth shook with controlled rage as frustration tears prepared for their debut. "Do you have any idea how ridiculous it sounds? You and Barton had a perfect love. Tom is *my* true love."

Myrtle took Beth's hands in hers. When she tried to pull them away, Myrtle held tight. "Barton was my second husband. My first husband, Josiah Harper, died two years after the birth of our son, Lucas. I loved them both with all my heart."

"What happened to Lucas?"

"Smallpox," Myrtle choked out. Swatting away the memory, she continued, "When I met Barton, he told me who he was and how the goddess had paired us to keep Ja'azul contained. The day sweet Josiah passed my heart shattered, but Barton helped me piece it back together. He also gave me another son, Solomon."

"So, you do understand," Beth whispered, her face wet. Someday she would have to choose between her two loves, but not today.

"Yes." Myrtle sniffled, wiping the tears from her cheeks as she offered Beth a napkin. "And I survived. Just as you will. When the time comes, don't close yourself off. Grady loves you, though he may not realize it yet. Give him time."

Beth felt like gravity had crushed her world beneath the hand of fate. The future she'd fought to keep was all for naught if Tom died. Why couldn't she have a normal life with the man she married? The white picket fence and kids laughing while running in the yard, the growing old together. It's what she'd always wanted. She never asked for any of this.

"It's not fair," Beth grumbled, wiping her nose with the silk. "To lose Tom now after all that's happened. It's-it's just not fair." She huffed with a bitter chuckle.

"Life seldom is," Myrtle replied, stroking Beth's hair like a mother soothing a child. "Dawn approaches, and I must go. Know that I am always with you. Anytime you need help, think of this place and call on me. Remain vigilant, daughter of mine."

Beth stepped out of Myrtle's embrace, and they walked outside. The cottage faded, and she was left alone in the darkness again.

Warmth brushed her cheek before she opened her eyes. She turned her head and found Tom sleeping peacefully on the cot next to her. A sad smile crept up on her face as she studied his handsome features. She eased out of her cot to kneel beside his. When Tom stirred, she brushed the hair out of his eyes and traced his jawline.

"Hey, handsome," Beth whispered. He peeked at her behind sleepy lids, eyelashes fluttering before he was fully awake.

"Beth," Tom whispered, wrapping his arms around her. His cot tipped, spilling him to the ground. He laughed, planting kisses wherever his lips landed.

"Oh, Tom," she whispered as he pulled her into his lap. Her knees squeezed his thighs. Her heart thumped against her ribs.

"I thought I had lost you," Tom murmured, placing his forehead on hers.

"You can't get rid of me that easily." Beth kissed him sweetly, memorizing the feel of his stubble on her chin, his soft hair, and faint scent of orange and sandalwood cologne.

Tom buried his face in her neck and hugged her tight. Her heart was full, but she was done with these woods. "Can we go home now? I could really go for an extra-long shower and some hot food, not necessarily in that order."

Tom tensed in her arms before replying, "Absolutely." He untangled their arms and stood, holding out his hand.

Accepting it, Beth smiled as he pulled her to stand. Tom must not realize that Grady was outside. Beth sensed him when she woke. Their connection, which had started out as a thin string, had grown into a thin rope with a warm and steady hum.

Like a heartbeat. *Their* heartbeat.

And that was worrisome.

Chapter 23

TOM

"ALL SET?" BETH ASKED as she tied her hair back in a ponytail.

"One more thing before we go." Tom squeezed the back of his neck while one hand braced against the wall. The air in their little haven was stuffy. "It's—I don't know how to break it to you, but—"

The door fell open. Tom turned to catch it and nearly fainted. His best friend's ghost stood inches away.

"Grady?" Tom gripped Grady's solid shoulder. There was no sign of a knife wound either. "You're real."

"I'm here, Brother." Grady clapped him on the back in their usual man hug. "I'm not going anywhere."

Tom pulled away to check on Beth. Grady's assessing gaze was on her before it settled back on Tom. Grady shot him a sheepish grin, and Beth cleared her throat.

Her cheeks were tinged pink, but her eyes sparkled like emeralds. Tom slipped his arm around her waist and tugged her into his side. "How are you so... You barely had a pulse, man. You were dying."

"Long story." Grady backed up to stand in the same spot where the panther slept. "I'll tell y'all all about it when we get back home."

"Fair enough. I'm just glad the two most important people in my life are alive and this mess is over." Tom kissed the side of Beth's head. She beamed at him, making his heart swell. "Whaddya say we get out of here, so we can focus on what's important?"

His wife was living and breathing, magic was a real part of their lives, and his best friend had survived. After a series of terrible happenings this weekend, going home seemed like his first good decision since saying 'I do' in January.

"We need to get our backpacks," Beth said, bringing Tom's focus back to the present. "If we can't get into our vehicles, we can't get into our homes."

"Do we still have the extra key in the hatchback?"

"We don't have to hike back out there or worry about extra keys," Grady interjected, pointing at the ground past Tom's feet at their backpacks. "I brought them with me in case I found you."

"You are full of surprises," Tom replied, handing them out.

Beth slid her arms through the straps and pulled them tight. As much as it pained Tom, his wife was a hugger, and she never missed an opportunity to get one from their friend, Grady. He tensed, awaiting the inevitable. They must've been in an alternate universe, because she didn't attempted to and didn't bring it up. Tom may have been more than pleased to have her glued to his side.

"Just being practical." Grady shrugged his shoulders before pulling on the backpack. "Let's not burn any more daylight."

"Sure," Tom replied. He fussed over Beth, not that she needed help. Near-death experiences had the power to make you reevaluate your life. A knot formed in his chest. "Ready, hon?"

"Yeah." Beth kissed his cheek. "Let's go home."

As they made the trek to Jeff's Honda, Tom snuck glances at Beth. Most of the time, she kept her head down, brows drawn in concentration. Occasionally, he would catch her eye, and she would smile. Tom let her work through whatever was going in her head. Once they were home, he'd offer his ear if she needed to talk.

"When we get back to the house, I'm ordering two large pies, two orders of buffalo wings, and some garlic knots from Benny's," Tom remarked, attempting to break the uncomfortable silence.

Beth slipped her hand in his and squeezed. "Sounds amazing, hon." She smiled, but it didn't reach her eyes.

Tom wanted to press the issue. He wanted to ask Beth if she was really okay, but he didn't. At least Grady wasn't making lovey-dovey eyes at his wife anymore. His marriage couldn't afford that kind of distraction while they were in the middle of making up.

Since the others weren't in the mood to talk, Tom was left to his thoughts. With Paul no longer a threat, why did he have the feeling something was unresolved?

"How do we know Jeff isn't waiting by his car for us? We haven't seen him since camp that first night," Tom wondered aloud.

Grady stopped; his head cocked to the side as if listening to something else. He turned, studying Tom like he had forgotten he was there. "There's only one way to find out. Parking lot is less than a mile ahead. You two stay out of sight while I scout." His eyes flickered toward Beth, but they quickly trained back to Tom.

"Right." Tom agreed. He took off his backpack in search of his cell phone and cursed, dropping the useless block of metal back inside. "Cell is dead. We'll give you a five-minute head start before we follow. You shouldn't have to fight him alone if he's there."

"Agreed." Grady started forward, but Beth put a hand on his arm. His bicep flexed as he turned slightly.

"Be careful," Beth whispered. She hesitated before slipping her arms around his waist.

Tom had never seen Grady delay in returning Beth's hugs, and he did for half a heartbeat before enveloping her. Seeing them this way brought Tom's jealousy back tenfold.

Grady lowered his nose to her ear and inhaled deeply. Tom's chest restricted at the same time his stomach turned into a pretzel. *Aw, hell…*

There was definitely something going on.

Chapter 24

BETH

GRADY HAD BARELY WALKED out of sight, but the silence between her and Tom was unbearable. Her husband was in his head again, meaning this would be the longest five minutes of Beth's life.

What could she say or do to make it better? She was genuinely concerned for Grady's safety, hence the hug. The magic drawing them together was like two strong magnets, but her heart belonged to Tom. It was time she reaffirmed this.

"Hon?" Beth lightly touched his arm.

Tom blinked a few times before focusing on her. "Yeah?"

His sad eyes and the worry lines etched on his face nearly broke her. Beth's bottom lip trembled as she cupped his face. "Being strapped to that stone table was terrifying," she began.

"Baby," Tom whispered. His worry lines softened as he placed his hand over hers.

"Do you know what I was scared of most?" she asked. He shook his head. "Losing you, Tom. I thought I'd never see your face again."

Tears slipped down both of their faces as Tom wrapped Beth in his arms. He trembled with her.

"Shhh. It's over now, hon. I'll never let you go," he murmured, pressing his lips against the curve of her neck. "We have forever to make memories, and I intend to start now."

Regret pierced the center of her chest. As soon as they made love, Tom would die. He could live years, but they wouldn't have forever. Magic had robbed them of that. 'The Talk' needed to happen sooner rather than later. However, in this moment she didn't want to think about magic or lines in the sand. She just wanted her husband.

"I love you, Tom," Beth mumbled into his shirt.

He planted a kiss on the side of her head while stroking her hair. "I love you, too, Beth. Forever and always."

"Forever and always," she repeated, squeezing him tight.

They stayed locked in an embrace for what seemed like an eternity before Tom pulled away. He gazed into her eyes; his lips curled up. Tucking the hair behind her ear, he kissed her forehead. Beth closed her eyes, cataloguing the warmth and softness of his lips.

"Time's up," he sighed.

Beth's mind went into a tailspin until she realized what he meant. Her tongue was still locked, so she nodded.

Tom laced their fingers, and they headed to the parking area. Ten minutes later, they broke the tree line to find Grady leaned against the hood of Jeff's car. His lips were set in a straight line as he stared at the broken lumps of granite near his feet. He absentmindedly twirled the keys on his finger. As soon as their boots hit the gravel, his gaze found Beth. Her stomach flipped, but he'd averted his attention to the ground as he pushed off the Honda. The sedan made a double 'bleeping' noise and the lights flashed.

"All clear. No sign of Jeff or anyone else," Grady addressed Tom, his face was unreadable.

"Good," Tom replied. His jaw twitched. If Beth hadn't been looking, she would have missed it. "Shall we?" He then opened the back passenger door for her.

She gave him a half smile and tilted her head before climbing inside. Tom patted Grady on the back a little harder than usual before getting in after her. Grady got into the driver's seat and adjusted the rearview mirror. The engine roared to life, and they were off.

Beth rested her head on Tom's chest, cuddled underneath his arm. She played with his hand, deep in thought. She worried this would be the last time she felt at peace around her husband. Once they got home and had their talk, would she and Tom be able to carry on as usual?

She was hopeful things would work out between them, but as the magnetic pull to Grady grew stronger, her optimism wavered. Beth couldn't avoid being around Grady, or Tom would become suspicious if he wasn't already.

Beth glanced at the rearview mirror, met by Grady's stare. She blushed and looked away. If Grady watched her so closely, no wonder Tom was pissed. Beth was acutely aware of Grady's presence. The fact she was somewhat calmed by it only annoyed her further.

So far, he'd kept to himself, but how long would that last? There were too many variables; it made Beth's head hurt.

"Are you okay?" Tom whispered.

Beth rubbed circles on her temple. "Hm? Oh, I have a headache." Tom didn't look convinced, so she added, "It's nothing. Really."

Tom nodded, stroking her hand with his thumb. She studied his face while he watched the trees pass by. Sorrow hung over his head like a dank, dark cloud. She hoped he wouldn't fall into depression again. From what Grady had hinted at, Tom's episodes varied depending on the situation. It was more information than Tom had given her. He wasn't one to talk about his mental health, insisting he had it managed.

Beth snuggled into Tom's side. He gave her a half-smile before returning to stare out the window.

Over several minutes, Beth's headache turned into a marching band wearing spiked shoes. Closing her eyes was the only thing keeping nausea at bay. Grady stopped tapping his fingers on the steering wheel.

"Hey," Tom whispered, petting her head. "Is it worse?"

She nodded, the pounding in her head persisted no matter how much she relaxed.

"Lay down and try to sleep. We have about forty more minutes." Tom lifted his arm so she could shift.

Once Beth was comfortable with her head in Tom's lap, he rubbed circles on her back while blocking the sun with his other hand. She hadn't been tired but fell straight to sleep.

"We're here," Grady announced in his deep, smooth voice.

Beth opened her eyes and yawned. Her limbs were loose, but the dull ache in her head remained. She sat up with a stretch and took in their surroundings. Grady pulled onto the gravel road where their hatchback was parked. Her stomach jumped at the prospect of going home.

Tom brought his arm around her shoulders. "Feel better, hon?"

"Mm-hm. A little. My head's still fuzzy." She rubbed the sleep from her eyes and slumped into Tom's side. "Nothing a hot shower, good food, and a solid eight in my own bed won't fix."

"I think we can manage that." Tom's lip ticked up at the corner before he kissed the top of her head.

Grady parked Jeff's Honda Accord next to their hatchback and got out. His shoulders shifted forward as he slammed a hand on their door, keeping Tom from opening it.

Beth craned her neck to see what was going on. Grady's hulking chest puffed in and out as he sniffed the air. When he finished, his gaze was on hers like a compass pointing north. Grady gave her the ghost of his lopsided smile before lumbering away.

Well, that was odd.

Tom hooked his finger under Beth's chin and tipped her face, so she was looking at him. His jaw ticked before he lowered, placing a tender kiss on her lips. Thoughts of Grady's muscular back were washed away like a sand drawing when the tide comes in. In its place were storm clouds over a raging sea as Tom plundered her tongue with lazy strokes. The man knew how to take her breath away.

"You okay to wait here while I load our bags?" he asked with a knowing smirk.

Beth's eyes were hooded as she traced his bottom lip with her thumb. "Yeah."

Tom pressed his lips against her forehead, lingering long enough that Beth had closed her eyes without realizing.

"Be right back," he whispered, easing out of the car and leaving the door open.

As Tom walked away, the air in the vicinity grew cold and thin. Beth sat up with a start. Someone was watching. There was an unpleasant tingling underneath her skin, as though something was trying to work its way out. She rubbed her arms and shivered. From the back of her mind, the knowledge came in a whisper.

Something evil lurks in the shadows.

Beth opened her mouth to warn the guys of danger, but it was like someone hammered a frozen pick into her skull. She fell out of the car onto her hands and knees.

Her brain was stuck in a wave of muscles spasms, blurring her vision. The buzzing in her ears grew from power-line pole strength to swarm of hornets above her head noisy.

She blinked her eyes rapidly until her gaze zeroed in on the thing short-circuiting her nervous system. Emerging from the forest next to Grady's truck was a snarling, black creature. Its heavy, tattered cloak shifted against the wind. Dark embers of pure hatred where its eyes should be bored into her soul. A wicked smile formed on its round, lipless mouth, showcasing rows of sharp, tiny teeth. It was evil incarnate.

The thing lunged at Grady and swiped with its gangly hand full of long, razor-like talons. He jumped and rolled to his feet, dodging the first attack. Beth blinked and the creature caught Grady across the back. He howled as four deep gashes bloomed rouge. When he crumpled to the ground, his body twisted and contorted. Beth's stomach sunk like the Titanic.

"No!" Beth wheezed, unable to move except to ball her fists. The paralytic hammering across her skull intensified. White spots clouded her vision. She fought past the pummeling agony, desperately seeking the thread between them. It was still there, faint but firm.

She glanced his way when he groaned. There was a glimmer of hope that his injuries weren't so severe, that he would get up to continue the battle using his magic. When Grady's eyes rolled to the back of his head, it was lost.

Beth couldn't watch him die. Looking away, tears stung her eyes as the jackhammers in her head worked overtime. Again, she pushed it down, gasping from the strain, and looked for Tom.

As always, her shining knight stood his ground against the odds. The tire iron he held must have come from Paul's truck.

"Back for round two, ugly?" Tom taunted.

Beth reached out for him, but it was like an army with a battering ram rushed forward, and her forehead was the gate. Her hand curled against her chest while her arm wobbled. Myrtle's words floated to the forefront: *'Don't fight the magic. Let it flow naturally.'*

"I can't," she sobbed. If she let it go, she would lose Tom.

As if the shadow creature was tuned to her thoughts, it turned its baleful grin to her husband. He went instantly still. A chill crawled down her spine to her toes.

This thing must have been what he saw at the waterfall. It was made of nightmares.

The men she loved were in danger and there was nothing she could do to save them without ruining everything. The nightmarish monster moved slower, its mouth muscles moving as if it were sucking the essence of her terror and savoring her pain.

A thunderous voice boomed inside her head, *"Stop fighting your destiny!"*

What was more important? Giving up or fighting to figure shit out another day? Beth glanced at Tom. His muscles strained against the hold as the creature from hell moved closer.

Beth closed her eyes and let go.

The pounding slowed to a stop, and she heard the same 'pop' from her dream. A familiar warmth of power surged and filled every crevice. The pain and tingling were gone, leaving only raw, magical strength seeping from her pores. The smell of pine sap, freshly dug earth, and petrichor from yesterday's rain filled her lungs.

She was on her feet, invoking the blue flame in a blink. The instant her right hand ignited, she flicked it toward the enemy. A fireball shot through the air and engulfed her target.

The shadow creature screeched with an unearthly animal-like pain as it writhed against the flames. Beth willed the blaze to burn hotter. It incinerated the creature where it floated. Eventually, it stilled, and a warm breeze scattered the ashes.

Beth's body went slack. As she fell to the ground in a heap Tom scooped her into his arms. His stormy gray eyes swam with wonder while his brows met in the middle.

Her sight went black, but her men were safe. She could rest now.

Chapter 25

TOM

"PLEASE BE OKAY. PLEASE be okay," Tom whispered.

His hands shook as he raised two fingers to her neck. This was the third time in two days he'd nearly lost her. A sob fell from his lips at the steady double-beat.

Tom kissed Beth's forehead twice before laying her down in the front passenger seat of their Subaru hatchback. Same as last time, she was in a deep sleep. He rushed over to where Grady had fallen and skidded to a stop. Instead of finding his friend, a large black panther lay in his place. Tom's eyes widened as he sank both hands through his hair.

"I don't believe it," he muttered, mustering the courage to kneel beside the large feline. He tentatively laid a hand on the panther's head. The cat was identical to the one last night.

"Grady?" Tom's face flushed hot, and he winced.

The cat opened its eyes and whimpered in pain. There were deep scratches along the panther's ribs. Dark red coated his fur coat, but the eyes were the exact sapphire-blue as his childhood friend's.

Grady's taken a beating and survived before.

Tom looked at the backseat of the car, and his shoulders fell. Beth's blue flame had healed them last night, but she was out for the count.

He studied his friend. The cat's breaths were shallow and fast. His whole body was suddenly tired. "What can I do to help? Beth passed out, and I don't have anything to wrap around your middle."

The cat's eyes closed in reply, and Tom bellowed in frustration. He'd load the panther in his hatchback, but they'd have to leave Grady's truck. Tom had barely gotten to his feet when realization slapped him in the face.

The Dodge had a tow hitch.

Tom loaded Beth into the front bench of Grady's Dodge. The panther he hauled into the backseat of his Subaru. Once he hitched his hatchback, they were off by the time the sun was retiring toward the horizon.

The drive home was too quiet, giving Tom's thoughts the space to wander. When Beth complained of her migraine, concern was etched on Grady's face. It was almost like he could sense her discomfort. Whatever caused the headache must have been magical. Tom hated feeling helpless and unable to comfort his wife in times like those.

The thing that bothered Tom more than anything was the way Grady *sniffed* his wife. Something about that action got under his skin. In a way it was territorial, making him want to punch his friend in the face.

Whatever caveman mentality taking over urged Tom to stake his claim on Beth. Hadn't he already done this when they married? They'd dated for over three years. She was *his* girl. The time for fighting over her affection was over.

Despite the testosterone-driven dispute he had going on with himself, a question niggled at the back of his mind. *How does Beth feel about Grady?*

Tom wasn't sure if he could even look at her again if she reciprocated Grady's feelings. The thought of his wife embracing his best friend awoke the darkness inside him. The fear of losing her to another man fed the beast waiting in the shadows of his mind. He let go of Beth's hand when his body's muscles tensed so hard he quaked.

Tom couldn't deny there was something there between them. He'd seen it before, but whatever it was had grown beyond their shared magic. If that was the case, why would Beth bother telling him she loved him if her plan was to be with Grady?

Thinking back over the weekend, Tom clung to all the times Beth reassured him of her loyalty and devotion. The shaking lessened, leaving him with cold chills.

Beth couldn't be unfaithful. She wouldn't.

They had the kind of love people see in movies or read about in romance novels. As soon as they were home, Tom would remind her why they say, 'together forever.' It had always been her, and it always would be. He'd never love another woman as long as he lived.

Beth whimpered in her sleep. Tom peeked to find her hand. At his touch, the frown lines on her forehead soothed. Even with her skin turned ashen and the color of her hair dulled to match, he still found her beautiful. He would do anything for this woman, and he *had*. This weekend had been a testament to his devotion.

If nearly dying for her multiple times wasn't true love, he didn't know what was.

BETH

BETH WAS WRAPPED IN SOMETHING soft and warm. It smelled like home. She blinked a few times until her eyes adjusted to the light. Flashes of an evil shadow creature caused her heart to beat wildly. She shot up to her knees with her fire hand ready to blast the monster to smithereens.

But there was no forest and no creatures. Only light beige walls with cornflower curtains blowing with the breeze.

Beth was at home in her bed, washed, and dressed in clean clothes. She fell back onto her pillows and sighed in relief.

Hushed voices came from the living room. Her head throbbed, making her wonder when she last had a drink of water. This time, Beth sat slowly, dangling her legs off the side of the bed before settling her bare feet on the cool laminate floor designed to look like hardwood. She wiggled her toes against the patterned wood grains, then padded across the room. Beth opened her bedroom door and stopped abruptly. Spread out on the floor in front of the fireplace was a large black panther with bandages around its midsection. It studied her as Tom came over with a glass of water.

"Here, honey. Drink up. Grady said you'll need plenty of water and food," he said with a relieved grin. "Let me know what you want to eat, and we'll order in."

She glanced at the giant cat and downed the water without stopping, gasping as her head absorbed the water quickly. The throbbing intensified before subsiding.

"More. Please," she croaked, handing the glass back to Tom.

Grady's presence was near, but it was different than before. She scanned the apartment for him, but the only other living thing besides them in their small apartment was the wild animal.

Tom was back in no time flat with another glass of water. She downed it with an *ahh*. "Thanks, hon."

He took the glass from her and placed it on the coffee table.

Nodding toward the panther in the room, Beth inquired, "Why do we have an injured wild animal in our living room, and where is Grady?"

A flicker of amusement crossed Tom's face. "That wild animal *is* Grady."

"C'mon, Tom." Beth raised an eyebrow and crossed her arms. "This is another joke. Spoiler alert: I'm not in the mood for any more pranks this year." There was no way Grady could transform into an animal, right? Tom was pulling her leg.

"I'm not kidding. After the fight with that shadow creature, I went to help Grady and this cat"—Tom gestured to the sleepy panther—"is what I found in his place. One hundred percent real, Beth."

Frowning, Beth uncrossed her arms and slowly made her way closer. The huge cat yawned, not appearing to be at all threatening unless you counted the rows of very large, very sharp teeth.

"This is the dumbest thing I've ever done," Beth murmured as she lowered to the floor beside him. The panther's bright blue eyes watched her with an intensity that made her body heat. She gulped. "Grady?"

Amusement danced in the cat's eyes as it licked Beth's hand. He laid his head on its paws and closed his eyes.

Beth shook her head. "This can't be for real."

"I dunno how but it is." Tom chuckled nervously and ran a hand through his hair. "Uh, we can communicate telepathically now...sort of. We practiced for a few hours, but we can only relay one or two words at a time."

She stroked the fur on the panther's head, and he purred loudly. Smiling, she closed her eyes and listened.

"I'll heal with rest, Beth, don't worry," Grady's voice said in her head.

Beth startled. Her eyes flew open, and she jerked her hand away. "What?"

Tom raised his eyebrows. "So, he can talk to you, too?"

"It's really Grady? You guys aren't shitting me?"

"No shitting you, baby." Tom studied the panther, and laughed in astonishment. "This is incredible."

If someone had told her this was possible last week, she would have thought them completely mental.

Beth continued petting Grady's fur, falling into a meditative trance. The peaceful tranquility she found in the forest radiated from his animal form, calling to her. It was so intense, she could smell the sap of pine trees with a subtle hint of wild roses. The serenity filled her limbs before going deeper into the stillness. The feeling of a rope around her waist tugged at her. Something was keeping her grounded.

Tom cleared his throat loudly, repeating Beth's name and snatching from her peace. His deep frown made her turn away quickly. She pulled her hand away from panther Grady, breaking the magic's hold. His absence left a hole in her heart.

"Sorry, hon. Guess I'm still tired," Beth apologized. She forced herself to make eye contact and smiled while offering her hands. "You were asking what I want for dinner?"

Tom returned her grin with a tired one of his own. He gripped her hands and tugged her to his chest, placing his hands on her hips. "Grady was very clear. You need to eat." He planted a kiss on her forehead. "Anything you want as long as it can be delivered."

Beth looked into his beautiful gray eyes, stormy like the raging sea at night. The normalcy felt nice, like old times. She leaned into him for a tender kiss as if they'd been apart for months. Resting her forehead on his, she chose the first food that came to mind. "I want a deluxe pizza from Benny's on Main. And wings."

"That's exactly what I was thinking." Tom leaned back, his eyes narrowed playfully as he motioned between them. "Are you sure *we're* not communicating telepathically?"

"Hmm. Let's just say it's intuition," Beth teased with a cheerful smile. "I think I know you well enough to know that Benny's pizza and wings fix everything."

The words left her mouth but soured on her tongue. The peaceful mood vanished in a puff of smoke. Nothing would be able to fix their situation.

Dismissing the stone in her gut, she kissed his chin dimple and excused herself to the bathroom. Tom kissed the top of her head, the space between his brows creased slightly.

In their vast world, full of wonder and all kinds of good, she was suffocating. Out of the billions of people on the whole damn planet, destiny had chosen her. Why? How long could she pretend to be fine when her desire for Grady grew?

She hated magic for destroying the one thing that had brought her happiness, for forcing her to love another man. Beth sat on the edge of the bathtub and quietly wept. She wasn't sure what to do. How would she broach a conversation like this?

Hey, Tom. There's something you should know before we have sex. Some three-hundred-year-old dead witch came to me in a dream and told me we can't do it anymore or you will die.

It sounded ridiculous. Tom would think she was trying to sabotage their marriage.

What about her attraction to Grady? She could blame it all on magic, doubling down on her choice to stay with Tom until destiny intervened.

No matter how she put it, a rose covered in shit is still gonna smell like shit.

On the flipside, Tom could remain oblivious to it all and die a happy man. They might even have time to try for a family.

The thought made her chest cave as a wave of overwhelming sadness sapped her strength. Either she was also sensitive to Grady's emotions or the stress of the weekend was catching up.

Beth's defeated sigh rattled her bones. No matter how badly she wanted things to be the same, deep down she knew it wasn't possible. It wasn't in her nature to live in denial. Her feelings for Grady continued to grow like weeds in a garden, but she loved Tom with all her heart. It had to be enough.

She stood and stared down the woman in the mirror. The dark circles underneath her eyes hardened her face. A faint scar had formed along the outside of her bicep where Paul's blade cut her after deflecting the blade. Underneath it all, the thread between her and her best friend hummed with need, aching to be united...to be wanted.

This wasn't a dream she could wake from. There was no time machine and no amount of wishing to fix it. This was her new reality. If her marriage and her friendship were going to survive, they'd need to adopt a new normal.

Beth finished in the bathroom. She washed her hands and splashed cold water on her face. Toweling off, she repeated the lie she kept telling herself.

You're doing the right thing.

When she opened the bathroom door, Tom was on the other side poised to knock. The creases on his forehead were deeper. "You were gone for a while. Everything okay?"

The corners of her eyes were tight as she forced a smile. Beth pulled him into a hug. "Everything is gonna be fine."

Chapter 26

GRADY

WHILE TOM AND BETH had shared an awkward but quiet dinner, Grady stayed curled up on the floor in his panther skin, drifting in and out of sleep.

Once all the lights were off and silence filled the apartment, Grady dreamed of the first ritual he had been dragged to. The usual anxiety and dribbles of sweat accompanied his nightmare.

He walked up the hill between Tom and Jeff, chatting excitedly and goofing off. When their dads stopped abruptly, their playful mood dropped like bad Wi-Fi.

There was the stone table fashioned out of boulders too heavy to have been built by man. Strapped to the top, a woman with a dirt-covered, tear-streaked face. Her wide eyes pleaded for help as she mumbled incoherent words into the rag stuffed into mouth.

This time, the woman morphed into Beth. Grady's body grew cold, and his heart caught in his chest.

Before he could reach out and save her, Louis Cooper drew the knife across her throat. Clear blue water poured from the slit like a spout.

Surprised shouts came from the men as they scrambled to get away. The water swirled around their feet, grabbing at their ankles. They tripped and fell repeatedly, only to stand and fall into the water again.

The forest filled up too rapidly. Water was up to their knees already. Grady was gearing toward panic, but the impossible rising river caressed his waist like a heated saltwater pool.

He searched for Tom and spotted a peculiar fox hiding in the tall grass. The same one from when Beth's power was released. The animal sprinted away from the waves rushing toward the forest's edge. It leapt into the brush as the water crashed into an invisible wall.

The water was up to their chests.

Tom was within arm distance of Grady. Worry creased the corners of his eyes. He caught Grady's gaze seconds before their heads went under.

They were trapped in an endless ocean. The bodies of the four fathers, Paul, and Jeff floated nearby. Their arms flailed while their legs kicked, trying to make it to the surface. Instead of going upward, they sank. Panicked hands grabbed at their throats. Their eyes bulged out of their sockets. Large air bubbles leaked from their open mouths as they were lost to the navy abyss.

Tom kicked toward the surface. Grady tore his gaze from where his father disappeared and followed. Swimming to the surface was effortless. When he breached the boundary between water and air, sweet oxygen filled his hungry lungs. He floated on the top, staring out into the black of night where faraway stars twinkled like technicolor kaleidoscopes.

Grady had been so mesmerized by the sight, he lost track of Tom and forgot all about leaving Beth's body underwater. He took a deep breath and dove back in. The water welcomed him, and he located the stone altar long before his lungs would tire.

Beth's eyes were closed as she swayed in the water with her arms above her head. Grady focused on loosening the rope around her ankles. With no small amount of effort, she was free.

He grabbed her around the waist, but she snapped her head to stare at him. Her eyes had gone completely white, glowing with such intensity Grady almost dropped her trying to shield his face.

"Beware the one outside of time. The harbinger has broken his bonds walks the earth. He will be the downfall of the universe." Her monotone voice was ominous. As she spoke, the loose skin where the knife had sliced fluttered in the current.

Before Grady could fully understand the meaning of her words, the light in Beth's eyes snuffed out. He held back a gasp and tightened his hold. With a few strong kicks, they were propelled to the surface.

As soon as his head was free, Grady sucked at the air greedily and opened his eyes. It was morning. He was at the Newman's apartment. It took him a few minutes to calm his thumping heart. Why was he sleeping on their living room floor?

A collage of images reminded him. The fight at the parking lot. Beth disintegrating the enemy after it filleted his chest. Her passing out.

Groaning, Grady rubbed the sleep from his eyes. A chilly gust of air skated across his bare skin, causing him to shiver. He looked down. Naked as the day he was born. Grady cupped his unmentionables with both hands and shot a peek toward the master bedroom door. It was closed.

A small part of him wished Beth had walked in on him. Grady wasn't a fitness model like Tom, but he wasn't an ugly man. Grady had worked hard for every hard line and swollen muscle. So what if he wanted Beth to see what she was missing?

Grady squashed that thought like a persistent mosquito. It didn't matter how erratic his heart beat when she smiled at him, or how his lungs worked better when she was wrapped in his arms. He couldn't have her. Tom and Beth were the only family he had left. His sorry excuse for a sperm-donor had seen to that when he murdered his mother and gave her pure soul to Ja'azul.

His shoulders were hunched as he got to his feet. It was as if his heart were an anchor that had been split in two. Once he was dressed, some of his dignity would return. Probably. He had a stash of clothes in the guest room. However, when Grady opened the drawer, he got a nose full of vanilla and lavender. He grabbed the top shirt and buried his face in the fabric. Taking a deep breath, Grady's center of gravity righted until guilt sideswiped his gut.

Yeah, he was screwed.

BETH

THE MORNING LIGHT DANCED over the bed, casting faint shadows across the room. Happy birds sang their wake-up song.

Beth inhaled deeply, denying a stretch for fear of waking Tom before he was rested. As she exhaled, his arms wound around her from behind. He planted kisses along the exposed skin near her neck. She hummed happily before rolling into him. A smile crept on her lips moments before those gorgeous gray eyes fluttered open.

"Morning," Beth whispered, voice slightly gravelly from a restful sleep.

"Morning." Tom brushed the hair away from her face and leaned in for a tender kiss. "Did you sleep well?"

Her body arched with a stretch. She grunted and sighed happily. "Yep. Like a baby. You?"

"Good," Tom murmured.

His gaze perused every inch of her body, making her region below the stomach warm. If Grady wasn't sleeping in the next room, Tom would be settling the issue of his morning wood. To confirm Beth's thoughts, Tom's gaze flashed toward the living room, as though he could see through the wall.

"What are you thinking about?" Beth asked in almost a whisper while running a hand through his dark blonde locks.

"I'm appreciating how fortunate I am to have you in my life," Tom replied with a smile. "And I'm wishing we were alone so I could start showing you."

Beth's heart hurt and her eyes prickled. She rubbed her body against Tom's, trying to distract from the negative. He took the bait, letting his hands travel down her waist, to her thighs.

She hooked her leg over his hip whispered into his mouth, "I love you so much, Tom. Don't ever forget that...no matter what."

For once, she didn't let a trivial thing like morning breath stop her from missing out on all the little moments. She breathed in Tom's sandalwood and orange scent, hoping her hungry kiss conveyed her wants and needs.

Tom slowed the kiss and pulled back. His gaze searched her face for hidden secrets, but Beth had locked them down tight. "I love you, too, hon, but we should stop before we give Grady an earful."

"I'd say I'll be quiet, but I'm not sure I'm capable." Beth nuzzled his scratchy chin, loving the roughness of his stubble on her cheek.

"No, but I wouldn't have it any other way." Tom placed a quick, feather-light kiss on the tip of her nose and pulled her into a hug.

The guest bedroom door shut. Drawers were shuffled through. The passion they had built simmered down as Beth lay in bed, clinging to Tom.

"I guess he's back to being a bi-ped," Tom quipped. He stole a quick kiss before climbing out of bed. "I'll get my morning stuff done."

Beth hummed in reply, watching her husband saunter off in his boxers and t-shirt until the bathroom door shut. She groaned when Grady's thoughts came flooding in. They were a jumbled mess of running through the forest, magic, fighting the darkness, and her. She'd hoped the whole telepathy thing was just a consequence of his animal form. Obviously, that wasn't the case.

Today did not look as promising as she'd hoped, and this was only the beginning. Beth grabbed Tom's pillow and placed it over her head. She wondered if she could get away with sleeping the rest of the day when a thought occurred to her.

What if this open telepathy goes both ways and Grady can read every thought going through her head?

Oh yeah, this is gonna be fun.

She didn't remember having this level of connectedness last night. Did close proximity strengthen the magical thread between them? She reached out for it like before. The thin rope had become much thicker, akin to the rigging on schooners. Much stronger, more secure. The longer she focused on their connection, the stronger her desire to be near Grady became.

Tom opened the bathroom door, giving Beth a toothy grin on his way to the closet. Her face flushed in shame. She hopped out of bed and rushed inside for her turn. Once the door was closed, she gulped.

Oh, God. I can do this. Don't focus on Grady...Don't focus on Grady...

After reciting her mantra, Beth went through her morning routine. While she brushed her hair, she wondered if blocking thoughts were possible. Trying would be worth it if it meant not listening to Grady ramble about how wrong it was to be attracted to her.

Here goes nothing.

Beth set the brush down and closed her eyes. Practicing the breathing technique Grady taught her, she calmed her brain. She imagined her mind was a sensory deprivation tank and sunk her thoughts into the cool water. As soon as the hatch closed, sweet silence. When she checked the magnetic pull drawing her to Grady, it was gone but the thread was still there.

Beth giggled at her astonished reflection. She'd successfully used her magic *consciously* for the first time.

I can't wait to tell the guys.

Her smile wilted. What would Tom think about his wife and his best friend having a permanent two-way radio between them? She couldn't say anything without explaining everything, could she?

"Tomorrow, I'll figure it out." she promised herself.

Tomorrow was the answer to all of today's problems.

Chapter 27

GRADY

HE STOOD IN FRONT of the mirror staring at his reflection. Sweat formed on his brow, but he wasn't shaking because he was cold. He had a fever—a *condition*—and the only cure was *her*.

This is hopeless, Grady thought, gripping the sink until his knuckles turned white.

There was no way he could function normally around the Newmans. Beth was everywhere. Her intoxicating perfume surrounded him, and her thoughts were so loud it was as if she were standing next to him. She was in his skin...and he enjoyed the feeling too damned much.

Grady wasn't hopeless in the relationship department. He'd dated a few girls in high school and several in college. Nothing serious ever came of them, not for lack of trying. He wanted marriage and a family one day. They didn't.

After his mother died, Grady didn't date for a while. After he and Beth became closer, he quit dating altogether. Until recently, he hadn't realized the truth behind why his past relationships hadn't worked out. Beth was his destiny, his person, but she belonged to his best friend.

Wetting a washcloth with cool water, Grady wiped his face and neck. He should have taken a shower, but that would have been uncomfortable. There was a level of privacy he needed in order to take care of...certain things.

With a groan, he pushed away from the sink. Today was going to be difficult enough to get through without him at full salute. Plus, Tom's reception wouldn't be so civil. Meditation wasn't going to fix this.

Grady recited the philosophy books he'd studied in college in alphabetical order until he was decent enough to present himself to the Newmans. He'd just finished when there was an icy jolt in the top of his brain. A chill spread through his head before cascading all the way to his toes.

His reflection paled; lungs seized. Beth had gone silent. He scrambled for the thread connecting them and clutched his chest. It was still there, but barely. The Beth-sized space in his heart was almost empty, mostly imprints of a memory. Grady's knees lost strength, dropping him on the toilet lid.

Burying his face in his hands, Grady took a shuddering breath. He stared through the door, trying to figure out what the hell Beth had done?

BETH

BETH HAD AN EXTRA BOUNCE in her step. Perhaps she could talk Tom into getting breakfast in town at the cute little coffee shop on the corner of Bradford and Chestnut. They hadn't been yet, but it was known for its outstanding homemade croissants. It was also a popular go-to place for the staff at Mayes Hill Elementary School.

She stepped into the living room at the same time Grady came from the guest room. He stopped abruptly; his jaw muscles clenched as his gaze bore into hers. Beth forgot what song she was humming.

"Morning, you two," Tom called from the kitchen. "Coffee is brewing."

Beth cleared her throat and continued to the kitchen. Tom turned to wrap his arms around her waist, pecking her lips.

"Hey. Um, I was wondering if you wanted to grab breakfast out?" she asked. The back of her neck prickled as though Grady's glower were a living, breathing entity.

"We can do whatever you feel you're up to doing. You're welcome to—" Tom looked over her shoulder and frowned. "Shit, Grady. What's wrong?"

Grady's knuckles were white where he gripped the kitchen bar. His skin was pale and sweat poured down his face in rivulets. His barrel chest rose and fell with heavy breaths. His blue eyes darkened to near black.

She gulped as Tom went to Grady's side. It's not like she severed their connection or anything.

"Do I need to drive you to the hospital?" Tom asked as he put a hand on Grady's shoulder.

"Don't touch me," Grady growled, swatting the hand away as he backed up and knocked over a bar stool. His gaze stayed on Beth. "Whatever you've done, Beth, it hurts. Stop it, now. Please."

"I..." Beth stared wide-eyed in disbelief. The whites of his eyes were glossy and red. Why was he acting like she'd keyed his truck? "I shut out your thoughts. That's all."

Grady groaned in anguish. He tucked his head between his knees, and tugged at the sides of his curly black hair, sobbing softly. A black bird cawed as it flew past the kitchen window.

Tom stared between them with deep grooves above his brow. "What the hell is going on?" he asked in a calm, steady voice.

"I'm not sure. This morning, I could hear *everything* he was thinking so I blocked his thoughts." Beth's nostrils flared. Her face flashed hot. She crossed her arms over her chest. "It didn't bother me, so I didn't think it'd affect him either."

Tom put his hands on Beth's shoulders. He frowned and sighed. "I'm not happy with any of this, and I don't understand what's going on, but can you *unblock* him? Clearly, it's causing him pain. Grady's had more practice with magic. He may know a less-hurtful way to do it."

Her anger flared once more. She didn't like how Tom sided with Grady, but, then again, he didn't have all the information. She caught the argument before the words left her mouth. Tom was trying to help.

"Please, Beth. I can't...the magic...too strong—" Grady's words were broken. It pinched her heart to see him like this, knowing it was her fault.

Beth nodded and closed her eyes. She opened the hatch on her tank and released her thoughts, banishing the image.

Grady sucked in a harsh breath and shook his head. When he rolled his shoulders back, most of the color had returned to his face. His thoughts came rushing through like a warm breeze. She exhaled slowly. His presence comforted her, but she wouldn't dare to let Grady know. She turned away.

Tom came up behind her. He wrapped his arms around her, putting his chin on her shoulder. "Hey, don't be upset. You had no idea this would happen."

Beth leaned into his embrace, nuzzling his head with hers.

Behind them, Grady cleared his throat. "Beth."

Tom turned them to face Grady. Something dark passed over his somber façade. It made Beth grip Tom's arms harder.

"Yes, Grady?"

"We need to come clean to Tom."

Chapter 28

TOM

"WE NEED TO COME clean to Tom."

The words ricocheted around in his head, smashing his half-mended heart.

Tom didn't want to believe it. Beth *was* cheating on him—with his best friend. It was the most logical explanation for how she tensed in his arms.

Tom's jelly arms fell to his sides. His legs lost feeling at the same time the world tilted on its axis. Muffled shouts came in slow-motion. The wind blew his tears sideways. *This is what dying feels like.*

He waited to hit the floor, but something stopped him. Raising his head, he was met with Grady's worried face. Not guilty—concerned. A ball in Tom's stomach ignited, snapping him back to reality.

Pushing Grady away, Tom used the momentum to gain his footing. He glared at his so-called best friend. How could he betray him and pretend like nothing happened? How could Beth do the same? He didn't know which was worse.

Tom's face was a furnace, radiating from inside and ready to burst. The noisy-ass bird who chose to scream outside their home further grated on his nerves.

"Tom, let me ex—" Grady started, but Tom's fist cracked against his jaw. It was like punching a concrete wall.

Beth screamed, but his rage was overwhelming, shutting out all but him and the liar.

"I trusted you, and you touched my wife! You were my *brother*!" He shook his throbbing hand. Tom brought his fists up, ready to throw another punch. Adrenaline pumped through his veins. He needed to vent. "Stand up and fight me, you bastard!"

Grady was bent at the waist with one hand on his thigh and the other nursing his jaw. He straightened his back and shook his head.

"It's not like that!" Beth shouted, then grasped Tom by his shoulders. "He never touched me!"

"Then, why the hell did you tense up when he said you needed to come clean?" Tom stared holes into Beth's eyes, his chest heaving. She stood her ground, holding his gaze.

"It's complicated." She pinched her brow. "Can we sit down and get everything out in the open?"

Tom studied her intently, searching for any sign of untruth. He was doing it again. Jumping to conclusions before hearing her out. His wrath lessened, remaining a cinder. He still wanted to break something, because those damned words had set him off like a ticking bomb.

"Fine. Explain," Tom commanded, his jaw squeezed tight.

Beth went to the freezer and took out two bags of frozen vegetables. She handed the mixed vegetables to Tom and tossed the peas to Grady.

"Thanks," he mumbled before applying the bag to his jaw. Grady wasn't making eye contact now.

Tom waited on the man to sit before he took the farthest seat.

"First things first," Beth plopped on the stool between them, scooting closer to Tom to face him wholly. "Grady and I are not having an affair."

He studied her, the sincerity of her demeanor instilled confidence. Beth held his gaze until her brows sunk. His chest still felt like he'd laid on a bed of nails and someone stomped on his back.

"Okay," Tom relented firmly. Normally, this was the point when he would hold her hand for support. The thought made his nose sting. He couldn't bring himself to touch her. "So, what is it you have to 'come clean' about?"

"There's a connection between us. Uh, Grady and me. A...thread. It's magical," Beth explained, her brows drew together and mouth screwed up. She glanced at Grady for help.

"What Beth is trying to say, Tom"—Grady flipped the cold bag over to use the other side—"is we are bound by destiny. She and I are light-bringer guardians, appointed by the Goddess. Our job is to keep the evil being, Ja'azul, from breaking free to save the world from absolute destruction."

"Wha—" Tom stopped and rubbed his temples. "Let's put a pin in this Ya-zool whatever and tell me how this 'magically bound' stuff works. When did it start?"

Grady eyed Tom, and peeked at Beth before answering, "A little over three hundred years ago."

"You've got to be kidding," Tom scoffed. He threw his hands up in the air and stood. If they weren't going to take this seriously, he was done. "Look, stop wasting my time and just tell me what the hell is going on. Otherwise, you"—he pointed at Grady—"can leave."

"Tom, please sit down. He's telling the truth," Beth pleaded. She stood and reached for him. Her hesitation was almost enough for him to walk out, but flashes of the hurt from their last fight kept him from bailing.

"Okay, I'll sit but tell me *everything*." Tom stared at Beth before turning to Grady. "No lies. No omissions." When his friend nodded, Tom returned to his seat.

"Three hundred years ago, the previous guardian died before giving birth to the next in line. Her name was Myrtle Brinstar," Grady began, "Her first husband, Josiah Harper, was one of Beth's ancestors. He perished shortly after the birth of their only son, Lucas.

"Then Myrtle met her second husband, Barton Cooper. He was also a guardian and my distant ancestor. They had a son, Solomon, but no daughter, therefore ending the line of female guardians."

Tom felt sick. His mouth had gone dry and his whole body shivered from the stress. All he could do was nod since his tongue was too big for his mouth. Beth called Barton's name in her sleep. Tom prayed it all a coincidence.

"Seven years ago, my magic awoke, and Myrtle was able to communicate with me," Grady continued. He scratched the back of his neck. "Then, last weekend, she told me Beth's powers would awaken soon. It's why we had to go to the Grove, so I could guide her to unlock her power. Unfortunately, Paul and Jeff got in the way."

"So, not only did you know Beth had magic, but you knew she was destined to fight this great evil." Tom had difficulty tamping the lid on his anger. It spewed around the edges. "What was Paul and Jeff's role in this magic stuff? They didn't seem to know y'all had magic either."

"Paul, Jeff, and our fathers serve Ja'azul." Grady's face grew grim. He tossed the bag of peas onto the counter. "As for Beth's magic, I only found out for sure two weeks ago. Myrtle looks a lot like Beth, so I had an inkling."

"Holy shit," Tom whispered, rubbing his face with a hand. "Why didn't you say anything before? About *any* of this?"

"Would you have believed me?" Grady challenged.

Tom thought back in earnest to seven years ago on that fateful day. The thought of sacrificing people for some witch's favor seemed wrong on so many levels. He didn't believe in magic then, so he'd have thought Grady was crazy. But later, after what happened to Gail Cooper. Maybe.

"What about after we found your mom? I'd have believed you then," he answered finally. He tossed his half-thawed mixed veg on the countertop.

Grady studied the bag of peas, rolling one between his fingers through the plastic. "Maybe. I dunno. Never could find a right time to bring it up, I reckon."

"You reckon, huh? You had plenty of opportunities," Tom scoffed. He needed to know more. "So, if you and Beth are guardians, what exactly does that job entail?"

"Well," Grady sighed, the bags under his eyes had darkened. "First, I'll need to teach Beth how to properly use her magic. Then, we need to stop our dads."

"Do you have anything to add, Beth?" Tom was concerned with how quiet she'd been.

"Um, well, Myrtle said there is a prophecy. Ja'azul will be freed and there is one who will have the power to stop it." Beth wasn't making eye contact. His stomach sank like the Titanic. "She also said that if you and I are intimate—now that my magic is no longer dormant—it'll slowly kill you."

"What do you mean your *magic* will slowly kill me?" Tom's heart cracked again.

Painfully, he managed to swallow and cradled her face in his hands. "Beth, honey, I don't plan on dying any time soon. We're gonna be together forever. You and me against the world."

He wiped the tears from Beth's face and gave her a weak smile. Grady cleared his throat. What little hope he had recaptured from his spiel dispersed like smoke snaking through his fingers.

"There's one more thing. The prophesied one, the one with the power to stop Ja'azul, isn't Beth," Grady added and dropped his head.

"That's not what Myrtle told me," Beth argued. "She said I was the one prophesied."

"The prophesy said the savior will be a child born of magic, Beth. We all know your parents don't fit the bill." Grady's voice was tired and gravely.

A knot formed in Tom's stomach. He wasn't stupid. Tom went to rest his elbow on the countertop and missed, falling off his stool.

"Tom." Beth sniffled and reached for him. He pulled away and shook his head. Fresh tears rolled down her cheeks. "I love you more than anything. I didn't want to say anything until we knew more because I didn't want you to worry—"

"It's my place to worry, Beth. Sickness and health...until death do us part. Or did those words not mean the same thing to you?" Tom shouted in reply, pain lacing his voice. He cringed at the insult and quickly looked away.

Hell, he was mad. Magic or no magic, Beth had every reason not to trust him after endangering her life. Her words only cut deeper because he was still raw from thinking she was unfaithful.

"Look, we didn't ask for this, so don't take it out on her." Grady jumped off the stool, frowning as his chest heaved. He was on Tom in a split second. His growly voice started low and grew to a roar, "You have no idea how much pain she is in knowing the man she loves will die just by being with her. She's devastated, and if you could feel even an ounce of what I do—"

"That's part of the problem, isn't it, Grady?" Tom interrupted, jumping up from his chair to stare the man down.

The defeat in Grady's eyes was crystal clear. Tom winced. This was his best friend, his chosen family; he would never betray Tom. Not on purpose. Tom took a deep breath. The raging storm inside him subsided to a rumble.

"I would do anything for my wife; you know that without being able to read my mind," Tom said quietly, slumping back onto the stool and burying his head in his hands. "But y'all need to keep me informed. I may not be much help magically, but I'll do what I can."

The pulsing behind his eyes was too loud, and it made his stomach churn. This day couldn't get any worse.

Beth's arms wound around him from behind. Warm, wet spots tickled the spot between his shoulder blades. She whispered, "I'm sorry my communication wires got crossed. Please don't be mad. I promise to do better."

Call him a fool, but he believing her was easier than trying to cobble together an end table from scrap parts, which was how he felt with the information overload.

Tom sighed and turned so he could face Beth. Her arms went limp until he slipped his around her waist, keeping her from escaping. "I'm...processing. It'll take some time, but I'll come around."

Beth's cheeks rounded as a hopeful grin spread. "Okay. And when I learn something new, I'll keep you in the loop."

"That's all I ask." Tom placed a quick kiss on the corner of her lips before turning to Grady.

His best friend looked anywhere but at them. Sometime during this weekend, Grady lost his signature Zen-like chill. He was almost folded in on himself, making his solidly built friend look smaller.

Beth became heavy in his arms as she went limp. His sluggish brain was no help, but his muscles worked on instinct to catch her before they tumbled to the floor. He lowered them so his back was propped against the kitchen island/bar.

"Oh, shit. Beth?" Tom tapped her cheek. She was unresponsive, so he looked at Grady. "What the hell just happened?"

"She needs food," Grady growled as he dashed to the kitchen. Cabinet doors and drawers slammed loudly.

With everything that happened this morning, they'd forgotten to eat. She often skipped breakfast except on weekends but never fainted. Whatever was happening had to be magical.

"Please," Tom begged as he pulled her into his chest. "Honey, wake up. You gotta be okay."

The microwave beeped.

Tom scooped Beth up bridal style and stood on shaking legs. He laid her on the couch and tucked a few of the fancy throw pillows she liked under her head. He sat next to her and held her hand, stroking her forehead.

Grady came around the bar with a bowl of steaming oatmeal. He gently blew on it while stirring.

"Beth, baby, you need to eat." Tom commanded roughly. Beth wasn't moving and his throat was clogged.

Grady knelt beside them. "Open her mouth. We'll have to feed her."

Tom carefully pried her mouth open, and Grady tipped the spoon. The oatmeal slid inside, but Beth's mouth remained slack. Tom plugged her nose with his fingers until her jaw worked slowly, letting go so she could swallow. Grady had another spoon ready.

After a few bites, her instincts kicked in, though she was still out of it.

The house phone rang. Tom swore. His gaze met Grady's. He didn't want to leave Beth's side, but the phone rang again. "Be right back."

Tom jumped up and bolted into the kitchen. The name on the caller ID, Mayes Hill Elementary, made him swear again.

Quick breaths in and out. Tom plastered on a smile and answered on the third ring, "Newman residence, Tom speaking."

"Hello, Tom! This is Peggy from Mayes Hill Elementary. How are you today?" the woman asked with a cheerful southern drawl.

"I'm good, Ms. Peggy," Tom replied and cleared his throat. "I assume you're calling for Beth." He looked at Grady for some help, but he was focused on feeding her. Worry still clouded his friend's face.

"Yes! May I please speak to her? It shouldn't take very long. Principal Arnold has some questions for Mrs. Newman before I email her roster and our schedule for the new school year," Peggy answered in a well-practiced, professional speech.

"We just got back from a camping trip, and she's taking a nap," Tom asked, running a hand through his hair. "If you could email the questions, too, that'd be great."

"Sure! I'll include them with the other stuff." Peggy's fingers clacked rapidly on the keyboard. "It'll be waiting in her inbox when she gets up. We'll need her reply by Friday."

"I'll make sure she gets it. Thanks, Ms. Peggy," Tom replied, hanging up and rubbing his tired face with both hands.

He'd forgotten the mundane things they were still expected to do. Most people weren't aware of the existence of magic, shapeshifters, or evil entities. The thought caused his shoulders to slump.

Tom headed back to the couch. Grady tenderly stroked Beth's cheek when he lifted another spoonful of oatmeal. The action was so loving, it awoke the prehistoric need to claim his woman. When Grady's understanding gaze met his, Tom shoved it back down. They were all victims here.

He stopped at Beth's side, watching her lips part. While she chewed, Beth's eyes opened. Her gaze found Grady's first, then Tom's. With a heavy blink, they closed again.

Tom didn't need to be connected to his best friend to know Grady was hopelessly in love with his wife. He tried to put himself in Grady's shoes, unable to have the woman he loved, struggling to keep on his side of the line. It sucked, but he couldn't help but be resentful. It was a foreign feeling. They had been thick as thieves most of their lives.

Beth, on the other hand, had never thought of Grady in a romantic sense. Whatever magical love linked her to Grady, she still chose Tom. It was the only thing that kept him sane.

At least neither Beth nor Grady wanted to change the dynamic between their trio.
For now, his inner demons chimed.

Unfortunately, Tom knew his weaknesses all too well. Beth was his greatest. He'd be waiting for Grady to step over that line, and when he did, it would be a day of reckoning.

A small smile curled up on Beth's lips. "Thank you. Both of you."

She drifted back into whatever meditative state she'd been in. Her passing out was as clear as a flashing neon sign. She needed to learn how to control her power, which meant she needed to spend more time with their best friend.

Tom's jaw clenched.

Grady cleared his throat and stood, handing the bowl of oatmeal to Tom. "Here. She should be fine in a few hours. Just let her sleep it off. I'm gonna head home to do the same."

Deep worry lines and a furrowed brow marred his friend's face. Taking the bowl from

Grady, he put a hand on the man's shoulder. "Thank you for being strong, and, well, for everything. I promise we'll figure something out."

Grady nodded sadly and slipped out of the door. His truck engine started a few minutes later and tires crunched on asphalt. The rumble grew smaller until it joined the cacophony of lingering tourists.

Tom sighed in relief.

Taking back his spot on the couch, Tom continued feeding Beth until she'd eaten every last bite. He swept a stray hair from her face and stood.

Beth grabbed his hand, studying him through half-lidded eyes. Their usual deep fern green had faded to a light sage.

"Please don't go," she pleaded in a weak voice. "Stay with me."

His heart leapt with joy. Beth continued to choose him.

"Of course." Tom put the dish on the coffee table and smiled.

Kissing her forehead, Tom lay down on the couch beside her, pulling her close. She took a deep breath and sighed happily into his chest before mumbling something. He didn't need to hear the words to know what Beth said.

"I love you, too," Tom replied in a whisper. Kissing the top of her head, he held onto the moment like it was their last.

Chapter 29

GRADY

As soon as his tires hit the road, Grady lost it. His heart split open, soaking the front of his shirt. Tom could barely look at him without glowering. Beth could hardly look at him, period.

That stubborn woman, goddess bless her. She thought she'd filtered her thoughts, kept her feelings for him locked tight. Once she opened back up, Grady knew. He wasn't making shit up because he wanted love so badly it hurt his soul. Gods be damned, Beth loved him, and not platonically.

He should have been ecstatic, but it was another sucker punch the universe had served him. This was his penance for not helping the victim who haunts his nightmares. His comeuppance for turning a blind eye to the other victims over the years.

The streets were quiet for a Monday afternoon. One hand gripped the steering wheel, the other shielded his face from passersby. No one needed to see his sorry state. Every damn cell in his body ached for Beth, draining the energy he had left. His home library might yield some answers to keeping their thread from being so *potent*. Beth didn't seem to be as affected by the magnetic pull. Could've been her magic wasn't developed enough.

By the time he pulled into his driveway, their connection was pulled tight like a string wound around a dowel too many times. Beth's loneliness slipped through. Grady squeezed the steering wheel a few times.

She misses me.

Grady forced the smugness into a cage and got out of his truck. As he made his way to the front door, he flipped through the keys on the ring. His arms were too heavy as he pushed through to the entryway, kicking the door shut. He tossed the keys on the console table and listened. The house was eerily quiet and lonely compared to Beth and Tom's apartment. The cloud of cigarette smoke that normally hung around the ceiling was also missing.

Good.

Grady wasn't in the mood for a confrontation with his old man. Louis preferred bending metal to his will rather than spend time with his son. Grady was grateful. They'd never been close. He'd only stayed because of his mom. After she died, Grady still couldn't leave. He'd rather be close to where she was buried, and to Tom and Beth.

He ambled toward the living room when his panther senses kicked in, freezing his legs. Grady tilted his head, listening for the intruder. Nothing. He searched, room by room, sniffing and tasting the air. He got a mouthful of stale cigarettes and cheap whiskey before ending up in the kitchen. Grady was still in stealth mode when he crept out the back door and checked the protective spells he'd placed around the house. Their faint orange glow remained, untouched.

His gut still swirled with unease. Grady hadn't eaten anything besides what he'd hunted the night before they left the Grove. It was probably stress and hunger.

Grady rummaged around the fridge, finding enough deli meat for a modest sandwich. He unzipped the package and gave it the sniff test. Seemed alright. There were a few slices of cheese, but he'd have to scrape the mayonnaise jar with a spatula.

He shut the fridge door with his foot and offloaded his fridge forage onto the counter. Out of the corner of his eye, a whitish translucent-looking form appeared. He jumped backward, hands up.

The spectre didn't attack or move. Grady stared at it for a long time, convinced he was hallucinating when it finally turned.

"Hey, Grady," Jeff said. His voice was wispy and far away as though he stood behind a thick curtain. Jeff looked to where his feet should be, but his legs faded away below the knees. Looking back at Grady, Jeff mumbled, "Dude, I think I died."

"Holy shit." Grady swallowed the mango-sized lump in his throat past the racing horses thumping against his chest.

Without taking his eyes off the ghost, Grady crept over. Jeff's eyes weren't glowing red, he had no black cloud surrounding him, and no long razor-like claws. Jeff was a legit ghost.

"I think you're right." Grady asked, the philosopher in him was reconsidering the notions of life after death. "Do you remember what happened to you?"

"I dunno. Last thing I recall was somethin' angry with glowing red eyes coming for me." Jeff paused. He had a faraway look on his face. "Oh, Paul was there, and I think my soul is missing."

Grady ran both hands through his hair. Jeff must have gone back to his car after he died. Once they started home, he probably hitched a ride back to town. Jeff was closer to him than Tom and Beth. It must've been why Jeff's ghost showed up at his dad's house.

"Do you have a message for me?" Grady asked finally. If Paul had a hand in Jeff's death, maybe he left him with one.

The ghost went still for a moment, and the room grew dark. Grady's senses went crazy when Paul's voice came from the shadows. It was like listening to an old cassette tape recording. He chanted a dark spell that Grady recognized. A powerful soul-binding incantation. As soon as it was finished, the light returned to normal. Jeff's dead, white ghost eyes stared at him. "Paul bound my soul for Ja'azul, the dark one. The bastard."

Grady frowned in concentration. He'd heard of the Dark Ones during his studies, but in which library? Running to the living room, Grady forgot about Ghost Jeff and his hunger in his quest to find the volume of Appalachian Folklore that mentioned the ancient gods. Skimming the spines of several books, Grady finally found the one he was looking for. His eyes darted over the pages, frantically searching for any mention of The Dark Ones or Ja'azul.

At the end of the book, Grady slammed it closed with a frustrated groan. When he looked up to think, Grady's hands flew up and his muscles jerked wildly. Jeff's ghost silently floated next to him. He clutched his chest when Beth reached out via telepathy, "*Are you okay?*"

It was a simple gesture to most people, but, to Grady, it meant the world. "*I'm alright, but Jeff is dead,*" he responded. He sensed her confusion, but she left it alone. As trivial as their interaction was, the corner of his mouth curled slightly.

"You've got to get to my soul before *he* does," Jeff said as his spectral form floated nearby, skimming the titles of the books on Grady's shelf. "Ja'azul only needs four to be freed."

"Wait, what? Four souls?" Grady repeated. The pounding in his chest picked up. They were running out of time. With creeping alarm, he demanded, "How the fu—never mind. Jeff, where's yours? Can you sense it or what it's bound to?"

The spectre turned back to face him. "Yeah, I think so." As soon as he answered, Jeff disappeared.

Swearing under his breath, Grady kicked himself for being so stupid. Alive, Jeff was never the brightest in the bunch. Death hadn't changed that.

Gathering books, research papers, and spell components, he stuffed them in a duffel bag on the way to his bedroom. Grady added a few clean outfits to the bag, along with anything else that looked helpful. The zipper echoed in the room as he pulled it shut.

Jeff popped up beside Grady, nearly giving him a heart attack. "Goddammit, Jeff! You can't keep doing that," he yelled, rubbing his temple. He tried to calm his breathing while convincing Beth that he wasn't in danger.

"Sorry, Grady." The ghost looked at him with sad eyes. "I'm not used to being a ghost."

Grady sighed and shook his head. "It's alright. Just make a noise or something. Announce yourself when you pop up, so I know it's you, okay?"

Jeff's spectral form glowed brighter as he smiled. "Sure, yeah. I can do that." He waited while Grady gathered his bags before adding, "Oh, yeah. I found my soul."

Grady stopped in the doorway. He swallowed the thick mucus that had built up in his mouth. "Where?"

"The signed baseball grandpa gave me." Jeff sighed. "Paul put my soul there. It's underneath the stone ritual slab."

Grady dropped the bags to the floor and rubbed his face. *Of course, it is,* he thought. The dread from earlier morphed into panicked fear. He chuckled bitterly. Looks like he'd be taking lunch to go.

For half a second, he considered letting Beth and Tom know where he was going. It was too dangerous, and Beth was still recovering. They needed to practice finding her limitations and learning how to draw energy from sources other than herself. For now, it'd be safer for him to go alone. To make sure Beth didn't follow, Grady pictured a brick wall between them.

He locked up the house and tossed his bags into the front floorboard of his truck. Once Jeff's ghost took a seat, Grady shook his head at the absurdity of it and drove away.

Grady steeled himself, trying not to think about what he was about to do to Beth. He wasn't entirely sure what would happen to their connection when they were so far away.

I'm so sorry, my love, but this is the only way.

Chapter 30

BETH

She awoke surrounded by a Tom's comforting warmth. Despite the heavy sorrow burrowing into her chest, a smile graced Beth's lips at seeing the sleepy, stormy-gray eyes of her husband staring back.

"How long were we asleep?"

"About an hour, I think." Tom kissed the tip of her nose before reaching behind him. He came back with his cell in hand. "Yep. It's lunch time."

Beth swept the lock of hair from his eyes, then cradled his face, drawing him in for a kiss. There was a light thud as something fell onto the fluffy rug. Tom snaked his free arm around her waist, sending the butterflies in her stomach fluttering when he pulled her body flush against his. Her arms moved around his shoulders to bring him as close as possible.

Having nothing between their skin was suddenly a priority.

When Tom pulled away for air, she whimpered in protest.

He chuckled. "As much as I enjoy waking up like this, we shouldn't neglect lunch. We'll have plenty of time for more of this later."

To drive his meaning home, he shifted his hips against her core, stoking the flames. The lustful longing mirrored in his eyes reminded her of what would happen if they went further. Either he'd forgotten Myrtle's warning or didn't take it seriously.

"Yes. Later, hon." Beth cleared her throat and pushed herself away from Tom. "Want me to heat up leftover pizza on the griddle?"

He studied her with a slight frown. She smoothed the broken moment with a quick peck as she got off the couch.

He swung his legs over the couch and reached for his fallen cell, not breaking eye contact. "You sure you feel up to it, hon? I can reheat pizza without burning it. Probably."

"I can do this," she answered, biting back her watery eyes.

Standing, Tom pocketed his phone and cupped her cheeks. His gentle gaze searched her face before pressing his lips onto her forehead. He inhaled deeply before pulling her into a hug.

"Okay," he whispered into the curve of her neck.

Tom's embrace engulfed her. When he sniffled, she tightened her arms. Clearly, he hadn't forgotten, and she'd hurt his feelings by pulling away. Her chest was too tight, but she held onto Tom, rocking to a slow song only their souls could hear.

The thread connecting her to Grady vibrated like a plucked string. Beth gasped and closed her eyes, listening to hear if he was trying to tell her something.

Tom pulled back. "What's wrong?"

"Grady. I think he was scared." She pursed her lips, bringing her brows together. "I'm sure he'll let us know if it's something serious."

"Probably," Tom agreed, though his frown returned.

Beth rubbed Tom's back on her way to reheat lunch. It was odd having the constant pressure of something tugging at her sternum. She rubbed her chest, wondering what Grady was doing.

Tom moved past her, placing a hand on her hip as he gathered plates to set the table. Her cheeks heated when he caught her staring, but not for the reason he thought.

"Like what you see?" He winked with a cheeky grin.

"I do, but don't get any ideas. The pizza will be done any second."

Tom set the plates on the counter and caged her in. "We can work up an appetite first."

Beth nipped at his bottom lip, causing him to groan. As his lips pressed into hers, Beth felt another jolt from Grady and pushed at Tom's chest.

"Wait."

"Again?" Tom asked, eyeing her while his jaw ticked. His fingers dug into her backside, not in a hurtful way, but more possessive.

Beth nodded and closed her eyes. Grady gently blew her off, promising he was fine.

"I asked if he was okay. He said something about Jeff being dead."

Tom grunted before returning to his task. The timer for the food beeped. The scent of melted cheese and spicy sausage made her stomach growl.

"Go sit. I'll get it," Tom commanded with a chin raise. His gaze looked like a thunderstorm would erupt any minute.

Beth kissed his chin dimple before settling in at the bar. Tom sat their plates down and kissed the top of her head as he took the stool next to her. The silence as they ate was like eating in high altitude, but the only way to rid her stomach of nausea was to eat. She'd forced the last bite down when there was a metaphysical yank against the thread. It felt as though it was wrapped around her heart and being yanked through her ribcage.

"Tom, it's Grady again. Something's not right."

"What did he say this time?" Tom asked, throwing his napkin down on the counter.

He jumped up and scooped their sneakers off the floor next to the door.

"Nothing." Beth shook her head. "It felt like he was having a heart attack."

Once their shoes were laced, they headed out. Tom handed her a protein bar and water bottle as they left. "Just in case."

"Thanks, hon."

Grady lived on the other side of town, about five miles away. Tom took to the side streets instead of going through the middle of town. The closer they got, the more Beth could sense Grady's unease. When he went calm and quiet, she tried calling his cell multiple times. He wasn't answering.

"Not picking up, either?" Tom asked as they neared the next turn, three blocks from the Cooper's house. He barely came to a stop before turning onto the next street.

Beth gripped the seat belt strap across her chest. Grady was moving away from them, fast. Their string was pulled so tightly she could barely feel it.

Then…it was gone.

She sucked in a deep breath, unprepared for the utter emptiness rushing into his space in her soul. It was as if someone had taken an ice cream scoop to her insides. She sobbed, trying desperately to grasp onto him or find some trace of where he had gone.

Is this how Grady felt when I shut him out?

Beth swore she'd never do it again.

When they pulled into Grady's empty driveway, Tom's jaw clenched and dark clouded his features. Without a word, he cut the ignition and used the spare house key Grady had given him to go inside. Beth followed closely as they frantically searched room to room for any clue of what happened. They found nothing.

Tom stood in the middle of the living room with his fingers laced behind his head, staring out the window. Beth couldn't focus with the gaping hole in her chest. Being surrounded by the scent of wood stain and cedar didn't help either. Instead, she retraced their short telepathic conversation in case she missed something.

"Jeff. Grady said something about Jeff." Beth looked around the room. "Do you think he took Grady?"

"No?" Tom raised an eyebrow. "Didn't Grady say he was dead?"

Beth sighed and slumped onto the couch. "I don't know what to do."

"Maybe he read something and needed to work?" Tom sat down and rubbed her back. The gesture was nice. It helped to take the edge of the pain in her chest. "You know how hyper-focused Grady gets when he's into a project."

"I do, but," Beth paused. She didn't want to tell Tom that there was a hole in her heart twice the size of Texas and it threatened to collapse her whole torso unless Grady was within walking distance. "Why did he go off without telling us first?"

"I don't know, Beth. Could be as simple as a grocery run." Tom tilted his head back, staring at the popcorn ceiling as his jaw worked and the muscles in his neck flexed. "Or, could be he needed space. Whatever the reason, we should probably just leave him alone."

Her airways closed and her face prickled with needles. No. Leaving Grady alone wasn't *right*. It was the opposite of what she should do.

"Myrtle!" Beth sputtered. "We're both connected to her! She said I could summon her if I needed help. This counts."

Tom buried his face in his hands with a long sigh and mumbled, "What can I do to help?"

"Close all the curtains and blinds, please."

When Tom stood, Beth rolled onto her back on the couch and made herself cozy, closing her eyes. The lights dimmed and Beth pictured the cottage, focusing on Myrtle. She called out in the darkness of her mind, and a small light flickered ahead. Beth walked toward the warm glow, and as it grew the path opened into a serene forest. Not much farther, the cottage appeared. Myrtle stood in the garden with her hands clasped in front.

"Hello, Beth," Myrtle greeted her with a hug and a warm smile. "I didn't expect to see you so soon. How are things with Grady?"

Beth's smile faltered. "He's why I'm here. Grady's missing, and we're worried he may be in danger. I was hoping you could help us find him."

Myrtle looked confused. "Can you not use your connection to find him?"

Beth looked away; her cheeks burned. "No. The farther he is from me, the less I feel him. He's so far away that the connection is gone. I didn't know what else to do," she explained, the tears falling freely.

"The connection is not gone, child, but you *must* finish it. I can sense you were close, but something—or someone—held you back," Myrtle replied. The cunning gleam in her eye told Beth she already knew the truth.

"But I'll lose Tom," Beth said quietly. She regretted coming here. Magic had saved her life a few times, but it was threatening to take so much more.

"You must if there is any hope for the future of this world!" Myrtle grasped Beth by the shoulders firmly. "Time is relative, Beth, but it is not a luxury you have...not yet anyway. Complete your bond with Grady and learn the ways of magic. Defeat Ja'azul the Dark One as the prophecy foretold."

Beth's heart collapsed. She understood the magnitude of what Myrtle said, but she felt like there were missing pieces. Beth sighed, adding her own condition, "I will complete the bond, but only after Tom and I spend what time we have left together. My heart will always belong to him."

Myrtle's eyes narrowed and her upper lip curled like she'd smelled something foul. "Do what you will, but remember your choice when the consequences come due."

"I'm not a stranger to paying my dues," Beth replied, straightening her back.

Myrtle gave her a curt nod and turned away. Her caramel hair swayed in the breeze. "Grady is here—in the Grove."

When Beth opened her eyes, Tom wiped her cheeks with his thumbs. He looked like a kid who was just told Santa Clause wasn't real.

"What did Myrtle say?" he asked in a low voice.

"Grady returned to the forest," Beth croaked. "He's back at the Grove."

Unease settled over her like an itchy insecurity blanket. She didn't want to go back to the woods, not so soon. But Grady needed them.

Chapter 31

GRADY

GRADY PULLED HIS TRUCK into an empty parking spot and threw the handle to park. Every fiber of his being screamed with the need to return to Beth. He white-knuckled the steering wheel so hard his fingers were surely stuck. For good measure, he dug his toes into his boots and ground them into the floorboard.

He thought the task of finding Jeff's soul would shield him from the misery of being disconnected from Beth. He'd never been more wrong. His heart was like glass, cracking and breaking off slowly, painfully, until it would eventually turn to dust.

With a pained grunt, Grady peeled his fingers away from the steering wheel. He grabbed his two bags and locked his truck before heading toward the path. Grady would've welcomed the serenity, but it was a false peace. He was here for answers, and they were at his library in the Grove. The slowed time bubble would allow him to research how to shield their bond and possibly how to release Jeff's soul.

Grady adjusted the straps on his backpack and slung the duffel bag over his shoulder. The thicket led him to the same trail he'd used for years after finding out about his heritage. He was surprised the path wasn't worn more than a typical game trail. Unlike the obvious dirt path leading to the ritual stone.

Aside from the occasional ruffle of leaves and bird song, the forest remained relatively quiet. The woods were darker than usual, as if the light were coming through a filter. This shroud would be unrecognizable to regular folks, but he was acutely aware of the dark one's influence, however faint.

Pulling the mossy curtain aside, Grady stepped between the stones with a small smile. This was his secret sanctuary. A safe space for studying the magical arts without any outside interference. He'd spent countless days here, learning from Myrtle and putting it into practice.

As soon as he stepped into the clearing, the warm sun hit his face. Grady closed his eyes and breathed deep. The thought of how much Beth would enjoy coming here to practice magic hit him like a pop-up thunderstorm. He doubled over, grabbing his chest as the cracks in his heart grew. They'd continue to crumble until he either died or went back to his beloved. Grady hoped he finished his research before the former.

Sweat dripped down Grady's face as he straightened. Putting one foot in front of the other was like walking through molasses. Eventually, he stumbled toward the twin cabins. There was so much work to do. He couldn't afford to get distracted again.

TOM

DRIVING THROUGH THE NORTH Carolina scenic hills, trees whizzed by as Tom focused on the road. They'd been on the road for over an hour, but Grady had a solid head start.

Beth stared out the window. He'd peek out the corner of his eye to find her picking at the hem of her shirt or wringing her hands. The closer they got to Grady, the less fidgety she became. She was the compass, and Grady was North.

The realization made Tom's palms sweaty and the neck of his shirt too tight. They'd hardly spoken a word, but Tom held her hand most of the way. Occasionally, he'd give it a gentle squeeze. Beth would smile in return.

Worrying about Grady was normal. He left that for Beth. Tom only had room for fury. That morning, they'd promised to keep each other in the loop. Then Grady left and kept interrupting Tom's tender moments with Beth. The worst part was how his best friend flippantly hurt her in a way Tom couldn't fix. It was unacceptable.

He wanted to be connected to Beth, to *feel* her every emotion. To be the only man she loved. When he and Grady were growing up, Tom never had a problem sharing. But Beth wasn't a possession. She was his *wife* by mutual choice. They promised each other forever in front of God, family, and friends.

Until death do us part.

According to some random witch's ghost, death would come swiftly. All Grady had to do was wait.

Before resentment took hold, Tom stuffed it inside the bulging box that resided in the darkest corner of his mind. It groaned, waiting to burst the second he lacked the energy to keep it all contained.

The twisted bright spot Tom clung to: Grady wasn't as perfect as he let on.

He secretly hoped Beth would notice, making Grady less in her eyes. It was a petty thing to want, but this situation kept eating at him.

"We're here," Tom murmured as he pulled onto the short dirt road that took them to the trailhead.

Beth sat up and placed her hands on the dashboard. When they saw Grady's truck, she craned her neck to see if he was still there. Of course it was empty, but Beth sat back with a huff as Tom pulled in next to it. He fought against frowning at her reaction.

Tom cut the engine and turned to his wife. He had a strong inkling Beth had feelings for Grady. Rather than admit it aloud, Tom held to the immature fantasy that her attraction was purely magical.

He cupped her chin and traced her cheek with his thumb. "Hey. I've got you, no matter what."

Tom hoped the encouraging smile would ease her worries somewhat, but the woman staring back at him looked like she had the flu. He shouldn't have driven after Grady. What if something happened and Beth was unable to protect them?

His poker face melted. He'd done it again, put his wife in danger because he didn't think.

"Maybe we should go back. Let you rest some more."

"I'll be alright, hon. We brought food and water," Beth reminded him with a half-grin. "Let's go find out why Grady left in a hurry, okay?"

Tom tucked a lock of hair behind her ear. There was no talking her out of leaving Grady to deal on his own. Tom had to be strong. Beth *needed* him to be. If he refused, she'd go by herself. Tom swallowed his jealousy. "Whatever we find in there, just remember, we can conquer it together."

Beth nodded and leaned in. Tom met her halfway to share a sweet kiss before resting their foreheads together.

"You ready?" she asked.

"No, but I'll do what I need to," Tom replied with a grim grin, grabbing one last peck before they exited the vehicle with their bags in hand.

The further they trudged into the woods, the more Beth's natural spark returned. She moved with purpose, and her normal pinkish color returned. However, unseen things in the forest tested their mettle, causing the hair on the back of his neck to stand on end. Beth seemed to know which path took them away from danger. He couldn't see anything but trees, but he was certain something watched from the shadows.

"Just ignore it and keep moving," Beth whispered, squeezing his hand.

Faint whispers followed the early setting sun. They were close to the Grove's entrance, but with dusk setting in, he'd have to rely on Beth to get them there.

"This way." Beth pulled him along.

Tom wanted a quick rest, but the thought of stopping made his heart race and his legs wanted to move faster. The path opened to a sparser forest. There, ahead, was the moss-covered stone.

Beth spared a look over her shoulder and beamed. "Almost there."

"I'm with you all the way." Tom's grin was flat, but hers was like the sun.

He was just glad Beth was back to her normal chipper self. It'd make him think twice about giving Grady a matching bruise on his chiseled face.

Chapter 32

GRADY

GRADY EASED THE BOOK shut. His chest tingled, pulled, like someone tugging a fishing line but the hook was buried behind his ribs. Beth had breached the Grove's barrier.

Beth would either be spitting fire or giving him the cold shoulder.

"Stubborn woman," he murmured, pushing away from the table.

Despite the frown, Grady's heart betrayed him, fluttering at the thought of seeing his beloved. He tamed the curly mop of hair with his fingers and took a deep breath before going outside.

Beth crested the hill. Her honey-colored hair shimmered like an amber beacon against the sunlight. Grady's stomach somersaulted...until Tom appeared. He'd forgotten for a blissful moment that they were a package deal.

Grady settled his gut with a heavy breath and reset his frown. As they neared, he dropped his defenses, bracing for impact.

Beth's fists were clenched at her sides. He grunted when her fury rolled over him amid the tempest of other circling emotions. His chest buckled under the pressure.

How can she feel so much all at once and still be standing?

Grady shouldn't have shut her out and left without an explanation. At least when she did it, good intentions were involved. He had no excuse other than he was an asshole.

"Grady Alan Cooper." Beth marched up to him, her chin wobbled, twisting the knife in his heart. "You're clearly okay."

"What are you two doing here?" Grady demanded, ignoring Beth's glare.

The butterflies swarming in his stomach didn't care. She dropped her fists to cross her arms over her chest.

"Beth thought you had a heart attack," Tom scoffed. "You can't just block Beth and leave like that. It was a shitty thing to do after this morning, and you know it."

"I'm sorry," Grady said quietly, glancing at Beth before addressing the ground at their feet, "I wouldn't have come back here if it wasn't important. But, now that you're here, we're *all* in danger."

"What kind of danger are we in *now*?" Beth came to Tom's side, slipping her arm through his. Grady's butterflies turned to angry bees. "Myrtle said we have a couple of decades before the big bad pops."

"While that could still be the case, I'm not so sure anymore." Grady furrowed his brows. It was best to toss them in the deep end. "Unfortunately, Paul was taking second helpings. He tied Jeff's soul—"

Right on cue, Jeff popped up next to Tom with a "Boop."

Beth and Tom startled, and Grady smirked.

"Hey, Beth and Tom," Ghost Jeff greeted as they stared, catching flies with their dropped jaws.

"Come with me. I'll explain everything." Grady held out his arm, pointing toward the twin cabins. When Beth scowled, he added softly, "Please."

Tom gave Beth a peck on the cheek and took off toward the cabins, talking Jeff's ghost ears off. Grady waited for Beth. Finally, she gave him a curt nod and walked past. He fell in beside her, hoping their fingers would brush. Beth kept a careful distance, watching Tom talk animatedly with ghost Jeff. The silence between them was deafening.

Grady couldn't stand it anymore. "Beth, I really am sorry. I shouldn't have left you like that. I didn't want to come here, but I needed you to be safe."

"Grady." Beth stopped and sighed like she does when she hasn't had coffee all day. "You know more about any of this magic stuff than any of us. I need *you* to help me understand it, to control it. You can't do that if you die." She roughly wiped the tears from her eyes and let out a shuddered breath.

Grady gripped her shoulders and ducked to look at her square on. "I know. And it was stupid. I thought I was doing right by y'all."

His thumbs caressed the sliver of exposed skin at the curve of her neck. Beth shivered. The icy stare she gave him melted.

"Fine. Just don't make a habit of being a jerk."

"I'll try, but you know what they say about teaching an old dog new tricks."

"Asshole," Beth mumbled playfully. She rolled her eyes and opened her arms.

Grady accepted the offered truce. He wrapped his arms around her the way he used to, but everything had changed. He wanted to drown himself in Beth's comfort as it penetrated the loneliness suffocating him. This woman was his security blanket, the missing piece of his soul. She was his reason to be the best version of himself, and his hope for the future.

The unfettered, magical connection was warm, reaching for Beth with swirling, lazy tendrils. The moment Beth's brushed against his, she stepped back. The connection receded, but Grady recognized the longing reflected in Beth's beautiful green eyes while he stood there shaking.

"Not yet," she whispered, looking over Grady's shoulder. "I'm not shortening my time with Tom."

Grady yearned for this woman. Everything he'd read about these magical ties to your destined soulmate said it was such a mighty, magnetic force that couldn't be stopped. Beth had broken all their rules. She'd stopped the connection from becoming permanent *twice*. He'd never had to struggle so persistently to keep his emotions in check. Knowing she had difficulty suppressing her feelings helped him keep from unraveling further.

Despite his aching heart, Grady nodded. He couldn't muster the energy to form words without breaking apart. Though he seemed okay outwardly, on the inside another small part of him withered.

BETH

GRADY'S HEARTACHE WAS CONTAGIOUS, but Beth had no words of solace. They would live in harmonic misery until Tom left this world. Her heart bled, torn between the love she fights for and the one she wars against.

Beth trudged along, letting her fingertips graze the tops of wheatgrass. She looked up to find Tom standing alone at the top of the hill. Ghost Jeff must have wandered off.

Where does he go when he's not hanging around here?

The thought flew from her mind when Tom locked eyes with her. His jaw twitched. Her cheeks flushed as she tucked a stray hair behind her ear. He must have seen her and Grady hug it out.

When Beth stopped next to Tom, he held out his hand. She wrapped her fingers around his and gave him a tentative grin. The light squeeze eased her worries.

Grady ignored them, going straight inside the cabin. The door slammed shut behind him.

"You okay?" Tom asked, taking her other hand in his. They were warm and soft. Smooth. His thumbs caressed the tops of her hands.

"Mm-hmm." Beth replied, glancing toward the cabin as if she could see Grady through the wooden walls. "He's having more difficulty adjusting than I am. I don't know what we're gonna do, Tom."

"We're gonna take advantage of the time we have left together because we don't know how long that will be." He dropped her hands to wrap his arms around her waist.

Beth's hands automatically went to Tom's biceps before slipping up to his shoulders. She should tell him what Myrtle said, but how would a 'maybe' timeline help anyone?

"Hon, you know what I mean." Beth frowned in thought. She inhaled slowly. "We can't leave Grady in a constant state of melancholy. If we get into another fight, we can't afford to be distracted."

Tightening his hold, Tom's warm breath fanned across her face. His minty freshness didn't fully cover the scent of garlicky tomato sauce and pepperoni. "Then what are you suggesting we do? You know I'd do anything for you, but I won't share you with another man."

The storm raging in his eyes calmed something deep inside Beth. She wasn't used to this version of Tom, but she confessed to having an affinity for his domineering, take-control side.

"I wouldn't dream of it. You are mine, Tom, as I am yours." Beth hugged him tight, ending the conversation before it turned disastrous.

THE DINING TABLE WAS covered with books. Most were in stacks; some were lying open near his notebook and pen. Besides the clutter, the cozy cabin remained the same as when they left.

Grady stood next to his workspace and wiped his hands on his jeans. "Okay, so, couple of things you should know first. Paul used a spell to bind Jeff's soul to his prized baseball. Said baseball was left at the stone ritual altar. I came here to retrieve it."

"Oh." Beth took a deep breath. Jeff's soul being bound to an inanimate object was unnerving enough, but thinking about Grady going out there to retrieve it alone made her skin hyperaware of the air. She rubbed her arms. "What else did you learn?"

Grady's gaze flitted to her before he sifted through the open books on the table. When he handed Beth the book, his fingers grazed her. His touch was like a warm, electric charge. Beth's eyelids half-closed. How did such a simple thing move her to wistful wants of a greater kind?

Tom's arm stretched across the back of her shoulders, lifting the fog around her senses. Beth cleared her throat, sending a silent thanks to her husband.

"Ja'azul, the god of chaos and death, *eater of souls,* and bringer of darkness," she read aloud, frowning. There was more to the passage, but her brain fixated on this. "Paul bound Jeff's soul for Ja'azul to *eat*? What does he do with the souls and-and *how*?"

"According to my research, Ja'azul is one of the lesser Dark Ones." Grady held his index finger up while thumbing through his notebook. "The texts say he is cunning and clever and wants to usurp his bosses. But the Elder Gods exist beyond time and space, and he's trapped here. He needs a way back. I believe Ja'azul enlists weak-minded humans to help him. Knowing Paul, Ja'azul must have promised him position or power because he's been doing more than one ritual per year."

"Do our dads know Paul is going over their heads?" Tom asked, his voice was rough like sandpaper.

"Yours and Jeff's dads? No. But Louis and Elliott? Maybe." Grady pinched the bridge of his nose. "Louis and I aren't exactly talking these days."

Beth's frown returned. "Wait. So, when Tom said you ditched us the past few weekends because you were helping your dad at the welding shop, you were actually—"

"Here. Tom told you what I told him." His sapphire gaze darkened when it pinned hers. "I bailed to get the cabins cleaned and stocked. I wanted your birthday weekend to be special."

Tom pulled Beth into his side. All he had to do was throw his leg over hers, and he'd be caging her into a ball.

"That's not the most pressing matter, though. If I'm reading this right, Ja'azul needs thousands of souls before he can escape his prison. When he does, Ja'azul will drain all the energy and life from this planet, making him powerful enough to return to his dimension and defeat the Elder Gods."

"How long has Ja'azul been imprisoned?" Beth's wheels were turning. "And how many of those did he have human servants serving him up yearly sacrifices?"

"He's been here a millennia, but there's no way to know exactly how many souls he's collected already." Grady sighed, plopping down in the dining chair across the table like an exhausted king. "When our dads told us about the ritual, there were four of them and only one sacrifice per year. Six, when they added Jeff and Paul. At some point during college, Louis stopped doing them, so who knows how many people Paul and Jeff murdered."

"Paul lured two people, sometimes three every year," Ghost Jeff spoke. His translucent pinkie was jammed into his ear like he was scratching an itch. "Said his pa warned him that they couldn't help cover up more than that."

Beth's stomach clenched. Aside from the news Ghost Jeff had relayed, he hadn't announced himself upon his return. Who knows how long he had been listening? Shivers crawled down her arms and back.

"How many people did y'all sacrifice, Jeff?" Beth's voice cracked. Some morbid curiosity wanted to know.

"Don't matter how many souls Ja'azul has, it's how many he still needs should be top of your worries." Jeff flipped the tip of his finger at some phantom matter.

The temperature in the room dropped several degrees.

"How many people does he need?" Beth's question was barely above a whisper.

"One, two, three." Ghost Jeff pointed at each person in the room as he counted, ending with himself. "Four. But Paul promised to bring me back. Caint do it if he's dead, though."

Grady slammed his fist into the table, making everyone jump. "That son of a bitch!" He ran both hands through his black curls, tugging at them before his gaze landed on Beth, locking her in place. His thoughts were loud and clear, *"The two people I love most in the world, now brought as lambs to the slaughter."*

Breathing heavily, he broke away. "We need a plan."

"Okay." Beth sounded like she was talking through a glass jar. Her face paled and her hands shook. She grabbed Tom's hand. "First, I need to talk to Tom. Alone, please."

Grady studied them for a long heartbeat. Finally, he nodded and stared at the spread of books on the table. "We'll be here a while, so y'all can stay in the cabin next door."

He had both hands on the table, brows furrowed into a deep frown as he returned to his studies. As Beth passed, there were two dark wet spots on the pages of his notebook.

Chapter 33

TOM

Tom gulped. Beth's fear was palpable, and he had no idea why she was so upset. Each step seemed like gravity grew stronger until his legs were filled with lead.

Beth sat at the table while Tom closed the door and set their bags next to the cot. Mustering a little courage, he stood behind the chair across the table from her. The woven wicker backing groaned when his fingers gripped it tightly.

"What do you need to tell me?" Tom asked, waiting for the worst. He tried to tense up in anticipation, but it was like trying to crank a toy car after it'd been cranked all the way.

"Before I begin it's important for you to know," Beth said with a sigh, placing her hands in her lap, "I love you more than life itself, Tom Newman, and I am *proud* to be your wife." She peered at him with watery green eyes. They shone with love, but her brows were pinched.

Tom gave her a weak smile and swallowed. He wished she'd just rip it off like a bandage.

Beth's chest shuddered with a breath. "When I spoke to Myrtle last, she urged me to finish the connection to Grady."

Tom's face turned into a furnace. He opened his mouth to speak, but Beth held a hand up to stop him. His anger had nowhere to go, so it stewed inside his emotional cauldron.

"I told her I choose you."

The fist around his heart unfurled. He could breathe again, but the ache remained because Beth wasn't finished.

"As you can probably guess, Myrtle wasn't too happy, but she didn't go against my wishes."

Large teardrops fell down Beth's cheeks, bouncing off her shirt and splashing in her lap.

"That's good news." Tom came around and kneeled next to her, tangling their hands. "So why are you still upset?"

Beth shook her head. "I don't want to say it."

"Baby, if you don't tell me I can't help you."

"Two years, Tom. She said you'll die in two years."

"What."

He still didn't believe that Beth's magic was gonna off him the moment they had sex, but Beth obviously did. The weight of it hung around his neck like a gallows, giving Tom's rage a new target. He'd never met Myrtle, but he hated her.

Beth's hiccupping sobs snapped him out of his head.

"Come here," Tom whispered, rising to wrap his arms around his wife. In an instant, his rage calmed at her touch.

As Beth cried against his shoulder, Tom smoothed her hair and rubbed her back. After a while, her sobs lessened to tiny hiccups. Somewhere along the way, his anger became a distant memory.

"Two years isn't much, but we'll make them count, Beth. I swear this to you," Tom murmured into her shoulder. The ache in his heart had gone deeper, seeding his doubts.

"Yes, we will, hon. Every single day." Beth leaned back with a weak grin.

Her red-rimmed eyes made him want to shelter her from every hurt known to man. How could he fight invisible threats?

Tom swept the hair from her face and pressed his lips to hers. Beth deepened the kiss as if she could swallow him whole, keep him forever. When they broke for air, he nuzzled foreheads, breathing in her perfume, cataloguing the taste of sweetened coffee and the softness of Beth.

"I love you, Tom, always and forever," she whispered against his lips.

"I know," he replied, unable to stop the cheeky grin spreading across his face.

Beth playfully smacked him. He grabbed her hand and placed a kiss on her palm. Holding it over his heart, he murmured, "I love you, Beth, always and forever."

Tom didn't want the moment to end, but Grady's patience had been thin lately. He forced himself to stand, bringing Beth with him. He wrapped his arms around her waist and gave her one last kiss before they headed back to Grady's cabin.

GRADY

BETH'S ALL-CONSUMING LOVE for Tom had brought Grady to his knees. It wasn't enough knowing Beth loved him. Not when he was the second pick, same as always growing up in Tom Newman's shadow.

Grady wasn't sure how long he could hold onto his feelings, keep them concealed, because forcing Beth to want him wasn't an option. He'd rather the world burn than make the woman he loved despise him. If only she and Tom had stayed away, given him space to breathe.

He was walking a groove in the floor when they finally came back to his cabin. *Don't look. Don't look.*

"What's going on?" Tom asked, squeezing his shoulder like he does when he's trying to be helpful.

Grady shook his head. His heart battled against reason. "Ja'azul needed four souls. He didn't get Jeff's, but I'm pretty sure Paul's ritual was far enough along that his was given when Beth did her thing. What do think will happen when Elliott and Curtis come looking for their sons?"

"They'll come looking for us," Tom supplied, glancing at Beth.

At least he and Tom agreed on one thing.

"Right, but we'll still be outnumbered and outgunned." Grady's tolerance was fading. The thought of them not being ready when Ja'azul came after them made it hard to concentrate on keeping his cool.

"You and Beth have magic. That's gotta be enough." Tom had his hands on his hips.

"In our current state? Barely. Beth hasn't accepted her mantle and until she does, we'll always be weaker." Grady's insides twisted, jaw twitched. The ugly parts he'd fought to contain bubbled to the surface.

"What are you saying?" Tom stepped up to Grady, almost nose to nose.

"Grady," Beth warned, shooting daggers at him.

"No, Beth. Let him speak his piece," Tom countered with his holier-than-thou attitude.

It may have dissuaded him in the past. Not today.

Grady's rational brain screamed for him to leave it alone, but the animalistic survivalist in him won. "If I'm right, and Beth isn't the child of prophecy, she'll need to be born soon…to *two* magical people, Tom. Either way, I'll be spending a lot of time training Beth and our daughter."

The sound of a slamming door barely registered in Grady's mind.

"You're an asshole, you know." Tom's chest heaved, fists shaking at his sides.

"At least I'm not an insecure asshole." Grady's nostrils flared as he took a step forward and shoved Tom backward.

Tom roared. His shoulder connected with Grady's abdomen, robbing him of air as his back hit the floor. The dining chair nearest them tipped over with a loud clatter.

Tom drew his fist back. Grady grabbed his elbows and flipped them. Tom bucked his hips, but Grady's extra eighty pounds of muscle weren't budging.

"Would you stop," Grady wheezed.

"Fuck you," Tom spat in return.

Grady backhanded his friend across the cheek. The back of his hand stung, but it was Tom's wide-eyed bewildered stare that stopped him. In the twenty-something years they'd been friends, they'd never thrown down in anger like this, not against each other. And they'd done it twice in one day.

Grady scrambled backwards until his back bumped into the door. His lungs were like a bellows being used in double time. Tom crawled away, leaning his back against the cot. The distance and quiet provided some well-needed clarity.

"You hit me," Tom stated, holding the side of his face.

"You hit me first," Grady retorted, holding his best friend's gaze.

Tom snickered. Grady cracked a grin. Tom's laugh was contagious and soon they had expelled the leftover negativity.

"I'm sorry," Tom whispered, picking at his collar. "I don't know what's come over me."

"I do, and I'm sorry, too." Grady scooted closer to Tom and placed a hand on his calf. "None of us asked for this bullshit kinda situation, but I'm working through it."

"I know." Tom raked his hands through his hair.

"I won't lie and say I don't love Beth, because I do," Grady added, watching his best friend closely.

"I know," Tom repeated. When he made eye contact, he winced. "You were in love with Beth before this cursed weekend. It was just easier to ignore when she didn't have a clue." He gave a shuddered breath and continued in a low voice, "And when she didn't feel the same about you."

"Tom...*Brother*, I promise to not act on my feelings for her. You two shouldn't have to worry about my shit when your time is limited." Grady hung his head and removed his hand to run it through his messy mop. "This is the hardest damn thing I've ever had to do, so try to be patient with me. Please don't take it personal if I get short with you, okay?"

"As long as you are patient with me, too," Tom replied with a sideways grin. He let out a heavy breath and stared at the ceiling, shaking his head. "We should probably apologize to Beth."

Grady nodded. "She ran outside right before we had our testosterone match."

"Shit!" Tom jumped off the floor to his feet and was out the door.

Grady didn't move from his seat on the wood floor. He dreaded Beth's return to the cabin. She would be upset with him...again.

His list of apologies was getting long.

Chapter 34

BETH

Grady *KNEW* SHE AND Tom had made the decision to have kids later. Tom had confessed as much when he asked their friend for advice. He'd wanted to start a family right away. Beth insisted they wait a year before trying. She was never against having kids. She just wanted a little time to be alone with her new husband before long nights, exhaustion, and years of sneaking sex into their chaotic life.

Her skin felt like she'd been standing inside a furnace, but her teeth chattered from the anger thrumming in her veins. Grady was an asshole. Beth knew this, but he'd seldom targeted Tom. She'd won immunity after years of enduring mean-spirited ribbing.

Y'all chose to be transparent. Grady's keeping his promise.

Beth grunted at the her internal rationings. They were right, but it didn't change the fact that her selfishness had cost her the family she and Tom talked about. Fantasies of golden-haired children with stormy gray eyes vanished. Before they could resurface with new images she'd had lately, of dark bouncy-haired babes with the bluest eyes you'd ever seen and chubby cherub cheeks, Beth turned it off. Pulled the beaded chain and locked them in the dark closet with the rest of her forbidden desires.

A root came out of nowhere, catching Beth's foot. She righted herself as agony flowed down her cheeks like a waterfall. The spring breeze, with its cooling affect, guided her behind the cabins. Her trajectory was automatic, carrying her through the woods. She didn't care where she was going, as long as it was away. Grady had lost his damn mind, and Beth needed to blow off steam or else she might say or do something she'd regret.

Ever since she set foot in the Grove, her feelings for Grady had given her whiplash. He consumed her thoughts. Every glance from those deep blue eyes and every whiff of his piney scent tested the walls she'd built. One day she'd buckle under the pressure.

Whenever they touched, their connection yearned to be complete. Beth couldn't allow it to happen. She knew in her heart of hearts where completing their bond would lead. She wouldn't betray Tom more than she had already.

Beth's heart ached.

Why can't things go back to the way they were?

Magic had set things in motion. There was no going back to the way things were.

She was done with magic, dark gods, and destiny.

The trees thinned and their barks became those of white paper birches. Magic tugged, warning she had reached the border of the Grove. Without stopping, Beth wandered alongside it.

She could find the exit; disappear.

All it would take is one step outside the boundary. Beth could put one foot in front of the other, keep running well into nightfall until her body collapsed. She could lose herself to the woods that had already taken everything else from her.

"I can't leave Tom," Beth reminded herself firmly, adding, "and there's the whole thing about saving the world."

Her body burned from the exertion and her breaths were wheezy. She slowed to a walk because—surprise, surprise—she was lost and still hadn't found the exit.

Beth brushed her fingers against the flaky bark of the white birch trees as she passed. She'd head back to the cabins. Take the long way back, which meant keep on trekking. If there was a border, she'd eventually end up where she began.

She passed a large thicket of brambles and ferns. The forest opened into a glade housing a small fairytale hut. It was the same cottage in the dreamspace with Myrtle except the grounds were overgrown and the curtains dark. Her chest did a funny flip and fizzed like it was full of soda pop.

Beth reached for the front door and eased it open on its own. The dust particles couldn't decide whether they wanted to be inside or out. She waved them away and studied the space from the doorway. Like the cottage in her quiet place, this one was bright and vibrant, down to the statue of the woman and her bowl.

Beth strolled inside and gingerly lifted the statue off the shelf. A small, dust-free circle was left in its place. Using the hem of her shirt as a dust rag, Beth wiped it clean, and a faint green glow emanated from the statue. A flash of white light filled the room so brightly she had to shield her eyes. When she peeked out from underneath her arm, the light had taken the dust with it. The books on the shelf, bottles of dried herbs, and the knick-knacks were pristine and new. The only thing missing was a cheerful fire in the built-in stone oven.

The feeling in her chest pulsed like a living thing. Beth replaced the statue, thinking she should offer *something* in return for the cleansing. She dashed outside and picked the first flowers she could find. Hurrying back inside, she placed them at the feet of the lady.

"Beth," Tom called from behind her. She turned to find him standing in the doorway, trying to catch his breath. One side of his face was red and slightly swollen.

"Baby," he whispered, taking a deep, steadying breath before straightening. His brows were pinched in apology. "I already knew what the prophecy meant for you and Grady.

But the thought of losing you makes me crazy, so I pretended it wasn't something. I'm sorry."

As Tom's words sunk in, Beth's composure crumbled. She gripped the stone wall when her knees buckled. Denial was easier to stomach what the prophecy meant by 'two magical beings' when Tom acted otherwise. Beth wasn't sure if she should be relieved or angry, so she stayed neutral.

"So, you're not mad?"

"Oh, I'm plenty mad, but being pissed off all the time isn't gonna fix anything. Besides, Grady and I talked things over. We've come to an understanding of sorts." Tom sighed heavily and came to stand in front of her.

He winced when Beth's hand tentatively cradled his angry cheek. "*Talked*, huh? Looks more like y'all had a wrestling match. I hate to see the other guy."

She meant it in jest, but Tom huffed, "He's gonna be okay."

He closed his eyes for a second before settling his beautiful gray gaze on hers. He encased both of her hands in his and held them over his heart. The thumping increased. "I know you have feelings for Grady."

"Tom," Beth started, shaking her head as if to deny it, but she couldn't. Her eyes filled with unshed tears. She tried to pull away, but her weak attempt was thwarted by Tom's firm hold.

"Please don't pull away." Tom dropped her hands to encompass her in a hug. She clung to him, nestling her head underneath his chin. "I hate it, you know. It's driving me mad with jealousy, but I understand. The only way I can keep from losing my mind completely over it is to recognize it for what it is—a magical love."

"I wish with everything I am that things could go back to the way they were." Beth sniffled, leaning back to look him in the eyes. "I love you first and most, magic be damned. You are all I ever wanted, Tom."

Tom rubbed her back and smiled before kissing her forehead. "You have no idea how happy that makes me."

Beth's shoulders loosened, but Tom remained rigid. "Was there something else, hon?"

"I'm still thinking through a few things," he whispered, tucking a strand of hair behind her ear. When she frowned, he added, "I promise to talk to you about it when it's appropriate."

"Okay," Beth replied with a nod as her gut knotted.

"Want to check the place out?" Tom asked, no doubt changing the subject on purpose. He wiggled his eyebrows enticingly.

"Actually, as intriguing as this place is, I'd rather wait. Grady would be beside himself if we explored it without him. Besides, *he's* the expert in magic." She rolled her eyes playfully.

"Then let's get back to the cabin. I'm not sure about you, but I'm starving." Tom kissed the side of her head and laced their fingers.

"Wait. How did you find me?" Beth asked. It was the question burning at the back of her mind since he found her at the cottage.

"Magic," Tom replied with a smirk.

Chapter 35

GRADY

AFTER TOM LEFT TO retrieve Beth, Grady started on dinner. Forgiveness came swifter with a full stomach. He chopped potatoes, carrots, onions, and the last of the dried venison. They all went into salted water. He finished the stew with a bit of dried thyme, parsley, and a few bay leaves.

He was wafting the rich aroma when a surge of magic made him gasp. The thread connecting him to Beth thrummed like a harp in a heavy metal song, vibrating his bones.

Grady stepped outside and drew a deep breath. He sorted through the different scents in the area, separating the familiar ones util he pinpointed the new. Whatever this magic was, it had a slightly tangy and floral scent he couldn't identify. The butterflies in his stomach were having a rave.

Grady fought the urge to leave the cabin, staring off in the direction of the intriguing newness. The steaming stew was nowhere near finished, but if he left to investigate, it would be ruined. So would his chances of softening Beth after his assholery. Not to mention, cooking on a wood stove took technique and skill. So, he waited.

He peeked out the window at least fifty times before finally spotting them. Seeing Beth and Tom holding hands as if taking a leisurely stroll through the park twisted his stomach.

Tom deserves his time with Beth. Don't screw this up.

"Easy, man. You can do this." He took a few deep breaths, plastered what he hoped was a smile on his face, then stepped outside to meet them. "Dinner will be done soon."

Beth wouldn't look him in the eye. She pursed her lips and nodded.

Tom, however, was all smiles and clapped him on the shoulder. "Great! I was afraid I'd have to go squirrel hunting for dinner."

"Venison stew," Grady replied. The question he wanted to ask Beth burned on his tongue.

"We found a cottage," she blurted out, staring at the cabin's roof. "There may be some useful things there. I didn't want to explore it without you. Didn't seem fair since you're the one who knows all this magic stuff."

"I appreciate y'all waiting for me." Grady's heart galloped like a racehorse and leapt in his throat. He swallowed it back down. "Maybe we can go after dinner?"

Beth finally lowered her gaze to his and nodded. Turning away quickly, she tugged on Tom's arm, pulling him inside.

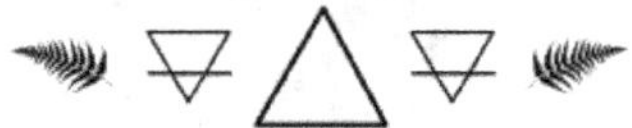

TIME SLOWED TO A crawl while they sat there, but Grady was too exhilarated to eat. He sent the two ahead with the excuse that he would clean up so they could spend time together. A partial truth. The whole truth was that he was suffocating.

Ever since Beth returned from the magical cottage, his skin crawled. It was as if her soul was a strong magnet and his was the metal, but a brick wall separated them.

Waiting as long as he could, Grady went outside and sprinted. When his speed was topped out, he leapt forward with his hands straight out and shifted midair. Bones cracked as sleek black fur sprouted all over his body. He landed on heavy paws, his tongue lolling out the side of his mouth. Panther form was his favorite part of magic. Freedom and speed. It was almost everything.

This shift was a bit different this time. Grady wasn't just showboating for Tom's sake, he was also seeking Beth's approval. He needed her to know he'd be a caring partner when the time came.

It wasn't possible to be picked first, but he was okay with second place. As long as he got the girl in the end.

BETH

BETH MEANDERED TO THE enchanted garden beside the cottage. It hadn't been renewed like the cabin, but there were smooth rocks surrounding the garden space with markings on them. They were faintly glowing green.

Tom was at her side. He jumped a foot off the ground before laughing. Beth turned to find panther Grady skidding to a halt.

His bones cracked and shifted as his skin changed into human form. Fur fell off him like black snow. It was both terrifying and mesmerizing to watch Grady twist and bow, finally reverting to his human self. He shook his head, and the shredded clothing was instantly repaired.

Grady had a wolfish grin as he walked over. "Panther form is so much faster."

His voice was innocent, but exuded arrogance. Beth's lower regions heated with need. She clenched her thighs together, hoping to control her urges, but Grady's smirk unraveled it.

Her cheeks flamed. Beth quickly turned away to find Tom, her anchor. He knelt next to the rock ring, eyeing them intently. His neck muscles tensed and jumped as he squeezed his fists. Beth rested her hand on his shoulder. He relaxed his shoulders, giving her a quick, tentative smile.

"What do you think these runes mean?" Tom asked, tracing the lines.

Grady knelt on the other side of Tom. "I've read about these. They're glyphs. Warding, protection, growth," he said, pointing to each symbol in turn.

Beth lowered to her knees and placed her hand on top of the loose soil, letting her fingers slip beneath. As she lifted a handful and rubbed it between her fingers, they tingled like they'd been dipped in warm wax. The glyphs glowed brighter.

Her hands adopted the same soft green light as the stones. As it spread to the rest of her body, the magic in the garden thrummed louder. She dug her fingers into the dirt and closed her eyes, speaking the first word that came to mind, "Grow."

The glyphs brightened with her, spreading the radiance across the garden plot. Everywhere the green light pulsated, little seedlings sprouted in its wake.

Grady wore a proud smile. Tom's gaze sparkled with wonder as his toothy grin brightened his face. Both men made her heart leap. When Beth went to stand, her legs buckled. Tom and Grady stood to catch her.

The shock from Grady's touch made her jerk away. Hurt hardened his features, but he gave her space. Beth wanted to take it back.

"Wow, what a rush." She chuckled despite her chest cracking open.

"Yeah." Tom answered, a frown forming against his handsome features. It was clear he didn't buy her act.

"You can't keep using yourself as the primary source of energy for your spells," Grady explained gruffly as Tom helped her inside the cottage. "I'll teach you how to recognize the energies surrounding us, and we'll continue our work tapping into them."

Beth sat on the small bed in the corner that was little more than a cot. Despite the makeshift mattress having been filled with hay and moss, it wasn't as uncomfortable as she expected. Tom sat next to her with one arm protectively around her shoulder, and the other holding out the spare protein bar.

"Thanks, hon."

While Beth chewed on the protein bar, she tried to think of ways to make Grady feel less ostracized. The only ones her brain came up with would drive a wedge between her and Tom. Their dilemma had a clear, easy fix: Give in.

Fucking magic.

GRADY

GRADY SURVEYED THE SMALL cottage, but he wasn't seeing much. Beth's thoughts were too loud. She wanted to share this experience with him, so he would pony up and pretend to be wowed rather than wanting to grant her every wish.

When his gaze landed on the statue of the lady, his eyes widened. "This...," he trailed off to carefully lift it off the shelf. "This is a statue Circe, the goddess of potions and herbs. I've read about her, but I've never personally known a devotee of hers."

He reverently placed the statue back upon the shelf, rearranging Beth's flowers, and uttered a prayer. The statue glowed green and hummed its approval, sending a euphoric wave throughout the space. Grady closed his eyes, letting the warmth settle in his core. His laughter spurred Beth's and Tom's.

Grady turned his attention to the bookshelf with twenty or more books stacked neatly on its shelves. He ran his fingers across the spines, stopping on a random book to read. It made a satisfying crackling sound upon opening. He carefully flipped through the pages, skimming the words as a grin split his face.

"Guys, these are Myrtle's journals. She wrote everything her mother, Addie, taught her and whatever else she learned," he announced as his body quivered with glee. "With them, we can find the answers we need about our ancestral magic."

"And maybe some way to stop broadcasting y'all's thoughts and feelings," Tom added, staring thoughtfully at the journal.

"Yeah, that, too," Grady agreed, but his heart wasn't in it.

As much as he complained about wanting what he couldn't have, Grady didn't want to give up the only closeness he and Beth had. He was already lonely enough.

Chapter 36

GRADY

"The words are running together," Tom complained, rubbing his eyes with the palm of his hand.

He'd been the most motivated of the bunch, pouring through page after page like a beast and bookmarking several things along the way. Beth had barely said a word, keeping her thoughts as quiet as a church mouse. When she was distracted like this, she didn't fight her feelings as hard. Working silently with Beth and Tom had a calming effect. Grady was a hundred percent sure this was why their research session lasted this long. They'd been at it for hours, carefully scouring every inch of every page as if they were in a race to be the first to find the golden ticket.

"We should take a break," Beth agreed softly.

She stood and stretched. Her shirt slid up just enough to give the room a peep show. Grady's fingers itched to touch her smooth skin, but Beth quickly tugged it back in place.

Grady closed the journal he was reading and stood; his back popped and cracked. He'd hardly slept a wink last night, and his stomach threatened to devour its neighboring organs. Another large cup of roasted black bean juice wouldn't hurt either. He rubbed the area above his heart, but it never soothed the deep ache.

"Leave the books. The cottage is protected. I'm not sure what would happen if we took anything outside."

"Okay." Beth nodded; her cheeks dusted with pink. "Do we have any leftover stew? Tom said the hardtack we found would be edible if it soaked up the broth."

"Uh, yeah. We can scrape enough together for a light meal." Grady scratched the back of his neck. Beth tucked her hair behind her ear and looked away. "Otherwise, I can make a vegetable stew."

Beth crinkled her nose. "Are we out of meat?"

"Yup. I'll go hunting after we find what we need." Grady's chest swelled. Knowing he could provide for his fated love was a win he'd gladly take.

"Are we even sure the spell exists?" Tom marked his place with a bookmark and tossed the journal onto the table, dislodging the stack underneath. "The only thing interesting I've found so far is Myrtle catching wind of her imminent death. She needed a way to pass the knowledge to the next guardian, so she created a spell to connect with her successor."

"May I?" Grady asked, pointing to the journal Tom referenced.

"Knock yourself out." Tom flipped to his bookmark and handed it over.

Grady skimmed the page, finding Tom's summary accurate. However, there was a passage that caught his eye. "She says the next guardian will either be the child of prophecy or 'will bear the one foretold to end the darkness and bring about a new age of magic.'"

"Right, and the prophecy bit we already knew. Beth is the key to defeating the darkness," Tom relayed matter-of-fact.

Grady felt Beth's gaze slide from the page to study him. Her attention made his heart do jumping jacks, but there were no right answers when the clues contradicted themselves.

"Myrtle can't keep her facts straight." Grady shrugged and rubbed his eyes. "I'd like to get a copy of this prophecy; read it myself."

"Whether Myrtle got it right or wrong, fact is I need to learn magic," Beth stated firmly.

Nodding, Grady glanced at Tom before turning his gaze to Beth. "We'll start first thing tomorrow."

"Oh, yay," Beth sassed, whirling her finger.

Whereas he was an early starter, getting up at the crack ass of dawn, Beth slept until the last possible minute. He cracked a smile.

"I've got about five more journals in this stack to go through," Tom said, counting each one by pushing them aside.

A few books down, one with a purple cover shimmered. Grady's pulse kicked his need for rest to the curb.

"Hold up."

He plucked it up and carefully flipped through the pages, skimming each one in double-time. Near the back, a title caught his attention: Magical Connections.

"Did you find something?" Tom asked, peering over his left shoulder.

"Maybe," Grady murmured, skimming through the passage.

"What does it say?" Beth asked over his right shoulder. "We know Myrtle was married before Barton."

"I didn't," Grady confessed, but it didn't matter. This was it. What they had been searching for all day.

"If Josiah was non-magical like me." Tom cast a frown in Grady's direction. "Why can't I hear Beth?"

"It's probably because she hadn't met Barton yet," Grady answered without missing a beat. He'd wondered the same thing. Since his best friend looked like someone had kicked his dog, Grady added, "Good job, Tom."

"I didn't do anything." Tom's frown softened.

"The journal was found in your stack. Has to count for something." Beth leaned into Tom's side, gifting him with a sweet grin.

Grady cleared the knot in his throat. "You ready to try it?"

He waited for the green light from Beth, otherwise he was happy to torture himself if it didn't mean being alone all the time.

She rolled her lips inward and nodded. "Yes."

Grady read through the spell a third time. He stood in front of Beth. She grasped both of his hands; the warmth and pleasant tingles caused him to shudder. He closed his eyes and gulped. Once his breaths slowed, he began:

"Though our lives be intertwined, by the power of above and below, may the goddess grant our wish to mute what is shared and keep silent what is known. So mote it be."

A gentle breeze and a soft golden glow surrounded Beth and him. Tom reached out, grazing the edge. The hair on his head stood on end like he'd touched one of those electrical current balls.

It was as if someone had trickled ice water on the top of his head in summer. The cold was snappy on impact, but warmed as it spread across his skull. The golden light swirled like a vortex above their chests, sinking in like being pulled through a funnel.

The candles in the room went out at the same time, leaving the waning sunlight as the sole source of illumination.

Tom broke the silence "Did it work?"

Grady opened his eyes at the same time Beth did. They stared at each other for a long moment. The connection was still there, strong, though it flowed more like a babbling brook rather than a flowing river.

He missed sharing every nuance with Beth, feeling the rightness of it all. This truth uncovered another, proving what Tom had already pointed out. Grady was head over heels for Beth. The magic amplified what was already there.

"Looks like." Grady let go of their hands. He stepped back and tapped his head. "It's just me up here."

"Same." Beth nodded in confirmation, glancing once more at Grady as Tom wrapped his around her waist.

Grady wanted to slap the smug grin off his best friend's face. It made him feel like he'd lost.

"Beth is excited to learn magic, and there are books I am looking forward to re-reading," Tom said, acting as if Grady hadn't seen his wife's deepest desires and struggled to keep her walls up.

"You two go ahead and get some food. I'm gonna go hunting." Grady slipped out the door, leaving the heady scent of Beth behind or else he'd suffocate.

He'd gotten no further than the rock step when her dainty hand grabbed his bicep.

"Grady," she breathed, concern etched on her soft features. "You should rest first. You didn't get any sleep last night."

Her gaze flitted to the ground as her cheeks flushed. She removed her hand from his arm and held it over her heart.

"Remember, this is my normal. I'm used to working days here without food or sleep. I'll be fine." Grady tried to give her a reassuring smile. A partial truth she could most likely see through.

"Well, in that case." Beth tilted her head and raised her eyebrow. "Go get 'em, panther."

She huffed a small chuckle as the corner of her mouth lifted.

"Be back before you know it," Grady whispered before he took off.

His panther smiled at her comment, tongue lolling to the side.

Grady may not be plugged into Beth like before, but something told him part of her missed the closeness, too.

Looks like he didn't lose after all.

Chapter 37

TOM

He wasn't sure what he expected after Grady and Beth weren't able to hear each other think, but he certainly hoped it would dull the connection. Grady still looked at Beth like she hung the moon, and Beth hadn't hesitated to stop Grady when he made to leave. Her concern was rational, but it set Tom on the edge of his own darkness. He stared into it before closing the door and locking it shut. Dealing with his demons wasn't on the table. Making himself useful was.

A bit of reassurance wouldn't hurt, and Tom chomped at the bit to get Beth back to their cabin. No matter how many promises his wife made, he was afraid her attraction to Grady went deeper than the magic tying them together.

Grady disappeared outside with a quick glance at Beth. She stared at the closed door. Tom couldn't wait any longer. He stood from his chair and sauntered over to Beth, sliding his arms around her waist from behind. She leaned her head back to rest it on his shoulder with a happy hum.

Taking this as a sign to continue, Tom trailed kisses from behind her ear to the curve of her neck. His hand slipped under her shirt, across her warm stomach. She shuddered at his touch, snaking an arm around his neck as she sighed contentedly.

"Now that we're alone, I think it's time to finish what we started at the house yesterday...er, earlier?"

When his hand moved up to cup her breast, Beth went rigid.

"Wait, Tom. Stop," she breathed, turning to face him. "Are you sure you want to do this?"

"Oh, I'm sure." He'd given this supposed 'dying in two years once you have sex' crap a lot of thought. He wasn't buying any of it.

"But Myrtle said—" Beth tried to argue, but Tom was sick and tired of all this mumbo-jumbo magical radiation nonsense.

"I don't *believe* what Myrtle said. And if she's right, who's to say I'm not already affected?" Tom was begging at this point. Not only did he want to be with his wife, but he *needed* this validation. "I want to share every possible second with you, Beth."

She rolled her bottom lip between her teeth. Tom hoped she'd see things his way. It's not like she didn't *want* to be with him. He understood that she was scared. What if he was wrong? No matter what happened, he wasn't missing out. He wouldn't die with any new regrets.

"You have a point," Beth finally relented.

Tom placed his hands on her hips, pulled her closer. He leaned in for a kiss.

"What about Grady? He'll know."

Her words were like a bucket of ice being dumped on his head, only instead of shivering from the cold, the water evaporated on contact.

"And this is a problem, how?" Tom scoffed. Dropping his chin to his chest, he flexed his fingers and cupped her pert apple ass. "You're *my* wife, not his. He can't expect us to not have sex. And if he does, well, he and I need to have another chat."

"Okay. Fine. You're right." Beth's head drooped back. She stared at the ceiling before clicking her tongue. "On one condition."

Tom's pants were painfully tight as he nuzzled her neck and whispered, "Anything."

"We can't be loud or I'm gonna die of embarrassment." Beth was dead serious. He almost laughed but nibbled her ear instead.

"Done." Tom steered them toward the door.

As soon as Tom closed their cabin door, he turned to watch his wife. There wasn't anything spectacular in the way she slipped out of her jeans or pulled her t-shirt overhead. It was the fact that she did it for him.

"You are so beautiful."

Tom slid his hands around her waist to her back. He kissed her neck tenderly while working to unfasten her bra.

"Tom," Beth breathed as her fingernails scratched his scalp. God, he loved that feeling.

Tom stopped to gaze into her eyes. "Beth, baby, you are my everything." His lips swiftly found hers, kissing her as though he were a starved man.

Beth melted into him, closing her eyes as she ran her fingers through his hair. Tom's whole body shuddered. Nimble hands worked quickly to finish undressing each other. He was eager for the unfettered passion they had before her connecting to Grady.

Tom lifted Beth up to straddle him and laid her on the cot in the corner. She pulled him down to kiss her, but he planted playful kisses on the tip of her nose, her cheeks, and her neck before bringing his lips to hers. Their hands explored each other, sending sensational ripples across their bodies. As Tom slid home, his sultry stare kept Beth's captive as they made love.

Something about this magical place made the experience much more intense, especially now, being truly alone. Beth's nails dug into his back as she panted through her climax.

Tom planted his hand on the wall for support, grunting quietly as he exploded with her to the point of seeing stars.

Tom pulled out and rested his head on Beth's chest while she rubbed his back, holding him close. He counted her heartbeats until they slowed and planted a kiss between her breasts. During the years they had been intimate, this one left him breathless and sated to his core.

Tom raised his head and propped up on an elbow. The sheen of sweat on Beth's skin had dried, but the rose-colored flush lingered. Her eyes were closed as he traced her cheek with a finger, marveling at the gorgeous woman who'd captured his heart when they were kids. Even after everything that had happened, she still chose him.

"Beth?"

Her eyes fluttered open in slow motion.

"What is it, hon?" Her soft words were slurred with exhaustion.

"I want you to know how much I love you." His heart heated, turning his ribcage into a furnace.

"I know, babe. You're my world, too." A sleepy grin spread on Beth's face as she stroked his head, ending with her fingernails on the nape of his neck.

"If I died tonight, I would die the happiest man on earth," he whispered, a knot formed in his chest.

Beth's eyes glistened and her chin wobbled. He wished he could cram the words back inside, but she pulled into a scorching kiss. He felt his very essence being imprinted on her skin. The tightness suffocating him vanished.

When Tom broke the kiss to breathe, Beth nuzzled his cheek with hers. Her soft breath tickled his ear. "I love you, Tom. Forever and always."

Tom fell to her side, slipping his arm around her waist. She turned her back to his chest so he could spoon her like always. Burying his face in her hair, he whispered, "Forever and always."

Tom awoke to an empty bed in complete darkness. He sat abruptly. The cabin was silent, and Beth's side of the bed was cold. His knee-jerk thought was that Beth had snuck out to be with Grady.

Stop being a dumbass.

He pulled on a pair of shorts and grabbed the flashlight off the table on his way outside. The glow from a large campfire flickered across the field.

At the top of the hill, Tom stumbled to a stop. In the light of the full moon, his naked wife danced with wild grace around the bonfire.

A wide grin spread across Tom's face, mesmerized by the sight until he saw another naked body dancing with her. He squinted and the man's face came into view. Tom's body tensed, the fists at his side flexed. There was fire in his blood.

"No way in hell is Grady gonna take Beth away from me. Over my dead damn body."

Tom broke out into a run with a roar. He swung his fist at Grady's face, but it missed. The second connected with air where his face should have been. All the while, Beth and Grady kept dancing as if he were invisible.

He stepped back, trying to get a hold of himself when he got a good look. The phantom dancers weren't Grady and Beth, they were their twins or clones. Tom could only assume he was seeing Myrtle and her lover, Barton. Their resemblances to Beth and Grady made his stomach sick.

Myrtle waved her hand. Everything around them faded until it was just them standing in the field under the stars. She walked toward Tom with a confident swagger, stopping barely a feet from him. He kept his eyes firmly on her face, not daring to look upon the bare, pale skin that glowed like the moon.

"It is good to finally meet you, Tom," Myrtle replied with a wry grin. "I am surprised you bedded your wife so soon, knowing the cost."

"You said it yourself; Beth is my wife. And I don't believe the, 'sex with your non-magical spouse will kill them,' bullshit," Tom answered coolly. He'd planned a slew of words to set Myrtle straight, but they disintegrated when her grin grew into a smirk.

"Oh, believe me when I say it's true. Of course, it took losing Josiah to learn the lesson." Pain flashed over her face for a split second before she straightened her back. "How much are you willing to sacrifice for your lady love?"

"I would do anything for Beth," Tom ground out without thinking, laying his cards on the table. His jaw ticked and his face grew hot, so he shot from the hip. "Even if it means dying for her."

"I am glad we are on the same page." Myrtle's smile softened. With a flick of her hand, a flowing lilac gown with white lace trim covered her body. "While Beth is holding back, Ja'azul sent three of his scouts—the Agnazar—to seek her out. You have already met his lesser creatures, the Ungenth, and barely escaped with your lives. The three of you will have to muster all the strength you can to defeat the Agnazar. They are terribly fierce beings with swift blades that will infect the blood with a boiling disease and mortally wound those without magic."

"Why are you telling this to me and not the others?" Tom asked, frowning. He didn't like where this conversation was heading.

"Because you will do anything for the woman you love," Myrtle replied sadly. She looked into his unwavering eyes and sighed. "I can give one of you the power to defeat the Agnazar, at the expense of your life. The world cannot stand to lose Beth or Grady. If they die, the prophecy will not come to pass, and the everything you have ever known and loved will cease to exist when Ja'azul is released upon this world."

The bubble of Tom's hopes for the next two years burst. Myrtle was giving him a way to save Beth's life by giving up what little time he had left. Tears stung his eyes. He turned away from Myrtle, closing them tight. He'd made peace with the fact that they wouldn't have a lifetime. He'd even accepted the reality that his wife would end up having the family they had talked about with his best friend. But to have days instead of years...it was unacceptable.

"I'm sorry, Myrtle, but I need more time. Beth will be devastated if I die now, and I'm afraid she'll refuse to make the connection with Grady if I do," Tom said, shaking his head before turning back to the healer. "There has to be another way."

Myrtle sighed in defeat, closed her eyes, and whispered something inaudible. When she opened her eyes, they glowed purple. She held out her hand, waiting.

Instead of grasping it, he stared, unblinking. So far, everything she said seemed honest, but Tom didn't trust Myrtle. Frowning in disappointment, she grabbed his hand and held it in both of hers.

"Tom Newman, I bestow on you Circe's Blessing, granting you the power to defeat the agents of Ja'azul. Only when you accept your fate and willingly surrender yourself will it activate. If, somehow, you manage to find another way to defeat the Agnazar," Myrtle's voice was ethereal as the power transferred to him, "you must return this gift to the goddess. In doing so, you shall secure the malevolence for another decade. As above, so below. May fortune smile upon you."

Tom felt a cold fire race through his body as purple flames engulfed him. He awoke with a start next to Beth. She gave a whimper before cuddling closer under his arm, snoring lightly in her sleep.

Taking a deep breath to relax, Tom turned his free hand around in the dark. It looked normal. He dismissed his conversation with Myrtle as a strange, albeit realistic, dream and wrapped his arm around Beth. As his hand passed through the moonlight, a hazy purple glow hung just on the surface of his skin.

"Accept your fate, surrender yourself, and save the woman you love." Myrtle's words were in the forefront of his mind before they faded.

Tom lay there listening to his heart pound, exhausted. There was no way he could go back to sleep.

Chapter 38

GRADY

RUNNING THROUGH THE WOODS with the wind on his face was almost heaven. Grady missed being in panther form like this. It had been weeks since he'd shifted for any length of time. In this form, his senses were heightened, making the thrill of the hunt all the more exhilarating. The scent of the forest's inhabitants, mixed with the muskiness of the forest floor, grounded him in a nurturing way. The tug of his sinewy frame when it tensed and snapped to catch his prey was empowering.

Grady was one with nature when he surrendered to the beast. All the human worries plaguing him vanished, leaving him with only the instinctual need to survive. Oddly enough, the need to breed wasn't a part of it. Which was fine. The only person he wanted to be with was...*the one person he was supposed to be forgetting about.*

No matter how hard he fought to delay their destiny, Beth was always with him. The only way to separate them was to sever the thread. When they completed their connection, it would be unbreakable. But, for that to happen, he would have to lose his best friend. Unprompted, images bombarded his thoughts. Curly-headed children laughing gleefully while running through fields of wildflowers, Beth's glowing face and round stomach, the adoration in her gaze. His lungs paused in reverence of what could be his future.

Grady's chest caved. His heart was beaten, battered, and bloodied, but he'd survive. He had to. Grady's broken self and all his pieces belonged to Beth. She was the only one who could heal him. He simply had to survive the next two years. Thank the goddess they'd found Myrtle's spell.

Panther Grady shook his head and focused on searching for game. They could always make a trip to town for provisions, but he promised to bring back meat. There was a primal *need* to provide for his family. At least that's what he was telling himself.

In his periphery, a family of deer grazed in a patch of ferns. Slinking closer, Grady let the silent predator take over his reflexes. He crouched, ready to strike, when their heads shot up, ears twitching. The deer bolted through the woods, away from his position.

There were no other animals nearby to spook them. He sniffed the air to pinpoint the source of the disturbance.

The wind carried the scent of humans.

Grady sped up the hill toward safety. Sitting on his haunches behind the cover of shrubbery, the black panther waited for the source of man-scent. His first thought was hunters, but that couldn't be right. It wasn't hunting season.

Still and quiet, he scanned the area with his night vision, catching a familiar scent—heated metal, gunpowder, and cigarettes.

His father was here.

From his perch, four men in orange vests with rifles came into view. Louis, Jack, Elliott, and Curtis. The four horsemen of Mayes Hill. If they were here, it meant they knew Jeff and Paul had failed.

Panic surged through Grady, making it difficult to restrain his animal instincts. He needed to get back to the Grove, to warn the others, but he'd have to wait until they moved out of rifle range.

Slinking in the opposite direction, Grady stopped when one of them mentioned the ritual stone. *Shit! We need to get the baseball before they do.*

Panther Grady flew through the woods back to the Grove, deftly dodging the forest obstacles on graceful legs. If they stood any chance of getting out of these woods alive, Beth needed to begin training right away. If his timing was right, it was morning there, and the couple should be awake.

Gliding through the rock opening, and through the secret path to the birch Grove, he made it in record time. He didn't stop until he was in front of Tom's cabin.

Halfway through the transformation back to his human form, Beth and Tom stepped outside. The morning sun bleached their skin, but their frowns were deep.

His lungs worked like hellish bellows, dragging oxygen across coals on every inhale. A simple loincloth was the only thing he could summon to keep decent, given Tom's sensitivity and all. Grady's broad, hairy, and muscular chest heaved, causing the last bits of fur to fall off.

"Dads here... in the woods..." he managed to get out before he fell to his knees. Taking a few heavy breaths, he added, "We're out of time."

BETH

BETH STUDIED GRADY AS he shoved food in his mouth. His body shook uncontrollably. Of course, she was concerned about his well-being, but with his bare chest and biceps on display, she found it difficult to focus on much else. Her cheeks warmed as she turned away. Thankfully, Tom was deep in thought. She moved behind his wicker chair. The space didn't help when Grady's natural musk of cedarwood and freshly tilled earth was everywhere.

Putting one hand across her forehead and the other on her hip, she sighed. "Grady. You need to rest. You look like death warmed over."

"Yes," he replied between bites. He wouldn't look at her. Instead, he hyper-focused on eating.

"Why are they here?" Tom paced behind him. "They've gotta be looking for Jeff and Paul."

Grady shrugged, and took a long drink of water before answering, "Maybe. I overheard them say they're heading to the ritual stone right now."

"Dammit! When are we gonna get a break?" Tom demanded, tugging his hair. "How soon will they be there? I mean, how much time do we have to get ready ?"

"They'll be at the ritual stones in three hours," Grady replied after swallowing. He paused with a spoon of stew lifted next to his mouth, "that give us—"

"Less than three days," Beth finished with a heavy sigh, "I've got two days to learn and practice something I could only manage when my life was in danger. How can you teach me when I can't fully grasp the concept?"

"Don't worry, you'll do fine," Grady said in an attempt to reassure her.

It was hopeless. There was no way they'd survive. Beth's face tightened as she fought tears. She didn't want to cry anymore, but it seemed to be the only thing she had control of lately.

Grady stood and started toward her, compassion covering his face. Beth's body warmed, bracing for the hug that would solve her problems, but Tom's glare deflected her comfort. Instead, Grady swerved toward his backpack. Beth shivered when the breeze of his passing teased her with his heady scent.

"Hon, I believe in you," Tom murmured, wrapping his arms around her. The tightness gathered in her ribs eased, but it wasn't enough. "I also believe in Grady. If he can teach me how to make an end table, he can teach you magic. You're a natural."

Tom knew all the right things to say to make her uncertainties disappear. She nodded, and he placed a kiss on her forehead.

"Let's get to it." Grady said, standing next to her.

Beth thanked the stars he was fully dressed, otherwise she wouldn't be able to stop blushing. Upsetting Tom wasn't an option, and failure was a luxury she couldn't afford. She needed to absorb as much magical knowledge as possible, so they had a better chance of survival. She would fight for their lives and save their love.

BETH SAT BAREFOOT IN the middle of a mossy patch. Her bent knees were pressed against her chest, and her feet were planted firmly on the ground.

"Concentrate on letting everything else go except the feeling of the earth beneath us," Grady instructed Beth.

"Once you've cleared your mind, see with your inner eye that everything around you has energy, life, and sustenance. Merge with it. Let the energy ebb and flow through you and within."

Beth closed her eyes and took a deep breath. She imagined little green lights spreading through the forest where the plants met the dirt. Roots drank the lifeblood of the earth while their leaves soaked in the sunlight. Beth breathed with them and sank into the soil, planting her own seed to take root. As she focused on the energy, it filled her up like a battery.

When Beth felt like she'd drawn enough, she opened her eyes. A green glow surrounded her, floating on the surface of her skin. The wind danced through her hair before racing circles around Grady. Then, it sped through the trees, rustling leaves in its wake.

"Excellent," Grady said quietly. "Now, give it to the garden. Wake up what's dormant in the dirt."

Beth froze. Now that she had the energy, she wasn't sure how to direct the flow. Her voice was meeker than intended when she asked, "Can you help me?"

"Of course." He crawled to the spot beside her, leaving enough space between them as to not upset Tom. "Can you sense the well inside of you? It could be as large as a pool or as small as a birdbath."

Beth reached for the source, but it was slipping into an endless sea. "I can."

"Good." Grady held his hands in front, palms up. Beth mimicked him. "Now, pretend your hand is the scoop and take some out."

She did as instructed, sending ripples across the surface. Her 'well' barely seemed tapped.

"You're doing a great job." Grady praised. His proud smile was wide, returning the youthfulness she'd missed. "Watch my movements as I direct the flow to that drooping cornflower over there."

He transferred the sparkling green energy to his off-hand and pinched some off the top. Grady flicked his fingers toward the wilted flower, sending a stream of what looked like the fairy dust from her childhood stories on the wind. When it touched the cornflower, the leaves and flower petals fluttered, and the stem straightened. The whole plant looked like it was behind a saturation filter.

"It all comes down to intent. See the outcome you wish to happen, fuel it with energy, then let it be," Grady explained, watching her face for understanding. The attention made her blush. He cleared his throat with a dip of his chin. "Your turn."

"Right." Beth rolled her shoulders back. She was determined to get it right his time. No more being the victim. "Visualize my intent. Energize. Make it happen. Easy."

She grabbed a handful of magic with her left hand and hefted it. The spillage sought Grady and sank into his skin. She focused on the cottage's garden and frisbee-tossed her magic at it.

C'mon. Go to your home. Grow into big plant babies.

Instead of a stream like Grady's, hers was a babbling brook. It raced to the garden plot like a kaleidoscope of butterflies during migration.

"It's so beautiful," she whispered with a hopeful smile.

When her magic surged into the dirt plot, the ground shuddered, and the rectangular plot shined like the Emerald City. From where she sat, Beth could already make out fully grown plants with ripening fruits and vegetables.

"Shall we go see what you made?" Grady stood and held out his hand.

Beth slipped her hand into his without thinking, and he pulled her to her feet. The energy lingering on their fingertips wound together like a vine. Grady kissed her knuckles and drew the power out, guiding it to a nearby fern that had been trampled. The plant stood straight as the leaves knit back together, appearing to sigh in relief. Grady placed her hand at her side.

"That was amazing," Beth marveled, not only at Grady's ability to make magic look as easy as breathing, but at the amount of restraint it took for him to keep himself in check. Her chest fluttered.

"You are amazing," Grady whispered, nodding to the cottage.

Tom stood outside the door. His arms were crossed, matching his surly gaze. Beth beamed with excitement, cheeks hurting from smiling to much. Tom's stance relaxed, and his face softened when she came to his side.

"I did it, Tom." She looped her arm with his, pulling him out of his grumpiness. "Come see."

She dragged Tom to the garden space with Grady following a short distance. There were fully grown and fruited tomatoes, squash, cucumbers, green beans, blueberries, and strawberries. More food than they could eat in a week.

As they walked around the lush garden, Beth spotted various herbs growing among the plants.

"Grady showed me once, and I got it on the first try." Beth was delighted, and she was hardly tired at all.

"Yep," Grady responded, putting his hand on Tom's shoulder and squeezing it. "Your wife is a natural."

"I know." Tom's short-lived grin looked strained. "Hey, uh, we need to talk."

Chapter 39

TOM

TOM RELAYED MYRTLE'S WARNING about the Agnazar to Beth and Grady. He kept the power she gave him a secret and didn't go into specifics about the dream, either. Grady wasn't convinced Tom had told them everything, but Beth assured him it was not the case.

He crammed his guilt into the overstuffed box. At this point, the only thing keeping it closed was a bungee cord, but it kept his weakening sanity more or less intact.

Watching Beth grow closer to Grady chipped at his defenses. Magic was something else he'd never get to experience with Beth. Try as he might, Tom rationalized that they were working to save the world. Resentment still lurked behind the door he kept locked, but its tar-like fingers prodded the cracks.

"Go. Practice and learn. Become the awesome savior of the world I know you are." Tom rubbed Beth's arms and cracked a smile. "I'll be studying the journals for anything helpful."

"If you're sure you'll be okay," Beth replied, but she made no move to leave.

She wasn't wrong to worry, for leaving him alone with his thoughts, but what else could they do?

"I promise I'll be fine." He passed a glance at Grady, who nodded curtly and stepped outside. His friend still wore a thoughtful frown. Since they were alone, he gave Beth a sweet kiss. Just because Grady no longer had a front row seat to everything didn't mean they would throw their public displays of affection in his face.

Beth sighed into him and relented. "Okay. But if you get bored, promise you'll come join us."

"I'm a history teacher, and these journals are history. I doubt I'll get bored." Tom's smile was genuine when she slapped his arm. "But I promise I'll join you if I do."

"Good." She gave him one last glance and a nod before heading outside.

Tom grabbed the first one on the stack and began. He wanted to know everything about Myrtle's non-magical husband, Josiah. Was their child normal or did he have magic? How did Josiah's death affect her?

More importantly, he wanted to know how Myrtle changed once Barton came into her life.

Among the recordings of her daily life, Myrtle had a smattering of spells and recipes. Tom copied them to separate notebooks so he could show them to Grady and Beth later.

He rubbed his eyes, had a good stretch, and turned the page:

"The nausea continues, so I went to see Mother today. She says I am with child! Josiah will be happy, but I fear for him. When we married many months ago, he accepted me and my magic. While my sweet Josiah has learned to cope with sharing our every thought and emotion, I see his suffering. My husband, the stonemason, is a resilient man, but I fear he will not be able to survive the pain of childbirth after nine months of suffering. He wears a brave face for my sake, but I have begun to create a spell to shield him. I pray for the goddess's guidance."

Tom skimmed to the end of the journal, where Myrtle had successfully come up with a spell. He bookmarked the page and tipped the book closed.

He wasn't blind to the math. Myrtle already had magic, therefore, Josiah was affected from the beginning of their relationship. This meant, Tom would have an extra six months if he was as 'resilient' as Josiah, the burly stonemason. How were they able to communicate, but Tom couldn't with Beth? Is it as simple as a timing issue? Beth was already close to both men when her magic awakened. He'd ask her to try with him. After.

Tom stood and stretched, staring out the window to the field where Beth practiced. She laughed at something while Grady stood with a forced scowl.

Suspicion ticked at his stomach, but he shoved it away. Beth had to learn how to use her magic and Grady had to teach her. Tom was doing his part by reading and recording. It wasn't an ideal setup, but it had to be this way. At least it kept his mind off the amount of time his wife and best friend were spending together.

With a heavy sigh, Tom dropped into the chair and grabbed the next book in the stack. For the next few hours, he continued Myrtle's story, reading about the birth of her first child, a bouncing, happy baby boy they named Lucas. To Tom's disappointment, Lucas was born without magic.

Furthermore, as happily as the couple welcomed their new child, Josiah's health took a turn for the worse. Any hope Tom had for the rest of his time with Beth deteriorated along with Josiah's health. The man lasted two days after Lucas's second birthday. That morning Myrtle wrote:

"Words cannot describe the pain of losing my love. Josiah was a wonderful husband, caring

and hard-working, and an ideal father. I tried to save him, but nothing worked. Goddess, help me, but I was powerless to stop his deterioration. The only solace I find is in knowing he passed peacefully in his sleep. His memory shall live on in our Lucas. For now, our son sleeps soundly in the cradle his father crafted while I grieve the loss of his father in silence. My heart is broken beyond repair. I fear it will never be whole again. For Lucas's sake, I shall persevere."

Tom sat back in his chair, staring at the centuries old, dried tear stains curling the page. A lump stuck in his throat and his lungs squeezed at the thought of Beth being left broken. Somehow, Myrtle had survived and met Barton. He placed a bookmark on this passage.

Flipping to the next page, and the next, Tom searched for any mention of Barton. He'd gone through another journal, learning of Lucas' tragic death from contracting smallpox before finding what he was looking for:

"Out of disparity, a light has appeared, bringing the hope I had lost from its depths. Today, whilst perusing the market, I met a man. The Coopers recently settled in our small village, and Barton is the eldest son. We were drawn to each other by forces unseen. But, I digress!

Purchasing flour from the miller's, I felt his presence like a warm woolen coat. He stood in the middle of the dirt road three houses down, staring at me with his piercing gaze. Curls the shade of raven's feathers and wide eyes of sapphire. The smile on his face caused my insides to flutter and warm. The moment our eyes locked, I knew he was mine and I was his, though I did not yet know his name.

We spent the day conversing like childhood friends. By the setting sun, the deep wounds inflicted upon my heart with Josiah's and Lucas's deaths began to mend. What I deemed an impossible task, Barton has exceeded. He has asked to see me again on the morrow, which I have gladly agreed. I pray he will not be another person passing by to leave me alone once more, for I believe him to be my true soulmate. Only time will tell. Circe, hear my prayer!"

The book fell from Tom's hands. He buried his face in his hands. He wasn't much of a drinker, but he could use a fifth of something stiff right now. Grady and Beth had been fighting this same pull for days. Tom scoffed, chuckling bitterly at his naivety. He'd been delaying the inevitable. Beth *will* end up in Grady's arms. The love they'll have will be a fraction of what Tom could provide. This was an unpleasant pill to swallow, but he knew what had to be done.

Myrtle was right.

A tear rolled down each cheek. Tom swatted them away. As long as he lived, Beth would choose him. She would not complete her connection to Grady. The sake of the world and every living thing here would suffer and die if they didn't. Myrtle had given him the means to ensure their victory and Beth's survival.

Tom faced his demons head on. Sacrifice himself to save his world or pray for a miracle to keep him alive only to die later. It would be a slow and painful death but guaranteed him the most time with Beth.

"You brat! You did that on purpose!" Grady yelled before the cottage door opened.

He was covered in mud from head to toe. Beth's clothes were as pristine as they were this morning.

"I wasn't the one slinging blocks of dirt around." Beth retorted, trying to swallow another bout of giggles. She ended up doubled over, holding her stomach while howling in laughter. "You told me to defend myself, so I did!"

Grady shook his head as he stomped to the kitchen sink. Cupping his hands, he splashed water on his face several times before the dirt washed away. He dried his face and hands on the towel, then tossed it on the counter. Grumbling, he pulled his caked shirt over his head and dropped it to the floor.

"If you don't want a show, I suggest you two wait outside." Grady held the button of his pants between his fingers. He cast a challenging glance at Beth, ignoring the scowl on Tom's face.

"C'mon, hon. Nothin' to see here." Tom placed a hand on the small of Beth's back. She snorted before turning to leave with him. He couldn't look at her face. If he saw an ounce of desire, the zip tie keeping his sanity intact would snap.

Tom turned to Grady before closing the door. The heat from Grady's stare burned. Frowning, Tom pulled the door shut.

Why do I feel like I'm the other man now?

After dinner, Tom and Beth made love. While they lay in bed, he lazily smoothed his hands up and down her body until she fell into a sound slumber. Sleep was not so easy for him.

Tom stared at the ceiling, hoping the Universe gave him another answer before the fight, otherwise he'd have to live up to his promise. There were worse ways to die than sacrificing yourself for the woman you loved.

Chapter 40

GRADY

GRADY REFLECTED ON THE day's practice, cleaning mud from his ears. Beth's aim was damn good, but she lacked the punch needed to take her enemy down. Grady wasn't a greenhorn. He could sling a chunk of earth and peg his target, but Beth's shielding abilities knocked his ego down a peg or two. It wasn't too bruised, though. It was under *his* guidance that Beth's natural protective instincts shone. The evidence was as clear as her spotless clothes.

But her inability to inflict hurt wasn't what had his stomach in knots so that everything tiny inconvenience got under his skin. Having all four dads mucking around in his woods took that cake.

Elliott Larson was as hard-laced and sour as the apple that fell from his tree. Word on the street, this year he'd have enough votes sway the win for the mayoral seat after a decade of trying. If Elliott was voted in, Paul would surely make a bid to replace the current sheriff, Eric Blaylock. If shit wasn't bad already, it'll be ten times worse.

Jeff's dad, Curtis Putnam, was a lousy piece of shit who liked the bottle too much and measured manhood by how many punches his son could handle. Too bad he was the best damn auto mechanic in the tri-state area.

Jack Newman, Tom's dad, wasn't a terrible man, but what he lacked for a backbone he made up for by taking Grady in when his old man didn't give a shit. If Jack died today, it would be like losing a father.

Which brought him to Louis Cooper. His old man held the title of 'Worst Father of the Year' for twenty-six years running. Grady didn't want him dead, but he wouldn't be bothered if the bastard vanished.

Grady finished his water bottle and popped another mouthful of blueberries in his mouth. While he chewed, he rifled through his bag for a clean shirt. Pulling on his black tee, Grady snuck a peek at the woman whose hands could make or break him.

Beth's honey-colored hair was tied back in a ponytail. A few tendrils had slipped the elastic, bringing his gaze to her slender neck. Her brows were drawn as she enchanted Tom's spears. Grady could watch her work all day, living in a Beth-induced stupor.

Tom cleared his throat, drawing his and Beth's attention. "I figured we could recap the plan real quick. Beth'll do her night-seeing spell, then we'll drink our 'invisibility' potion. Once we get to the ritual stones, y'all will keep a watch out for the Agnazar while I find Jeff's baseball."

Jeff popped up next to Tom with a *"Howdy!"* They'd not heard from him in the past few days, but that wasn't anything new. What was odd was how Ghost Jeff could come and go as he pleased. Grady was a smidge curious where his deceased friend's spirit went when he wasn't haunting them.

"Nice of you to join us again, brother." Tom smirked as he continued, "Long as things go smoothly, we should be back here at the Grove, safe and sound."

"But Grady said the dads have shotguns. I redirected a thrown knife once, but four men shooting buckshot sounds a lot more involved," Beth reminded them, her face tight and drawn.

Grady's gaze flicked to the raised scar on her bicep. He'd been bleeding out on the ground when it happened, but it still made his blood boil. "If there's any sign of the dads being anywhere near the stones, we have no choice but to bail. Sorry, Jeff."

The apparition shrugged his translucent shoulder. "Not like I got much say in the matter, being dead and all. I's just tryin' to keep Audrey safe. Still, I appreciate y'all trying."

In a blink, Jeff's ghost was gone.

"Who's Audrey?" Beth asked.

"Not sure," Tom replied with a shrug.

They looked to Grady.

"No idea." Grady shook his head. "Haven't been on talking terms in several years. Anyway, the longer we dawdle here, the likelihood of running into the dads increases. I think we're as ready as we're gonna get."

"Right. Let's move on out," Tom agreed, pulling his arms through the straps on the pack.

"Grady?" Beth gnawed on her bottom lip and wrung her hands. Her nervous habits. "I think we should open back up. Being able to speak without words will give us an edge, and you can help walk me through what to do if we end up fighting."

Tom hung his head, jaw ticking and fists curling around the nylon strips at his sides. Grady knew this was a sensitive subject for his best friend, so he treaded lightly.

"You're a quick study, Beth. I think you should trust in your abilities." Beth's hopeful grin fell, breaking Grady's stance. "But if it'll make you feel better, I'm okay with dropping the spell temporarily."

"Thank you." Beth placed a hand on Tom's shoulder and the other on his. "You two are the most important people in my life. Upping our chances of survival is worth it."

Grady's cheeks warmed and his chest filled with the urge to keep Beth far away from danger. But this was her fight, too.

"How do we undo the spell?"

Beth's fern gaze glittered with hope. Grady would move heaven and earth to hold it there, to keep her optimism from fading. But he was also a realist.

Before Grady could offer a middle-ground, Tom sniffed and gripped her chin. He didn't need to use force other than the sway of her heart to garner her attention.

"I'm gonna step outside, okay?" Tom waited for her to nod before giving her a simple peck on the lips.

Grady saw it for what it was, refreshing the brand. A reminder that Beth was Tom's girl. Grady couldn't forget.

"M'kay," Beth moved her hand over Tom's heart, making Grady's limbs weak. "Meet you out there in a sec."

Tom's thumb traced her jaw; his mouth was set in a possessive line. He cast a quick, warning glance at Grady before heading outside. The door was left cracked open.

"Is he going to be okay?" Beth asked in a hushed whisper.

"I don't know, Beth." Grady busied himself with fastening all the zippers and buttons on his backpack. "Keep an eye on him. We can't afford for Tom to fall into depression, not until the current fucking issue is dealt with."

The last of his statement had a bite he hadn't intended to let slip.

"I'm sorry." Beth's voice was barely audible.

Grady paused to gather his calm. He turned his softened gaze to Beth. "None of this is your fault. We were left to clean up a thousand-year-old mess without instructions and a magical bond with the worst timing, but we'll manage. Right?"

"Yeah," she huffed, the memory of a smile curling the edges of her full lips. "We'll manage. Now, do we just will the spell to end or what?"

"Pretty much."

They closed their eyes. Before he finished his next exhale, Beth's jumbled thoughts filled his head the way a nice bath mixed with his favorite bath oils calmed his soul. He was nearly whole. Beth placed her hand on his chest, over his heart like she had with Tom. His eyelids popped open.

"Beth," Grady croaked, fighting the need to slip his hands around her and never let go. His pectorals twitched at the thought.

"Shhh. I have something I need to say."

Grady swallowed the lump in his throat, digging his toes into the floorboards to keep from moving closer.

"You've respected my boundaries without complaint, showing your strength and loyalty not only to Tom but to me. Thank you."

I would do anything for you. He couldn't say the words aloud, fearing if he moved a single muscle his control would snap.

The sunshine beaming from Beth's face took his breath away. When she removed her hand, it was like opening the door on a spring day to let the wind through. Grady's breaths were haggard, but Beth's appreciation, her transitioning love were his anchors.

Tom's head popped up when Beth exited the cabin in front of Grady. Deep thoughts wore heavy lines on his friend's face, but they dwindled and softened when his gaze found his wife.

"Let's do this."

Chapter 41

BETH

THE ARCHWAY TO THE outside shimmered when the waning light slid over its surface. Funny, it didn't do that the first time they left the Grove.

"Your magic is awake now. There's so much more to discover." Grady's velvety voice coated her insides like a soothing balm.

"I'll step through first, make sure it's safe," Grady said aloud, tapping his head. "Beth will know."

He stepped between the birches and disappeared.

When Beth turned around, Tom grabbed her. One hand cradled the back of her neck while the other cupped her backside. He kissed her like this would be their last, setting her skin on fire with desire. Heat lay waste to her bones, rendering them to nothing. And when Tom broke away, Beth's eyes were still closed. Her chest heaved. If Tom didn't have his arms around her, she'd be putty on the ground.

"Wow. If you were going for a brain-stuttering, goo for insides kinda kiss, you hit the mark."

Her lips still tingled when she opened her eyes. Tom studied her with hooded eyes. A contented smile perched on his lips.

"Good." He rubbed noses with her before placing a feather-light kiss on the tip. "Call it our good luck kiss before battle."

"Come through when y'all are ready," Grady relayed, a tiredness in his voice Beth wanted to chase away.

"It's safe." Beth laced fingers with Tom. "Let's not let all that good luck go to waste."

One moment, they were in a dimming globe near the throes of springtime dusk. The next, they were thrust into a midnight forest full of watchful eyes. Her skin chilled and broke out with goosebumps.

"Everything good?" Grady asked before her eyes adjusted.

"Yeah. It's just a lot darker than I thought it would be."

"Right. I think you-know-who is optimistic about tonight," Grady grumbled. He reached into a pouch and pulled three 'invisibility' potions free. The reddish-brown syrup clung to the sides as he handed them out. "There's activity all around, so I'm having trouble pinpointing anything."

"We'll all double our efforts to keep our eyes and ears open," Tom replied he took the top off his potion and made a face.

"Bottoms up on three." Beth popped the cork. It fizzled as she counted down, "One...two...three."

The trio tipped their potions back and the potion slid down Beth's throat. The combination of blackberry, rosemary, and birch bark wasn't entirely unpleasant. It reminded her of an unsweetened sassafras soda.

Tucking the bottles back into the outside pocket of their packs, Beth took their hands in hers. "Follow my lead."

She raised her hands and faced the sky. The full moon was glorious, sending a ripple of power as she bathed in its light. Beth drew from its energy on a slow inhale.

On her exhalation, she cast the spell, "Oh, Blessed Moon Mother, round with radiant light, grant us the gift of Nightly Sight. Allow us to see, as your nocturnal children do, every branch, every leaf, every speck of dust clinging to dew. So mote it be."

Beth lowered her arms to her sides. The guys still held fast to her hands, providing her with a comforting strength. At some point, she'd squeezed her eyes shut.

Moment of truth.

Relaxing her lids, they opened slowly. It was like looking at the world through sharpening lenses. She could count the individual needles on pine trees ten feet away, and tell the difference between the groves of deciduous trees scattered between patches of ferns. Even colors were a richer shade.

"Whoa. I can see *everything*!" Tom was peering around like a kid who was visiting an amusement park for the first time.

As much as Beth wished to celebrate the small victory, they were burning resources and time. "Let's move out, boys."

Beth accepted a spear from Tom, and Grady led the way. They moved eastward on swift, light feet, covering two of the three miles before the effects of the cloaking potion began to weaken.

Eventually, the whispers grew louder as the forest dimmed further, putting them back on an even playing field. A whiff of rotten eggs floated on the breeze, getting stronger. Beth's neck hairs went stiff a heartbeat before everything went still and silent. Goosebumps prickled all over her body in warning. The hair on Grady's and Tom's arms were raised.

She gave them a curt nod and took formation. The guys stood back-to-back with her. Holding the enchanted spears at the ready, they scoured the area for whatever evil hunted them. Their breaths came out in white puffs as the air turned frigid.

Fear radiated from their group. Beth reined hers in like guiding a stubborn mule. No matter how much determination she built, her legs still shook. A black form swooped in and out of the trees, inches beyond her reach.

Beth tightened her hold around the spears shaft, causing the binding to creak. Her tongue darted out, moistening dry lips before gritting her teeth. Beside her, Tom stabbed the space in front of him with his spear hitting nothing.

A grinding cackle echoed in the darkness.

The Agnazar slipped out from the shadows, making Beth gasp. The books did not adequately describe how grotesque and inhuman these beings were. She was caught in a waking nightmare.

The thing reeked of sulfur. This creature was a larger shadow being than the Ungenth and supposedly faster. Like the Ungenth, its 'robes' moved despite the wind, which was dead still now. A super-intelligent malignance studied them as if they were insects to be exterminated. Its long, thin teeth turned up in a lipless smile. Gnarly hands gripped a thin, obsidian blade dripping a viscous, green substance that scorched the earth where it landed.

"We come for the female," it hissed with a deep, grating whisper as if speaking the words aloud pained it. "Give her to us, and no harm shall come to you." The Agnazar flew around the trio, stopped in front of Beth, and extended a hand.

In perfect synchronization, Grady and Tom thrust their spears, tips piercing the Agnazar on either side. It recoiled with a high-pitched, unearthly scream. More of the green substance flowed slowly from its wounds, coating their spears. Seconds later, the tips of their weapons sizzled. The pestilent ichor bubbled, dissolving everything it touched. Reflexively, they tossed the burnt remains to the side before the poison could spread to their hands.

The Agnazar twisted around and howled before charging straight for Beth. She reared back and hurled her spear, using the wind to correct its path. It landed deep in the creature's chest with a sickening thud. Screeching in agony, it dropped its sword to claw at the spear. Beth took a deep breath and transferred enough energy from the forest to produce the blue flame. The ball barely fit in her palm, but when she threw it at the Agnazar, the fire was ravenous. Writhing as it burned, the screeching threatened to burst her ear drums. She covered her tender orifices. There was no way the dads hadn't heard the screams.

As the Agnazar disintegrated, and the forest returned to normal, Beth took stock. There were two more of these creatures to take on. The only weapons they had were the few spells Tom had found, but he didn't have the magic to protect himself. They were fucked.

"Nothing in the texts spoke of them having acidic blood," Tom said as he started away from the area. "Myrtle only mentioned the boiling blood disease."

"It's best to assume any information we don't have firsthand is outdated," Grady said, eyeing the fallen weapon.

Beth grabbed his arm. "Don't even think about it."

"It might be okay, as long as I don't touch the green stuff," Grady argued without looking at her.

"Don't risk it. We'll just have to hit them with magic instead," she said, terrified it would curse him if he simply touched the hilt.

"Yeah," Tom agreed, "I'll fashion some makeshift spears or coat my knife with the fire potion we made. Don't risk it."

Grady studied Beth and Tom before taking his pack off. He brought out a pair of work gloves and pulled them on. Beth placed her hand on his shoulder, pleading with him to reconsider, "*Please don't.*"

"I'll be fine. Trust me." With a gloved hand, Grady touched the handle with a single finger.

Beth sucked in a breath when he wrapped his hand around the hilt. When Grady lifted the sword off the ground, the acrid smell of scorched earth burned their nostrils.

"See? It's alright," Grady remarked, holding the otherworldly blade out in front of him. "Let's go."

Beth shot him a disapproving glance when he tested the weight of the blade. Her disapproval turned into a smirk when the blade shattered into ashes with an oily green sheen, drifting on the breeze.

"*Now* can we go?" Beth huffed. Tom shrugged apologetically before he pushed past Grady.

She rolled her eyes and followed Tom while rifling through her pack. The longer they lingered here, the more her resolve broke. The Agnazar freaked her out more than she cared to admit.

The sound of Grady's boots pounding the earth stopped next to her. Without a word, Beth shoved a bottle in his hands, and he sighed.

One day soon, she'd have to have a heart-to-heart talk with Grady. If they were responsible for the fate of the world, they needed to lay some ground rules.

Tightening the strap on her backpack, Beth shut down the thought of what life would look like without Tom. She needed to focus. They had some Agnazar to kill...and four angry, armed dads to contend with.

Chapter 42

BETH

THE FASTER THEY MADE headway, the more tree limbs caught her hair or tugged at their clothing. It was as if the forest deliberately tried to sabotage their expedition. They'd been following a worn dirt path for some time now. Surely, they would be there soon.

Tom and Grady paused at the edge of the woods. When they continued, the clearing up ahead was empty. Beth's stomach knotted. They hadn't run into the other two Agnazar or the dads, so where were they?

Every ruffling leaf, snapping twig, and flickering shadow had Beth on edge. It was like winding a jack-in-the-box without the warning song.

Grady curled back his lips and sniffed the air. Seeing him less than half as anxious as she was helped to slow her racing heart.

Tom knelt in the grass, sharpening the point of his makeshift spear. His surprisingly confident demeanor put a smile on her face. After he closed the knife, he slipped it into his pocket and caught her staring. He gave her a lopsided grin and popped the cork off the fire potion, coating the point. The tip glowed a bright red before dulling to a sheen. Her husband was somewhat protected, but Beth was still worried.

She'd learned a lot about magic in a short time, and Grady proved to be a patient teacher. However, testing what she'd practiced in theory against a very real and dangerous adversary was entirely different. The possibility of losing the men she loved had doubled. Beth would not have the strength to do what was necessary if it weren't for them.

Tom and Grady came to her side holding their potions near their mouths. "Together," they said in unison.

Gripping the small glass bottle, she glanced between her guys. Warmth blossomed in her chest.

There it was. The spark of hope she needed to restore balance. It spread like wildfire, consuming her, and burned away her worries.

Beth lifted her potion. "Together."

The three tipped the bottles, drinking every last drop of the protection potion. The sour tang turned peppery, leaving her mouth feeling like cotton. The empty bottles were discarded in a drawstring bag on Tom's hip and tucked away. Beth slid her left hand into Tom's, and her right hand into Grady's. The light of the guardians emanated from them as they made their way to the ritual stone.

While this area of the forest hadn't been exactly welcoming days ago, the trees had become barren and gray. The land was visibly darker, as if an umbrella of evil had descended upon it. They neared the ritual stone to find the other two Agnazars floated on either side of it. A shiver ran down Beth's spine. They snarled and hissed at the bright light being brought into their midst.

"Your struggle is futile. How long before your shield loses power?" the Agnazar voiced in unison with the same, bristly whisper as the one from earlier. "You cannot stay behind it forever, humans. Give us the girl, and we will make your deaths quick. Otherwise, Ja'azul will consume your world, leaving it to burn."

Hearing one speak was bad enough, but both speaking at the same time sent the chill from her spine into her knees. They shook as fear tightened her chest. Beth would have fainted if the guys didn't have a grip hold on her hands.

One of the Agnazar approached their protective bubble, sliding the edge of its blade along the barrier. The bright white sparks reminded her of when Grady welds. They landed on the Agnazar's skin, hissing and burning with the acrid scent of burnt toast slathered in spoiled mayonnaise, then cooked over a tar pit. Her stomach bubbled and churned.

Defeating these creatures was her destiny; it was what she was born to do. If she couldn't be brave now, with her two guys backing her up, there was no hope. She wasn't a pushover.

Beth straightened her back, standing taller. The power radiated from her, causing the air to thicken and the pressure to drop.

"Whatever we do, don't let go of Beth," Grady said through clenched teeth. He adjusted to link fingers with her.

"Right." Tom squeezed her hand.

Tingles shot up her arms. The sensation was spectacular. Magic flowed between the three, pulsing like some sentient being.

Beth used this boost to project the light shield further. If they could reach the top, they'd use Grady's incantation to close the gate. Any power the Agnazar drew from it would be cut off. Theoretically.

As they began their uphill march, Grady chanted his first prepared spell, and the ground shook. Roots burst loose from the packed earth, whipping toward the creature nearest them. The Agnazar hacked away at endless tendrils.

Beth concentrated on holding the shield, but Grady's display was mesmerizing. When one of the roots got past its sword strokes, it coiled around the creature like a snake. Grady dragged the Agnazar into the light. The extraterrestrial horror thrashed, screaming vileness in an unknown language that felt like nails on a chalkboard to her brain. Not soon enough, it had burned to dust and the ashen remains fell away. The screams continued to echo long after it was gone.

A tug came from Tom's side. He grunted as the spear loosed from his hand. The tip was a flaming ember, igniting as it soared through the air. At the last moment, the Agnazar shook its head and dodged out of the way, hissing as the spear grazed its arm.

"Foolish humans. You were warned," the creature spat with its scratchy alien voice. It then howled a series of guttural sounds and disappeared into the fissure.

Beth dropped her head in relief, thanking the goddess that the creatures had gone. They were safe... Well, *safer* once they finished.

"Let's close this damn gate and find Jeff's baseball-bound soul." Beth kept her eyes on the altar stone.

It was almost over. She looked forward to finding their new normal, whatever it was. They just had to survive the next part of their task.

TOM

WHEN THE LAST AGNAZAR left, a weight lifted from Tom's shoulders. He hadn't used the power Myrtle forced on him. He'd take whatever time with Beth he could get. A year or two, however long it took. He forced the nagging at the back of his mind back into another box. One-handed, he pulled the square of fabric from his pocket. Using his mouth to grab one corner, he readied it to house the ball under the stone.

Ducking his head revealed no baseball. Tom's position was limiting the search. "*Where is it?*" he thought in a panic. He would have to let go of Beth's hand and crawl underneath to get a better look.

"No, Tom!" Grady screamed, but it was too late.

As soon as Tom let go, Beth's light shield dimmed to that of a cheap nightlight. He didn't think it would make that big of a difference. It was a shitty time to assume because he'd exposed them all. He finished the job, scooping Jeff's baseball with the square of cloth and tucked the corners around it.

"I'm sorry. That was stupid of me, but I got the baseball." Tom's gut twisted. Even his apology sounded lame.

"What's done is done," Grady grumbled. The protective shield shimmered and flickered until it was gone.

Beth shot Grady a pinched look before addressing them both. "Don't worry. We can build it back. Just let me—"

The loud boom of a shotgun ricocheted off the stone pillars standing at the four corners. Tom pushed Beth behind him. Grady wore a murderous frown.

Standing less than ten feet away were Jack Newman, Louis Cooper, Elliot Larson, and Curtis Putnam. How the hell had they gotten so close without them knowing?

Jack frowned at his son, pointing his rifle at the ground at Tom's feet. Curtis stood behind the others, wringing his grease-stained baseball cap. His rifle was tucked haphazardly under his armpit while he stared blankly at the ground.

Louis Cooper and Elliott Larson, however, aimed their rifles at chest level. Grady's dad wore a smirk that oozed contempt while Paul's dad's maniacal grimace could curdle milk.

Tom reached for Beth's hand at the same time Grady did. For a second, Tom experienced their hearts pounding in unison before it was just his own. He could have enjoyed it more if there weren't four angry cultists glowering at them with trigger-happy fingers. No matter what happened, he had the power to protect Beth. He wasn't sure if the blessing Myrtle gave him would work on their fathers, but he'd try. *If* he was capable of unleashing such devastating power against his own father.

"Step away from the stone table and give us the baseball," Elliott Larson demanded, his hate-filled glare falling on Beth. "Or I will end you where you stand."

The dark circles under his bloodshot eyes cried grief, but the building veins across his forehead and sinewy arms promised to tear the world apart to avenge his son. Tom wasn't much of a poker player, but he knew a lost hand when saw one.

Chapter 43

GRADY

"Mr. Larson," Grady began, holding his free hand up non-threateningly. When the man pointed the barrel of his rifle at Beth, he joined Tom to give her more cover.

"Don't start with me, boy," Elliott growled, cocking his rifle to drive the point. "Now, you kids step away from the stone, nice and slow."

Not surprisingly, it was Jack Newman that came to Grady's defense instead of his own father. "Calm down, Elliott. They'll listen if you put that away." He raised his chin toward the gun barrel.

Paul's dad didn't take his eyes off Beth the entire time but lowered his rifle. "Jack, I thought you, of all people, would be pissed that your daughter-in-law is a damned devil-worshipping witch. Obviously, she's bewitched your boy and Grady to save herself."

Even though Tom's dad believed in the rituals he'd participated in each year, he was an otherwise sensible man. Grady urged Tom to try, "Tom, if anyone can make your dad see reason, it's you. Talk to him."

Tom glanced at Grady and nodded in understanding. "Dad, please. Beth hasn't bewitched anyone. If it weren't for her and her magic, Grady and I would be dead, too."

Before Jack got a chance to respond, Elliott interrupted with spit flying from his mouth, "You admit to killing Paul, is that it?" He raised his gun again, pointing the rifle at the three, and took two long strides toward them. "Tell me what happened, or the whore of a witch dies now!"

"Don't you dare call my wife a whore!" Tom commanded, fuming at the accusation. He let go of Beth's hand to advance on him.

Grady held his ground in front of Beth, his fists tightening. He let Tom worry about Paul's dad. Staring down the barrel of his father's rifle, Grady met Louis Cooper's icy glare.

He didn't trust the man. Grady knew if he moved, his father would fire on Beth without a second thought. Louis Cooper didn't care if Grady loved her or not. Beth stood between him and his quest for power. Hell, now they both did.

Out of the corner of Grady's eye, Jack wrestled the barrel of Elliott's rifle to the dirt. Beth's power pulsed. She pushed the shield to cover Tom as he rushed forward.

Grady flinched when Elliott's rifle went off, peppering the ground with buckshot mere inches from his feet.

Tom punched Mr. Larson square in the jaw, rendering him rigid before falling to the ground. Tom kicked Mr. Larson's rifle out of reach and turned to his dad.

"Son, be reasonable—" Jack Newman pleaded. He went to embrace his son.

Tom shoved him away. "Don't pretend like everything's okay! Do you even *know* who you've been sacrificing to all these years?" he asked, backing up toward Beth.

Grady's gaze flicked to Tom and Jack's confrontation. It was enough time for the viper to strike. A heavy hand shoved him from behind. Grady stumbled forward, flapping his arms for balance. When he turned around, his father stood over Beth with a triumphant sneer. She sat on the ground, rubbing her red arm. Her eyes were wet with unshed tears.

"Of course he knows," Louis Cooper answered, grabbing a handful of Beth's hair. He shoved the twin barrels of his rifle against the side of her head.

The edges of Grady's sight were tinged in red. His blood boiled, singing the music of magic as it crackled around him. Grady lifted his hand and drew a breath. The earth rumbled at his command. Jack and Curtis aimed their rifles at Grady.

"I don't think so, son," Mr. Newman said firmly.

Tom moved to help Beth, but a hand fisted his shirt. Elliott was back up, nursing his jaw. He shoved Tom toward Jack. Tom's dad caught him with his free arm, but Tom wrenched free, glaring at his father in disgust.

"How can you stand to be part of this sick practice?" Tom sneered.

"You wouldn't understand, son." Jack hung his head.

"Who do you think helped me coax Gail here for her sacrifice?" Louis goaded, the slimy smile crossing his face angered Grady to a level beyond anything he'd ever experienced.

His dad's confession caused something inside Grady to snap. All his life, his father never seemed proud of anything he'd accomplished. He'd always degraded Grady for becoming a scholar instead of a welder like himself and his father before him. Said he was wasting his time and should do an honest man's work. Growing up, Grady spent a lot of time at Tom's house while his mom took all the shit from his dad to protect him. She'd always encouraged Grady to do the best in whatever he chose to do, and his dad had finally killed her for it.

Grady's heart exploded into pieces. Screaming in rage, the fire beneath his skin broke through the surface and his panther tore free quicker than a blink. The fear in his father's eyes as he pounced on him was unforgettable. Louis Cooper kicked and screamed as the panther tore him to shreds.

TOM

TOM AND HIS DAD stared in disbelief at the gruesome scene. The blood and crunching bones made him want to hurl.

He'd come to terms with his best friend being able to shapeshift into a panther but hadn't considered Grady would obey the more animalistic urges. Tom couldn't blame him, though. Grady had been devastated by his mother's death four years ago. Hearing Louis confirm what they'd figured out brought all that pain rushing back. Tom didn't blame his best friend for getting his revenge.

Tom tore his eyes from the gory spectacle. Beside him, Jeff's dad, Curtis, gagged and spewed chunks into the grass.

"Dear god, I don't wanna die. I'm outta here!" Mr. Putnam clutched the baseball to his chest and disappeared into the woods.

Tom barely registered what the man said. He hurried to Beth's side to finish what they started while his dad was distracted.

"Tom!" Jack shouted with the authoritative voice from his childhood. Tom stopped and half-turned, keeping Beth safely tucked at his back.

Elliott stood at Jack's side. Both men aimed their rifles as they advanced. "Don't be a fool, Son. Come home with me now. Your mother has been asking to see you...she's worried sick."

"I'm not leaving Beth, Dad," Tom said with finality, squeezing her hand. "Tell Mom I'll call her as soon as I can."

A cruel smile spread across Elliott's face. The irises of his dark blue eyes were swallowed by white. They look like black pinpoints. Tom had a sinking feeling in his gut.

Mr. Larson kept his slow advance, rifle raised at chest height. "Ja'azul can give you immortality and riches beyond imagining. Can your witch wife do that?" He spat. Foam gathered at the corners of his mouth.

Sweat ran into Tom's eyes. It stung like hell, and he blinked as much as he could to clear it without losing focus.

Beside Elliott, Tom's dad, Jack, sighed. Fear closed Tom's airways when his dad aimed his rifle at Beth.

"Dad?"

"My Son, I will free you so you can see reason again." Jack's voice broke as he cocked the rifle and set it against his shoulder.

Tom jumped in front of Beth at the same time the pressure of Beth's shield touched his back. There was a loud bang, and his head felt fuzzy. His chest felt like someone had thrown hot coals against it.

"Nooo!" Beth screamed.

"A son for a son," Mr. Larson snarled, but it sounded as though he was talking through a tube.

Tom's legs went limp. His breaths were wheezy. Something liquid filled his lungs, making the oxygen scarce.

I think I've been shot.

His whole body was tired. He clawed against the tunnel as sleep dragged him downward. Beth wasn't safe. He couldn't leave her, not now. His attempts slowed until the pinpoint of light at the end fuzzed into shadow.

Chapter 44

BETH

"No, no, no." Beth stared in horror as small red dots spread across the back of Tom's shirt.

Her eyes blurred and the world came to a screeching halt around her. Why hadn't she shielded him sooner?

Tom wheezed and fell backward, limp into her arms. The weight sent them both tumbling to the ground, but Beth managed, landing on her backside again. She cradled Tom's head in her lap, but her hands were too small to keep all the holes in his chest from weeping.

"Tom, baby, stay with me."

Beth blinked furiously and swept away the hairs stuck to Tom's forehead with shaky hands. The squeezing in her chest made it more difficult to breathe between sobs. Agony ripped her soul in half.

A muffled scream followed another gunshot. Beth was too stricken with grief to even bother looking. Tom lay dying in her arms, and the man responsible for it was dead.

But Beth had a use what was left of his pathetic life. If she could draw energy from the earth, she could draw it from a man.

She sniffled and slipped out from underneath Tom's head, making sure he was stable. He reached out for her.

"I'm gonna fix you, baby." Beth cupped his cheek, leaving a bloody handprint. "Please, stay with me a little longer."

Tom's watery eyes and wordless pleas stoked the anger consuming her compassion. Beth kissed his forehead. "Don't you dare leave me yet. I'll be back as soon as I can."

Beth her eyes with the back of her hand and stood, letting the magic take over. As her feet left the ground, she searched for the man whose life was forfeit. Elliott laid on the ground, a bloodied hand applied pressure to his thigh. Beth balled her anguish into a harpoon and shot it at Elliott Larson's black heart.

He screamed and jerked as blood poured down his chest. Beth needed it all, but she couldn't give Tom anything tainted. She used the metaphysical rope attached to her harpoon as a conduit, sending her white-hot cleansing energy into the vessel. Elliott's screams grew louder and more frenzied as he scratched frantically at his chest; fingernails bloody and filled with gore. When his eyes began to bleed, he thrashed on the grass before stopping abruptly with a choking gasp. Beth grasped the life energy before it was wasted and drew it into herself.

Elliott's back arched until he exhaled his last breath and went limp. The grass beneath Mr. Larson's lifeless body was matted by a pool of blood. His empty eyes stared at the night sky.

The satisfaction she received from watching the light dim from his eyes should have scared her. It did not. The power she held rejoiced at another source of evil being snuffed out, but there was another to be dealt with.

Beth turned her fury toward the man who had become a second father to her. Unlike Elliott, she searched Jack's heart for any shred of goodness—for his wife's sake. Lilian had been Beth's role model. She wouldn't needlessly take Jack's life if there was something redeemable.

Jack was at Tom's side, applying pressure to his chest. The blood hadn't slowed. The damage was spread too wide to cover. Jack stared at Beth with wide eyes, terror-stricken with remorse, and mouthed the word '*please.*'

The man had held a rifle to Beth's heart, intent on taking her life. Still, she could not stop the pity welling up inside. Jack and the others were the monsters; she wasn't.

"Only for him." Beth's voice sounded like several recordings playing at once. Jack nodded, tears streaking his face.

Lowering to the ground opposite Jack, Beth placed her hands above Tom's chest. The energy brimming inside her was effortlessly converted into the warm, healing blue flame.

Closing her eyes, Beth focused on pulling out the projectiles she could find, starting with the major organs. After each bullet was removed, Beth healed its space. Tom screamed in agony as the black bits of metal fell out of the holes they had created. He was drenched in sweat and blood. Soon, his breathing became quick and shallow.

"Don't leave me yet, hon...Hold on a little longer." Beth shook uncontrollably, but she'd never done anything like this before. Once they made it to the hospital, the doctors would have some questions.

Those were worries for later. She wouldn't stop until every last fragment had been removed.

GRADY

HIS MOTHER'S DEATH HAD been avenged, and justice delivered. The partial victory was bittered by the knowledge that his mother's soul had been consumed by Ja'azul. The only way of having complete retribution was to defeat the Eater of Souls for good.

Grady changed back into his human form, studying in the bloody scene surrounding him. Paul's father was dead. His face was twisted in agony and body soaked in blood.

His gaze trailed the carnage to where Tom lay in Beth's arms. His best friend's sticky, red chest caused gravity to shift, taking the ground out from underneath Grady's feet. Jack blotted Tom's forehead with a handkerchief, while Beth worked to repair the extensive damage.

Choking back a sob, Grady stumbled to Beth's side and placed his hands above hers. Channeling the earth's energy, he sent it to her. "Take it."

She gave him a strained smile. He gulped. Her eyes were a pale gray, and her skin was colorless. Grady prayed he wasn't too late.

The thought of losing Tom gutted Grady. If he lost Beth...there would be no reason for him to exist anymore.

"Done." Beth breathed in relief. Her grin had scarcely reached her eyes when she collapsed on top of Tom.

"No," Grady's choked command wasn't enough to will her to breathe. He had to work quickly or they'd both be lost.

Grady grabbed Jack by the shoulders and stared him straight on. "Make sure Tom keeps breathing."

Jack nodded in understanding. Grady turned his attention to Beth, pulling her into his arms, he checked for a pulse. It was weak but steady. He picked away the hair plastered to her face and held his palm above her mouth. Her breaths were faint, but, by the grace of the goddess, she was alive.

Grady hugged her limp body against his chest. He searched for their magical connection, for the melody he'd become familiar with. It had gone silent, but the thread remained.

Sobbing in relief, Grady placed his hands on either side of her head at the temples and closed his eyes. Concentrating, he drew on the life energy around them, hoping it would be enough to replenish what she'd used.

"Please don't leave us, Beth. I love you. I need you."

BETH

SHE'D NEVER BEEN SO sleepy. Beth wanted to lay down and rest as much as she needs coffee to function in the morning. The only problem was the near-imperceptible hum. There was no way she could sleep with its constant racket.

Beth opened her eyes and blinked, but there was pitch black everywhere. Wherever 'everywhere' was. Beth stumbled to her feet and focused on the sound since her sight was useless. She walked toward it, following the source until it grew louder. She thrust her hands into the dead air, searching for anything tangible to grasp. Her fingertips brushed against something pulled taut. She waved her hands in the general area, intent on finding the object. She was sure her life depended on it.

"Aha!" Beth's fingers curled around a thin, floating stick. She kept her hand around it as she searched for its end. After what seemed like forever, she reasoned her stick was actually a rope. Either way, she needed answers to why and where *this* was and continued her search.

The humming grew, and Beth saw a light ahead. When she focused on it, her body tingled with anticipation. Her feet led her down the rope to the mouth of the light, which was a lighted archway. Blinding, white light shone through, bleaching everything on the other side. She squinted until the outline of trees came into view.

There were familiar-looking people huddled around bodies.

Beth fought the urge to step through. Something bad happened here and she was frightened. Recoiling, she took a few steps back. Curiosity kept her from wandering too far, but fear stopped her from jumping through.

A deep, soothing voice echoed around her. It cracked with equal parts pain and need. It called to her, igniting a deep longing inside. Whoever the voice belonged to needed her. She was the only person who could take the pain away, but it meant going through to the place that frightened her. The voice vibrated the string tethered to her soul, becoming farther away and softer. It was dying. If she didn't leave now, the voice would be gone forever and that thought caused her heart to crack open. On that thought, Beth ran to the light. She embraced it and the feeling of home that came with it.

Beth's eyes flew open, met by the worried stare of the most gorgeous set of deep blue eyes she'd ever seen. Joy, love, and hope swam in their depths. A part of her wanted to drown in those waters. She cupped his cheek, and the rest of her brain caught up.

She remembered what she'd been doing before getting lost on the way to her permanent exit. Tom's chest blooming rouge, the bullets, so many holes. Beth moved her hand from his face to Grady's bicep. He made no move to let her go.

"He's okay. You saved his life," Grady replied, tenderly stroking her hair.

That simple act sent Beth's emotions into a swirling tempest. She wanted to throw herself around Grady in comfort, but Tom needed a hospital...and they had an audience.

"Are you..." Beth trailed, sitting up and putting distance between them.

"I'm okay." Yearning passed over Grady's face. He stood, dusted his hands on his pants, and extended his hand. "Come on. Let's get you two to the hospital."

Beth accepted his warm and callused hand. When Grady helped her up, the hillside spun like a top. He caught her, as he always did, hands gripping her elbows.

"Careful. You dipped too far into yourself to save Tom." Grady's firm voice wavered at the end.

Beth noticed the blackened ash under their feet. Her gaze followed it all the way to the tree line. She gasped. A circle of devastation swallowed every living thing within her eyesight. The sickly trees that had given the hilltop evil cemetery vibes had been erased. How much effort had Grady put into keeping *her* alive?

The space inside her chest was too small for the emotion building up there. Some spilled down her face.

"I remember. Sort of. I followed the string, and you were there. You saved me, Grady." Beth slipped her arms around Grady's waist in a crushing hug. "Thank you."

"I will always protect you," he murmured into her hair before breaking free of her embrace. His tired smile made her heart flutter.

She sniffled and returned his smile before turning her attention to Tom.

Jack's wary gaze analyzed Beth's every move as she knelt next to her husband. Her face still leaked excess feelings. Tom's breaths were steady, but his heartbeat was weak.

"I'm sorry it took me so long." She wiped as much of the sticky blood from his cheek as she could with the hem of her shirt and cradled her husband's face. "Thank you for being so brave, baby."

Tom didn't move or answer. He slept, resting after the trauma to his system. She'd done what she could to save him and she did. Most importantly, they'd survived.

Beth glanced around at the bodies on the ground, lingering on Elliott's ashen face. Well, the ones that mattered had survived. And that was good enough for today.

Chapter 45

TOM

Tom was in a small, white room with a single curtain and faint beeping noises. He blinked against the dim light until his eyes focused. Tubes ran from his arm to a bag feeding him intravenously. In the chair next to his bed was a sleeping lump with a mop of curly black hair. Grady's head rested in the crook of his arm at an odd angle. Tom's heart warmed at the sight of his best friend.

When he realized they were the only ones in the room, panic rose in his throat.

"Beth," Tom croaked. Tears stung his eyes at the thought of losing her.

The bed next to his squeaked, and the curtain moved aside. "I'm here, honey," she whispered. Beth's under eyes were dark and heavy; her usual deep green eyes were pale. Tom gulped. He wasn't the only one who dodged death's scythe.

She shuffled toward him with outstretched arms. The room twisted and contorted like the walls were melting from extreme heat. The lights flickered rapidly, plunging Tom into darkness.

His eyes didn't have time to adjust before the lights came back at half brightness. When they did, he yelped at the sight. Beth's eyes were black, and her legs were wispy black shadows. A hideous cackle came from her lips before she morphed into one of the Dark One's agents.

"Ja'azul sends the light-bringer a message," it snarled with its sharp rounded rows of needle teeth. Pointing a gnarled finger at him, it continued, "you will be our messenger."

Tom's skin crawled. His lips were glued together of their own accord as the monster continued.

"Three souls, Tom Newman, and Ja'azul will haunt more than just your dreams," it growled before cackling again. "Three more souls and Ja'azul will have your Beth." It accentuated the 'th' sound at the end of her name. Whether on purpose or because of its unnatural speech, it was unnerving.

Tom blanched. The being knew their names. He tried not to show how shaken he was by gritting his teeth. He pulled his lips apart with a pained groan.

"What do I call you?" he asked, looking to glean any information he could since the rest of his brain had shut down.

"My master calls us Ungenth, but this knowledge will do you no good," it growled. "Wake now and tell your Beth that Ja'azul comes for her soon."

The Ungenth faded into nothing as the lights flickered on again. When Tom jolted awake from his nightmare, he blinked against the glare of white lights against white walls. Blotchy figures blocked some of the light as they moved closer. The incessant beeping next to his head gave him a headache.

The shapes above him came into focus. Grady and Beth stood next to his bed, deep frowns etched across their faces. Tom raised his hand toward Beth, but the two nurses working to calm the machines sent her and Grady out of the room. Beth glanced over her shoulder as Grady guided her with his hand high on her back. She mouthed, "I love you," before the male nurse blocked his view.

GRADY

GRADY SAT BESIDE BETH with one arm curled protectively around her shoulders. She stared numbly at the floor. Lillian Newman sat on Beth's other side, patting her hand while willing Tom's door to reopen with her intense stare.

When Tom's heart monitor went crazy, Grady worried they were losing him again. They'd barely made it to the nearest hospital before he'd gone into cardiac arrest. The staff rushed him to the emergency room for surgery. Seventeen hours later, the surgeon approached, shaking his head with wide eyes and all the color drained from his face, talking about miracles.

Tom had cheated death twice tonight.

Grady wasn't sure how to feel about it. Holding Beth's limp body in his arms was enough to break him. She belonged to him, destined to be his partner, his lover, the mother of their children. She was everything he ever wanted and more. But he couldn't have her because Tom survived.

Of course, he didn't want best friend to die. Beth wasn't the only one who would be crushed. This was the first time she'd left Tom's side since they arrived. Grady had a front-row seat to her grief, broadcasted in real-time. Underneath it, almost entangled, was her need for him. Beth's mental health was Grady's priority. He would be her unyielding lighthouse amid the thunderous storms raining destruction.

Beth leaned forward, resting her elbows on her knees. Grady rubbed her back in big, slow circles. The rhythm must have helped, because the tightness in her shoulders finally loosened. To his surprise, their bond was quiet, as if the magic knew she was not in the right frame of mind and was respectful of her wishes. The thought was fascinating.

While he pondered the possibility of sentient magic, the door to Tom's room opened. Beth sat straight, her hands clasped in her lap. The young female nurse took Tom's chart and headed off.

The male nurse stayed and addressed the four, "Mr. Newman has stabilized on his own. It appears he was having a nightmare, which is normal after a traumatic experience."

"How long will it be until he's awake?" Lillian's eyes and nose were red. She held a tissue in her hand, poised to wipe them.

The nurse smiled kindly. "He is awake now. You may go in. One at a time, please, and only for a few minutes. He still needs plenty of rest."

Lillian didn't wait for them to choose turn order. She was on her feet before the nurse finished his statement.

Jack shook the nurse's hand. "Thank you." He busied himself reading the fliers on the bulletin board.

Beth broke the silence, "Jack, you can go in next, and then Grady." The man nodded grimly and turned back to reading fliers.

"Why are you going in last?" Grady asked, leaning forward to rest his elbows on his knees. He was beyond exhausted—they both were—but the need to be strong for Beth overruled everything else.

"Because," she replied with a sigh. "Jack and Lily are beside themselves with worry. *We* know Tom will be okay. Between our magic and the hospital, he shouldn't have much permanent damage."

Grady nodded as Lillian came through the doorway with a relieved grin. Jack met her halfway, stopping for a hug before entering Tom's room. She came to sit on the other side of Beth.

"Thank you both, for helping save my boy. The doctors are still baffled at how you managed to get so many pellets out so quickly, but...I know. Jack told me everything," Lillian whispered as she blotted her eyes with a new tissue. She leaned in close to Beth's ear, hugging her lightly. "If there's *anything* you need, just ask," she murmured before heading to the water fountain.

Grady and Beth took a deep breath together, letting it out with a nervous chuckle. They sat quietly while Tom's dad took his turn.

When Beth rested her head on Grady's shoulder like she used to, his stomach fluttered. He took this moment and stored it with the other fantasies squirreled away in the part of his heart reserved for Beth. They'd keep him company over the next few years.

A short while later, Jack came back out with a similarly relieved grin for his wife. They spoke in hushed voices before Lillian excused them to get food from the cafeteria.

"Will you be okay out here by yourself?" Grady fought the urge to hold Beth's hand and played with the frayed edge of his shirt instead.

"Yeah. It's only for a few minutes." She nodded, sitting up and arching her brow. "Plus,

I'm not really alone, am I?"

"No, not really." Grady stood, kissed the top of her head, and sighed. "We can probably get away with you coming, too."

"I don't want to break any rules," she replied with a weak grin. "Go on. He's waiting."

TOM

TOM GAVE GRADY A recap of his dream, who relayed it telepathically to Beth. He thought they would be more upset, but he figured the constant stream of impending death had them all worn. "What I want to know is, where did the soul come from?"

"Jeff." Grady said with a growl. "Curtis must've waited for us to leave. We haven't seen his ghost since yesterday."

When Jeff's ghost didn't pop up, Tom felt like he was missing a small part of himself. One of his lifelong friends was truly gone. When Jeff wasn't following Paul around like a lost puppy, Tom got a brief glimpse of the real version. The one who sketched pencil drawings of flora and fauna when he thought no one was watching. Tom was gutted knowing Jeff's soul was given to Ja'azul. His friend deserved better.

"The Ungenth didn't say when Ja'azul was coming?" Grady asked, frowning while picking at the skin around his thumb.

"No, but we need to keep Curtis from killing three more people," Tom replied before nervously admitting, "and I might have a way to stall him."

"How?" Grady's steely blue gaze pinned him in place.

Tom drew in a deep breath, shuddering at the sharp pain in his chest. "The night Myrtle warned me of the Agnazar, she gave me something else."

Grady rested his elbows on his knees and raised both eyebrows as if to say, 'go on.'

"She 'gifted' me the power to stop them."

The chair tipped back as Grady jumped to his feet.

"You're telling me Beth and you almost died for nothing?" His best friend asked through clenched teeth. "Jesus fucking Christ, Tom."

An urgent knock came at the door. Tom winced when Beth stormed inside, a ball of fury and determination. She thumbed over her shoulder.

"Grady, out."

"If I don't use it to defeat the Agnazar, I'm supposed to offer it to Circe, so she'll seal the gate for ten more years," Tom blurted, the weight on his chest lifting.

Beth and Grady's silence was deafening.

Grady studied Tom for a long time. Finally, he squeezed Tom's shoulder in support and headed toward the door. He paused beside Beth.

"Don't be too hard on our boy," he whispered loud enough for Tom to hear. Grady hooked his pinky finger with hers and wiggled.

"No promises." Beth patted Grady on the bicep with her free hand.

These small, meaningless interactions bothered Tom on a new level. He willed the jealousy to the farthest corners of his mind, but the box where he kept all his dark thoughts tucked away was fully open.

It seeped into his mind like a poison.

Beth studied Tom before coming to his side. Her delicate features were marred by exhaustion, but her frown had gentled. As she sat, her warm hand covered his.

"What happens if you use this gift?" Beth's voice was soft and even, but Tom could see her pulse in her eyes.

He swallowed the rock-hard lump in his throat. Beth squeezed his hand. He didn't deserve her support. "The way I understood it was, if I used the power to defeat the Agnazar, I'd die immediately." At the time, he hadn't thought to ask.

"And if you give it to Circe to shut the gate?"

"I don't know," Tom whispered, but it echoed in the room like the hollow promises he'd carried since Myrtle cursed him. Even now, the magic bubbled deep, slowly burning him from the inside.

Beth's shoulders fell. She wiped the tears away with one hand and sniffled. Tom snatched a clean tissue from the box on the bedside table and handed it to Beth.

She dabbed her red nose. "What happens if you use it on Curtis Putnam instead?"

"I don't know." Tom hated those words. He should have asked; Myrtle should have told him. In fact, her lack of offering clarification spoke volumes. Tom was tired of being underestimated.

"If blasting the Agnazar with the power will kill you instantly, then it's safe to say doing the same to Mr. Putnam will, too." Beth chewed the inside of her cheek. "Giving the power to Circe is our only option. We'll deal with Jeff's dad on our own."

Beth tilted her head as if listening. "Grady agrees."

Tom's chest warmed knowing his friend had their backs. His father said Grady saved both of their lives. Tom was surprised, at first. He was the only thing standing in the way of his friend being with Beth. But that's why he did it. For her.

"Good, then we'll go as soon as I'm released," Tom said, not wanting to hesitate any longer. The sooner they put this mess behind them, the sooner they could get on with their lives...even if it meant without him.

Chapter 46

TOM

"That should be it." The lady at the nurse's station reviewed the signed release form and set it down on her desk. She handed Tom a small, white paper bag with a piece of paper stapled to the front. "Make sure you take these antibiotics as instructed for at least two weeks to ward off any infection. If you have any pain, take ibuprofen as directed on the bottle. Otherwise, drink plenty of water and get lots of rest."

"Thank you," Tom said with a tired grin. He scratched his scruffy chin while the orderly wheeled him out to the curb. Beth walked beside him, her hand on his shoulder.

Grady sat in the driver's seat of their hatchback, turned sideways. Worry lines were prominent on his face.

Beth hurried to open the front passenger door, then leaned over so Tom could wrap his arm around her shoulders. His legs wobbled, but he managed to keep most of his weight off Beth. As she eased him into the front seat, the landmine of bandages across his chest tugged. He sucked in a sharp breath through his teeth.

"Sorry, hon." Beth winced.

"It's okay, love," Tom countered, squeezing her hand. "It doesn't hurt now that I'm settled."

Beth and Grady tag-teamed buckling him into the seat. When there was nothing left to fuss over, she gave him a peck on the cheek, and hopped in the back seat. Tom didn't enjoy feeling like an invalid, but the doctor had given him explicit instructions to move as little as possible. His wife took this as a personal quest.

"Are you sure we can't wait a few more days?" Beth asked, her soft hand lightly rubbing his shoulder.

Shaking his head, Tom clutched her hand in return. "We've lost days already, and

Curtis Putnam can't be allowed to roam free without a contingency. This has to be done today."

Tom was more than willing to heal in bed while Beth doted on him, but the urgent need to return to the Grove was like a noose tightening around his neck. He'd never been so compelled to go somewhere that he lost control of his body. He had a better understanding of how magnets worked.

Beth gave a non-committal nod. The woman was stubborn, having made the same argument at breakfast. She said there was a nagging feeling in the back of her mind. She didn't want to risk going back to the forest so soon after his release. He understood, but they were out of options.

"Maybe we could perform the ceremony at the park instead of making the trip out there," she suggested. The helplessness in her voice made Tom's heart ache.

"As much as I'd like to do that, we can't take chances. Too many things could interfere. This boon from the goddess is too valuable," Tom replied, squeezing Beth's hand lightly before she pulled away.

Grady shot her an apologetic glance before focusing on the road. Tom read between the lines, getting a dose of helplessness from his best friend. Whatever Beth and Grady had done to save Tom had tied him to them. Beth noticed it this morning while helping him get dressed. She described the dull ache and tightness in his chest. When he focused on Beth, he could taste her sorrow like it was an aged wine served in a plastic cup. The sweetness was ruined by the synthetic material.

While his connection wasn't as strong as what they shared, it gave Tom the closeness he craved. He wasn't ready to leave Beth. Her feelings were mutual, validated by her reluctance to return to the Grove.

Tom stifled a yawn and stared out the window. These past four and a half years with Beth were the happiest of his life, but guilt still ate at him. If he'd had any sense at all, he'd have put off the hike for another year and taken her on a real vacation.

But then the world would've burned.

Despite all the nightmarish things they'd encountered, Tom couldn't be prouder of Beth's strength and bravery. He wished he could see her come into her power. Knowing he'd miss it only fed his depression.

Shutting those thoughts down, Tom closed his eyes and focused instead on the happy memories with Beth. His mind buzzed too much for sleep to find him, so he listened to the road noise and faint top twenty country music playing on the radio.

"I wish we lived closer," Beth murmured after a long silence.

Tom opened his eyes and caught Grady staring at Beth in the rearview mirror.

"Shouldn't be much longer. The hospital isn't far from the trailhead." Grady returned his gaze to the road and raised his chin. "We're here."

Tom sat straighter, grunting when a sharp pain cut through his chest. His torso ached when the road came into view. Grady slowed to get a better look at the wooden police barrier that had been raised, keeping the public from entering. Their woods were now a crime scene.

Grady cursed quietly and continued for a few miles until he found a pull-off. Putting the car in park, he turned sideways and rubbed his face.

"There's a dirt road I know of...well, it's more of a service road, a bit bumpy, but I think the hatchback can handle the first mile or two. We'll have to walk the last five or so miles from there," Grady offered warily. "There's also a slight possibility your car might be towed."

Beth sighed and pulled out her phone.

Did he want to risk destroying their car and being stuck in the woods seventy miles from home? No. It's not like Beth could magic another one outta nowhere, and getting another vehicle wasn't within their budget.

"I know." Tom cleared his throat. "We can drive out to the dam. There's a parking area there and, if we go off-trail, the distance to the Grove is about the same. Plus, no abandoned or towed vehicles."

"I don't like that either, Tom. We should wait a few days. I'll have you fully healed, and then we can come back when the police are done," Beth argued again.

He wouldn't say she misunderstood the importance of getting this magic to the Grove, because she did. There was the lowkey feeling of panic saturating the cabin of their hatchback.

"Baby," Tom said with a pained grin, "If there's a chance we can temporarily close the gate or whatever so Curtis can't complete anymore rituals, we need to do it now. The Ungenth are visiting my dreams. Next time it might be Ja'azul. I don't want to be susceptible anymore. This is the only way we can be sure. Please."

He was right, and she knew it. Beth squeezed his shoulder and wiped the tears off her lower lashes. Sitting back in the seat, she whispered, "Okay."

Grady nodded and shifted around. Making a U-turn, they made the forty-five-minute drive to the dam. If Providence was kind, they'd be able to slip in without being detected, spend a few days at the Grove so he could heal, then make it home in time for dinner with his parents tomorrow night.

THE DAM'S PARKING LOT was empty. Grady pulled into the spot closest to the trails. As soon as the engine cut, Beth was out and at Tom's side. Putting his arm around her shoulders, Tom gripped his ribs as Beth helped him to stand.

"We'll do what we can to ease your pain as we go, okay?" Beth reminded him.

Tom grunted in reply, tipping his chin toward the trail. He wasn't going to stop for anything, not when the insistent pull of the Grove eased up the closer he got. He could breath easier each step they took.

Grady unloaded their gear and locked up, while Beth waited with Tom at the trailhead. The trio headed back into the woods, keeping to the gentler slopes. They'd traveled a mile before sweat soaked Tom's shirt. Beth called for a stop.

"I'll be alright. Just keep moving," he said, trying to brush her off. Tom knew Beth wouldn't budge, but he always had to try.

"You sound like a broken bagpipe, Tom. Give me a few minutes. I can ease the pain," Beth said firmly, gripping him by the shoulders and pushing him down. "Sit here until I finish. No arguments."

Tom lowered to the fallen log, casting wide eyes at Grady. He shrugged, looking to say, *"What do you want me to do?"*

Beth closed her eyes and held her palms up on either side of his face. The air smelled as though a honeysuckle bush had been smacked with a bug zapper. She opened her eyes and gave him a chaste kiss, placing her hands on his chest. His torso flooded with the warmth that chases a hefty gulp of hot coffee. He'd stopped wheezing and didn't feel like he'd run a marathon uphill both ways through a forest fire.

"How do you feel now?" Beth asked with an eyebrow raised.

"Like I could fly." He kissed her temple before pulling back. "Let's go."

While Beth's radiant smile lifted his mood, Grady intently studied a moss-covered rock as if it had the answers to the Universe's quandaries. Tom wanted to ask Grady if he figured anything out, but he couldn't bring himself to bother him. There wasn't anything to do for his brother, not unless he was ready to lay down and give up. Tom glanced at Beth, watching her ponytail swish with each step. His ribs shrank. He couldn't do that either.

Tom breathed a sigh of relief as they pierced the rock's veil and stepped into the ring of birch trees. It was like coming home. This was Tom's first experience with that feeling.

His chest hurt a lot less, but there was something else different. He closed his eyes, listening to the wind rattle the leaves. The pull toward the cottage nearly stilled his breath.

"I need to go to the cottage," Tom whispered harshly as his legs careened in that direction.

The closer he got, the stronger the pull became. It was like waking up on his birthday, knowing his mom had made his favorite breakfast of blueberry waffles and bacon drenched in maple syrup. The way he automatically hurried out of bed and downstairs without caring that he'd forgotten to brush his teeth. Everything else waited until after waffles.

As soon as the cottage came into view, Tom slowed. Myrtle stood outside waving to them. *Why is she here?*

Grady was the first to embrace Myrtle. Beth stayed by his side until they were at the door. She went in for a hug, but their laughter turned his stomach. Tom still didn't trust Myrtle; he never would.

A bright purple glow came from inside, pulsing as it awaited him. Tom's thoughts were left behind. He plucked a pure white lily from the garden and faced the door.

Myrtle stepped back, her face beaming. "This is a rare occurrence! The goddess, Circe, has allowed me to be with you for the remainder of this day in exchange for the power Tom offers." She studied each of them with pride. "You are most brave for a mortal, Tom Newman, and resilient. Circe awaits, my child." With a warm smile, she waved her hand toward the open doorway.

There were things Tom wanted to say, but they all got caught in his throat. With a longing glance at Beth, he nodded and stepped inside. The others stayed outside to watch through the open window.

He knelt in front of the statue, placed the lily at its feet, and opened his arms in a half-circle, palms up. It seemed like the right thing to do, so he went with it.

"Circe, I offer this power to seal away the darkness. As freely as it was given to me, I give to you." The words flowed naturally from him, forming in his head without him trying. Tom was unsure what else to say or do, so he waited.

When he looked up, the statue of Circe had disappeared. Instead the goddess herself stood in front of him. Tom gasped at her beauty. She was in a simple, forest green, renaissance-style dress with an ornate gold sash tied around her waist. Intricate symbols were embroidered into the light gold trim around the neck and sleeves of the dress. Circe's long, floor-length, dark red hair glistened like starlight, as did her smooth, porcelain skin. The way her dark purple eyes twinkled reminded him of Beth and how hers did the same. The magic consuming him from inside slowed to a pulse, like a second heartbeat.

"You have a pure heart, great compassion, and a fierce strength, Tom Newman." Circe's beautiful, celestial voice caused his heart to rejoice.

Her ruby lips curled up into a gentle smile. She placed her open palm on his forehead, and the power Myrtle had given him moved through his body toward it. He was flooded with overwhelming joy, causing tears to stream down his face. When Circe drew the last of the magic from him, her body took on a soft, purple glow before fading. Her eyes, however, remained luminous.

"For your sacrifice, I shall grant you three days to say goodbye to your loved ones. At the end of that time, your spirit will rejoin the forest."

Circe kissed his forehead. The inside of the cottage exploded with light, bursting into a blinding array that spread throughout the Grove.

When it dissipated, Tom sat alone. His weakened body slumped over while he quietly wept. When Beth's tender hand came around his back, Tom leaned into her, wrapped in the blanket of her comforting arms.

The numbness in his heart crept through his whole body. The demons lurking in the shadows of his psyche lapped at it like hungry wolves. Tom no longer had the strength to hold them back.

Chapter 47

GRADY

GRADY TURNED AWAY FROM their display. Myrtle gave him a sympathetic smile. She tucked her arm in his, guiding him away from the cottage.

"My son, enjoy these last days with your dear friend. Tom has done well to have received such a gift," she began, smiling at the sun. "You and your destined one will be together soon enough."

Grady pursed his lips and nodded. Words failed him. Seeing Beth in a broken mess pushed him past his limits. Everything they'd done to keep Tom alive was for nothing. Grady was going to lose his best friend. They had three days to prepare for something they'd accepted to happen in two years. There was too much Grady needed to say.

"Will you show me the outside world? I would very much like to see how much has changed in three hundred years," Myrtle asked suddenly. Her childlike wonder and glee reminded him of Beth.

With a strangled chuckle, Grady smiled and took out his cell phone. "This device is called a cell phone. It's our way of communicating over distances, long and short. It's also a way of capturing moments in still pictures," he explained as he scrolled through the photos.

Myrtle's eyes grew larger by the moment. She smiled at the pictures with all three of them, pointing at the one from three years ago. One of their earlier fishing trips together. "You are very close."

"Yeah. We grew up together." Grady didn't elaborate. His attention was glued to the shot.

The oblivious grin on Tom's face, the awkwardness in Beth's smile caused by Grady's wariness. It was never dislike. He'd fought his feelings even then. Would things hurt this badly if he'd pursued Beth, knowing Tom was in love with her, too?

No matter the outcome, the future his brother had envisioned was still gone. Beth would become Grady's future. He'd be eager to begin except for the stab wound in the center of his chest. Survivor's guilt was a bitch.

Myrtle waved the phone away and sniffled. "Thank you, Grady. I have seen enough." She cleared her throat and asked about the modern advances in medicine, travel, and technology, which Grady happily obliged.

"So, you must travel great lengths in order to get here," she concluded, brushing a small speck of something off her shoulder.

"Yes. Beth and I were wondering if there was a way to create a portal. Something that would allow us to step through a doorway from wherever we are." Grady welcomed the subject change. The pressure building behind his ribs shrank until he could breathe again.

She put a finger over her pursed lips in thought. "It is possible, but we will need to find the original texts from when the Grove was first built. They are hidden here, somewhere in the Grove." Myrtle tapped her chin. "I can sense them, but I know not of their origin. Only of a brief note of its existence."

Grady stopped to catch his breath. They'd have *all* the answers. "Do think you can find them?"

Myrtle sighed. "It is a place hidden in plain sight. The original guardians wanted somewhere to keep the archives safe, in the event of the darkness breaking through the protective barrier. This place had to be in what could be described as a pocket, something attached to this plane but separate. It is also a place that exists outside of time, in order to preserve knowledge. A pocket dimension, if you will."

The sound of a throat clearing came from behind. Beth and Tom headed toward them with puffy red eyes.

"There's an old roadbed behind the twin cabins. We haven't had time to explore it, but it has to go somewhere," Beth suggested.

"It's worth a look," Myrtle smiled. "But, first, let us eat. I am eager to taste food again and we all will need our strength."

Her reminder summoned the fatigue they'd dodged. Going through hell and back with barely any food or sleep caused his bones to ache.

Grady and Tom gathered wood for the stove, with Grady doing most of the work. The girls chopped vegetables. During dinner, Myrtle listened to their journey of learning magic so far. It was surreal to Grady, having his distant magical ancestor sitting there with them instead of in a dream. He wished for more time to learn from her. He had so many unanswered questions.

As usual, time was against them. The sun would be setting in a few hours, and they had a cave to find.

Myrtle stood and straightened her apron before clapping her hands. "Come, my dears, and make haste." She squirreled out the door, not waiting for the others to follow.

When they got to the end of the roadbed, Myrtle placed her hand on the border. "This is surely it. Perhaps one of you would be so kind? I fear, in my current state, I lack the power to summon the door."

Grady stepped up to the border. He raised his hand just as Beth's slender hand slipped into his. Tom gripped her free hand.

"Just in case," she said with a wry grin.

Grady nodded coolly even though his insides were throwing a rave at her touch. He placed his free hand on the border and pushed. Something solid and unyielding was underneath his hand, but there wasn't anything there. He needed a key.

He looked over his shoulder at Beth.

BETH

BETH'S FINGERS TINGLED WHEN Grady touched the invisible wall. He gazed over his shoulder at her, and the word 'key' popped into her mind.

"I'll try."

She stepped up beside Grady and placed her hand on the border next to his. Beth gasped as a surge of electricity coursed through her fingers and traveled down her arm to her toes.

"Did you feel that?" she asked Grady.

"Yeah," he said in a hoarse whisper. "Can you open it?"

"I think so."

Beth closed her eyes, recalling the white-hot energy she'd summoned by accident. Her eyes grew warm as beams of light shot from them, hitting the border. The rectangular shape wavered slightly. She pushed more power into it, and like the water-revealed coloring pages from her youth, a single wooden door with a small, iron pull-ring appeared.

"Cool." Grady beamed.

"Well, don't just stand there," Myrtle urged with a nudge to her back.

Beth tugged the wooden door. It opened soundlessly to their own Narnia in the form of a small, dimly lit cavern. Flickering candlelight illuminated several bookshelves. The comfortable ambience promised safety and solitude.

A shadow crossed the room as someone or something moved past the light. Beth took a step back and onto Grady's foot.

His "ouch" echoed, and the shadow stopped.

Beth held her breath, her hand on the door, as a woman stepped into the light. She had long, black hair, piercing, icy-blue eyes, and a slender build, wearing a simple blue cloth dress. In her hands lay an open book.

Without looking up, she addressed the newcomers. "Don't just stand there. In or out!"

Beth shared a look with Tom. When he shrugged, she led the procession inside. Myrtle was the last to enter, shutting the door behind her. The strange woman held up her finger as she finished reading the last page of the book she was holding.

With a snap, she closed it and looked at each of them in turn, stopping at Myrtle with a raised brow. "Ah. *There* you are. You are *late*, Myrtle Brinstar...three hundred years late."

Myrtle was taken aback. "I did not know I was expected. Who...who might you be, sister?"

The raven-haired woman's face softened; her eyes darted around. "I know. It was not your fault, but the enemy's." She straightened, training her intense gaze on Myrtle. "I am Heliotta Rayon, first of the light-bringer guardians, and Keeper of the Vault."

"It's nice to meet you, Heliotta. We—" Myrtle was mid-sentence when the woman turned away and strode further into the room.

There were wall-to-wall shelves going from floor to ceiling, holding thousands of books and hundreds of series. In the middle of the room were two red velvet couches surrounding a small, hand-hewn table.

"Excuse me," Beth prodded on Heliotta's heels. "But we're kinda in a hurry."

Heliotta whirled on them, making Beth stop short or tumble over the slight woman. Heliotta shoved into Beth's personal space with her squinty gaze analyzing every inch of her like she was a science project. When she gasped, Beth startled. Grady gripped her arm before she could accidentally walloped the eccentric guardian.

Tom was slower on the draw, placing his arm lightly around her waist. Heliotta plucked a hair from Beth's head and stuck it in her mouth.

"Hey! Why'd you do that?" Beth whined, rubbing her head with a scowl.

As Heliotta treated Beth's hair like mouthwash, the lights flickered. Her pale skin was almost translucent when she gasped again. "By the goddess! The prophecy has begun, and we are not prepared...Come! Quickly! There is no time. You must learn about magic: the duties and expectations of a light-bringer guardian, the coming battle against Ja'azul for the salvation of their world, and your role in bringing about a new magical age with the birth of your children."

Heliotta stopped pacing, turning abruptly on the couple. "You two have not completed your connection?! You must do it now!"

The woman grasped Beth's arms. The wildness in her wide eyes causing Beth's midsection to cramp.

"We will, just not yet. My *husband*, Tom, has limited time with me...we want to spend our last days together," Beth explained coolly, narrowing her eyes in challenge. Grady had turned to stone beside her.

Heliotta squinted her eyes and studied Tom. "I see. You are stubborn like your ancestor." Turning on her heel, she was off again.

"I hope this isn't a habit," Tom chimed in, his voice breathy as though he'd been running.

Beth's heart skipped a beat. She slowed, catching Tom by the elbow.

Grady and Heliotta passed them to follow Heliotta.

"Are you feeling okay?" Beth asked, but Tom's fury hit her in the chest.

"Just peachy." Tom rolled his eyes. "I'm dying and you're gonna move on with my best friend. How do you think I feel, Beth?"

Beth's eyes pricked with tears. "I'm sorry. I shouldn't have asked."

Like the coward she was, Beth hurried to meet up with the others. Tom's footsteps were quicker. His arms wrapped around her from behind, stopping her short of the chamber where Grady's voice echoed.

Tom buried his face in her neck as he tightened his embrace. "You're fine to ask. I had no right to snap at you and I'm sorry. I'll try my damnedest to wrangle my asshole remarks."

"It hurts, Tom," Beth whispered as she turned in his arms. Staring into his bloodshot gray eyes were like peering into an angry storm of blood and stone. "We were supposed to have more time."

Tom cradled her face in his hands, his nostrils flaring as he fought back tears. "I know, hon. But I'm determined to make the best of it, yeah?"

"Yes." Beth nuzzled noses and breathed, "I love you."

"I love you, too, Beth." Tom's broken whisper shattered her façade.

Their kiss was like salted caramel. Bittersweet and gone too soon.

"Let's join the others." Tom placed a kiss on her forehead, making her chest gallop.

When they caught up the rest, Grady's gaze quickly found something else to study as he scratched the back of his head. Guilt was her constant companion these days. It ate well.

This chamber was twice as big as the first with twice as many books lining its walls. They were all color-coded, and when Beth took a closer look, she saw they were also grouped by year.

Heliotta pulled a large, gray book off the shelf, flipped it open, and handed it to Grady.

"This is what we're up against. Everything you need to know about the enemy is in this record," Heliotta told him before turning to Myrtle.

"It's all here, the missing pieces," Grady murmured, skimming the pages with his freakishly fast reading skills.

When he raised his head and looked at Beth with fascination sparkling in his deep pools, the world upon her shoulders stopped feeling so damn heavy. Her cheeks flushed, and she cleared her throat.

"Perfect. We just need to find a way to reconcile them with Myrtle's books at the cottage." Beth chewed on her bottom lip. When she caught Grady watching intently, she quit.

"Speaking of, I will need you to bring her writings here for the archive." Heliotta's prompt interruption helped break the tension.

Grady shook his head and frowned. "I thought we weren't allowed to bring the books out of the cottage?"

"Whatever gave you that idea?" Myrtle giggled. She waved her hand like he was joking. "Good news. Heliotta has invited me to stay here, so you'll have an extra set of hands to help with whatever you need."

"Like portals that allow us to teleport places and back here?" Tom supplied.

"Precisely," Myrtle said with a gleam in her eye.

Chapter 48

GRADY

"Did someone say portals?" Heliotta exclaimed with a delighted sparkle in her eyes. "Follow me."

Tom grabbed Beth's hand when she darted forward. Of course she was excited about portals; who wouldn't be? But Grady's feet were rooted to the ground as he stared longingly after Beth.

"Be patient." Myrtle placed a hand on his shoulder. She gave him an encouraging grin and squeezed. "You are almost done with this chapter."

Nodding in response, Grady's feet were free. Patience was a struggle he was losing, but the alternative made him feel like a right bastard.

They followed Heliotta to the end of the hall, where it opened into a deep cavern with a two-foot-wide stream running through the middle. The thirty-foot-high ceilings were home to many stalactites and a strange, glittering ceiling providing a soft bluish light. It gave the cave an ethereal look.

On this side of the stream, dozens more bookshelves lined the walls. Across the water there was a crude laboratory with carved rock tables and lots of vintage alchemical implements and tools.

They hopped over the stream and headed to the lab where Heliotta checked every jar and basket on the shelf as though she raced against a timer. The walls here were smooth with recessed shelves filled with bottles, skulls, and the like. The collection was similar to what the cottage had, but much larger, and the variety of materials here gave very impressive collection vibes.

"Here, we will answer your riddle. This book"—she waved an old, black leather-bound book around and placed it on the table—"contains spells for the creation of the Grove's time bubble as well as the protective barriers."

Heliotta snapped her fingers and the candles on the walls ignited, illuminating the area. "Shall we get to work?"

This woman's chaotic energy was exactly the spark Grady needed to get out of his mental slump. Heliotta was extra in so many ways, but knowledge oozed from her pores like a siren's call. He wanted to learn everything.

"We shall start with your current knowledge. What do you know about stones?" Heliotta held up a basket of various sized rocks and crystals.

Before Grady could run through his basic knowledge, Beth raised her hand. He covered his mouth with a hand, hiding his amused grin. She was adorable without trying.

"Well, gray moonstone would be ideal. For instance, it's known as the Traveler's stone and has been used for grounding, protection for travelers, and as a focus in astral projection."

"An excellent choice," Heliotta agreed with a smirk. "Now, choose your moonstone."

Grady stood on the other side of Tom while Beth rooted around the basket. She chose three stones roughly the same size that would fit in their pockets.

He turned the oval stone around in his palm. It was half the size of a golf ball and cool to the touch. The light gray surface had a shiny luster, giving it the appearance of soft, brushed nickel.

"Hold it in your dominant hand and focus your intent: creating a space through the void and connecting it to a familiar space. Visualize a passageway and wave it over the incense three times in a clockwise manner," Heliotta instructed, watching them with eagle eyes.

She wafted the smoke trails above the small, black cauldron atop their workspace. The scent of Ash leaves, comfrey, and mugwort created a tangy and woody smell that was sharp. It wasn't unpleasant, but it made his nose itch.

Moving the moonstone in a clockwise motion over the smoke, Grady counted three times while concentrating. After the third rotation he opened his fingers. The gray moonstone had taken on a mesmerizing pearlescent aura. He could stare at the stone for hours.

"The spell took hold!" Heliotta exclaimed, clapping happily.

Tom's stone had the same glow, but Beth's shined brightest. She always had.

"May I borrow our guests, Heliotta?" Myrtle stood off to the side with her hands behind her.

Grady glanced at Tom, whose frown could curdle milk. He didn't trust Myrtle, but Grady couldn't fathom why.

Beth tugged at his shirt and tipped her head toward their teacher. Once they stood in front of Myrtle, she placed a necklace over each of their heads. Grady's thoughts quieted, and his heart was left with his own mess.

"These gifts are a little late but are much more convenient. May your thoughts and feelings be your own, so long as you wear these," Myrtle said with a happy grin.

"It's beautiful. Thank you so much," Beth said, taking hers in hand, and turning it around. As the fluorite caught the light, brilliant rainbow-colored ribbons shone throughout the speckled green and white stone.

"Thank you," Grady whispered. Myrtle returned his thanks with a pat to his cheek.

Tom frowned as he turned the stone in his fingers. His watery gaze sought Grady, then Beth, ending with Myrtle. To Grady's surprise, his best friend wrapped Myrtle in a tight hug.

"Thank you. This means a lot."

Myrtle patted his back. "It's the least I could do. You are a good man, Tom Newman. I am happy Beth had the chance to share her love and light with you."

Tom sniffled and stepped back, nodding as he studied the gift. Without being able to read his best friend or know his feelings, Grady was at a loss.

At least he had a short reprieve from Beth's growing desire. Thing was, he still didn't breathe easier without her in his head because she was a permanent resident in his heart.

Chapter 49

TOM

"Well, try it out." Myrtle waved at the archway, her eyebrow arched as she pegged him with her unwavering gaze.

Tom's stomach flipped as he held the smooth, gray stone in his hand. He pictured his and Beth's bedroom, then directed his focus at the doorway, speaking the incantation.

"Exgradi."

The stone glowed faintly, pulsed three times, then...nothing. His chest throbbed and it wasn't from his surgery. The intrusive thoughts burrowed deep. It didn't work because he didn't have magic.

"The archives are closed to travel," Heliotta announced. "Leave and try again. Remember to clearly visualize the place you want to be and speak the word just as you did." She used her hands to shoo them toward the front door.

"We'll be back to let you know if it worked," Beth promised as she guided Tom out of the caverns with a hand on his lower back.

Tom couldn't help but feel slighted. He wanted to be included, to experience the rush Grady and Beth seemed to have after practicing magic. Growing up, hey were inseparable as kids, mostly because Louis Cooper was an abusive asshole. He'd always included Grady in what he was doing. Being unincluded didn't seem fair, and Tom felt like a jerk thinking it.

He'd try again for Beth's sake and because Heliotta could be right.

Back at Grady's cabin, Tom opened the door and readied the moonstone.

"You've got this, hon." Beth's positive tone peeled away the top layer of doubt which clung to him like sticky fly paper.

He visualized their bedroom, letting the peace he shared with Beth in the space fill him, and tried again. "Exgradi."

The stone glowed brightly, warming his palm. The air in the doorway thickened with a pearlescent, opaque film similar to the aura of the stone itself. It shifted in slow swirls, causing it to shimmer. When Tom touched it with a finger, it flowed like liquid but left him completely dry. He smiled crookedly and eased his whole hand through.

"It feels cool to the touch...and kinda tickles," he relayed before pulling his hand back out. Turning it over, he examined it closely. It was still his normal hand. He smiled at the others. "Here goes nothing."

"Wait!" Beth grabbed the back of his shirt and pulled him to a stop. Her arms wound around his waist. "Don't you dare step through without giving me a proper goodbye. What if you end up in some other dimension and we can't—"

Tom turned to embrace her, unable to let her finish. He, too, worried about ending someplace other than home. The thought of dying alone terrified him, but *he* had to be the one to test it. His expiration date was days away, making him expendable. Shooting a glance at Grady, his friend took the hint and turned his back to give Tom and Beth some semblance of privacy.

Resting his cheek on her head, Tom murmured, "Have faith. Heliotta said the magic worked. She's had centuries of practice. If we can't trust her judgement, whose can we trust?"

"You're right. I'm being stupid. I just...it's difficult, Tom." Beth sniffled and straightened. "Go, we'll give you exactly thirty seconds before I come through after you." She tried to chuckle, but it came out more like a hiccup.

God, I'm out of time. He wished they had more.

Lifting his hand, Tom grazed her cheek with his thumb. "Be back in a flash," he whispered, then stepped through the veil and into his bedroom. Or so he hoped.

GRADY

IMAGINING HOW SOFT BETH'S neck would be against his lips as he hugged away her worries should have been the last thing on his mind. But it wasn't.

Her heavy sigh snapped his rational thinking back in place.

Beth gnawed on her nails. Grady unconsciously pulled her hand away. Pleasant tingles spread from his fingers to his arm. His heart skipped a few beats when her glassy fern gaze looked at him, so lost and weary. Touching her hand had been torturous enough, but his free hand moved to stroke her hair, to rub her arms. He tucked an invisible hair behind her ear instead.

"He'll be fine," Grady promised, giving her his lopsided grin.

The hard lines on Beth's face softened the same time Tom's head popped through the doorway.

Grady stepped back, feigning surprise.

"It worked. Come on through," Tom beckoned with a smile before disappearing again.

"Ready?" Beth offered her hand.

Grady hesitated, but the thought of going through two at a time seemed like a logical thing to do.

For educational purposes, of course.

He nodded and took her hand. Grady gritted his teeth against the need to pull Beth into his arms and kiss her the way they do in his fantasies. Thankfully, the passageway provided ample distraction. When they stepped through the portal, it was like being in a pool of water without getting wet. There were sounds in the dark space outside their bubble, whispers or something like them. The noise was muffled by the pearly-white substance they passed through. In seconds, they stood hand in hand in Beth's bedroom, with Tom giving him a cocked eyebrow. Grady's face flushed as he dropped her hand.

"Great. It works with singles and doubles." Tom clapped Grady on the back. He held the stone up to the doorway. "Claudere." The portal whooshed closed, and the living room appeared on the other side.

Grady cleared his throat. "Um, I'm gonna go to my house...gather my things and give you two time." He wasn't sure what to do with his hands, so he pulled the stone out of his pocket, and thought of home. Speaking the word, the portal opened. Grady glanced at Tom, then at Beth.

With a curt nod, Grady stepped through and closed the portal behind him. At least with the necklaces he wouldn't feel them.

TOM

"WHEW!" BETH SAID, LETTING out a big nervous chuckle. "How do you want to spend the rest of our time today?"

Tom's eyes were hooded as he wrapped his arms around her waist. "Oh, I can think of all manner of things we can do," he said in a low, sultry voice before kissing her intimately.

Beth melted into him, running her hands up his chest and around his neck, tangling her fingers in his hair. When he let her catch her breath, she managed to ask, "Are you sure you're up for it? You just got out of the hospital."

"Is that a challenge?" Tom growled and picked her up, ignoring the dull pain in his chest as he carried her to their bed. "Sounds like one. Guess I'll have to prove to you how good I feel." Beth giggled loudly as he attacked her with an onslaught of kisses.

An hour later, Tom lay in bed with Beth sprawled across him playing with his chest hair. They'd needed to stop once so Beth could ease his pain, but tonight had been no exception to the wonderful lovemaking sessions they'd had lately.

He wished they could keep to themselves. After dinner with his parents tomorrow night, he should spend some time with Grady. There were things they needed to discuss before his permanent departure.

"Tomorrow for breakfast, I think we should go to that little coffee shop on the corner of Bradford and Chestnut we've never been to," Beth said, breaking him out of his thoughts. "Then we can spend a few days at the Grove and be back in time for dinner with your parents."

He lazily ran his fingers up and down her back. "That sounds nice, hon. I'd like that a lot." He kissed the top of her head and hugged her tightly. "Let's get some sleep. The next couple of days are gonna be busy."

Beth gazed at Tom with her impossibly gorgeous green eyes and nodded. She kissed his lips, then his chest before snuggling up to him with a happy sigh. He waited until her breathing had slowed before closing his eyes and whispering, "I love you so much."

A grin spread on his tired face when she responded in her sleep, "Love...you...Tom."

Chapter 50

GRADY

WHISPERS IN THE DARKNESS surrounded Grady as he tossed and turned. Hundreds of voices overlapped in various volumes. When he focused on one, he still couldn't make out what they were saying.

He walked in what felt like a straight line, but the feeling that someone watched him never ceased. Several times he called out to the invisible crowd, but his voice was drowned in the multitude.

Wherever he was, it was full of rage, seeping into any open cracks in Grady's defenses. His fists clenched at his sides, knuckles white from how tight he kept them. He willed his fingers to relax.

The heated pressure in this hell built, baiting him. His fists balled again, short nails digging into the flesh of his palms until they pierced his skin. Blood dripped from his open wounds, but he didn't feel pain. All of his emotions had been converted into one ball of fury, growing every second until he couldn't tell where it ended and he began.

The whispers coaxed him into facing things that ought not be faced, to let loose the unbridled anguish he'd been hiding since that fateful day during college. The memories seeped from the vault in his mind, one by one in reverse.

His murderous father lay shredded on the ground, his mother's unmoving body, Ja'azul crushing her soul.

The scabs over deeper wounds were ripped off.

The woman he needed more than breathing, stolen by his best friend. Tom Newman, the 'Golden Boy,' always got what he wanted. Everything had been handed to Tom without his having to work for it. The only reason he put up with Grady all these years was because he liked being the hero. Tom's life was so perfect that he *wanted* to rub it in

Grady's face every chance he got. Tom pitied Grady for having a piece of shit father who cared more about his next paycheck and drink than his own son.

Grady's chest heaved from the pent-up rage inside him, waiting to explode as soon as he gave it permission. How could he have been so blind? How had he fallen for Tom's goody-two-shoes act for so long?

Get a grip! It's not like that at all, Grady scolded himself. He shook his head, trying to force out the sinister thoughts trying to displace his own. How could he be so weak and let the enemy poison his mind?

A rhythmic grating noise surrounded him, like something between nails on a chalkboard and a poorly tuned violin. As the racket grew louder, Grady realized it was a cackle. The heavy scent of sulfur burned his nostrils. Two large red orbs the size of tires appeared several feet in front of him, devoid of anything but fire and cold emptiness. They glowed with an unnatural light and seethed with hatred.

Underneath the orbs there appeared a circle of dark, yellow teeth. They were unusually long and looked like thin razors. Greenish saliva dripped from the bottom of what he assumed was a mouth, hitting the ground with a hiss. Grady's skin crawled, and the stench turned his stomach. The creature reminded him of the Agnazar but was much larger, more alien, and seemed a hundred times more dangerous. There was only one creature this could be.

"Ja'azul." Grady's voice echoed in the sudden silence. The name sent a shiver down his spine and twisted his insides.

"Pathetic little guardian. Weakling. You do not wield your fullest power. How do you expect to protect your beloved? You couldn't even save your mother or the woman who haunts your dreams," the entity rasped, lips unmoving. It cackled again at Grady's fear. "The world as you know it will cease to exist. I will burn everything and everyone you ever loved to cinder and ash. Let me show you what is to come when I break free, and you will despair, knowing you are powerless to stop it."

With a rattling, wet sigh, Ja'azul's rancid breath changed the current landscape. The darkness melted, bubbling like thousands of tiny blisters. Flames licked it away to reveal a picture of the future.

Everything as far as the eye could see was ruined in a crimson haze.

Buildings toppled into rubble, some turned to ash. Broken cars upturned or abandoned on roadsides alongside dead bodies. Some victims lay mangled and scorched, others had faces frozen in terror with smoking, eyeless pits. One body was curled around a smaller form, a parent protecting their child from an inevitable doom.

Survivors were hunted by armies of Agnazar, Ungenth, and other larger, four-armed, creatures whose skin was armored. Humans who'd fallen to a spear or sword wound were picked up and held by their throats, feet left dangling. Ja'azul's denizens unhinged their jaws and covered the victim's faces with their mouths. When they swallowed, it was like sucking mud through a straw. The sound reminded Grady of a starved dog wolfing down wet food. When they finished siphoning the souls and remaining life force of their victims, the bodies were tossed aside like garbage.

Grady's stomach turned at the sight. His face was dry with trails of tears evaporating as soon as they rolled down his face. His knees were weak. He stood only by sheer force of will, lumbering into the road. Nothing looked familiar until he saw a downed sign next to what looked to be a parking lot. The smoking pile of rubble and the scorched hill behind it were what was left of the grocery store in downtown Mayes Hill.

The place where Grady was born and grew up was gone. Is this really what will happen if Ja'azul gets free? What will become of Beth?

Ja'azul chuckled and waved his grotesquely misshapen hand. The scene shifted, taking them to the ritual stone in the woods.

A pregnant woman lay on the altar stone. Her tattered white dress was stained with large dark red splotches and black soot. Her skeletal limbs were covered by paper-thin skin that had withered and dried as if vacuum sealed. Dull, gray hair was plastered over her face, barely covering her sunken eye sockets.

Grady studied the woman's face as he edged closer. His insides dropped to the pit of his stomach. It was his beautiful Beth, or, rather, the husk of who she'd been. A long wail escaped his quivering lips.

When her dull eyes focused on him, Beth held out her hand. The action must have taken all the energy she had left by the way it wavered and sank.

He ran to her side, but she and the altar stone stretched beyond his reach. No matter how fast Grady moved his legs, he moved in slow motion. The ground became like mud, pulling at his feet.

Beth choked uncontrollably as her body convulsed. A gurgling sound came from deep in her throat. Grady pumped his legs harder, desperate to help her and their unborn baby. Heavy sobs stole his precious breath, making his lungs burn.

White foam fell from her open mouth, and her eyes rolled to the back of her head. She violently convulsed upon the stone and a pool of blood gushed between her legs. As Beth's round stomach deflated, she expelled her last breath and collapsed still as a statue.

The hold Ja'azul had on him was gone and the altar was next to Grady in a nanosecond. He scrambled to Beth's side, nearly falling to his knees when they buckled. He held her hand and swept away the hair covering her face with his other. His body quaked with terror at the sight of his beloved's death and at the loss of their child. The pain of losing them ripped through him in waves, but he couldn't look away.

Beth's empty gaze stared up at him as if asking why he didn't save them.

"I'm so sorry," Grady managed to whisper through strings of saliva. He lowered his forehead to the cold hand he held. This couldn't happen. He refused this possible version of reality.

Wiping his wet face with his free hand, Grady picked his head up and looked around. Ja'azul had gone, the fires had been extinguished, and the smoking rubble faded into darkness. Only the altar stone, Beth and himself remained.

Out of the darkness, Ja'azul boomed, "You cannot save the woman you love or your unborn child. Give up now or I will make you relive this moment until your eyes bleed."

The voice faded into a whisper, leaving Grady shaken, but his anger grew into something white-hot and righteous. The enemy hadn't won yet, and he wouldn't accept defeat. The goddess as his witness, he *would not* let Ja'azul take their world from them.

Beth's head jerked toward him and rasped, "You let us die!"

Grady woke with a start, sitting up. His t-shirt clung to his skin like he'd showered with it on. He clutched his chest and struggled to slow his breathing. The vision of Beth's horribly deformed and emaciated face slowly faded, but it would never leave him completely. The sight of her was scorched into his memory as a reminder of what was at stake.

The clock on his bedside table read a quarter past three in the morning.

Groaning, Grady tossed his legs over the side of the bed. There was no use trying to sleep. He wiped his face and stretched. The muscles in his body twitched, the remnants of the torment still fresh.

Some contrast hydrotherapy was in order, and then he'd buckle up for three days of hell.

Chapter 51

GRADY

Grady spent most of the morning gathering most of his belongings and boxing them up. His home library had been packed away, along with most of his clothes and sentimental things.

He stared at the half-empty space. His childhood home had become devoid of life when his mother passed. With Louis gone (he refused to call his sperm donor by an honorary title), the house felt lighter, but it wasn't home anymore. Somebody else was. The corner of his mouth tipped upward.

Next on the list were tools. His grandfather taught him everything he knew of woodworking. The man had made all of his tools, including the awl Grady was fond of using when a project needed precision. It would come in handy when fixing up the cabin.

Though Ryland Cooper was a welder by trade, carpentry had been his passion. The summers spent with his grandpa at the shop were the only times he enjoyed welding.

"Steel is strong, stubborn, and cold. You have to dig it from the earth, and then it has to be purified. Once tempered, it'll last for ages," his grandpa explained one summer when Grady apprenticed at the shop.

The scent of burnt leather and metal dust were scorched into his brain. *"Wood is versatile, beautiful, and proud. You cut a tree down and plant the seed; another grows in its place. And wood is good to craft damn near anything useful or build a house. Ain't no better feeling than building a house with your own hands. 'Course, your memaw said I did such a fine job building her cabin, she wanted furniture to match."* His grandpa winked and flipped down his shield, letting Grady weld the next joint together.

Most of Grady's carpentry tools were kept in the same worn leather bag his grandpa had used. It didn't take long to toss in the few tools Grady had bought new. The rest were kept in a tool chest. It would stay here until he could build a shed in the Grove.

Grady added the leather tool bag to the growing pile of boxes in the corner of the living room.

The rest of the afternoon was spent going through the dusty bankers boxes in his—*Louis's*—room. An old, black leather notebook was wedged under stacks of financial documents. Grady pulled it loose, flipped it open, and scanned the pages. His eyes widened with each page. "What the..."

Rows of names, politicians and others, were scribbled between the lines. Affairs, unpaid debts, embezzlement...the list went on. Louis had dirt on everyone and used it to cover up years of murders.

Grady's stomach soured, reading the names of folks he'd known all his life.

He snapped it shut and shoved the notebook into his backpack read through later. Grady didn't want any outstanding issues popping up later and causing trouble.

The rest of *Louis's* things were stuffed into boxes and stacked in the corner of the office to be shredded or burned. Grady put the lid on one of the cardboard boxes when his phone dinged with a text. His stomach lurched.

Did Tom die? Is Beth hurt? A number of concerns bombarded his brain as he ran to the living room for his phone. Grady picked it up and flipped it over, sighing as he read the name.

Jack Newman had texted, *"Dinner will be done an hour early. Tom's not answering. Will you let him know? Thanks."*

A new kind of dread welled up inside Grady.

He wiped his face with both hands. Tom messaged him this morning to give him a heads up. He and Beth would be spending several hours at the Grove and wouldn't be back until an hour before dinner. The couple were surely up to some very personal business, and he *absolutely* did not want to bother them. Their situation was awkward enough without his walking in on them and seeing Beth while she was...

He shook his head to get the image out of his head.

"Think, Grady...maybe they'll get the text, and you won't have to worry about it," he wondered aloud before sending a text. *"Dad called. Dinner earlier. Please respond."* As soon as he pressed send, the band around his chest loosened. Setting the phone down, he wrapped picture frames in newspaper and packed them into boxes.

Once Tom's days were over, Grady would move to the Grove permanently. Money wasn't a concern. After Louis passed, Grady inherited the house and the workshop. He'd sell both. The money they'd save from living off the grid would more than pay for the cabin's upgrades. And Beth's income from teaching could be used for supplemental groceries or anything else she wanted.

As for the impressive wealth Louis had amassed over the years—blood money, as Grady deemed it—that part of the inheritance would be used to fund their campaign. Anything left over would be given back to the community. It seemed like the right thing to do.

With Tom still around, it felt odd thinking about a future with Beth. But then again, Tom had always been a planner. Grady figured this was no different.

An hour passed and neither Tom nor Beth had responded.

"Goddammit," he cursed under his breath. They had a little over half an hour before they needed to be at the Newman's house for dinner.

Taking several deep breaths, Grady removed his charm necklace and braced for feedback. First came the sudden, splintering heartbreak at being so far away from Beth. Then, the rush of pleasure rolled through him, causing his body to shudder. Beads of sweat formed on his brow. He bit down on his fist to help him focus enough to form a coherent thought. *"Beth, check your phone,"* he sent through their connection.

Grady waited approximately ten more seconds before the necklace went back on. The crushing weight over his chest eased enough that he could breathe again, but the ghost of a certain ache remained. His only choice was to go to the Grove.

How much time has passed, and where would they be? He wondered as his reluctance expanded.

Grasping his stone, Grady stood in the doorway to his bedroom. *They'll most likely be at the cabin.* Imagining the cottage, he spoke, "Exgradi."

The doorway changed into the pearly sheen he'd gotten used to. He faltered.

"Just do it. Go...and stand in the middle of the field. Scream their names. Just...get it over with..." Grady said aloud, trying to pump himself up.

With gritted teeth, he stepped through.

TOM

BETH'S HOT BREATH WAS against his neck. Their bodies glistened with sweat as they continued testing the cabin's cot. Beth's face flushed a beautiful shade of dark pink. Tom groaned loudly. For a profound moment, the world ceased to spin and their hearts beat as one. Unable to prop himself up any longer, he eased next to Beth, laying his head on her breast.

The exertion from their jaunts had caught up with him, but Tom was determined to cement himself in Beth's forever memory. Two blissful days of reaching ecstasy together were two days he'd trade for nothing. He listened to her heartbeat while running his hand up and down her thigh, up her hip and across her waist. *Silky, smooth, and soft. My baby has always had such nice skin.*

"I have a thought," Beth murmured, pressing a kiss on top of Tom's dark blonde locks before running her fingers through them. He closed his eyes, savoring the feeling. "Let's skip dinner and everything else to stay here for the rest of time." She hummed in contentment.

"Might need to." Tom chuckled at the thought.

They hadn't been this active since their honeymoon. Life had been too busy for them to settle down earlier, as Tom had planned. When they'd made the joint decision delay starting a family until after they'd been married a year, Tom struggled. Beth's logic made since when their schedules seldom lined up, and they had to steal time where they could. The choice would have haunted his last days except for the crux printed in black and white that he'd tucked away.

"Hey." Beth lightly scratched his scalp with her nails, drawing him out of his thoughts. "You were stuck in your headspace, hon. Want to play another round of Yahtzee? Winner chooses the next *game*." The sparkle in her eyes said those of the non-paper variety were included.

"You're on, but I'm winning this round." After a break and some food, he should be ready for whatever activities she had in mind.

Tom kissed between the valley of her breasts down to her stomach.

"Or we can stay in bed." Beth wiggled underneath until he blew raspberries on her belly. Her laughter egged him on.

"Nope." Tom took a deep breath and buried his face over her belly button. He was full-on blasting her stomach while her legs kicked the air.

"Tom! Stop!" Beth giggled then stilled. She pushed him by the shoulders. "Hon! Hon! Stop."

"What's wrong?" Tom lifted his damp face. His smile fell at seeing her pursed lips.

"Grady's here." Beth's words snuffed out his happiness.

Tom flexed his arms around her midsection and dropped his forehead to conceal his displeasure. Grady wouldn't bother them unless it was an emergency.

Pushing himself up by the forearms, he hovered over Beth and gazed intently into her green eyes. When she smirked, he placed a lingering kiss on her lips. She whined when he pulled away. "Alright. Let's get dressed and go see what's up."

As they threw their clothes on, Tom tried once again to hide his annoyance, but Beth knew him too well. Before they left the cabin, she grabbed his hand, pulled him back, and kissed his palm.

"Hey. He wouldn't be here if it wasn't important," she said, hugging him to her.

"I know." Tom stroked her head softly, feeling her power thrum soothingly. "And if I was serious about keeping you all to myself, I shouldn't have silenced our cell phones."

Grady's shoulders were hunched so low and tightly, he looked like a tree stump. As soon as they came within yelling distance, he raised his head.

"Check your fucking phones! Dinner in thirty!"

Without waiting for their response, he turned and stormed back through the portal.

The thought of Grady reaching his limit gave Tom a sick satisfaction, which brought on a slew of embarrassment.

Tonight's dinner would be more than interesting since Grady had been invited as well. Tom hoped it wouldn't be a nightmare.

"There they are!" Lillian called in her sing-song voice as soon as Jack opened the door.

"Hi, mom."

She accosted Tom before he made it to the welcome mat, holding his face in her hands. Her eyes twinkled and her lips were pursed in a half-smile, half 'I'm not gonna cry' curve as she looked him over. "You're okay? Looking a little peckish, dear."

"Let him breathe, Lily," Jack intervened, placing a hand on her shoulder. His smile was warmer than usual, but the tiredness in his eyes gave Tom pause.

"Dad. How are ya?"

"Good." Jack embraced his son with a light pat on the back and pulled him further into the house while his mom greeted Beth and Grady. "Had a terrible dream last night involving you three. I didn't tell your mother; she's had enough on her plate. Just keep your eyes peeled, son. It feels like the wind has shifted. Something bad is coming."

Tom's gut was an anchor tied to a boulder and sinking fast. "Sure thing, dad."

Jack gave him a curt nod and refreshed his smile. "I don't know about y'all, but I'm starving. Let's retire to the dining room where Lily has cooked us a Michelin Star dinner."

Beth slipped her hand in his. "Everything okay with your dad?"

"Yeah. Just checking in." Tom squeezed her hand, glancing at a somber Grady. His face was scrunched in a light frown as he fidgeted and shifted on his feet. "Come on. Smells like mom made her gruyere mashed potatoes."

Beth followed his gaze, squinting in worry. "Grady? You coming?"

"Sure." He passed them without looking at either.

Tom's mental barriers rattled against the ugliness battering against his control. He was losing it. As long as Beth stayed by his side, he could make it through tonight.

And no more curveballs.

Chapter 52

BETH

BETH FOUGHT THE URGE to lick her plate clean.

"Beth, dear, will you help me bring out dessert?" Lillian asked with her usual radiant smile.

"Of course, Mrs. Newman."

"Please, call me Lily," she insisted. "You're family now."

The guys leaned back, resting their hands on their stomachs while she helped Lillian clear the dishes. Every time she leaned over the table, Beth caught Grady or Tom stealing glances at her. She tried to ignore them but her face blushed harder each time.

In the kitchen, Lillian cleared her throat. "Is it just me or is Tom not able to keep his eyes off you?" she asked slyly while Beth rinsed the dishes.

"Well," Beth began carefully, "we have been spending a lot more time together while he recovers."

She wasn't sure what her mother-in-law was getting at. Any time Tom smiled tonight, it barely reached his eyes. His mood had been dropping ever since their early departure from the Grove.

Lillian chuckled knowingly. "Hopefully, you two have spent some of that time thinking about...*children*," she said in a low voice with a giggle.

Beth choked on her tongue and laughed nervously. "You would need to talk to your son about that." She couldn't help her face growing hotter, making Lillian laugh heartily.

"My girl! This is nothing to be ashamed of. Jack and I are just hoping for some grandbabies sooner rather than later," she replied, patting Beth on the back lightly. "Besides, I couldn't help but notice Grady was having a hard time keeping his eyes off you, too."

Beth froze in place. She had hoped no one else noticed, or else things would be awkward, *exactly* like this. Her red face darkened. When Lillian snorted and chuckled, Beth's confusion must have shown.

"They say, when a woman is fertile, her pheromones attract males. It would appear you are *ripe*, if you catch my meaning," Lillian said, raising her eyebrows in suggestion.

"Oh!" Beth said loudly, a relieved chuckle escaping her lips. "I totally understand. Fingers crossed," she replied, doing just that.

Beth also wondered if Tom had left behind a mini-him. Only time would tell. Either way, about being pregnant with his child while having a relationship with his best friend gave her mixed feelings. Pushing it from her mind, she focused on getting through the rest of the evening.

Beth and Lillian returned to the dining table with dessert plates and cheesecake in hand. She placed a dish in front of each person, while her mother-in-law came behind with slices.

The mood in the dining room was awkward, made more so by the lack of conversation. The sound of cutlery clinking on the chinaware grated on her nerves.

Beth poked a strawberry before bringing it to her lips. Her eyes were glued to the plate.

Tom squeezed her thigh under the table and leaned in close. "Are you okay?"

"Yeah." Beth couldn't bring up the conversation with Lillian. Instead, she deflected with a weak smile. "Tired."

"I'll take care of you when we get home." He kissed her cheek and winked before getting back to dessert.

Beth's heart skipped a couple of beats. The knot in her stomach loosened so she could finish a few more bites of the cheesecake. Lillian was an amazing cook, and this was probably the last meal her mother-in-law would make for her.

Jack stood with an ear-to-ear-grin. "Since we have all you kids here tonight, Lily and I have an announcement." Lillian stood and slipped her arm through her husband's arm with a happy smile. "After recent events, we've decided it's time for us to retire. We don't have many more years on this earth, but you young'uns have bright futures ahead. Tom, we are so proud..."

Beth's ears hummed a ringing tune. The room shrank and all the oxygen was sucked out in an instant. She couldn't feel Tom's hand on her leg anymore. All her nerve endings had gone numb. *Please don't...*

"...which we hope you and Beth will fill with many grandchildren," he finished, raising his glass.

Tom grabbed his chest like he'd been punched. Everyone glanced at him with worried looks, but he picked up his glass, stood, and raised it high. "To the future."

A heavy gloom settled over him. Tom forced a smile, motioning for Beth and Grady to raise their glasses.

Beth's watery eyes never left his. She stood, lifting her glass, and whispered, "To the future."

She didn't need a metaphysical connection to tell her Tom's heart had shattered.

Grady was last to rise. With pursed lips, he nodded, avoiding eye contact with everyone at the table.

Jack furrowed his brows in confusion, cleared his throat, and repeated, "To the future." Then brought the wine to his lips.

As Tom threw his wine back in one huge gulp, Beth shivered as if someone had walked over her grave. She always hated that saying, but the ominousness of it was fitting, even if the universe walked over the wrong one.

LILLIAN FUSSED OVER TOM before they left, which was directly after dessert. He didn't brood often, but when he did, it was grueling. Beth geared up for a short night.

Tom was quiet as he drove them to the apartment. The only conversation Beth had in the twenty-minute drive home was texting with Tom's mother:

"Tom seemed to be down."
"He may just be tired but keep an eye out."

"I will. If he starts going downhill, I know what to do."

"Make sure he gets plenty of sleep tonight."

"Of course. And I'll make sure he drinks plenty of water."
"No more alcohol."

"If he starts to withdraw, call his doctor."

"I will. Thanks."

It killed Beth that Tom was in such a dark mood. He spent so much energy making their time at the Grove magical. Outside of going at it like rabbits, they spent a good amount of time playing board games, taking long walks through the woods, and having romantic picnics.

She wished she could ask Grady for advice, but he was in a funk, too. Her support circle was exhausted.

As soon as they were inside their apartment, Tom mumbled something about the bathroom and made a beeline for their bedroom, slamming the door shut. Beth jumped at the sound, putting a hand over her heart, and tried not to cry.

His mood was not her fault, but it was difficult not to feel that way. It was even harder to not be upset at Jack and Lillian. They had no idea. *Why couldn't they say they were moving to Hawaii?*

Beth busied herself looking for a bottle of wine. At this point, any bottle would do. She could get a glass or two down before he came back out.

She crouched to search the back of the pantry when a loud crash came from the bathroom. She jumped, bumping the top of her head on the bottom shelf. Stepping backward, her foot slipped on a near-empty bag of potatoes. She twisted and fell on her face with her hands sprawled out in front of her. Her arms wobbled as she pushed off the floor onto her hands and knees. Her chin and nose nose stung. Blood dripped onto the white tile. Lightheaded, another drop of blood splashed as second crash came from their bathroom.

Beth scrambled to her feet and ran to the bedroom door. She expected the window to be broken and for there to be an intruder. Instead, Tom was curled in the fetal position next to the bathroom door. He sobbed heavily, his hands covered in blood. She clutched her shirt over her wrecked heart. It hurt to breathe.

She rushed to his side, dodging the broken glass mirror and items scattered over the floor. Her bare feet were miraculously untouched.

"Tom, baby, tell what I can do to help," Beth pleaded as large tears fell down her cheek, trying tentatively to check his hands for wounds.

Tom jerked away from her and curled up tighter. "Go away!" he yelled sharply.

Beth crawled backwards away from him, the snot building up in her nose burned as it mixed with blood. Since she couldn't reach a towel, she had no choice but to wipe her tender nose on the hem of her shirt.

She stared helplessly at the broken man in front of her. She'd never seen him this bad off. She trusted Tom when he said he had his condition managed. This was well above anything she was capable of dealing with. When her husband let out a loud wail, the chills across her skin activated her action button. *Call the doctor.*

Beth scrambled to her feet and hurried to the kitchen. They kept important numbers on the refrigerator. Her hands shook uncontrollably as she scanned for the number, but the words and pictures blurred beyond recognition. She whimpered when frustration squeezed her lungs like wringing wet clothes.

With ragged breaths, Beth fumbled for her cell phone. She was barely able to press send, calling the one person she knew would be able to help.

"Beth?" Grady answered, on alert at hearing Tom's wailing in the background.

"Please, Grady," Beth cried over the phone, her voice cracking. "Help him."

She didn't hear any response but instead the whoosh of a portal opening. Seconds later, Grady's soothing voice came from her room. "Hey, Brother. Breathe and relax…let it all out…easy now."

GRADY

TWENTY MINUTES AFTER HE arrived, Tom's wailing had quieted to a soft sob. Grady left him sitting on the floor leaning against the wall to check on Beth. He couldn't imagine how she must be feeling. Dismissing the portal, he gathered what little strength he had left.

"Thank you. I couldn't find the number. Lillian, she said to call the doctor, but the numbers weren't there. I—" Beth held herself and tightened her arms. Another round of tears streamed down her face.

Grady's face heated at seeing her bloodied nose. He squeezed his fists a few times, taking deep breaths to settle his nerves and rushed to her side.

"Beth."

Her gaze found the floor more interesting.

He gingerly placed his fingertips on her cheek, turning her face from side to side to assess the damage. Because her touch was calming, his eyes and fingers lingered longer than necessary. His eyes burned, thinking the unimaginable. He glanced back at Tom to say something but stopped. There was no reasoning with him in his current state.

"He didn't hit me, Grady. He would never do that," Beth scoffed, wiping her nose with the back of her hand.

While she explained what happened, the flaming vice gripping his torso snuffed out and let go.

"It looks worse than it is, really," Beth added softly.

Grady's face softened when she finished. "Let me have a look at your head."

Lowering her chin to her chest, Beth pointed to the spot she bumped. Grady rested her forehead on his collarbone to keep her still. He carefully parted her hair to get a better look. To his relief, there was a small knot, but the skin wasn't broken.

Grady breathed in her perfume and stepped back. Lifting her chin, he smiled warmly. "You're right, but I recommend not hiding wine in the pantry anymore."

"Lesson learned." She gave him a curt nod and half-chuckled. "And no more potatoes."

There's my girl. Beth's green eyes glistened as she studied his face with a look of comfort and longing. His daydreams were causing his eyes to play tricks on him. He took a backward step toward the bedroom.

"I'll grab you a clean shirt," Grady offered, thumbing over his shoulder toward her room. He needed to put space between them before he did something he'd regret.

Beth simply nodded and wrapped her arms around herself comfortingly. Grady understood how she felt, having dealt with highly emotional outbursts from his dad whenever he was home, and helping Tom with his depressive episodes in the past.

He darted into the bedroom in search of Beth's clothes. Tom had made a knee and arm cocoon. He didn't move at Grady's intrusion.

Glancing around at all the glass surrounding Tom, Grady wondered where it came from. With as much as there was, he guessed the bathroom mirror and supplies were Tom's victims.

Grady crept over to the dresser. His hand was on the top right drawer handle when Tom spoke.

"What are you doing?" His gravelly voice was barely audible. Tom watched him with swollen, red eyes.

"Beth needs a new shirt. She had a nosebleed," Grady answered quietly.

Tom raised a shaky hand and pointed to the dresser. "Second drawer on the left." He shoved his fingers into his hair at the roots and sobbed quietly, mumbling something incoherent.

Grady couldn't remember a worse depressive episode than this. He'd always admired Tom's strength, especially after the hellish hike. Obviously, he wasn't alright, having built a damn convincing facade or else Grady would have noticed sooner. Grabbing a matching shirt and shorts, he crept out of the room.

Grady found Beth exactly as he left her, staring blankly at a wall. She blinked awake when he came to stand in front of her.

"It's been twelve years since Tom had an episode even close to this. This is the worst one by far," he murmured.

She nodded and clutched the clothes to her chest. "Thank you."

Grady studied Beth. Even though the necklaces Myrtle gifted them blocked her feelings, the sorrow was shared in the vacant expressions. "I can clean up the bathroom if you need me to." Beth's lower lip quivered as she nodded.

He couldn't bear seeing her like this and pulled her into a firm hug. She burrowed into his chest, gripping his shirt at his waist. Shushing her quietly as he rocked them, Grady whispered, "I'll get Tom into bed and clean up while you change, okay?"

Beth nodded with a whispered, "Okay."

Grady pulled away, damning the growing distance when every fiber of his being urged him to care for her. The only way to convince his heart was to remind it cleaning up the mess and letting Beth rest *was* caring for her.

The weak smile she managed splintered his heart. He kissed her forehead, lingering on a long blink, then nudged her toward the guest bathroom. He watched her well past the door closing, and uprooted from his sentinel spot to check on his best friend.

Tom was still curled up in a ball, but his breathing had almost returned to normal. He wouldn't look at Grady when the man helped him stand. As he guided his best friend to the bed, Tom's body shivered. Once he was under the covers, he curled up on his side, and resumed weeping.

With Tom settled, Grady grabbed the broom and dustpan from the kitchen along with a paper bag and a plastic trash bag. He swept a path to the larger pieces of broken mirror. It took him a solid hour to carefully clean up the mess. By the time he went to put everything back in the kitchen, Tom snored lightly.

It pained Grady to see his best friend broken like this. What killed him was knowing it was his fault.

Chapter 53

BETH

When Grady came back into the living room, Beth was on the couch with her knees tucked beneath her and a cup of calming tea in her hands.

"I made you a cup, if you like," she mumbled, her eyes puffy and red. She pointed to a steaming cup on the island.

Realization dawned on Grady's face, and he nodded. "Thank you. I'll just, and then I'll be..." He nodded toward the kitchen, holding up the trash bag and broom.

Beth simply nodded absentmindedly and continued to stare at nothing. How could she have let Tom get so bad off? In the past, if Tom felt an episode coming on while they were on a date, they'd call it an early night, and Beth went home. He'd call the next afternoon, and things would go back to normal.

This was the first time he'd been depressed since they got married, and it was a whole other level she wasn't equipped to deal with. If she'd seen any of the usual signs on the way home, maybe she could've gotten Tom help sooner. Lily and Jack's announcement was a dangerous distraction that'd cost them precious time.

Beth blamed her lethargy on stress. Cleaning up Tom's mess was something she didn't want to touch with a ten-foot pole, not if it meant getting yelled at again.

Grady washed his hands and grabbed the cup of tea on his way over. He took the seat opposite her and rested his elbows on his knees, gently blowing the liquid.

She was both relieved and comforted by Grady's presence, and not just for helping Tom. He made her feel safe and cared for, the way her husband did.

The hold she had on her feelings for Grady was slipping. Her want and need to be with him was tearing her apart, but she had Tom to help her stay grounded. Grady had no one, so it was twice as difficult for him. Guilt was her constant companion these days.

"So…Tom is asleep," he began, taking a sip of tea. "I cleaned up all the glass I could find in your bathroom, but you should sleep in the guest bed. The last time he got this way…he, uh, didn't want anyone to touch him for a few days."

Beth's face twisted. "He doesn't have a few days though, does he?" She fought the floodgates from reopening. This was not the way she wanted to remember her husband.

Placing her near-empty cup of tea on the coffee table, it sloshed around the rim and onto the surface. Beth rushed into the guest room and closed the door. She shoved the wood like they were her feelings and landed on the corner of the mattress. Fisting the comforter as she lowered to the floor, it pulled free, pooling around her. Propped against the bed, she let the tears loose.

If she cried hard enough, maybe it would numb the pain.

The gentle pull of Grady's presence was on the other side of the door. Every fiber of her being wanted to open the door and fall into his arms, but she didn't. Instead, she clutched the duvet to her chest, breathed in Grady's scent, and wept.

GRADY

HE WISHED HE COULD take it back. Beth's reaction split Grady's heart in two. After all the years denying his love for Beth, tonight was the tipping point. The emotions were too big to fit in his skin anymore.

Grady rested his forehead on the cold wood. One hand gripped the doorknob. Beth was in pain and every muscle in his body needed to hold her, to make her feel like she was treasured, wanted. *He* wanted her…more than anything.

He'd be able to show her soon.

Grady pulled strength from the last of his reserves and knocked on the door. "Beth, please forgive me. I should've thought before I spoke. I'll, uh, be at the house if you need me."

Hearing the bed shift, he waited, but she didn't open the door. Sniffling, Grady wiped his face, and turned to leave. His hand gripped the portal stone.

"Please don't go," Beth whispered, easing the door open. She wrung her hands together. He understood, she didn't want to be left alone in case Tom had another episode. "I should be apologizing to you. I-I'm sorry…" Her red-rimmed eyes met his with the most pitiful gaze he'd ever seen.

"If you want me to stay, Beth, I'll stay," Grady murmured. He'd messed up more than he'd helped, so he'd take this lifeline.

"Thank you," she squeaked, relief flooding her eyes. She hugged him tightly.

Another part of his heart crumbled.

TOM

TOM WOKE UP AROUND three in the morning with a splitting headache. Once his eyes focused, he saw the empty space beside him, and panicked. The memory of the dinner and afterward replayed on loop. His chest constricted.

The night before my last day with my wife and I have a fucking breakdown...

Taking his time, Tom slipped out of bed. He went to the bathroom for water. The bandages on his hands had him fumbling to turn the faucet on. There wasn't a glass—not that he could hold it, so he drank straight from the spout.

His head felt like a dry sponge absorbing water, making his eyeballs pulse. After downing another few gulps, Tom wiped his mouth and looked at his reflection. Dried adhesive and bits of glass clung to the drywall. *Oh, shit.*

Tom winced. He'd pushed Beth away when she tried to help. Of course, she called Grady. She was right to do so, but it still bothered him.

He cracked the bedroom door and peeked out into the living room. Grady was asleep on the couch. His head was tucked into the crook of the arm covering his eyes. Behind the couch, the door to the guest room was closed. Tom's heart ached, knowing how heartbroken and helpless Beth must be feeling. For once, he was glad for the necklaces.

Tiptoeing through the living room, Tom eased the guestroom door open enough to enter. Closing it, he turned to see Beth sleeping on her side with her lips parted.

Coming to her side, Tom cleared away the wad of tissues in her hand so he could sit next to her. Frowning in remorse, he swept the hair from her face, thanking the goddess she had stayed and not left for her parents' house. As he placed a kiss on her forehead, Beth startled awake, shrinking away from him with a worried face. His heart panged like she'd taken a hammer to it. *I did this to her.*

"It's okay, honey. I needed to make sure you're alright," Tom whispered consolingly. He reached to hold her hand. Beth snatched his arm and pulled him underneath her.

Burying her face in his chest, she cried softly. Tom eased the rest of the way onto the bed to wrap his arms fully around her. Her body shook. Stroking Beth's hair, he placed another kiss on her head.

He was halfway sitting up, which was slightly uncomfortable, but he didn't care. He should never have let himself get that upset. Settling in, Tom rubbed her back until her breathing slowed.

"I'm sorry, baby. Forgive me?" His hoarse whisper cracked.

"Of course." She sniffled and cuddled closer, gripping his shirt like he would disappear. He was afraid she wouldn't fall asleep if he didn't settle in. Shifting to lay flat on his back, Beth curled up on his chest.

Only when her grip on his shirt loosened and her body slackened against his, did he allow himself to follow.

Chapter 54

BETH

BETH AWOKE THE NEXT morning in the guest bedroom with a warm body at her back. She tensed, unsure whether her dreams last night of Grady were more than fantasy.

After all her careful knots, tying and trimming and keeping her love for Grady contained, she feared it had finally broken free. Her stomach clenched, lungs seized. His strong arms had soothed her aching heart. His kiss lingered on her forehead long after he stepped away, making her soul sing.

She had welcomed Grady into the guest bedroom and begged him to make her forget. He'd asked what she wanted to forget, and without a beat she answered, "Everything."

What was she trying to forget?

She scratched an itch on her nose. "Ouch." Her fingers came away with dried, red flakes underneath the nails.

No. Beth hadn't invited Grady to her bed. She'd run away. After...

Tom's breakdown.

Memories of last night came flooding back. She turned her head at the sound of soft snoring. Tom's eyes were still puffy and the dark circles under his eyes were almost purple. She vaguely remembered him joining her sometime last night, but thought it was wishful thinking.

Happy tears filled her eyes, and her heart skipped a beat knowing he had come to her on his own. Closing her eyelids, they ran paths toward her pillow. Beth inhaled his familiar cologne while listening to his shallow breaths. She'd almost drifted back to sleep when Tom awoke. With a big yawn and stretch, he wrapped his arm around her waist. Tom placed a kiss on her forehead, but didn't stop there. Beth was fully awake when he shifted in the bed to continue kissing down her face to her neck. She sighed, sinking her fingers in his soft hair.

"I'm sorry for last night. Let me make it up to you." He positioned himself on top of her, kissed her lips, and pressed his pelvis into hers. When Beth started to undress, Tom shook his head and whispered, "In the shower."

He slipped out of bed and crept over to the door. Shutting and locking it, he explained, "Grady's gone."

Tom kicked off his jeans, and took off his shirt, beckoning her with a hooked finger. Beth bit her bottom lip at the sight, slipping out of bed to join.

The hot water soaked her bones, releasing the stress of last night as ribbons of red raced down the drain. When the water ran clear, they took turns washing each other with tenderness, scrubbing away the remnants of the unpleasant evening.

Once the memories faded into the fine mist, Tom took full advantage of having an empty apartment. The steam from the shower poured out into the small bathroom, filling it quickly as the couple's heated romance built. Tom pulled out all the stops trying to make her forget about last night. He'd made her climax at least twice before the hot water ran out.

Beth's handprint was still on the glass door when Tom turned the water off. He shook his head, letting the water fly all over the place. Beth couldn't help but giggle. As they toweled off, he stole as many kisses as she'd allow, which was as many as he wanted. The constant attention and affection improved her mood until she had a perpetual grin.

Wrapped in a bath towel, Beth grabbed her phone from the kitchen on the way to their bedroom to check the time. Her mother-in-law texted earlier this morning asking how Tom was.

Beth answered, *"A good night's sleep did wonders."*

She went to the bathroom to brush her teeth and paused. Two new toothbrushes and a tube of toothpaste sat on the wasteland of their bathroom sink. "Thank you, Grady."

Beth had just finished when Tom joined her side with his cell phone.

"Grady left a message. He's inviting me to spend a few days at the Grove with him."

Beth finger-combed through her long locks. "Did he say why?" There were probably things they had to talk about that Grady didn't want to say in front of her.

Tom shook his head. "No, but he's my oldest friend. He probably wants time before..." His smile eased the tension. "No matter, it'll only be a few hours. Maybe you can spend time catching up with your parents?"

Beth shook her head, scrolling through the messages her mom sent the week before last. Neither of her parents had bothered to wish her a happy birthday. "They're still somewhere in the Bahamas with Bill and Deb." Tossing the phone onto the bathroom counter she turned away so Tom wouldn't see the tears.

He grunted and put his phone down. "Forget them. That frees us up for more time together." He placed his hands low on her hips and kissed her intimately.

Her arms snaked around his neck. Tom started to deepen the kiss, but she pulled back with a pout. "I wanna be greedy for all your time, but I can't."

Tom's chuckle sent the good kind of chills to her toes. His lips were back on hers in a flash with his hands roaming her body. Lifting her to sit on the counter, Tom deepened the kiss until they were breathless.

"As long as you kiss me like that when you get home, he can have you for a few hours," Beth relented, kissing her favorite chin dimple. The scruff didn't bother her as much as she thought it would.

TOM

"I MAY HAVE TO grow a beard while I'm gone," Tom teased for old time's sake. He kissed her forehead, leaving his lips to linger. "I love you, Beth."

"I love you, too, Tom," she replied with a sniffle before leaning back to give him a brave smile. "Let me fix your hands before you go."

Beth removed the gauze and did a quick breathing exercise. His hands were bathed in soft blue light. Tom watched in wonder as the tiny abrasions slowly knit back together until there was nothing left but his soft, normal skin.

"All better." She kissed the backs and palms of both hands.

"You're amazing, you know." Tom hugged her tight, burying his face in the crook of her neck. "What are you gonna do while I'm hanging with Grady?"

"I'm gonna finish the questionnaire for Mayes Hill and memorize my schedule," Beth replied, running her hands through the hair at his nape.

"If you're sure." Tom pulled back to cup her cheek. He was hesitant about leaving her alone, knowing full well tomorrow was his last day.

"Go! I'll be fine for a few hours, hon." Beth stared into his eyes with such conviction, he folded. "Have fun with your best friend doing whatever you guys do when I'm not around."

"How did I get such a charming and wonderful wife?" Tom gave her his megawatt smile. His heart had never been fuller.

"Have you already forgotten? You got smacked by a dodgeball in sixth grade." Beth smirked and shrugged. "Chosen by process of elimination."

"Oh, you think you're being clever, don't you?" Tom squeezed her close, nibbled her ear, and whispered, "How do you know I didn't let you win?"

"In your dreams, Eagle Scout." Beth chuckled, her green eyes sparkling. Soon, he'd never get to see her dazzling smile or get lost in her eyes again. "Don't stand Grady up. Go pack."

Tom groaned but left to get his overnight bag ready. He made sure to pack a pen and notebook to write a letter to Beth for after he was gone. It was something that had weighed on his mind since reading about Josiah's death. There were things he needed to tell her, but the words wouldn't form, not aloud anyway.

Lastly, Tom searched for his lucky fishing cap. He wanted Grady to have it. Every single time they took Beth fishing with them, she would end up wearing it, and would reel in the largest fish between them. After a ten-minute search and no hat, he gave up, making a mental note to add it to his letter.

Beth sat on the barstool with her laptop at the island. Her hair was twisted in a messy bun. A wooden pencil with deep grooves on most of its surface was wedged between her teeth.

"You ready to go?" she asked as he placed a kiss on the back of her neck.

"Mm-hmm." Tom turned her stool so she was facing him. "You don't have to be alone. I'll tell Grady you're coming with me. You can hang at the cottage, and we'll meet for dinner like old times."

"I dunno, Tom. I'll probably be a distraction." Beth shrugged, blowing away the loose hair in her face.

"No way." He shook his head, but knew she was right. "What if you spent time with Myrtle and Heliotta?"

Her eyes brightened. "If I hang out with the girls, technically I won't be missing time with you, right? Well, not exactly." She pouted with her face scrunched in thought.

"It's settled, then." Tom kissed the tip of her nose and sat on the stool next to Beth. She swiveled back to her laptop while he texted Grady, "Beth is coming to hang out with the girls."

Tom distracted himself by playing with her hair or stealing the pencil from her mouth. A few minutes later, his phone dinged with Grady's response: *"Okay."* Tom frowned. *What's his deal?*

"That's Grady." He hopped off the stool and kissed the curve of her neck. "Ready to go?"

"Mmm," Beth replied with a shiver. He loved her reaction to his ministrations. "Almost. I'm nearly finished with the questionnaire, then I'll be along. I'll text before I go to see Myrtle and Heliotta."

She craned her neck to kiss Tom goodbye, but he turned the stool around to get a full kiss. Her arms went up around his neck as he deepened it, promising more intimate things later. A tiny whimper came from Beth as Tom ended the kiss with a loud smack. He rested his cheek on hers.

"Don't forget me while we're apart," he teased, murmuring against her jaw before he kissed it.

Beth's chest heaved. Her fingernails lightly scratched the back of his neck. "Never," she whispered.

"And let me know as soon as you come through." Tom's arms tightened around her. His feet were rooted to the ground as the rising fear of leaving her alone grew.

"I promise." She nuzzled his neck, kissing his Adam's apple before pushing at his chest. "Now get going. I'll see you soon."

Tom turned the moonstone over in his hand as he backed away. Stuffing his trepidation into whatever dark hole he could find, Tom opened the portal and stepped through.

Chapter 55

UNKNOWN

A WAVE OF EXCITEMENT rippled through him when Tom stepped through the portal. *Finally!*

He had been waiting days to have a moment alone with Beth. These guardians were so naive it was painful to watch at times. When Tom was shot, he was sure the man would die, but the male guardian, Grady, saved his life.

The boy must relish the torment of seeing his beloved in the arms of another man. If Beth were mine, the husband would have disappeared the moment I found her.

Swooping behind her apartment complex, he transformed into his natural form. This was their first meeting. He wanted her to see *him*. For his plan to work, he needed her absolute trust and it would need to be quick. Perhaps he could procure one of their clever portal stones.

Smoothing the lines of his doublet, he shook the black feathers from his hair, and ran a hand through his long, wavy auburn locks. A hot flash tore across his skin. *Why am I so nervous?*

He practiced his best bewitching smile and took slow, deliberate steps until his legs were used to the movement again. By the time the staircase came into view, his muscles had acclimated to being human.

Standing at the bottom, his nerves got the best of him when her power wavered. It called to him like a siren. All coherent thought was swept away upon the oceans of serenity due to her mere presence. Apprehension gripped his courage, holding it hostage against reason. *What will I say?*

Despite his bout of turmoil, he found his fist poised to knock. *For love and revenge.*

BETH

KNOCK, KNOCK.

Beth's face flashed with pins and needles. It was ten-thirty on a Sunday morning. Most people were at church. Maybe her parents had come back early. What if something had happened to them? Her heartbeat quickened.

"Coming!" Beth's voice cracked.

She sent a silent prayer to the goddess and opened the door. The scent of spiced cranberries and cardamom assaulted her senses. The man looked to be dressed for a renaissance fair in his black and silver doublet, billowing white long-sleeved dress shirt, tight black leggings, and slightly worn black leather boots. His auburn hair touched just below his shoulders, framing a devilishly handsome face. His mustache and beard were short, neat, and well styled. What was most striking about the stranger were his hazel eyes. They reminded her of the forest and seemed to pierce through to her soul.

Beth's gaze ended on the stranger's lips. She blushed at the smirk he wore. *Oh, God! I'm ogling a stranger!*

"I'm sorry," she giggled nervously. Sweat formed on her brow and upper lip. The heat must be getting to her. "I-can I help you? I mean, yes? Gods, I'm babbling."

The man's smirk warmed into a dazzling smile. She struggled to take a breath. "My name, dear lady, is Fennick Rayon, but you may call me Fen." He bent at the waist, flourishing his arm in a deep bow.

Beth's heart skipped two beats when he raised her hand to his lips. His mustache tickled her knuckles where he placed a soft kiss. His fingers lingered in hers, leaving a barrage of sparks when he released her hand.

"Um, pleased to meet you, Fen." Her words were breathy. She mentally kicked herself and cleared her throat. "I'm Beth. Have you recently moved into the complex, or..."

"No," he answered. An emotion flashed across his face too fast for her to catch, "but I intend to. I am new to the area and thought I would inquire if there were any vacancies."

"Oh. You'll have to call the landlord and speak to him. I can get the number for you, if you want?" Beth motioned over her shoulder. Something about this stranger seemed, well, strange.

"That would be lovely, Beth. Thank you," Fen replied, stepping inside before she had a chance to close the door.

"Certainly." She forced a smile and wiped her sweaty palms on her thighs. She hadn't gathered any energy for a shield and the man set off all kinds of internal alarms. Why didn't she stop him?

Searching the kitchen for pen and paper, Beth secreted a glimpse at Fen. He studied her apartment with idle curiosity and amusement. Scrolling through her contacts, she found the number and wrote it down.

"Your home is quite lovely, Beth, but not as beautiful as the tenant." Fen's smile, while handsome, set her teeth on edge, and made her skin crawl.

"Thank you, my husband and I decorated the space together." Her emphasis on the word husband was not lost on her guest.

He chuckled and placed a hand over his heart. "Oh, no, my dear, you misunderstand. My sincerest apologies. I meant only to compliment, not to cause aggrievance. Pardon my more flamboyant way of speech. It has been too long since I have conversed with another. Will you forgive my lack of decorum?"

Beth swore his eyes glowed purple for a split second. A trick of the light or something else. She dismissed it and headed to the door. He'd not stepped foot outside of the square of laminate that served as the landing.

"Here's Mr. Jameson's number. He may not answer the first call since your number is unfamiliar. Just hit redial, and he'll pick up." Beth held the edge of the paper between her middle and forefingers. Fennick found a way to brush his fingers against hers when he took it.

"Wonderful. You have my thanks."

Beth stopped herself from wrenching the door open. The smile she gave the handsome devil of a man did not reach her eyes. Whoever this Fennick guy was, she'd had enough of his exuberance.

"Perhaps we shall see each other again soon." Fen winked as he left.

She shut the door so quickly she was surprised his foot hadn't caught.

Chapter 56

TOM

"Are you sure?" Tom sat across from Grady with his face in his hands. "She's his only child."

Beth is going to be crushed.

"I'm afraid so." Grady sighed, tossing the black leather notebook on the table. Sitting back, he crossed his arms over his chest. "When Anthony Harper's name popped up on the page, my brain stopped. I read it ten times, Tom. I can't believe the man would sell his kid's soul to pay off gambling debts."

Grady stood and kicked the dining table leg. The wood cracked, giving the solid table a slight tilt.

Tom understood why Grady was so upset. He was livid to find out what his father-in-law had done. He'd never liked Anthony or Laura Harper, but he got along with them for Beth's sake.

Tom stared at his friend through his fingers. The cloud hanging over Grady's head darkened with his scowl. They had until tomorrow to come up with a plan to protect Beth after he was gone. His body was already fatigued, but not enough for Grady or Beth to notice yet. Coffee was a wonder.

"Are there any other names listed in your dad's notebook besides influential people in the community? Who else owes him favors?" Tom asked. Changing the subject didn't help his brain reconcile Anthony Harper's actions.

"More people than I care to admit. Look, I haven't finished reading through them all, but there's a lot." Grady stared at his father's ledger like it would come to life at any moment.

A chill spread over Tom. They'd forgotten about Curtis Putnam, and Beth was home alone. He kicked himself for ignoring his internal danger alarm.

"Grady." Tom's voice was thick with fear. "Curtis is still out there. What if—"

"Beth is in danger." Grady finished, jumping to his feet. His face was as white as a sheet. "Fuck."

BETH

"AAAND, DONE!" Beth clicked send. Her email made a whooshing sound.

Popping the last kettle-cooked potato chip in her mouth, Beth wiped her hands on a napkin, and powered her laptop off. She slipped off the stool and headed to the bedroom to pack a few things for the Grove.

Knock, knock.

Beth stopped and rolled her eyes.

"I swear, if Fen tries to flirt again, he's gonna get punched in the throat," she mumbled under her breath.

Knock-knock-knock.

"Coming!" Beth called. These were more insistent than the others.

She flung the door open, wanting to put Mr. Flamboyant off-guard this time. Instead of Fennick, a raggedly dressed man stinking of alcohol and ill intent glared at her with white eyes.

"Witch!" he spat, charging inside after her. He kicked the door shut with his foot as he shoved Beth against the wall. A muddy baseball fell out of his pocket.

"M-Mr. Putnam?" She squeaked before his arm pressed across her throat.

"If you'da died when you were suppos't ta, my boy'd be alive!" Curtis shouted. Spittle flew in her face, causing her to gag. When he raised his other hand, there was a flash of silver.

Panic rose in Beth's throat and time slowed. She willed the magic to come to her aid, but it was like there was a very large pool cover over her well.

Curtis's arm crushed against her esophagus. Beth clawed at the arm, filling the room with copper. She tried to jerk her knee upward, delivering damage to his crotch, but Curtis was too close, pinning her with his larger body.

His gaunt face split into a triumphant yellow grin. He held the knife up with his free hand so she could see it. Placing the tip on her cheek he rasped, "I'm gonna cut out those pretty little eyes and leave them for your pussy-whipped little boys to find. The master'll give me my boy back when I give him what's left of you."

Black spots appeared in her vision and her sight blurred. She tried to think of another way to get out of the situation, but her brain felt fuzzy.

Suddenly, the pressure on her throat disappeared. Beth gasped for air and fell to her knees. She tried to focus her sight, to see her rescuer, but it was impossible. A coughing fit had her in tears. Her throat felt like she'd swallowed boiling water.

Between coughs, Beth heard scuffling and grunts. Someone cried out, and metal clattered to the floor. There was more shuffling and heavy breathing before the front door slammed shut.

Seconds later, a whooshing sound came from the direction of the guest bedroom. "Beth!"

Her vision was still cloudy, but she recognized the dark curls at her side. He held her shoulders as his shape moved from side to side.

"It was—" Beth tried to speak but her throat was swollen. She closed her eyes. It hurt to swallow.

"I'll get some water." Tom's voice came from her other side. His sneakers squeaked as he rushed to the kitchen.

"Who did this?" Grady demanded, his voice shaking with anger. His hands fell to her elbows, pulling her to stand. Beth opened her eyes so she wouldn't stumble and was happy to see his features more clearly.

"Give her a minute! She can't talk yet." Tom scolded, taking her by the arm and guiding her to the couch. As soon as they sat, he wrapped an arm around her protectively.

"Goddammit!" Grady grumbled as he paced. "I'm going to check outside. Be right back."

"Here, hon. Drink this. When you can speak, tell us what happened." Tom helped guide the glass to her lips.

The cool water helped a little. Beth took several small sips, letting her thumping heart calm. Now that she wasn't being strangled to death, she was able to focus. She closed her eyes and placed her hand over her tender esophagus, wincing. Magic flowed through her fingertips, dulling the pain until swallowing wasn't like passing a grapefruit through a smoothie straw.

"Did you heal yourself?" Tom asked, taking the empty glass from her hands, and placing it on the table.

Beth nodded, leaning into his side. He tightened his hold and pressed a kiss to her head.

The front door opened, and Grady entered with a frown. Shutting and locking the door behind him, he turned to the couple, shaking his head. "I didn't see a thing. The fucker—"

"It was Curtis Putnam." Beth's body shivered at the thought. She'd had enough near-death experiences for one lifetime. "He blamed me for Jeff's death."

Grady knelt in front of her, the rage in his eyes burning in waves. "He'll never get close enough to hurt you again, Beth. I swear, when I find him, I'm gonna rip his fucking head off."

"He may have gotten away, but I guarantee Beth left a scar." Tom rocked her in his arms.

Beth shook her head. "The magic didn't come. I was going to die, and it wouldn't come." Tears welled in her eyes then rolled down her cheeks. "Someone else saved me."

What good am I going to be against an all-powerful being if I can't even save myself?

What if my magic won't help again when I need it?

"Who, baby? Who helped you?" Tom cupped her face in his hands.

"I'm not sure, but I think it was Fen. He came by earlier. I thought..." She couldn't finish. The feeling of helplessness still afflicted her.

"Who's Fen?" Grady asked, his face hard. She could only imagine what was going through his head.

She shook her head and closed her eyes again. The scent of spiced cranberries still lingered in the air. Fennick Rayon may have saved her life, but he was still a stranger. One she now owed a debt to.

"I don't know." Beth sniffled and opened her eyes to stare at the front door. "But I'm tired of needing to be saved."

Chapter 57

GRADY

Grady was not usually one to resort to violence of this magnitude, but Curtis Putnam had crossed the line. The world hid behind a sanguine filter as Grady imagined Curtis's blood draining from his body.

"Fen came by asking if any of the apartments were open for rental. I gave him the landlord's number and he left," Beth explained to Tom.

"Well, that's random. Did he say or do anything else? He didn't seem like a creep?" Tom continued his line of questioning.

Grady agreed with Tom. People didn't simply come up to an apartment building. *Unless they were from out of town.* "Anything else you can tell us will help."

"Um, okay. I heard a knock on the door. It was odd because most people in town are at church. I haven't heard from my parents, and I was worried, so I opened the door and there he was. Dude looked like he was going to Medieval Times or stepped out of a Rennaissance fair." She shook her head and scrunched her face in thought. "Anyway, he said he was passing by, but it was odd."

"What's Fen's last name? Did he say?" Grady urged. He couldn't shake the feeling of something being horribly wrong. *Calm down, man.* Mr. Putnam had him worked up.

"Fen...Fennick. Um, Fennick Rayon," Beth recalled with a triumphant grin. "The way he spoke was strange, a little archaic even; like he was performing Shakespeare. It was annoying, really."

While Grady pondered the name, Tom asked the question perched on the tip of his tongue. "How do you know it was this Fen guy who pulled Curtis off you?"

"His cologne is distinct." Beth's cheeks turned pink. "Spicy like the cardamom muffins your mom makes. I got a whiff of it when the door shut, right before you guys came in."

Rayon...where have I heard this name before? The notebook?

"I'll be right back. There's something I need to grab from the Grove." Grady sped to the door with the portal stone in hand. He stopped and spoke over his shoulder, "I won't be long."

His feet barely touched the floor before he had the notebook in hand and was back through the portal. He ignored the look of disapproval on Tom's face as he sat on the fireplace hearth. Flipping through the pages, his eyes searched for Fen's name, but it wasn't there.

"What are you looking for?" Beth asked. Her voice still croaked, and Grady was reminded of the anger swelling inside.

"His name. Rayon. It's not here, but I know I've heard it somewhere." Grady gripped the folded notebook until the leather creaked under the pressure. "There are other names in here, Beth. I think you should know—"

"Grady! Not now!" Tom stood in front of Beth, always her Champion. "She's been through enough!"

"She needs to know, Tom. We need to figure out what to do next." Any other time, Grady would have agreed, but given the circumstances.

"For the love of Pete..." Beth rolled her eyes and pushed past Tom. She grabbed the notebook from Grady's hands before either man could react. As she flipped through the pages, her frown deepened. "What is this?"

"My—Louis's notebook. The names of everyone who made a deal with him are listed there," Grady explained as disgust replaced part of his rage. "Your dad's name—"

Beth's hand cupped her mouth as she sobbed, her glassy eyes wide in disbelief. "He didn't."

"Honey, you don't have to read it." Tom came to her side and reached for the notebook, but she jerked away, tears streaking her cheeks.

"Anthony Harper...Paid. The soul of his only child: Elizabeth Marie Harper." Beth's finger shook as she traced the line.

"Your dad owed a lot of money to a lot of people. He'd been embezzling money from work for the past four years to pay off gambling debts, but it wasn't enough. When my dad gave Anthony a way out, he sold your soul to buy his freedom." The pit of Grady's stomach turned, making him sick.

"I hate him," Beth whispered.

She snapped the notebook closed and threw it onto the table like it had bit her. Flopping onto a cushion, she sighed and buried her head in her hands. She mumbled something, shaking her head.

Tom carefully removed her arms and ducked his head to look her straight on. "What did you say, love?"

"I said, I don't want to do this tonight." Beth's face sagged in tiredness. She pursed her lips but her bottom lip quivered. Taking a deep breath, she continued, "It's Tom's last days with us, and we have missed two movie nights. Right now, I want to forget everything else, order pizza and wings, make popcorn, and watch a movie. You know, do *normal* stuff."

Tom hugged her tightly and glanced at Grady, pleading with his eyes. He needed this as much as Beth did. Grady couldn't say no. Curtis Putnam was a threat who needed to be dealt with as soon as possible, but Tom would be dead in hours. Strength in numbers, and all that. He'd deal with Curtis tomorrow.

"Okay. Fine." Grady threw his hands up. Someone had to pretend to be the responsible one of the bunch. "Movie night is on."

Chapter 58

TOM

TOM WAS GLAD BETH had talked them into movie night. Listening to his best friend and wife argue over which movie to watch was exactly like old times. After the events of the past week, this was the normalcy he needed before reality took a nosedive.

"We've seen Gladiator *fifteen* times, Grady!"

"It's Tom's favorite movie!"

"We should watch something new."

"Tom, which do you want to watch?"

"Whatever you guys want." Beth cocked an eyebrow at his answer, so Tom changed it. "Gladiator is fine. It *is* my favorite movie."

Grady let out a victory 'whoop' while Beth stuck her tongue out.

Just like old times.

While Grady fired up the DVD, Beth placed the bowls of popcorn on the table. She kissed Tom before snuggling next to him. Before he could reach for popcorn, she had some at the ready.

"Open up, you." Her green eyes sparkled when his lips wrapped around her fingers, tongue flicking out to keep the popcorn in his mouth.

"Y'all nasty. Beth needs to wash her hand before putting it back in the bowl," Grady said jokingly, but his blue eyes had darkened to a navy.

"Fine. I'll be right back." Beth licked her fingers clean and swayed her hips on the way to the kitchen.

Tom followed her with his gaze. Grady watched her, too, his hand halfway to his partially open mouth. Most of the popcorn had fallen back into the bowl.

Surprisingly, Tom wasn't bothered by this. The realization made him gulp. His time must be near its end.

He prayed to whomever was listening to let them have this last normal night.

When Beth returned, Grady started the movie. Tom tucked her into his side with his arm around her shoulder. He kissed the top of her head and settled in, stifling a yawn.

About fifteen minutes into the movie, Tom's thoughts wandered to earlier at the Grove...

"Grady." Tom clasped hands with his friend, pulling him into a side hug. "So, uh, what did you want to do for the next two...days?"

"I wanted to make sure we had everything in place for–for when the time comes." Grady's grim demeanor diminished. "And to spend time with my best man, of course."

Tom nodded. Melancholy colored his mood gray. *Business first, then.*

"Where's Beth? You said she was gonna visit Myrtle and Heliotta." Grady looked behind Tom at the open portal. Disappointment flashed in his eyes.

"Oh, she's answering the email Mayes Hill Elementary sent last weekend," Tom explained, scratching his jaw. The beard was beginning to drive him nuts with how itchy it made his face. He'd have to shave it when they finished. "Beth said she'd text when she's on her way."

"Cool, cool. First, I figured we need to talk about your soul. There are things you need to do, so Ja'azul doesn't end up with it. Then, we'll prepare. After all that," Grady paused, rubbing the back of his neck and averted his eyes, "I need to go over some personal stuff, you know, about Beth."

Tom wiped his face, holding his chin. *Yeah, I saw the last part coming.* "Sure, thing. Let me get settled, then we'll start on keeping my soul safe."

The men made their way inside Grady's cabin and settled at the table. Tom was thankful for the coffee his friend had thought to make ahead of time. His energy was waning. It was his fault, though. His inability to keep his hands off Beth for longer than a couple of hours at a time had taken its toll. He was a starved man, needing as much of her as possible in the next twenty-four hours.

"Okay, so, to keep Ja'azul from ending up with your soul, you have to take your last breath in the Grove. There are protective magics in place to keep your soul from wandering outside of safety." Grady held his cup of coffee with both hands, studying Tom from across the dining table.

"When I die here, will I be able to visit your dreams like Myrtle visits ours?" he asked, a smidge of excitement in his voice. The prospect of being able to see Beth again made his stomach flutter.

"I'm not sure. Your case is special because of the magic Myrtle imbued you with to defeat the Agnazar. Since you gifted it to Circe, there's a possibility." Grady frowned as he stared into the black circle encased in his hands. "We'll prepare a resting place, and use the burial rights Myrtle found. It's a simple process."

"What happens to my body after I die?" Tom was barely able to ask. His voice wanted to hide, as if asking questions made his impending death more real. Whether he talked about it or not, it didn't change the fact he was going to die tomorrow.

"Well, Beth and I will bring you back to the apartment and lay you in bed. She'll make the call the next morning. With everything that's happened, I doubt there'll be much of an issue with the paramedics," Grady explained.

"Will you stay with Beth through it all? I don't want her to be alone. I can't—" Tom's sobs snuck up on him. He'd been keeping his emotions bottled up, but the thought of Beth going through his death alone was too much.

"Of course. I'll stay in the guest bedroom...after you give me the 'all clear.'" Grady's face flushed. His face screwed up in pain as the hand he had on the table next to his coffee squeezed into a fist.

"I am so sorry." Tom placed his hand on Grady's arm. His friend shuddered, dropping his head.

"All I ever wanted was what you and Beth had, but no one ever made me truly happy. I tried, dammit. I really did, but the other girls *felt* wrong. I guess now we know why." A sobbing hiccup escaped Grady's carefully constructed shield, but then he shook his head with a short chuckle. "In the beginning, I couldn't stand Beth. She never gave you the time of day until college. I never understood it, but I didn't care. She was a self-absorbed bitch. Well, that's what I thought...until my mom passed away.

"Beth never once belittled my pain or got angry at you for spending time with me. She could tell how much I was hurting and did everything she could to help. Afterward, I felt like shit for treating *her* like shit. Then she kinda grew on me, and, well...you know. I love her, Tom. And it's not because of magic or destiny. Fuck." He dropped his forehead to the table.

"I prayed for you, you know. You are the most real and good person I have ever met. You deserve to be happy." Tom used the handle on his mug to drive it to his waiting hand. "My parents go to church every Sunday, so I thought, 'What harm can come of it?' I mean, even as kids, you talked about having a beautiful wife, lots of kids, and having your own woodworking shop. You wanted to build the house with your bare hands like your grandfather...and I *wanted* you to find it. I guess you did, just not how you'd hoped."

"Yeah," Grady whispered as he raised his head. He lifted the coffee to his lips and took a gulp. "The other thing I wanted to talk about. I don't want to... Damn, this is hard. Look, there are certain things what belong to you and Beth. I don't want to upset her by thinking I'm trying to replace the memories you two made together. Does that make sense?"

"Yeah. Yeah, it does. You don't have to do that, but I appreciate your consideration." Tom gulped. The slurry of confusion, partial relief, and bone-deep injury made for an odd emotional cocktail. "Trust me, Beth won't forget me, but she'll heal a lot faster than you expect. If it helps, I'll make a list."

The rest of the day was spent preparing a space in the meadow for the ritual tomorrow. While Tom lay on the ground, Grady took a length of rope to outline his form in an oval. They then picked wildflowers from the meadow and placed them around the outside of the barrier. Once there were enough, Grady put the flowers in a stasis so they wouldn't wilt until the appointed time.

After dinner, Tom lay in bed with his pen and paper. Throughout the day, he'd written a list of things to tell Beth in his goodbye letter. There was so much he had to say, but this was a start.

Tom's stroll through memory lane was interrupted by the sweet voice of his love. The woman who had captured his heart as a youth, and still held it captive.

"Hon, you okay?" Beth's hand cradled his face. Her thumb caressed his smooth skin.

"Yeah. A little tired, that's all." He tried to smile, but the look on her face said she didn't believe him.

"We can stop the movie and go to bed if you need to." Fear flashed across Beth's face.

"Naw. I want to stay up with you and Grady." Tom put his hand on hers, turning his face to kiss her palm. "And stop worrying. It's not time."

Grady came around the couch with two bowls of popcorn. He handed one to Tom and lounged on the loveseat with the other. His feet wiggled happily.

Tom sniffed the bowl and sat it on the coffee table. "It's burnt. How can you eat that?"

"It's not burnt! A little over, sure, but it eats fine." Grady shrugged at Tom and winked at Beth, digging into his popcorn and watching the movie.

Beth snatched the bowl and grabbed a small handful of popcorn. She shoved it in her mouth and hummed in contentment.

"Not you, too! Not fair. Y'all are teaming up on me." Tom shook his head in mock anger. Beth giggled as he took a handful from her bowl. Popping one in his mouth, he groaned at the taste. These two were crazy. The popcorn was definitely burnt. "Gross."

Tom headed to the kitchen to spit it out, dropping the popcorn he still held in his hand on Grady's head as he passed.

"Hey!"

A popcorn fight ensued. The sound of raucous laughter filled the small apartment while the movie continued to play in the background.

Chapter 59

BETH

THEIR LAST NIGHT TOGETHER was wonderful, albeit bittersweet. Beth held onto the laughter and fun-filled evening for strength to get through the hours to come.

When she asked Tom if he would rather spend the rest of his time at the Grove, he declined.

"I *want* to be here. Tonight has been the closest thing to what life was before magic. I need this to be the last memory we share together," he said with a sniffle.

"Then we stay, Brother," Grady replied, hugging Tom until he protested.

When they made it to bed, Tom could barely keep his eyes open, but it didn't stop him from trying to be intimate. He finally agreed to cuddling when he fell asleep during their make-out session.

Beth barely slept. She kept jolting awake with every single noise, worried that Tom had stopped breathing. Mostly, she lay facing him with her head on her pillow, watching for his chest to rise with the next breath. When her eyes grew too heavy to keep open, she fought sleep by rapid blinking or pinching her arm, only to startle awake with the next sound.

A crow cawed, and Beth's eyes flew open. The first rays of the sun's light peeked through their bedroom window. Fully awake, she shifted to watch Tom's chest rise and fall. Panic rose in her throat when he didn't take a breath. Her eyes stung with tears, but she had to make sure.

Beth placed her hand on Tom's chest above his heart, desperate to feel something. His body tensed, eyes flew open, and a guttural scream tore from his throat. Tom's handsome features twisted in pain as he gripped the sheets, clenched his teeth, and struggled to catch his breath.

"Tom!" Beth cried, getting to her knees beside him. "What can I do?"

He stared at her helplessly as excruciating pain forced his features into a deep grimace.

Without breaking eye contact, Beth quickly drew energy from the sun. She placed her hands above Tom's chest and poured the healing magic into him as fast as she dared. "Hold on, baby. I'm trying to ease the pain."

The bedroom door flew open. Grady stood in his sleep shorts and tank top. His wide eyes took in the scene in front of him. "Tom."

In a flash, he was on the other side of Tom, giving Beth the energy she needed. His gaze went between her face and Tom's. She never looked away from her husband, though. She needed to focus on him, or she would break. Yesterday, she was helpless, and her magic was useless. Today, she would redeem some of her confidence.

As her energy waned, Tom's breathing became regular and his body relaxed. She stopped when Grady shook her loose.

"Beth. He's okay now. You can stop." He was studying her with gentle eyes. "You did good."

"It's time," Tom whispered. His voice was hoarse from screaming.

Words failed her. He couldn't leave now. There were things Beth still needed to say. She wanted to tell him he couldn't leave. She wanted more time.

"We need to get him to the Grove. His soul is in danger here." Grady's words snapped her to attention.

"Okay." Beth didn't recognize her own voice. It sounded like it was coming from another room.

"Open the portal. I'll help Tom stand," Grady commanded with gentleness.

"Okay." Apparently, her vocabulary was empty except this one word.

No! There's something I need to say to open the portal. Say it and get Tom through!

"Ex...Ex...Exgradi." The word seemed foreign to her tongue. *Is this the first time I've used the spell?* The irony was not lost on her.

"Good. Now, Beth, help me. I can't carry Tom alone." Grady grunted as he lifted Tom with one arm around his shoulders and the other around Tom's waist.

She nodded and wrapped Tom's other arm around her shoulders. His feet dragged between them, but they made it through.

Grady closed the portal behind them. "We're going to the field. Everything's been prepared."

Beth wanted to ask what had been prepared but nodded. Focusing on carrying Tom to the meadow was all she could do to keep from falling apart.

They came upon a ring of wildflowers in the middle of the field just large enough for Tom to lay in the center. At the head and feet lay pure white lilies crossed at the crown.

"We need to place him in the middle without disturbing the flowers, okay?" Grady instructed. "Head up here and feet down there."

Beth lowered Tom's feet inside the base of the ring. "What now?"

Grady sat at Tom's right. "Sit across from me and follow along," he instructed, raising his hands over Tom's body then stopped, adding softly, "we can say goodbye first."

Beth sat on her knees, careful not to disturb the floral ring. Taking Tom's hand in hers, she cradled his face with the other. His skin was pallid and cool to the touch. "Tom, thank you for everything. You taught me how to love, truly and deeply. The few years we've spent together have been the happiest of my life."

Tom smiled at Beth, his eyes glistening. He hooked his hand behind her neck and pulled her down for a last kiss. It was tender and sweet and salty.

When he let her go, he caressed her face and then faced Grady. He took his best friend's hand and put Beth's hand in it, saying, "Be happy," as he blinked away tears.

Grady nodded at Tom as rivers ran down his chin, soaking the front of his shirt. As soon as Tom closed his eyes, Grady sniffled, and held their hands above Tom's chest.

Raising his other hand, Beth did the same as Grady chanted:

"Blessed Circe, hear us. We bind this soul to you, may it pass in love and peace."

When Grady repeated it, Beth joined in. At first, she could barely form the words. They came out in a cracked whisper. The thought of sending Tom's soul away safely and the meditative hum of Grady's voice somewhat soothed her. Finally, she fell into a rhythm, and their voices joined as one.

A white glow surrounded Tom's body. Beth paused, but Grady nodded to continue. The glow brightened and Tom gave a long sigh. A marble-sized spark lifted from his chest, mingling with the waning sunlight. It dancing playfully like a child on the first day of summer above their heads before bursting into a million tiny specks of glittering light. Tom's soul spread out among the Grove, leaving them feeling warm and calm.

In the eye of the emotional storm, time froze. Outside of the stillness, Beth was numb. She stared at Tom's peaceful face, the image now a permanent stamp on her soul. The only sound was the rushing of blood to her ears, drowning out everything else.

The rush of sadness didn't hit her until Grady placed his warm hand on her shoulder, pulling her into his embrace. Beth gasped, her face warm with fresh tears. She fisted the back of Grady's shirt as wails tore from her chest.

Her Tom was gone.

Chapter 60

BETH

Beth gazed at her reflection in the small mirror propped up on her sink. Her face was pale, plain, and stony behind a simple, black veil. The plain black dress she wore with simple black flats comforted her somewhat, knowing that some things remained plain...and simple.

Otherwise, she was a husk. The world had turned dark, empty, and cold. There was no more joy, no more laughter. All the happiness had been sucked away the moment he was gone. Her sweet Tom.

Since Tom's passing, Grady had come to the apartment seconds after asking, night after night. They'd sit on the couch, and she'd cry herself to sleep on his shoulder, clinging to him. Her heart broke further for him. He'd lost his mother four years ago, then his father and two of his oldest friends last week, and now, his best friend.

Despite everything, Grady remained strong. A rock. Her rock. She didn't have the emotional capacity to show him how grateful she was for his being there in her time of need. She'd feel his tears, though. They were heavy when they rolled off his chin and onto her head, making her cry even harder.

Knock. Knock. The soft rapping startled her.

"Beth, it's time to go," Grady said through the door.

Outside, the light patter of raindrops fell on the roof. They tapped rhythmically on the bedroom window. It was almost soothing.

Beth opened the bathroom door, switching the light off before stepping out. Her usually bright green eyes were a dark gray-green. She peeked at Grady; his sad blue eyes studied her closely. She'd bet anything he was trying to decide if today was a clingy-tearful day or a stone-faced, empty, tired-of-crying day.

In his charcoal suit, Grady had one arm raised, leaning it against the door trim. Resting his head against his arm, messy black curls fell across his forehead with one lock in his eyes. Beth wanted to brush it away, to see his whole face, but she didn't. Not here. Not when she could still smell Tom's cedarwood and orange scent in this room.

Her fingers twitched.

Beth didn't speak; she couldn't. Then again, they didn't need to. Everything that needed to be said was conveyed in the pain on their faces, the plain black clothes, and the gloomy rain outside.

When she broke eye contact, Grady lowered his arm and offered his elbow. Beth slipped her arm in the crook, and he lead her to the living room.

"I put extra tissues and hand sanitizer in the truck for you," Grady said as they made their way outside the apartment.

He handed Beth an open umbrella. She held it over their heads as he locked the apartment door. At his truck, Grady opened the door for her, making sure her dress was inside before shutting it. When he came around to the driver's side to get in, Beth stared straight ahead, rigid and unmoving.

Did every widow burying their spouse feel like they were being swallowed whole by a bleak vortex?

GRADY

THE FUNERAL HOME WAS a short drive. Grady was glad the noise from his truck's engine was muffled by the sudden downpour. He watched the road carefully, finding some comfort in the rain until the windshield wipers squeaked. He glanced at Beth, making sure it didn't disturb her, but she was a statue. Weeping silently, but seemingly unbothered by the sound.

At least she's grieving well. This was important to Grady. Whatever future they were going to have, he wanted it to be authentic, not filled with the duty to fulfill some prophecy.

He promised himself not to push her, to let her have time to mourn Tom's loss. When Beth was ready, he would still take his time making sure she was happy, because he wanted to have what she and Tom had. Deep down he feared it wouldn't happen. If they had even a fraction of that happiness and love together, he swore it would be enough. Whatever it took to see joy in her smile again.

Grady pulled into the funeral home, parking at the front of the line behind Jack and Lillian's SUV. He cut the engine, watching the rain slow to a drizzle.

Grabbing the umbrella, the small messenger bag with extra tissues, and hand sanitizer, Grady got out and opened Beth's door. She sat there, shaking lightly. The front of her black dress had darker splotches.

Grady placed a hand on her shoulder, speaking softly, "Take your time and cry as long as you need to. I won't let anyone bother you."

Beth sniffled and dotted her puffy red eyes. "I'm sorry. Thank you, Grady," she whispered.

She held onto his arm as he helped her out of his truck, leaning on him heavily as they made their way to the back entrance. Grady had hoped to sneak around the bigger crowd, but they arrived later than anticipated. The viewing room and hallway were full of people there to pay their respects to Tom Newman, the well-liked young man of a well-respected family in their small town who had a bright future as a teacher.

The first person to catch sight of them was Lillian. She intercepted them before they could enter the viewing room. "Oh, my poor dears," she choked out, hugging both Grady and Beth.

"I'm sorry," Beth whispered when Lillian stepped back, and pulled them to the side.

She smiled at Beth, sad and lost. Turning to Grady, Lily smoothed his black tie and straightened his collar. "I thought Tom was feeling better after his downer. Was this because of his depressive episode?"

"He was, this was sudden," Beth explained as fresh tears fell down her cheeks, her eyes glossing over. "Tom and I had Grady over for movie night, and he said he was tired. The next morning, he just...never woke up," she explained barely above a whisper.

Her bottom lip wobbled. Grady handed her a clean tissue. Otherwise, he was helpless to console Beth. The funeral home wasn't her apartment where he could let her cling to him all night.

"Oh, you poor thing," Lillian consoled quietly, hugging her daughter-in-law. She withdrew to cup Beth's face. "Let's take you to see Tom before the service starts."

Grady sniffled and followed behind, shaking a few peoples' hands on the way. He never lost sight of Beth. When he caught up with her, she stood over Tom's casket, smoothing his tie and doing her best to keep from unraveling completely.

Tom looked good, like he was sleeping and would sit up at any moment. Grady reached into the pocket of his suit jacket and took out the signal whistle Tom had given him for his twelfth birthday. He'd told Grady to call on it anytime he needed him, and he would come, *'Because that's what brothers do.'* He couldn't remember how many times that summer he'd blown the whistle and Tom showed up...every time. Grady twisted the silver metal cylinder between his fingers and hummed before placing it in his brother's pocket.

In case you need me, too, Brother.

BETH

BETH RESTED HER HEAD on Grady's shoulder. It wasn't much consolation, but it's all she could give right now. Being here was a vivid nightmare. One she couldn't wake from.

She thought back to the day Tom died. He looked so serene then, too.

Grady had picked up Tom's body and carried him back through the portal, the pain silently leaking down his perpetually damp face. Beth turned the bed sheets down so Tom could be positioned as if he was sleeping. She washed his face, neck, and arms with a warm washcloth while Grady stepped into the living room. With every swipe of the cloth, portions of her grief were gradually replaced by calm.

She lay next to Tom for a while, studying his face, and pretended to see the slow rise of his chest so her heart didn't break into even tinier pieces. When she couldn't stand it any longer, she rumpled the covers and got up.

In the living room, Grady sat in the crook of the couch arm with his elbows resting on his knees. He glanced at her with glassy eyes and lips turned down in a deep frown.

"I'm going now, but when you call, I'll be here in five minutes." Grady stood and pulled the moonstone from his pocket.

She nodded and made the call as he stepped through. "My husband won't wake up. Please, hurry!"

When the police arrived, her face was red and puffy. They were taking her statement when Grady pulled up in his truck. He played the role of frantic and worried friend well enough that he was allowed to console her as long as he stayed in the living room.

The coroner's report showed that Tom's heart had simply stopped. They said he felt no pain and had died peacefully in his sleep. Knowing how he truly passed nullified their assurances.

That afternoon, Beth slumped onto the couch next to Grady and heaved a ragged sigh. His warm arm tucked around her shoulders and she leaned into his side. Neither of them said a word for hours. They simply held each other until they fell asleep.

The next morning, Beth woke up in the guest bedroom. She wanted nothing more than to lay there, numb, until the sadness lulled her into false peace.

"If everyone will gather in the chapel, we'll begin the service."

Beth startled from her thoughts when the funeral director made the announcement. Family and friends shuffled into the next room with somber faces and weak smiles among the low chatter. Walking behind Beth, ever vigilant, was Grady. He stayed by her side until they sat down. Leading her to Jack and Lillian's pew, she smiled sadly at the family and joined them.

When Grady turned to sit in the pew behind the family, Jack cleared his throat. "Grady, you sit with us. You're just as much family as Beth is," he said with a pursed smile, making room for one more.

Squeezing in next to Beth, Grady had to put his arm across the back of the pew to fit. She cast him a supportive smile before staring at her hands in her lap. His warmth was comforting, but she tried to focus on the sermon.

The preacher was from the Newman's church. He told everyone to hold onto hope, to not give up faith, and reminded them of the promise of eternal life. His words rolled into one never-ending hum, droll and dragging. Beth sank lower and lower into the comforting blanket of the darkness around her. She shut everything around her out until there was nothing but a small, marble-sized light above her head. It grew smaller and smaller.

"Beth, wake up," Grady said firmly, gripping her shoulders as her head flopped to the side.

The light flew wide open as Beth sat up, gasping for breath. She studied the horrified expressions of the faces around her. There was fear in Grady's eyes before he cleared his throat.

"You passed out, dear. We couldn't get you to wake up," Lillian said as she checked Beth's pulse, then put a hand on her forehead. "Have you eaten anything today? Your blood pressure is really low, I think. And you feel cold."

How could anyone *eat at a time like this?* Beth wanted to ask, but snapping at Lily wouldn't be fair. Especially when Beth wasn't sure she'd eaten anything in days.

"No, I couldn't. Not today," she answered, trying to ignore the scolding look of disapproval Grady gave her.

"Here." Lillian thrust a package of chocolate covered peanuts into her hand. "To tide you over until after the, uh...later," she added, trailing off.

Beth started to pocket the candy, but Grady raised an eyebrow. She mouthed okay, rolling her eyes like it was no big deal as the crowd shuffled outside for the procession. Beth ate the entire package before standing.

Grady soothingly rubbed Beth's shoulder. "The procession is about to start."

Beth nodded, and let Grady lead her outside. His truck rumbled to life just as the hearse pulled away from the funeral home. The Newman's car started after it, with Grady's truck close behind. The rest of the procession filed out of the funeral home, heading to the cemetery a few miles out of town.

The whole ordeal was quick. Only half of the people at the funeral home came out due to the rainy weather. The preacher said some words over the gravesite as the funeral director lowered Tom's coffin into the ground.

It was surreal burying her husband. Oftentimes, she thought he would outlive her. Sniffling, family and friends took turns dropping their white roses into the grave, covering the casket, along with offering their thoughts and prayers.

Beth stood over Tom's casket listening to large raindrops fall on the roof of the popup pavilion in chaotic patterns. She twirled a single red rose in her hands, her legs locked into place.

What if I can't walk away, Tom? The sooner she left him here in the dirt, the sooner she could start to heal...with Grady's help. They had to save the world, but she also had to grieve. Grady would understand. He always did.

The whirlwind of emotions made her dizzy. Beth glanced at the man who'd promised to pick up the pieces and care for her the way her late husband had. He stood next to his truck, wiping his face with a white cloth. When Grady caught Beth's gaze, he tucked it into his suit pocket, pursed his lips into a semi-smile, and nodded.

It was now or never. She teetered slightly and took a shuddering breath.

"Goodbye, my sweet Tom. I'll always love you," she whispered.

With one last look, Beth held the red rose over the bed of white and let it go.

Chapter 61

GRADY

GRADY'S LEFT HAND WAS on the wheel, his right hand on his leg. His chest was as hollow as his bones. Tom was gone. He'd never see his best friend again, never go fishing or call him up to shoot the shit whenever he was lonely. His nose tingled and burned, heralding another onslaught of tears.

The reception was nice. He couldn't remember what he ate or how the food tasted, but there was a nice spread. Beth hadn't eaten much. She picked at some fruit, nibbled on a sandwich. Halfway through, Lilian ushered them out, saying they needed rest. She promised to bring leftovers by the apartment later.

Beth grabbed his free hand, squeezing it between hers as fresh tears fell. Grady recognized where this day was headed, and steeled himself for the long afternoon ahead.

He parked at the apartment complex and helped Beth inside. While she curled up on the couch and cried, Grady looked through her nearly bare cupboards for food. *No wonder she hasn't eaten. Aside from the obvious.*

Making toast with the single piece of bread he found, Grady managed to scrape the grape jelly jar clean with a spatula. He made a mental note to buy groceries first thing tomorrow morning.

Beth traded the toast for a weak grin. She practically inhaled it, washing it down with a glass of water.

"Thank you, Grady." She placed the dishes on the coffee table and cuddled into a ball beside him.

Beth rested her head on his chest. Her hand curled up over Grady's heart. He put his arm around her and kissed the side of her head. Same as he'd always done.

Something heavy weighed on him. Several people gawked at them during the funeral, sparking concern about rumors spreading. There were already whispers in corners today. They stopped abruptly when Beth walked past.

He didn't particularly care what people said about him; it was *her* reputation that worried him. Beth was supposed to start teaching her first class this fall. Two and a half short months away. What would she do if a great number of her students' parents asked for their children to have a different teacher because Beth was labeled an adulterer?

He could already imagine the whispers.

"Tom's not even cold in his grave, and she's flaunting his best friend around."

"I wonder how long that's been going on?"

"Are you okay?" Beth interrupted the spiral of his thoughts.

Grady sifted through the voices in his head, focusing on hers. Usually, she would cry herself to sleep while curled up on him. Grady would carry her to bed afterwards, then sleep on the couch in case she had a nightmare. She sounded more like herself than she had in three days.

"Grady, are you okay?" Beth repeated. Sitting up, the hand on his chest flattened. Her worried eyes were more green than gray.

He removed his arm from her shoulders, causing her to sit cross-legged to face him. "Just thinking about a lot," he answered, standing so he could put distance between them.

Beth stared up at him before a bitter chuckle came from her lips. "You heard them, too. Gossiping biddies whispering in corners and pretending like they didn't want to be heard." She pulled her knees to her chest, wrapping her arms around them. "Honestly, Grady, I don't care. Those people know nothing about what we've been through the past week."

He shook his head and sat on the couch opposite her. "I won't let your reputation be tarnished, Beth. You need to have a good relationship with your students and their parents, especially in a small town."

"So, what're you gonna do? Leave and stop coming over?" Beth asked, her voice cracking.

Grady hated to see more tears welling up in her eyes. Tears he put there. He furrowed his brows and rubbed the back of his neck, waffling for a split second. Despite the sharp ache in the center of his chest, he stood his ground. "Yeah, I guess I am."

Beth stared for a long time before nodding. Her lips were pursed when the tears finally broke. The betrayal reflected in her eyes was too much.

Grady turned away. "Look, I'll, uh, bring some groceries by tomorrow, but I think it's best if we're not seen together for a little while at least. You can still call me anytime." When he turned to leave, Beth fell forward and grabbed his hand.

Grady could see the words swirling behind her eyes, begging him to stay. She studied him for a long moment, then let his hand fall to his side. Her eyes followed him as he backed away.

When Grady got to the front door, he opened it partially. A tear fell down his cheek. Then another. His heart screamed how wrong it was to leave her, but he'd convinced himself this was the best course of action. This was best for both in the long run.

"Please know I'm doing this for us, because…I love you, Beth," Grady whispered before stepping out the door. As soon as he was through, he gently shut it and hurried to his truck before he changed his mind.

Gripping the steering wheel, Grady left for his house, not once looking back. Every bit of distance he put between them would help her, but it hurt like hell.

When he pulled into his driveway, his head fell forward onto the steering wheel. It was like he had the flu, the sweating and shaking and clammy hands. Grady's song of agony left his throat raw. He took a shuddering breath that left his chest heaving. Even with the necklaces on, their grief bled through.

This is wrong. She needed me to stay, but I left. You promised Tom.

Grady slammed the palm of his hand into the steering wheel several times until he had pins and needles up his arm. He willed himself to go inside, but his hand went to the ignition key.

One turn and five minutes. That's all it'll take, then you can beg for forgiveness.

It was much more difficult to keep his distance now that Tom was gone. The only things keeping them from being together at this point was formality and the gossip mill. Beth had been looking forward to her first job as a first-grade math teacher. He wouldn't take this opportunity from her.

Slipping out of his truck, Grady was physically ill, but he made it inside. The quiet house was disheartening. He'd have to keep it until he figured out how to build and plumb a shower at the Grove. He planned to stay at the cabin and update everything while Beth grieved.

He'd check on her once a month by Grove time. For her, it would seem like he was popping by every other day through the portal. No one would be wiser.

By the time she started teaching, everything would be ready and they could live happily at the Grove. It was a solid plan; a good plan.

Grady felt better about the whole thing.

For a whole five minutes, that is.

He took the brown-bottled liquor with the Lion and Fox label off his dad's shelf and poured two fingers. The liquid burned, but it didn't numb the throbbing in his chest.

He'd just have to finish the bottle.

BETH

TOM WAS DEAD, her parents were dead to her, and Grady—her rock and the one fate designed specially for her—had abandoned her.

For the first time in her life, she was alone.

Beth stared at the door where Grady had declared his feelings for her aloud for the first time. She wasn't sure how to process the mix of emotions churning inside, but she knew this wasn't the way she expected to hear the words that were meant to heal and cause her soul to soar. It kinda pissed her off.

She fully intended to grieve Tom, but she'd grown dependent on Grady's support. Until today, she hadn't considered how their interactions must look to everyone else. He must've heard something worse than she had for him to leave so abruptly.

Grady should have stayed and talked things over with her. Hell, he could've drove his truck home with the promise to come back via portal. He was bullheaded by nature, but he didn't have to nope out as soon as he made a decision *for* them rather than together.

Beth inhaled until her lungs pushed against her ribs. Being alone was the last thing Beth wanted, but maybe it was exactly what she *needed*. Her chest burned with the need to expel the spent air. On a long exhale, she found strength in her loss and anger at the situation and used it to burn the last of her nerves.

Wiping the tears from her cheeks, Beth forced herself to get up and change out of her plain black dress. She would still mourn, just in something more comfortable.

Beth would re-evaluate her life, starting with this apartment. She couldn't stay here long, not with how much it reminded her of Tom. He'd picked out the light beige color on the walls when they'd moved in. That was a brighter time, though, when the promise of a lifetime full of laughter and happiness was still theirs.

Beth opened her laptop and searched for paint colors until she found a light gray that the landlord wouldn't complain about. She measured the bathroom mirror—and measured twice, then wrote the numbers on a piece of paper, along with the paint color she'd picked.

An unholy growl came from her gut. Beth opened the fridge, staring at the foil-covered dishes. Nothing in there appealed to her. What she really wanted was the Benny's they never got. She ordered a small pizza, buffalo wings, and a six-pack of beer calling it 'Tom's memorial dinner.'

Tonight, she'd rest. Tomorrow, she'd keep busy picking up the pieces to her broken life. The day after, she'd begin putting them back together, whatever that looked like. If she couldn't depend on Grady to help her through her mourning process, then, by the gods, she would get through it on her own.

Chapter 62

GRADY

GRADY REGRETTED RAIDING HIS dad's liquor cabinet when he woke up the next morning with a splitting headache. He'd been so sure of his decision, but no matter how much alcohol he drowned in, the second thoughts mocked him with visions of Beth's bleary-eyed face, the defeat. The loneliness she feared with his leaving.

What kind of asshole tells his girl he loves her before walking out the door and hours after burying her husband? *Apparently, this guy.*

Grady cringed. He'd make amends today. Buy her groceries, putting kettle-cooked chips and vanilla-bean ice cream at the top of the list. If the mood was right, he'd finally kiss her in the hope it erased some of his stupidity.

It was an okay plan.

The small corner grocery store was on the way to Beth's apartment. He hated the four-way stop and the difficulty getting in and out of the tiny parking lot, but it was too convenient not to shop there. The other option was driving ten miles to Ridgeville for the big chain grocery store, but he was in a hurry to make things right.

Grabbing a basket, he grabbed a few major staples and easy-to-prepare canned items. Lastly, he went down the cereal aisle for some oatmeal. He heard hushed voices in the aisle next to him.

"She wasn't even trying to hide it," one woman said.

"Mm-hmm! I heard they planned the whole thing after he caught them in bed together," another said.

The first woman gasped in mock surprise. "I don't doubt it. Her daddy is known to mess around. Must run in the family."

The second woman laughed scornfully but was shushed by the first. "Lillian and Jack must be devastated knowing their only child married a floozy."

That was it. Grady had heard enough. His face was a furnace when he stormed to the front of the store, forgetting anything else. He was naive for thinking that the town wouldn't gossip for a few days. He'd left Beth a mess last night for no reason. He just prayed she would forgive him.

The grocer rang Grady's items up with a holier-than-thou smirk on his face. Without a word, Grady quickly paid and headed out with the two paper bags.

Beth and Tom's apartment complex was a short two-minute drive away. When Grady pulled into the parking lot, the hatchback wasn't there. Throwing the truck in park, he sat there with the engine idling while he pulled up Beth's number.

"At the apt with groceries. Where are you?" Grady texted.

He could unlock the door and put her groceries away; he had a key. He'd be intruding, though. Like a vampire who'd had his invitation revoked. Waiting in the parking lot for her to return would give him a better gauge on Beth's mood. He rolled down the windows and turned on the radio. The words 'you're about to miss your shot, you gonna kiss me or not' blared through the speakers. He hit the scan button for the next station to come up. 'Just a kiss on your lips in the moonlight.' Grady turned the radio off with a groan.

Ding. His phone lit and Beth's response twisted his insides into knots.

"on my way"

That was it. No explanation, no playful banter. Just three simple words that weighed Grady down even more. Begging wouldn't cut it. Groveling had to work.

Ten minutes later, Beth parked next to Grady, ignoring him when he waved. She stomped up the stairs, unlocked the door, then stomped back down to the trunk of her car. Grady shut the door to the truck with the two bags of groceries in his arms when she emerged with two cans of paint and a bag of paintbrushes and rollers. Unsure how to proceed, he followed her up the stairs and placed the bags on the island. Beth paused at the door when Grady started putting the groceries away.

"Stop. You don't have to do that," she said firmly. All the softness in her eyes was gone, only anger and hurt remained. "I'll put it away."

Grady tried to gather the courage to explain but ended up stepping further into shit. "I want to help—"

"If you wanted to help, you would have stayed yesterday when I needed my *friend*," Beth shot back, emphasizing the last word. "Thank you for bringing the groceries, but I think you should go before someone gets the wrong idea."

She wasn't pulling punches, but he deserved it.

Grady's chest caved in as he wondered how he'd messed up so badly. *She's stubborn and you gave her a target.* "Beth, please. I shouldn't have left like that. I'm sorry."

He came around the island to stand in front of her, but she turned on her heel and disappeared outside. He ran his hand through his hair, head spinning when the hatchback door shut. Beth stormed past him, putting the last load of paint supplies on the fireplace hearth.

Grady followed and tried again, "Look, last night it seemed like the right thing to do, but I felt like shit this morning. I'm here now. I'll always come whenever you call. Can we just go back to how it was, and forget about how stupid I am?"

Beth turned on her heel, her face twisted in an angry frown. "We can't go back to anything, Grady. You told me you loved me then abandoned me in the same breath. Whatever we were, the slate has been wiped clean. You helped me see that clearly last night."

The knife lodged in his chest plunged deeper. He was going to lose the woman he loved if he didn't figure out how to fix his fuck up.

Grady dropped to his knees, fisting his hands over his heart. "If I had a way to turn back time, I'd never have left your side. What do I to fix this? To fix us?"

Her shields crumpled. Longing seeped through the cracks for a split second. But when Grady thought he'd gotten through to her, she straightened her back and reinforced her defenses.

"I need time, Grady," Beth said quietly, adding with a shuddered sigh, "You've been my rock during this whole thing. I wouldn't have been able to stand without you and I love you more for it. But I can't depend solely on you."

She'd thrown his words back, so that the gut punch took his wind, too. Beth was a stubborn woman. Groveling wasn't going to fix things. All the nights he'd spent consoling her had brought them closer together, but his stupidity had driven a wedge between them two miles wide. At the moment, it seemed unmovable.

"Beth—" His voice broke, clogged by his dying heart.

"Stop," she whispered.

He did, but his sad blue eyes bore into hers. He hoped she would change her mind, but the empty gaze staring back told him she wouldn't.

After an eternity, she placed her warm hand on his cheek. Her thumb swiped his stubble, spreading the wetness. He leaned into her touch as if this was his last.

"Two weeks."

The clouds parted and he could breathe again. She'd given him a way back into her heart, so he'd take it. Grady confirmed, "Two weeks."

Two weeks was doable. It would pass in no time while he worked on renovations for their forever home. He held her hand in place with his and stood. Beth swallowed hard. Her tongue darted out to wet her lips. His gaze followed the movement as he caressed her soft cheek.

"Give me two weeks to find my own ground. Afterward, you can visit either by driving over or by portal, I don't care. You'll get what you want, and I'll have what I need. We'll go from there."

"What I *want* is you, Beth," Grady pleaded. *Kiss her...* Before he chickened out, he lowered his lips, ghosting hers when she turned and gave him her cheek. For a breath, the world clicked into place. He closed his eyes and rested his forehead on her temple. "But I'll do as you wish. If you need me for anything, and I mean *anything*, call me. I don't care what time it is or what I'm doing, I'll come. Promise?"

BETH

"I PROMISE."

The truth was she *wanted* him to be here. If she'd let him kiss her, she'd never let him leave again. Grady was the only person she had left, the only thing keeping her grounded. If something happened to him, Beth would lose her tether to reality completely. She'd be lost. This terrifying thought was the reason she needed to find a way to ground herself. Grady had unknowingly given her an out.

"I'll be at the cabin in the Grove."

"Okay."

"If you feel the need to visit, you don't even need to give me a heads up."

"I won't." His hiccupped sharply, and his shoulders tensed. She added, "but if I change my mind, I know where to find you."

Beth prayed Grady would understand. Any more than two weeks on her own and she'd go insane. Tom was buried now; all that remained in finding closure was going through his belongings. And time. She loved Grady but giving him the broken half of herself didn't seem fair. Time heals all wounds, and Tom's sacrifice had given them several years.

Grady was first to pull away. Determination lined his handsome face, but his glossy gaze gave everything away.

"See you in two weeks, Grady," Beth murmured as a cold chill claimed her body with the loss of his heat.

"I promise." His jaw ticked as he backed away. "I mean it, Beth. Don't hesitate if you need something." He made the hang-ten with his hand and used it as a phone.

"Okay."

She resisted the urge to wring her hands, holding them in front like the proper ladies with fancy dresses in historical drama movies. No external signs of her insecurities were allowed to surface.

Grady pursed his lips as if he wanted to say more but couldn't find the words. She understood. His love was written in every crease of his face, the intensity of his gaze. Every tense muscle holding him back. Fumbling with the doorknob, he finally got the door open. His body moved forward, but his feet seem planted to the floor. Beth nodded, and it was like he was released from whatever force held him in place.

As soon as the door closed behind him, she counted to ten before letting the floodgates open. Her broken heart imploded. Her stomach felt sick from all the stress.

Mourning her husband, saying goodbye to her destined one, and standing at the edge of loneliness in order to conquer it would take more strength than she felt she had. But she'd already survived against astronomical odds. This was a stepping stone to a better version of herself.

Beth went to the window, peeking through the sheer curtains as Grady's red truck pulled away. She watched him until he disappeared around the curve, opening the curtains a crack. The gray sky promised no sunshine again today, but the clouds had no more tears to shed either.

She was Elizabeth Marie Harper-Newman, an ancestral child of Myrtle Brinstar, a light-bringer guardian, and a powerful green witch of prophecy sent to save their world. It was a tall task, but she could do this.

Epilogue

FENNICK

After meeting Beth in person, tasting her power, and realizing she had not come to her full potential, Fennick's need for her grew. But all his machinations hinged on gaining Beth's trust.

Fennick stood at Beth's doorstep and knocked. The plain black T-shirt, well-worn jeans, and black combat boots he wore fit him well. He had opted to try a man-bun, with minimal success. Hopefully the change of wardrobe would aid in easing her earlier hesitations.

"Just a minute." Beth's melodious voice came from inside. His stomach fluttered in excitement.

When the door opened, Fennick's black heart lodged in his throat. Beth's power had diminished along with her beauty. As if someone had taken a rough metal brush to delicate glass, taking the shine and leaving it thin and brittle edged. The splotches of gray paint on her hands and clothing had more pigment than her pale skin.

This will not do. Fennick would have to nurse her back to health.

"Good afternoon," Fennick smiled warmly, hoping the magic inside her recognized its kin.

"Fen? Um, hi. What brings you to the neighborhood?" Beth asked, her cheeks tinged with pink. Her eyes traveled the length of his body, ending with his messy half-bun. The corner of her lip upturned and she visibly relaxed.

"Well, I guess you could say it is also my neighborhood," Fen replied. His grin widened when her eyebrows scrunched as she processed his words. *She is quite adorable.* Clearing his throat, he leaned in and added, "I moved in next door yesterday."

"Oh! Ha!" Beth's eyes widened and her face lit up in a way only hers could. "Welcome to the neighborhood." She still checked him out, which he did not mind at all. He loved to see the blush of her skin.

Fen could not help himself. She presented such an easy target. "Is something the matter? You look at me like I am a stranger." It worked. Her face turned red. *Delicious.*

"I'm sorry! I can't believe—" Beth chuckled and covered her eyes. Her hand went to her hip as she shook her head. Once composed, her shy gaze met his. "It's just, you look...normal. The first time we met–it's like I'm seeing you for real for the first time. Gods. That sounds so lame."

"No, I understand. I should have changed before I came looking for apartments to rent," Fen chuckled, crossing his arms over his chest and leaning against the railing. "And you are not lame."

Beth's eyes softened under Fen's gaze. Something flashed across her face, a memory pushing through her grief.

Fen straightened and put his hands in his pockets. "I only wanted to pop over for a bit, let you know I am here if you need anything or want to hang out sometime. I should head back, finish unpacking."

"Sounds great. I'll be seeing you, Fen," Beth replied, chewing her bottom lip in thought.

"See you later, Beth." Fen turned to leave. He had made it to the bottom step when she called out. He hid his smile before turning to face her.

"Fen?" Beth's timid voice matched her demeanor as she fidgeted with her hands.

"Yes, Beth," Fen responded, trying to sound breathless without seeming eager.

"Would you like to join me for dinner tonight? Say six?" She sounded more sure of herself now.

"That would be lovely. I have an unopened bottle of red Moscato somewhere, or would wine be too presumptuous?" Fen asked, having the providence to blush. *This is a rare occasion, indeed.*

"Not at all. Red Moscato is my favorite." Beth radiated with a brightness that caused Fen's heart to skip. Her power pulsed in response, and some of the color returned to her face. *Interesting.*

"Perfect! I will see you at six." Fen returned her wave and she shut the door.

Things were looking up. When he was sure Beth would not open the door again, he hurried to the store to buy a bottle of red Moscato.

GRADY

AFTER LEAVING BETH'S APARTMENT, Grady pulled into his driveway, but he didn't get out of his truck. Somewhere in the swirling sadness and despair, a nagging feeling seized his mind. He'd forgotten something important. His emotional battery was drained. In these times, manual labor helped him focus.

Turning the key, he cut the engine and got to work. The first thing on the Grove's to-do list was to make the loft space into a bedroom. The cot was fine for one, but they'd need the extra space after Beth moved in.

Making sure the toolbox had a steel mill file, Grady grabbed his hand saw and some extra lumber. It took him several trips to get everything through the portal.

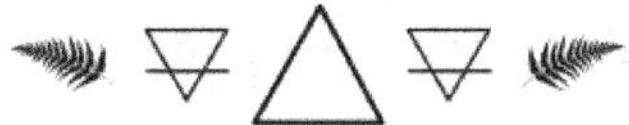

During the twenty-something days Grady spent working on the cabin, he purged his grief in trails of sweat from sawing wood and hammering nails. Building things from scratch had always been therapeutic, but he'd run out of scrap wood. If he was gonna surprise Beth with a front porch bench swing, he'd need to go back.

Grady swallowed the last sip of coffee and placed his mug on the dining table. His heart fluttered with the thought of seeing Beth again.

He portaled to the house and stepped outside. The springs in his driver's seat squeaked when he climbed in. He ignited the engine and the nagging feeling from before clawed at the recesses of his mind to gain purchase.

The memory jolted his brain like an electric fence. Grady hadn't forgotten some simple thing, like forgetting to turn off the coffee pot. He'd forgotten something pertaining to life and death.

Curtis Putnam.

"Fuck!" Grady threw the gear into reverse.

He'd left Beth alone again like the idiot he was.

Grady barely missed the curb when he slung the truck around onto the road. Slamming it into drive, his tires squalled as he burned rubber.

The Putnams lived on a sizable one point five-acre lot about ten minutes outside of town. Curtis fixed cars in his home garage. People tolerated his odious attitude because he could tell you what was wrong with a vehicle by sound alone.

Their neighbors were older folks who kept to themselves for the most part, except for the weekly quilting circle Jeff's mom, Marla Jean, was part of. He knew because his momma had been a member, too.

Grady parked behind one of the three cars in Jeff's driveway and cut the engine. He slid out of his truck and stared at the house. It was eerily dark and quiet. He was used to the noise from at least two televisions and country music blaring from the garage while Curtis worked.

The garage door was closed, as well as all the curtains. The neighboring houses echoed the stillness, causing the pit of his stomach to squeeze uncomfortably.

Glancing at the neighbor's driveways, the knot loosened at seeing them both empty. Grady pocketed his keys and started for the front door. He stopped on the front step when struck by the thick and sweet coppery scent of days-old decay.

Grady struggled with calling the police or going inside. The names of several people on the police force were listed in his father's notebook. His safety or innocence were forfeit, especially if they found him at the scene of the crime. The odds didn't look good either route.

Besides, how are the police gonna fight against magic?

Grady backtracked and acted natural as he made his way to the backyard like he'd done for a decade or better. Jeff's bedroom was a converted utility room situated on the corner and had a separate entrance. The door was unlocked. He cast a quick glance around before slipping inside.

Seeing the movie posters and photos of their middle school through high school years, brought on a surge of nostalgia and loss. Grady's concentration broke and his nose prickled. He sniffled and that's when the scent grabbed his attention.

Anyone else would have missed it, but Grady's heightened senses went beyond the blood and decay. Paint. Oil to be exact. Intrigue plucked at his curiosity.

A quick search led him to Jeff's closed closet. His hand gripped the cool metal doorknob, and with a quick breath to dispel the disquietude, he pulled it open. Stacked in the back corner were several painted canvases covered with a cloth. He carefully lifted it free to find at least thirty paintings, mostly landscapes. They were good enough to be on the wall of the local art gallery, at least.

Flipping through, one in particular caught his eye. Grady pulled it free for a better look. He expected it to be a self-portrait or Jeff's mother, but it was neither. A wry smile crept up on his face.

It was Ms. Pebblebrook, their high school art teacher.

Audrey.

"Jeff, you dog." Grady whispered as he admired the portrait. Her likeness was astonishing.

He'd found out who Jeff's mystery woman was. *I can't wait to tell Beth.* The thought kicked him in the chest. He had to move or he wouldn't be sharing anything with his girl.

Grady returned the painting to the closet, careful to leave everything the way he found it. He tip-toed across the room and eased the bedroom door open. The squeaky hinges made him flinch. Grady stilled, listening for movement. The house remained silent.

Creeping down the hallway, Grady followed the strange scent. As it got stronger, he covered his nose and mouth with his shirt. The stench originated from the kitchen.

Grady turned the corner and went through the living room, noting the rusty spattering on the walls. It looked as if a can of brick-red paint had exploded near the dining room.

His eyes burned from the pungent smell of rotting flesh. His stomach rolled and pitched, causing bile to rise in his throat.

When his eyes landed on the kitchen floor, the words flew from his mouth, unbidden. "Fucking hell."

Acknowledgements

Katie Bell, Jeanea Blair, Jana Rose, and Carter Elise Key…

Y'all! Thank you for being my cheerleaders from the beginning of BDA Publishing until the bitter end and beyond. We've all grown so much since the second edition, but your friendship, support, and Chemical X (just kidding on that last one) provided the special serum for my growth as a writer. While we've all had to navigate the sudden changes, I am so excited to cheer you all on with whatever new adventure awaits. *Hugs! - KP

***Azshure Raine ***

Since Awakening's conception, we jived so well with our love of fantasy and storytelling, that you became my idea-bouncer, best friend, and editor. I am so thankful for your Tom x Grady comments, unrelenting support, and pushing me to be a better writer, otherwise Beth would have been wandering the woods with complicit murderers—like a sweet summer child—and would have been eaten by a bear. Thank you for being the awesome person you are, and for taking a leap of faith to befriend this awkward human.

A huge thank you goes to my awesome beta readers.

This story wouldn't be as well-written if it weren't for their attention to detail, grammar, and my overuse of pronouns and adverbs. They also didn't let me get away with lazy writing. Your friendships were an added bonus: Matthew Poslusny, Caroline Fleur, Jennifer Lee from SacredEarth.Love, and Sarah K. Rhine.

Also, a big thank you to my ARC readers!

Your support and reviews helped get my book seen by readers. K. Thomas, Michele Quirke, Kristi M. @flash_mama, Kim Morehouse @kdmorehouse, Angie Dokos, Alan Denney, Jessica Price, and P.L. Stuart.

Fortuna Lux

Thank you for putting together a magical plan to help me make Awakening's third edition relaunch shine. Hugs! – KP

Lastly, I cannot forget my original proofreader, Pam Willson from the Picky Bookworm.

Thank You for Reading Awakening, Book One in the Between the Birches Trilogy!

If you enjoyed the story so far, please consider leaving a short review on Amazon, Goodreads, or on social media. Your support helps to spread the word for indie published authors.

OTHER TITLES FROM LUNAR RIDGE PUBLISHING:

Harbinger, Book Two, Between the Birches Trilogy by K.P. Roberson (2025)

Zenith, Book Three, Between the Birches Trilogy by K.P. Roberson (2027)

https://www.lunarridgepublishing.com

About the Author

K.P. Roberson is a Georgia native living in the southern Appalachian Mountains with her very handsome and nerdy spouse, their two teenage spawn, and a very rotund cat who answers to 'Kitty.'

K.P. loves science fiction, fantasy, thriller, romance, and horror stories, especially if they are character driven. Her writings align with her tastes, but she also composed Stardew Valley fanfiction on Archive of Our Own (K8eCre8s). When not pounding away at her keyboard with a string of illicit words, she enjoys watching movies, listening to music, reading on her Kindle, gardening, hiking, and crocheting...which explains her love of weaving a good tale.

Where to find K.P. on Social Media:

Threads – @authorkproberson
Instagram – @authorkproberson
Facebook – @KPWritesFantasy
TikTok – @author_kproberson
Goodreads – K.P. Roberson
www.AuthorKPRoberson.com